Sunday Falling

Sunday Falling

An Alba White Mystery

Martin Hurcomb

The manufacturer's authorised representative in the EU for
product safety is Authorised Rep Compliance Ltd,
71 Lower Baggot Street, Dublin D02 P593 Ireland (www.arccompliance.com)

Troubador Publishing Ltd
Unit E2 Airfield Business Park,
Harrison Road, Market Harborough,
Leicestershire. LE16 7UL
Tel: 0116 2792299
Email: books@troubador.co.uk
Web: www.troubador.co.uk

ISBN 978 1836283 812

British Library Cataloguing in Publication Data.
A catalogue record for this book is available from the British Library.

Printed and bound by CPI Group (UK) Ltd, Croydon, CR0 4YY
Typeset in 11pt Adobe Garamond Pro by Troubador Publishing Ltd, Leicester, UK

To James and Matthew,
my boys

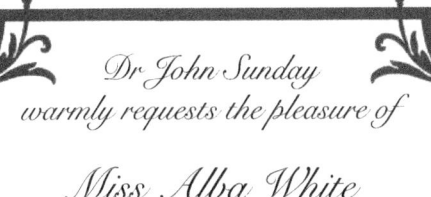

Dr John Sunday
warmly requests the pleasure of

Miss Alba White

To join him, Miss Eleanor Evans and his
wider family at

Kingsbourne Manor
Kingsbourne
Wiltshire

For his midsummer House Gathering

Wednesday 16th June ~ Tuesday 22nd June 2004

R.S.V.P.

*

Miss White, for your information as a friend of
Miss Evans, Dr Sunday's wider family consists of:

Anthony and Johanna Sunday and their grown-up
children Henry and Connie

Isabel Sunday

Hugh and Alice Sunday and their
grown-up daughter, May

Contents

CHAPTER 1

Sunday Falling

It was a greater drop than it looked from up there. As they all stood around Dr John Sunday's body, Alba found herself gazing up to where he undoubtedly fell from – that section of the Manor's roof which one could walk out on to.

When he had shown it to her – just a couple of days ago – and together they had stood up there looking out over the gardens and the gently upward sloping farmland beyond, it somehow had not felt so high as it clearly was when viewed from down here. Maybe that misperception was because her anxiety about why she had been invited, as an outsider to this family gathering of Dr Sunday's, had eased. Maybe it was because she was in the presence of her most adored former University lecturer or maybe it was simply because she had never looked directly down. Whatever the reason, it just had not felt as high as it undoubtedly was. Or perhaps just looking out across the estate, gazing towards the hills which the house nestled within and marvelling at the broad summer sky above them, simply had stopped her from considering just how far up they were.

Yet now, as she and his family stood on the gravel path which circumvented the house – a somewhat pale grey colour of gravel, which, unlike some rich, golden, 'Cotswoldy-in-colour' warm stone, seemed in its drabness appropriate for the moment – Alba reflected that whatever the reason, when viewed from down here it clearly was a considerable drop and anyone falling from that height would be killed outright.

So, here she stood, amongst Dr John Sunday's family. Here were his brothers Anthony and Hugh, their wives Johanna and Alice respectively and their grown-up children. His sister, Isabel, was also present. Alba looked up once more from where he had fallen.

That section of roof – lead covered, accessible from that discrete door in Dr John's study – had been a wonderful surprise when he had shown it to her on Thursday morning. She had been marvelling at a framed pencil drawing of Eleanor of Provence – Henry III's Queen – which hung behind his desk, then at Dr John's vast collection of books, including several on Chaucer, Gower and Langland, those great medieval poets, and then at an ornament on his desk, seemingly of a sleeping knight, when suddenly he had opened a previously unnoticed door and invited her to step out onto part of the roof of Kingsbourne Manor. It was in no way anything like stepping out on to a section of felt covered flat roof of a 1970s extension to your average urban post-war dwelling house; this roof was as solid as any other part of the Manor. The solid oak roof, completely covered in lead, with an agreeable slope to it to allow the water to drain into the gully which ran around the base of the parapet, was as secure a structure as anything Alba had ever stood on; it had felt more secure out there on that surprising section of roof than anywhere in her own home – her little cottage back home in the village where she lived on the Surrey-Sussex border and a village at the far end of which stood Hillstone Hall.

Being out on the roof with Dr Sunday was two days ago. It was, Alba considered once more as she glanced up a final time, a great drop from which to fall. A movement beside her brought her gaze back down. She turned as Anthony knelt and, having slipped his own jacket off, placed it over his elder brother's body.

As he did so, Alba instinctively placed her arm around Connie's shoulders and held her just a fraction closer to herself to comfort the young woman. In that moment, however, Alba acknowledged that she, Alba, felt comforted by Connie's presence and Alba realised she – as well as Connie – needed comforting. It had been over a year since Alba had last seen tragedy – that time it had been at the foot of a metal staircase outside 'The Jupiter Hotel' one bright morning. Since then, she had tried, if not to forget Martha, at least to forget that last awful sighting of her. Yet now that memory became ever so real once again, almost as if she alone could see two bodies lying battered and still before her.

On top of that, of course, there had been that other loss back home in the village not so long after her return from the West Country and the resultant gulf – well, maybe if not gulf then at least an awkwardness – which somehow, imperceptibly at first, had opened up between herself and Andrew. They had talked about the loss and thought they had planned for it. She had even spoken about what they all knew was coming with the Reverend Quinn, the vicar from her village, and still, somehow, it had tripped her and Andrew up. There was a distance between them now; there was no malice or animosity which underlay it, it was just that their – especially his – lives were now so different.

So, all in all, Alba accepted, she valued Connie's close proximity as much as she hoped Connie appreciated her 'sisterly' embrace. Alba had only known Connie a very brief time but nonetheless regarding her as someone akin to a younger sister seemed entirely correct. Connie, nineteen years old, waiting on exam results before heading off to university, had long brown, straight hair, a fuller figure than Alba had been herself at that age – though Alba regarded Connie as more beautiful for it – and a confidence about her that Alba, at a mature thirty-two years in age herself, felt she still herself lacked.

*

"Why would he have jumped?" almost screamed Eleanor. "Why? We were so happy. We would have been so happy."

She was answered with silence; a stoney, awkward, almost embarrassed, silence. It was, Alba felt, far from a natural shocked silence – there *was* an awkwardness to it. Indeed, after the last couple of days, as she had watched and lived alongside this family group, to pretend anything other would be misleading, disingenuous even.

For as much as anyone here, save for Eleanor and Connie Alba reflected, might on one level grieve for their brother or uncle, there was so much malice, greed and a sense of entitlement amongst the remaining family members that on another level they were all looking beyond the scene and seeing opportunities finally opening up, financial rescue or some distorted sense of justice. The Sundays were a nasty, vindictive family and not many of them would shed genuine tears now.

"Why?" repeated Eleanor.

"Who knows someone's final thoughts in such moments," offered Isabel, the dead man's sister. "Something troubling him I guess."

Eleanor turned to look at Isabel, anger instantly replacing shock; Eleanor addressed the other woman:

"Something troubling him? Of course there was something troubling him. You lot – yes, that's right – the whole sorry lot of you. Each of you resented my arrival in his life, were annoyed that I made him happy and were beside yourselves that we were to be married. All of your plans, hopes for an inheritance and whatever else you were conspiring together to bring about, you could see disappearing with me being around."

Eleanor paused before addressing one face within the crowd:

"Don't look like that Isabel; don't try and fain innocence. You might think you're a brilliant actress but you've never been able to act – you just worm your way into Directors' and Producers' lives and somehow end up being given bit parts in theatrical productions."

"How dare you!" Isabel responded. "I've appeared in London's

West End. You little upstart and as for anyone worming their way into someone's life, I think you Miss Evans ought to examine yourself!"

With that Isabel moved her shoulders back a fraction more than they were already and, with a slight lifting of her chin as she turned her head away from Eleanor, made her dislike of the younger woman abundantly clear. Her head already turned in the direction of the house – and specifically the billiard room – Isabel's body then also turned and she went in.

"I haven't wormed my way in," called out a defiant Eleanor to the departing figure. "John loved me. It has been toxic all the time these past few days here. Between the pathetic lot of you, you have driven him to suicide."

Finally, Eleanor slumped to the ground. She reached out to where John lay and placed her right hand on Anthony's jacket, on the spot where John's heart was, and wept.

Alba, her own composure more settled than it had been a few minutes ago and definitely more settled than anyone else's present, released her embrace of Connie and went and knelt by Eleanor. Alba winched as she did so, as one particularly sharp random piece of gravel embedded itself into her bare left knee.

As she comforted the distraught form, Alba spoke to those still gathered, suggesting someone needed to call for an ambulance, someone to have hot drinks produced and set out in the dining room and for the house staff to be alerted. Once some of the group dispersed, each in turn announcing what 'task' they were heading off to do, Alba asked the rest to leave Eleanor alone for a few minutes:

"Leave Eleanor to grieve her fiancé quietly for a bit, please, all of you. I'll sit with her but I think – as she has just made clear – she would rather have some time apart from you all."

Of all those who still remained, they all, whatever their inner feelings, heeded Alba's request. Hugh, though, keen either to have the last word or out of a dislike for an 'outsider' to have taken charge, called back to the two women on the ground that he would also call

John's university department to let them know, in order that they could have a press statement ready.

As Alba withdrew Eleanor's hand from John's body and took both the other woman's hands in her own, Eleanor, although still staring at the jacket covered body, spoke:

"I hardly think worrying about the media angle is the priority at the moment. That is what this family is like, though, rotten to the core. Self-centred and heartless – the whole miserable lot of them."

"I couldn't really comment," said Alba, trying to be as neutral as possible. "I hardly know them. Perhaps there are some tensions and it's been a slightly tense few days but all of them? What about–"

Alba, though did not have to finish her sentence. This was because, and as if to prove her assessment that at least one of them was not quite as Eleanor had just made out, Connie returned carrying a couple of cushions she had taken from one of the window seats within the billiard room. She was also lugging a very large folded sheet, the one used to cover the snooker table in the inappropriately named 'Billiard Room'.

"I'm not staying – it is right you want to be alone. However, I've brought you a cushion each as it can't be very comfortable down there on the gravel. I've also brought something more appropriate to cover Uncle John's body; looking at his legs and arms protruding can't be very pleasant."

Having handed the cushions over and as Alba and Eleanor made themselves a fraction more comfortable, Connie took the heavily folded sheet and unfolded it a couple of times and placed it over the full length of her uncle's body. Given the size of a full size snooker table, it was quite a thick covering but Connie endeavoured to tuck it in as best she could around the still form. Satisfied she then stood up. For a brief moment she paused and looked at the now heavily shrouded form and then silently departed once more.

"See, they're not all bad," observed Alba. "Connie at least seems to have a heart."

Eleanor did not answer Alba. Alba simply heard her quietly say '*oh cloth, you hide a merry jewel*'.

*

They had sat there time enough for an ambulance to arrive. The following police car was clearly a surprise, if not to Alba, to Eleanor. Alba was grateful that, between those who had just turned up, she and Eleanor were ushered away from John's body and 'encouraged' to go into the house.

Such was the time they had been sitting outside on the pale grey coloured gravel, by the time Alba and Eleanor – two women of similar age, Alba in her early thirties, Eleanor in her late twenties – made their way into the dining room, the rest of the family had vacated it. The pots of coffee and tea were at best lukewarm. Not that Eleanor had a hot drink, she opted for water but such was the state she was in Alba had to pour it for her, as Eleanor's hands shook too much for her to work the metal release clip on the large bottle of water – the clip which held the ceramic stopper tight to the rubber ring on the neck of the glass bottle.

As she endured a lukewarm, stewed, cup of tea, and softly patted out some gravel dust from her polka dot navy blue dress, Alba was still grateful none of the family had sought to do the 'right thing' and bring the two of them a drink whilst they had still been sitting out by Dr John Sunday's body this Saturday morning. It was clear that Eleanor felt she had not been welcomed into Dr Sunday's wider family and that, in return, Eleanor regarded them as not nice people. Alba herself had been made welcome enough – a little bit superficially but, to be fair to the family, they were all slightly puzzled as to why this 'outsider' had been invited to this family gathering. In fact, if truth be told, Alba herself was still slightly puzzled about her presence here.

Having finished their uninspiring drinks, Alba took Eleanor back to her, Eleanor's, bedroom, along the long landing which they had so carefreely walked together late the previous evening – passing comments as they did so on the large tapestry, on the aged, cracked, oil paintings which hung along the walls and on the mesmerising effect that the light from a solitary candle had on one painting in particular. As they walked along the same landing this morning, Alba did not notice the tapestry, the paintings nor the candlestick with the now set red wax around its base. Instead, she found herself preoccupied thinking about the letter Terry had sent her. She decided she would, once back in her room here at Kingsbourne Manor, re-read it yet again to see if she could make any more sense of it this time.

Yet, whatever sense she might make of it, neither she nor Terry – a friend from Alba's university days and who was Eleanor's brother – would ever have imagined that within the midst of her stay here, during this glorious month of June, Dr Sunday would take his own life.

CHAPTER 2

A request for help

Seated by the stone mullioned window in a surprisingly comfortable tapestry-covered chair, Alba held Terry's letter in her left hand. She had her legs tucked up underneath her, in a way that meant she was almost – but not quite – sitting on her ankles. Her positioning forced her upper body to be off centre and her left shoulder and elbow, secure against the chair's dark wooden armrest, were taking the extra force.

It was not an uncomfortable position even though there was just a hint of a lady from times gone by sitting side-saddle – although any hint was somewhat offset by Alba's above the knee polka dot dress.

Nonetheless, an imaginative individual – observing Alba from the shadows – might have seen beyond the spotted dress and perceived the romantic, where the woman before them did indeed have an air of a medieval lady-in-waiting; perhaps one riding side-saddle whilst out on her mount. Maybe the tapestried chair – depicting images of deer, woodland trees in full leaf and hares – added to that impression. Of course, a less imaginative and somewhat casual observer in that moment might have simply observed a modern thirty-something-year-old sitting off balance in a chair whilst a more practical *voyeur* would have simply worried for the blood supply to Alba's lower limbs.

Yet, however viewed, the observer – imaginative, casual or practical – would quickly be taken beyond their first impression of the lady before them and, instead, be drawn to Alba's puzzled look. They would be observing Alba alternatively rubbing her right hand across her forehead and then the same hand dropping down to her bare feet to allow her fingers to run themselves along her toes, almost as if the fingers were caressing the keys on a piano. The observer would also have noted Alba's pursed lips, ones lacking their normal velvety-redness, and, perhaps more than anything else, would have sensed Alba's intense concentration.

There was, though, no observer in the room and Alba was wholly alone. She decided to read the correspondence she was holding once more.

*

As the fingers on her right hand once more ran themselves along her toenails, tapping out another silent tune, Alba read Terry's letter from the very beginning. This time she hoped to get closer to what had driven him to write to her from Tashkent, that distant, unknown, almost 'Lord of the Rings' sounding capital city of Uzbekistan. That central Asian nation Terry had, about a year after they – Terry, Helen and Alba – had finished university, moved to. He had gone in response, so he said, to a calling to be a missionary there.

She started the letter where it began.

My dearest Alba,
It was wrong of me not to write before now and for that I am sorry.
I am also aware that this letter will appear as if I am only

writing to you as I want a favour from you – a considerable favour – and but for that I would not be writing to you.

It may appear so but please believe me that that is not the case and you have been on my heart for a long time. I have so wanted to write but each time my work, my time, my calling out here allows me to sit down with pen in hand, words somehow fail me. I put my pen back down and just find myself staring at a blank piece of paper. Then somehow another day, another week, another month slips by and still I have not written. But I have so yearned to write.

I accept, though, now I am having to write for I need your help. It is almost too big a favour to ask of anyone but somehow, if one person can help me in my helplessness, it is you, Alba.

To put you at ease though, it doesn't concern my work out here in Uzbekistan. My job with the 'European Business and Communication Advisory Board' is going well. Our task remains to grow smart and resilient links in the energy and research sectors between the European Union and the Republic of Uzbekistan. It is not a straightforward task – President Karimov is as suspicious of Western interest as much as he fears Russia reasserting itself over his country. Let's just say he is very aware his country's natural gas supplies are attracting outside interest now Uzbekistan is an independent State. We are treading carefully; we have to.

We are working closely with the European Bank for Reconstruction and Development and, where Karimov's government allows, some private investment and involvement. As you may realise, my time working for 'Blake and Malone' in the City of London after we finished university, is proving invaluable in that regard.

Enough though of my job.

Nor am I writing in connection with any other reason a man may have for being out here. You will understand it's best I don't say too much on that. I am certain you will remember who called me out here – your memory was always impressive.

I am blessed to have been sent here. As much as I love the rolling hills of the Downs, the Kentish Weald and the draw of London (you'll remember that time we met at Marble Arch), Uzbekistan is a beautiful country. That said, I cherish the times when I can get away from Tashkent itself and travel south west towards Qarshi. There's an openness there that I can't quite describe. Nor is Qarshi as frenetic as Tashkent and the people are so hospitable – I am constantly humbled by their generosity. If ever the saying 'those with the shallowest pockets, are the most generous' applied to anyone, it is to the beautiful Uzbek families of Qarshi.

I guess now though, I must tell you why I am writing; a man can only string you along for so long before you give him a certain look. I've seen you with that look so best I say why I'm writing.

My request relates to my sister, Eleanor. You will remember Eleanor – she came and 'bunked down' on my floor often enough in our student house. To begin with, as you know, it was my parents' way of introducing her to university life in a calm way. Well, maybe not as calm as they imagined but definitely she was always safe with us, wasn't she? Of course, after her first few visits – as her sixth form studies allowed – she came and visited of her own volition. She loved academia. Fell in love with it and she couldn't wait to complete her A-Levels and come to the same university as we were just finishing at; shame we didn't have just one year which overlapped.

Fell in love with it, as I say. She thrived in her studies, once she got there, and said she lived in the university library. Eleanor marvelled at the wealth of resources that were suddenly at her fingertips: the books, the journals, the centuries old manuscripts of medieval poetry that she 'purred' over. Not my thing at all but she just lapped all that old stuff up. She had found her niche, her calling, her passion, call it what you will, but she had most definitely found it. It used to exasperate mum – so dad would tell me out of mum's earshot – that Eleanor was never back in the student house at the time mum had arranged to call her each week. Mum would get so worried something horrible had happened to her girl, whereas in reality Eleanor had simply lost track of time yet again and was immersed in one of the 'Canterbury Tales' in some quiet, remote part of the library. Dad, in contrast, simply worried Eleanor wasn't eating enough.

Yes, she fell in love with her studies but – and this bit I don't think even you or Helen will have gleaned through the university grapevine – she fell in love with one of her tutors too. And he her. They were almost three decades apart in age but, so she's tried to explain to me in numerous letters she has sent me out here, neither of them saw it or, if they did, bothered for their difference in years. Perhaps if you're both passionate about medieval England – what's that six, seven, eight hundred years ago? – your heart can easily broach thirty years.

I won't pretend it wasn't a shock for me and I'm just her big brother. But it was 'shock and some' for mum. She was beside herself with anxiety and fear for her little girl – mum had convinced herself that some nefarious, lecherous and debauched academic had entrapped her child. That spider-like, he had entwined her daughter in some web which Eleanor could neither see nor have the strength to escape from. Dad, too, was worried but I think he became almost as worried for how mum was coping or, more accurately, not coping as for any seismic mistake his daughter was making. Yes, it was tough on dad I could tell – he never told me as such but I knew from our telephone conversations he was struggling. It wasn't so much what he said to me, more when he fell silent on the phone, not saying anything in response to one of my questions about what my sister was doing. Yes, dad's silence was very un-dad-like. Poor dad. He was too proud to share it with me, too gentlemanly to share it with mum – in his belief he had to be solid, stoic and sensible for her – and too reserved to share it with his few friends.

Needless to say, Eleanor, despite mum's tears and dad's nervous quietness, persisted in her relationship. Perhaps what had started as an affaire de coeur – an affair of the heart – between them duly became something real and it was something passionate and intense by the time Eleanor shared things with mum and dad.

Yet, Eleanor was not trying to isolate or ignore mum or dad. She, as I do, care for them very much and would never wish to cut them out of our lives. She asked them to travel to meet the person she'd fallen for, be it to have a meal together or just to walk through the university grounds together. Yet that suggestion was too much, too soon for mum. Mum knew she would have to meet the man eventually but not in a way Eleanor proposed. It was dad who decided that Eleanor and her man – you will have of course, Alba, have worked out by now that I'm talking about Dr Sunday – should come to mum's and dad's house for afternoon tea. That way, dad knew, he was ensuring mum was somewhere familiar, somewhere safe; it gave mum a chance to go and 'busy herself in the kitchen' or potter in the garden if it all got too much for her.

Thankfully it worked. I won't pretend my parents weren't still worried for the age gap but they began to see how at ease Eleanor and Dr Sunday were in each other's company, how equal they were in mind and they appreciated how respectful Dr Sunday was towards them as Eleanor's parents.

As an aside, I suppose if he's my sister's boyfriend I should be calling him John and not Dr Sunday but that still feels a bit odd for me even though I never studied under him, given my degree was in economics as you well know. So, for a while still I will keep referring to him as Dr Sunday but that's not out of disrespect or my trying to keep him apart from our family, rather simply recognising I need time myself to adjust to their relationship. That will come; maybe it's a bit harder for me being out here as I am, unable to meet him at some university function or even informally over a pint one Saturday afternoon.

Critically, though, if they love each other, they will have my blessing – and they will have mum's and dad's too, I hope. It will take time but it will come.

So, yes, we'll get there as a family – we'll welcome Dr Sunday to our bosom. However, I can't say I'm as confident concerning his family in welcoming Eleanor into theirs. I accept I've never met them but, and this is hardly reading 'between the lines', from what Eleanor has said about them, they are a fractious, self-serving and untrustworthy bunch. Slick and polished on the outside – seemingly carrying off some successful careers and business ventures along the way – but harbouring some dark hearts and running businesses built on some precarious financial footings on the inside. Eleanor has shared that with me but she's been unable to tell our parents just yet. Eleanor said it's a delicate task getting mum and dad to accept Dr Sunday, to get them to accept his family too would be nigh on impossible at this junction in time. Eleanor has clearly been embarrassed sharing this with me but she needed to raise it with someone in her family she said. 'Someone needed to know', she said but that it couldn't be mum or dad. Eleanor stressed though she had fallen for Dr Sunday and that was what mattered; how his family reacted to her, to him or to them as a couple was separate.

Dr Sunday's family will react to her, I am sure. From what Eleanor has shared with me they will most definitely react. His two brothers, sister, nephew and two nieces will not be happy. After all, so Eleanor informs me, Dr Sunday is a wealthy man.

Yes, a wealthy man. His money doesn't come from his work

at the university. Yes, he earns a good wage from his job there and there will be some royalties from his books along with fees earnt from his lecture circuits to America – what is it with Americans and their love of 'old England'? – but none of those make him wealthy. Comfortable, yes, but not wealthy. No, his wealth, apparently, comes from a bachelor uncle who made his money mining in southern Africa. No doubt, Dr Sunday's siblings resent not being given a share of the inheritance. Perhaps the mining uncle could see the others for what they are and wanted his money to go to someone better. Perhaps but who am I to judge? Within the seventh chapter of Matthew's Gospel we are told not to judge and – oh, look, there I go, trying to witness to you. It never was your thing when we were at university, was it? So, I'll leave the 'Sermon on the Mount' for the people of Tashkent to reflect on.

Suffice to say, Dr Sunday's family were not impressed when John chose not to share his uncle's wealth; he opted instead to acquire Kingsbourne Manor and then to respectfully, authentically, compassionately – is that a word one can use when referring to a building? – restore it. Eleanor has spoken a lot about Kingsbourne; apparently some of the Manor's foundations have been dated to the mid-thirteenth century. I understand the rest of it is newer by several hundred years but that hardly makes it a new build; all in all, major renovations were required. The manor's restoration took a good chunk of the inheritance and I would surmise maintaining it will take the remainder. I sense – from Eleanor's comments – his family would still rather a share of the money that's currently left than having the contentment of knowing a lovely country manor house has been saved from dereliction and can in time be left to a group of trustees on a solid financial footing. I really don't think they care a jot for Kingsbourne even though they shamelessly make use of the manor house whenever they like.

Eleanor, by contrast, loves the place. She describes it as –

*

Alba looked up from Terry's letter. Having read the letter before she knew how he recounted Eleanor's description of it.

Indeed, Kingsbourne Manor had made the same impression on Alba as it had on Eleanor – it *spoke* to them in the same way. As she gazed out the window, not really seeing the honey bees working their way around the herb garden nor the bright lemon yellow self-seeded Calendulas – English Marigolds – at the edges of the gravel paths which interspersed the herb beds, Alba tried to reconnect to that first impression of Kingsbourne Manor. Alba attempted to rekindle the sounds and to the aromas she experienced when approaching the property along its grand lime tree drive. She tried to remember but could not, for the image of Dr Sunday's cloth covered body was inevitably still forefront in Alba's mind.

She decided to return to reading Terry's letter – skipping the paragraph which covered Eleanor's assessment of Dr Sunday's country home.

*

...and yet the best view of it, according to my sister, is as you first see it when approaching the manor through the lime tree drive.

So, yes, Eleanor loves the place even if she objects to how Dr Sunday's wider family shamelessly use it given their resentment towards him.

That resentment will only grow with Eleanor's arrival in his life. They will not take kindly to her; they will – as I've said – react to her.

And that is what worries me. Worries me, especially so, with what Eleanor has just telephoned to tell me about. Apparently, there is to be a family gathering over several days, at Dr

Sunday's request. As much as his brothers and sister make use of Kingsbourne, they will take exception to being summoned there. They will take umbrage with Dr Sunday's expectation that they will turn up at a time of his choosing and they will particularly object to Eleanor's introduction – for Dr Sunday has said to Eleanor he wants to introduce her to his family. They will see her as usurping all of their positions and that is what worries me. Yes, it worries me greatly.

Eleanor and I spoke at length about it. She knows she will feel vulnerable moving around a country manor house and gardens, at risk of being accosted whenever by herself. She is conscious of not having myself or my parents to watch her back – were we to also be invited – but equally conscious of not wanting to be seen as Dr Sunday's 'lap dog' unable to leave his side or sight. Eleanor knows she has to go to Kingsbourne to meet his family but, in talking to me about it all, was searching for some way to mitigate those concerns.

I suggested she ask Dr Sunday if a friend could accompany her – to bolster the numbers on her side, so to speak. That might be useful on those occasions when Dr Sunday gets caught up in meetings with potential trustees or the estate manager as he will inevitably be at stages over the several days they are all scheduled to be there. My suggestion was listened to by Eleanor. Yet she conceded she'd never kept any trusted friends at university. She'd either been dropped by them as they'd signed up for student accommodation which wasn't quite big enough for them all and she was the first from the group to be dispensed with or dropped by other friends, as they learnt of her attachment to her tutor.

So, she couldn't see any 'mileage' in my idea. However, when I put to her that I could ask you to accompany her, she was willing to consider it. Now I know you're hardly best friends with her but you do know her, she likes you and, critically, you know Dr Sunday. It could work.

Yes, it could work.

To be clear, I haven't committed you to anything. I simply said to Eleanor that I would write to you and ask you to consider it – to go to Kingsbourne Manor for four or five days in June and accompany my sister.

It would so put my mind at rest. Also, in time when we tell my parents about whatever 'goings on' take place at Kingsbourne over those days, it will reassure them that Eleanor had had a confidante with her that first time. I'm not asking you to go and talk Eleanor out of her relationship. Neither am I wanting you to build bridges between her and Dr Sunday's wider family – that will best come from Eleanor herself. Nor am I asking you to simply keep my sister from encountering Dr Sunday's brothers, sister and their children at the Manor. Rather, I'm asking you to go and be my eyes and ears, to be a supportive presence but most of all to go and be yourself.

I know you will offer wise counsel to anyone who consoles themselves in you and if you are there, things will be better. You and Eleanor…

*

'Better' re-read Alba. The word somehow now broke what had been the natural flow of the letter. She paused her reading of Terry's letter and closed her eyes. '*Better*' mused Alba to herself. She considered the word once more. Terry had assumed things would be better if Alba was present at this house gathering and yet, with Dr Sunday lying dead under a covering for a snooker table and with his newly announced fiancé having just been escorted – broken and distraught – back to another bedroom, Alba could not in that moment believe things could be any worse.

Alba opened her eyes.

"Better," she said out loud. Seemingly she spoke to herself

but perhaps it was to no one, for she was alone, and there was an emptiness around her. Death was proving to be a lonely and ungiving 'companion' to be in the company of. Yet, perhaps in another sense, she was actually speaking to Terry, despite the thousands of miles which separated them.

Whoever it was she was speaking to, if anyone, Alba continued –

"I don't see how I'm making anything better. I've been a slight comfort to Eleanor this last hour or so but that is all. Terry, oh my dear Terry, I don't know what you were hoping from me but I've failed you miserably."

With tears welling, she endeavoured – through moisture laden eyes – to continue reading the remaining short section of his letter.

*

If you are there, things will be better. You and Eleanor always got on well and she will trust you and take reassurance from your presence. Of course, I also hope – if you go – you are able to enjoy yourself. Kingsbourne Manor sounds a beautiful place, you will appreciate the gardens better than most and I gather there are some fine walks to be had, including one out towards Ludgershall Castle.

If you decide to go, you will have to speak with Eleanor direct; if you write to me to ask me to arrange things with my sister, we might not have time. The post is reliable out here – in that things do get delivered – but not necessarily as swiftly as one might wish; the postal workers are good, honest people but they operate within a cumbersome, bureaucratic system. A legacy of the Soviet days, perhaps. Yes, good people, in a wonderful country who are beginning to value some outside involvement which is enabling them to better stand on their own feet as a nation.

So, if you are up for it, please liaise with Eleanor – you know her address. I hope I have captured within this letter what it is I am asking. I've set out my fears, my thoughts and sense of powerlessness being out here when she would benefit from my presence back home. Yes, I am a long, long way from where I'd like to be in June. So, I ask – nothing more, nothing less. I just ask. You can say no and Eleanor might be absolutely fine all by herself and it turns out I'm just a big brother worrying over nothing.

Yet, as I say, I'm nervous for her. It feels 'high stakes'. He's introducing her to his family, they are not nice people and Eleanor's anxious. So, five days at a country house out in the wilds of Wiltshire is what I'm asking. If you go, may I express my thanks here, in advance, but you don't have to go. Your decision but you have a way of seeing things and of understanding people so I hope –

Sorry, there I go again. Your decision.

I will write again soon – promise. When I next write that will be without further favours being sought from myself. It will be just a letter, telling you a bit more about life out here and, as importantly, asking how you are and what you are getting up to these days. Are you still volunteering at that stately home in your village, owned by that ageing Lord? Do you still see Helen there? If so, pass on my best to her. Separately, thank you for the postcard you sent me of Restormel Castle – said you were staying at your favourite Cornish hotel once again, 'The Jupiter'. From the date you put on it, it took a long time to find its way to me here in Tashkent. I treasure it and use it as a bookmark.

Now though I must conclude if I am to make today's postal collection. I will close by saying, as I said at the start of this letter, it has been remiss of me not to have written more often. I miss your friendship – fancy a drink sometime?

With my love and prayers.

Terry

x

Philippians 1:3

CHAPTER 3

Worlds Apart

Alba placed the letter down on the small octagonal wooden table next to her. As she unfurled her legs from underneath her, she stretched out her arms either side of her and then arched them upwards until her hands met a distance above her head, as if she were performing some delectable sequenced ballet routine.

As her hands returned to her lap, Alba found herself doubting something. It was not something directly emanating from what she had just read nor was it a doubt about what had happened here at Kingsbourne overnight. Dr Sunday, driven to act by a toxic family around him, had jumped to his death having realised his family would never accept his fiancée; believing they would make Eleanor's life a misery if she stayed with him. Thus, to spare her that life but unwilling to live without her, he had taken his own. Tragic. Perhaps it was, as he stood on that lead-covered roof, seemingly 'heroic'. Either way troubling but nothing about it was placing any doubt in her, Alba's, mind.

Doubt was there though – or was it 'doubt'? Was there not some other emotion or factor which had suddenly unsettled her – unsettled her in a different way to what she, along with everyone else staying here these few days, had witnessed outside. Something was troubling *her* – something was not *sitting right* with her.

It was there deep within her and, up until this moment, she had been reluctant to accept it or even to countenance it as a possibility. Others back home – that small village on the Surrey-Sussex border where she lived – had observed it and had tried to discuss it with her but she had dismissed them. A pang of guilt pulsed through her body as she conceded to herself, as she sat in the tapestry-covered chair, that 'dismissed' was probably too sanitised a word. She had cut her friends short, she had placed a distance between herself and them and had made it obvious she had been unwilling to even listen to their opinions.

*

Alone and with no one else to talk to but herself, she had to question why she had in fact come to Kingsbourne. It was something she should have done all along, something her friends had tried to help her with and yet only now was she willing to consider why she had come.

Terry had made it abundantly clear it was her decision whether she came or not and she definitely had not felt he had forced her into it. She knew he wanted her to come and to be here for Eleanor but that was different to him *forcing* her. There was no compulsion, no emotional 'arm twisting', no playing a guilt card; that had never been Terry's style. He had always given those around him the space to make their own decisions even if he had first opined what he felt was the right thing to do.

No, she had most definitely come of her own volition – she had *wished* to come. She had wished to help Terry, a friend from her university days, and she had wished to support Eleanor and yet something was troubling her as she finally stood up and gazed once more out of the mullioned window before her.

'And yet' she found herself musing over, as she leant towards the window, looked down and observed two police officers engaged in a hushed conversation as they strode through what they had not appreciated was the Manor's well-stocked and well-maintained herb garden. 'And yet' was a phrase of sorts which Alba could not shake. Was she really here because she had chosen to come out of a desire to help a friend who was unable to act for himself? Here out of a keenness to support an acquaintance through an awkward few days? Here because of the pull of being allowed to stay in a country house? Were any of those reasons why she was really here? Was it really that simple that things had drawn her here to do the right thing?

She moved over to her bed and pressed the button above the bedside table before returning to stand by the window.

'No,' she conceded. 'No. Yes, there were things which had rightly, compassionately, drawn her here but there was another layer to it,' she inwardly said to herself. It was not just that things had attracted her to coming. Something had pushed her away from home. Something had made the decision for her or at least had made making the decision to come, so much easier. Something had made taking time away from her cottage, from the village, from her voluntary work at Hillstone Hall easier. She had come – and Alba winced at herself as she came to accept the fact – as she was running from something. Alba had been grateful to have been given a reason to get away for a bit and she had taken it.

An excuse to leave for a short while had made things so much simpler back home. She had been able to say to Andrew that she was going away to help a friend of a friend, whilst all along it masked the reality that it was in fact Andrew who she was needing time away from. Maybe that was a bit harsh on Andrew, 'yes, it definitely was too harsh on Andrew' Alba immediately corrected herself. Time away from them as a couple, was that more accurate?

Not that they were a 'couple' couple, for he still lived at Hillstone Hall, the ancestral home of successive Viscount Hartfields, with its sunken garden, an Orangery and its once grand music room, and she in her little cottage with its sash windows, wisteria growing up and around the tiled front porch and a hall table with an ornament no grander than that of a lady with a cat on her lap, on it. In other regards, though, they were a couple – they were soul mates, best friends, boyfriend and girlfriend call it what you will, they got on. Well, they did get on.

She had been a volunteer gardener at Hillstone Hall for a good while before she had ever spoken to him and it was only the tragic death of Vaughan, a couple of years ago, which had brought them together. Despite Andrew being heir to the Viscountcy, he had helped her search Mrs Taylor's home, he had stood up for her during that dénouement – that unknotting – of what had happened to Vaughan and he had, another time, travelled to Cornwall to surprise her when she had been holidaying by herself. He was, when they had first met, due to his father predeceasing his, Andrew's, grandfather, heir apparent; Andrew was destined to be the 8th Lord Hartfield. Alba, in contrast to his being the Honourable Andrew Chapman, was simply Miss Alba White, with no lineage, history or money behind her. Still, though, they had got on. For a couple of years they had been getting on and yet things were different between them now.

Of course, it did not take a genius to work out what was different now. Edward Chapman, Andrew's grandfather and 7th Lord Hartfield, had died at the turn of the year and Andrew had duly inherited the peerage. Andrew – the 8th Lord Hartfield, a Viscount and rumoured by some that he was being lined up to be a working hereditary peer with a position within the Foreign and Commonwealth Office – was now just busy. To begin with, he had tried to include Alba as much as he could. She had enjoyed learning the difference between 'letters patent' and a 'writ of summons' and she had sat beside him and his grandmother during the 7th Lord's funeral, which had taken place in St Mary's, the parish church and conducted by the Reverend Quinn.

It was just that Andrew was *so* busy.

Not busy because he was struggling with what now lay before him; he had been well tutored by his grandfather and Andrew was entirely up to the task. He wanted to take Alba 'on the ride with him'; he had, and Alba knew he had, tried to involve her in decision making for the estate grounds, in personnel matters and he had frequently voiced his appreciation for the companionship she had offered his grandmother.

Yet Andrew was having to 'ride on a train' which was travelling – having to travel – too quickly, far too quickly, for Alba. She had done her best, given this was to all intents and purposes an alien world to her, but she came to feel that her best was not good enough for what he needed from her. It was not that she could not understand it all. She knew what the limitation on the remainder meant for this particular Viscountcy. She knew his title ranked below an Earldom and she even grasped the subtlety of the tradition which meant Andrew did not *take* his grandfather's title until after the latter's funeral. It was just that it did not interest her enough. She loved Andrew but maybe she was too much of a free spirit, maybe her yearning to be outdoors, with her hands in the soil or walking the Downs, was too much of a draw for her. The closeness they had both felt to begin with, as she stood over Andrew as he sat at what had been his grandfather's desk and signed official letter after official letter, had waned. She came to realise that she was not offering him enough in those moments and, if anything, was slowing him down as he kindly, patiently, sought to explain what each document was truly about.

Inevitably, she had started to make her excuses. She found reasons why she could not join him on certain days. To begin with it had been driven by her desire to allow him to make greater administrative headway by himself but it all too soon became apparent that she was relieved not to be involved and in time Andrew stopped inviting her to join him. Inevitably, more and more decisions about running the estate, which at one stage he had endearingly wanted her involvement in, were made quickly, sensibly, by him but by him alone. Thereafter, he had stopped even trying to encourage her to join him and, after her umpteenth rejection, no longer offered her a paid role within his estate team to replace the volunteer's position she still technically undertook.

They had drifted apart.

There had never – never, Alba resolutely reminded herself – been a cross word between them. It was just that they seemed to be living worlds apart and whilst teleporting between planets in that iconic 1970s science fiction television series of 'Blake's 7' was simple enough, in the real world, moving between her cottage, Andrew's study within Hillstone Hall and Westminster was anything but simple – if only she had Kerr Avon's teleport bracelet but she did not. She had had to navigate moving between such worlds by herself and she, not intentionally, maliciously or without regret, had failed to adequately do so and so she and Andrew had grown distant.

'Maybe they were not different people but the circumstances in which they now found themselves in, were,' Alba found herself musing.

At that moment there was a knock at her manor bedroom door.

*

Alba, opening the door, was greeted by Sandy, the housemaid. It was a visibly upset and unsettled younger woman who Alba found herself looking at.

"You rang, Miss White," the person standing in the corridor stated but she did so without any energy in her voice and without any colour in her cheeks.

"I did," replied Alba apologetically. "I'm so sorry to trouble you."

"No trouble at all, miss," broke in Sandy completely unconvincingly.

"I know it's an intrusion, Sandy, what with what has just happened. We're all totally shocked and saddened."

"Oh, miss, it's awful, just awful," and with that Sandy burst into tears and fumbled for a handkerchief in her dress pocket.

Alba, able to produce one from her own pocket quicker than the maid – a person hardly out of her teens – opposite her was able to, offered it to Sandy. Then, having taken a step towards her, duly put her arm around her and ushered her into the bedroom. Alba sat the crying girl in the chair she, Alba, had been reading Terry's letter in just a few moments ago and then duly lifted the hardback desk chair over from the other side of her bedroom to sit with her.

"It's horrible, so ghastly and horrible. Just horrible," said Sandy.

"Yes, it is," replied Alba.

"Horrible," repeated the young maid – she was young, if not in her own mind, then definitely to Alba.

Alba nodded in agreement and allowed Sandy time to cry. There was little else Alba could do. She did not know Sandy – beyond having briefly spoken to the maid on the day of Alba's arrival at Kingsbourne and seen her at work around the manor thereafter. Alba could not even offer her a cup of tea, for that was the reason she had rung for her.

One of Dr Sunday's quirks had been to not have hospitality trays in guests' bedrooms but to employ sufficient staff to cater for his guests, even down to having shoes polished if so desired by those staying. He had explained his reasoning to Alba shortly after she had arrived and she could see what he was trying to get at even if some might misinterpret it. Perhaps, so Dr Sunday said of himself, he was old-fashioned; he claimed it was all about giving employment to local people, especially those who had fallen on hard times. Old-fashioned or not he said he was keen to support people where he could and build them up rather than simply giving out charity. He also said he wanted those who worked for him to feel a degree of ownership of the place too. Finally, he said that some people simply had a flair for serving others. He had acknowledged to Alba that he knew such a stance was open to challenge and resentment by those who did not share his views, especially by other locals who had been refused similar positions or sacked after he had given them their chance, but that he was persevering with his approach regardless.

Whether Alba agreed with Dr Sunday or not – be it a way to get cheap labour, even if it was all nicely wrapped up in clever altruistic language, or a way to offer employment that was underpinned by a genuine, compassionate, desire to build up his fellow man, to 'help the weary traveller' – in this moment, Alba was unsure. What she was far more sure of was her silent wish that she had bothered to pack a little kettle to enable her to have her own hot drinks as and when she wanted in her bedroom here at the manor, rather than having to trouble the house staff every time she wanted something; and Alba was particularly conscious of burdening Sandy, who had seemed timid from the first time she had met her, with her desire for a cup of tea in a moment like this.

*

"I'd only just started working here in April," stated Sandy. "Even though Dr Sunday had heard about me not making it through my first year at university, he still got his housekeeper to approach me and ask if I fancied working here. I'm still on my sort of probationary period but I'm so grateful he did offer me something, I need all the money I can get – for starters I have loads of rent to pay on my uni accommodation which I'm obviously not using but which I am contracted to pay for until the end of August."

With that, Sandy suddenly looked across to Alba and said defiantly:

"But please don't think I got kicked off the course for doing anything bad – I didn't take drugs or said anything unkind to anyone else – I just kept failing my assignments. I just struggled to fit in, I missed home and–"

Her voice died though and she simply looked at Alba.

"No need to explain, Sandy," offered back Alba sympathetically. "University is not for everyone. For what it is worth, I really struggled at university myself to begin with."

"Did you?" asked Sandy with surprise in her voice. "But you seem so confident and had the other guests here all doing as you told them as you were playing that garden game yesterday. I saw, you see, I was watching through the dining room window as you were bossing the others around. Oh, please don't think I was spying, it was just as I was laying the table – I wasn't snooping, promise."

"Please don't worry yourself; looking out of a window is hardly a capital offence and there were definitely some raised voices to be heard as we played."

"Strange game, so it looked to me, what with all those wooden blocks – I've never seen it before, what's it called?"

"Kubb," answered Alba.

The blank look Alba got in reply prompted Alba to add some details.

"It's – well I think it is – a Swedish game in origin. There are two teams and each has to knock the other team's posts over and then the 'King pin' before the other team gets all yours."

"Oh," expressed a slightly but only slightly less puzzled Sandy. "From where I was watching, it looked like you were throwing those rounded wooden batons at one another's shins."

"Given all the arguments which have been going on this weekend–"

Yet Alba paused as she noticed that that comment had triggered just a faint momentary half smile on the young woman's face. Once it had faded Alba continued but felt she needed to explain herself first:

"Please don't think I'm making a joke of today or our whole time here."

"No, no," concurred Sandy. "I knew you weren't trying to be funny as in 'laugh out loud funny'. Plus, well, between you and me if I may break the upstairs-downstairs code of the staff never discussing anything with the guests, it seems to me that a lot of the people staying here really don't like one another."

"I think that's a bit of an understatement," agreed Alba. "I'm sure if Anthony and Johanna, if they'd been on opposing teams, would have happily thrown the batons at one another's shins whether it was within the rule book or not; thankfully they were on the same side."

"And Henry," added Sandy. "He's been angry the whole time."

To that, Alba simply nodded an agreement, for Henry, the elder child of Anthony and Johanna, and brother to Connie, did indeed seem to have an impatience, a frustration with the world, which had flared up several times since Alba's arrival on Wednesday evening.

"But no," Alba wished to clarify. "Within the game of Kubb you're not throwing at the people in the opposing team – well, you're not meant to be – rather at the opposing team's wooden blocks. You're throwing at their 'kubbs' and then finally at their 'king'. I guess it was the angle you were looking at us from, that made you think we were simply throwing things at each other."

"I suppose," agreed Sandy. "Enjoy it? The game I mean not necessarily the company you played it with," she clarified.

"A wise distinction," said Alba as she tucked some of her own loose hair behind her left ear. "I am sure with that kind of discerning eye, you would have sailed through uni had you had the right friends around you and a tutor to take you under his wing," added Alba for the other's encouragement – for Alba sensed this petite woman opposite her needed building up. "Thankfully, I had Dr Sunday as one of my tutors and some good friends around me to help me through some of my darker moments; Eleanor's brother for one."

"You were one of Dr Sunday's students, then?"

"Yes," confirmed Alba. "As you will have had during your time at uni, we had several lecturers and tutors but, yes, Dr Sunday was one of them. A very knowledgeable man but without being so bookish or ivory towered as to be unable to teach. He was creative in how he taught us but methodical with it."

"He was tidy, too," added Sandy, keen to offer her assessment of the man who in life and now in death had brought her and Alba together in this moment.

"Tidy? I suppose that's another way of saying methodical," mused Alba.

"No," corrected Sandy. "I wasn't just redefining 'methodical' I did mean something different – he was, on a practical level, a tidy, ordered person to work for. He liked things to be put away, not left to be picked up later, not scattered."

"Really?" reflected Alba. "I never got to see that side of him – I just saw him in lecture halls and tutorial rooms."

"Oh, yes, he liked things being tidy. Please don't get me wrong, not in some obsessive way but he did prefer order and neatness. Said he believed it helped us, as his staff, be efficient but, as I say, on a personal level he liked things to be neat, never random or just ramshackle."

Yet on looking at Alba, Sandy was suddenly unsure whether to continue or not. After a pause, Sandy spoke again:

"Sorry, miss, was I boring you? You looked rather uninterested."

"Was I? Sorry, I was just – oh, never mind. Let's get back to what's important – to you, shall we?"

"Me? I've never been important."

"Don't keep putting yourself down – we're all important – and we were considering your time at university. I really think with different friends and tutors around you, you surely would have settled and progressed," insisted Alba.

"I really don't think I–"

"As I say, don't keep putting yourself down," cut in Alba. "You've been such a hard worker; I've seen you. Always there in the background tidying things up, helping people with their coats, finding lost handbags–"

"I didn't take those earrings!" pleaded Sandy.

"I wasn't inferring that you did. Sorry, not the best example to build you up with. I just meant to say, you are efficient. You have things ready when needed, you cater to our whims and, I suspect, you've a good eye for judging people's characters. You're more talented than you let on. So, don't let not continuing with your studies be your defining feature; that course or that academic institution wasn't for you. Don't let that dictate who you are."

"You think–" but Sandy hesitated, unsure of herself or the confidence Alba was trying to instil in her.

"Absolutely – you remind me of a young friend of mine back home, Sam. She started off helping in the tea shop of the local stately home and now is their head of catering and events. She's only got a few years on you, so you persevere, that's my advice to you."

"Really?"

"Really," insisted Alba. "And yes to answer your original question, I enjoyed the game. I'd played 'Kubb' before which helped and it is reasonably simple to explain when it's laid out on the grass in front of people who have never previously played it. Plus, there's a bit more strategy to it than you first think. It's a nice garden game for the summer days we've had whilst we've been here. Well, it would have been if there hadn't been so many rows."

Sandy, having regained her composure and keen to reassume her role of taking care of her guests rather than the other way round, this time consciously refrained from adding her own opinion to Alba's final comment. Instead, she brushed her black dress down and stood up. She spoke to Alba:

"A drink, was it? The reason you called me?"

"Yes but I really don't want to trouble you," insisted Alba. "I really don't mind popping down to make it myself."

"No, miss," said Sandy. "You're a guest here. I'm quite alright now to get it. Milk, I presume, sugar?"

"No, no sugar, thank you."

With that Sandy made for the bedroom door. As she stood with her hand on the heavy curved metal door handle, she turned to Alba and, with her composure already waning, anxiously spoke once more:

"Please don't tell any of the family I've been discussing them with you. Don't tell the housekeeper either. I can't lose this position, especially not for something negative and looks really bad, like breaching my employer's confidentiality. If I suddenly had to look for other work already, oh dear, it would be, er, well, er, a disaster. So, you really can't tell. My prospects are limited as they are, what with dropping out of university for starters, as I say. Seriously, I mean seriously, you can't tell anyone."

With that, Sandy fell silent and simply looked to the other, desperate for some reassurance.

"Of course not," said Alba. "You haven't said anything about the family I haven't observed for myself so please don't worry yourself."

"Oh, miss, thank you. I do worry, you see, what with—"

"It's fine," said Alba.

"You see, I just can't be sacked for bad behaviour. I mean, I guess, er, we'll all – I mean us staff – will all lose our jobs before too long. The master has just killed himself after all; there won't be much work for us now, will there?"

"I suppose not," agreed Alba.

"But I need this position for as long as possible – for as long as they, er, Dr Sunday's brothers and sister I guess – want the staff around. As long as possible and at least when they do dispense with me, they will give me a good reference; Hugh should, given all the attention he pays me; though, at times, he does get a bit close, as you've noticed. It's not pleasant. Really it's not but I've tolerated it because I need my position here, given I've got that rent to pay."

"Still?" queried Alba – this time opting to momentarily revisit that issue with the other.

"Yes," replied Sandy. "I'm paying until the end of August. Hardly seems fair to me and I'm sure the accommodation office will have put someone into my old room by now. However, they said I'd signed a contract and so I had to keep paying. It's not fair, if you ask me and what with the other money I owe to people, well, I need to stay on here as long as possible."

Alba, sensing Sandy was close to tears once again, went over to her and took the young woman's hands in her own. As she gently held them, Alba said:

"I've said I won't tell anyone, so I won't, got it?" With that, Alba ever so gently tugged on Sandy's hands to make the point. "Got it?" Alba repeated.

"Yes, miss."

"That's one less thing to worry about, then, so that is good. As for everything else, money worries, what will happen here at Kingsbourne now, I can't say but you're a small team here and you yourself seem very efficient, as I've already said, so I'm sure they will hold onto you for as long as they can. Just keep doing your job over these difficult few days ahead and someone will see your worth. I can't promise, as you know, but 'stiff upper lip' and all that."

"Yes, miss. Thank you, miss."

"And if you feel yourself wavering, come and find me and we'll have a quiet walk round the garden or something – just you and me. After all, the roses are just lovely out there, aren't they? OK, not quite the rose garden at Hever Castle but where is? Still, the roses here are pretty good."

"Alright, miss. I'll bear that in mind – I'll look out for you if I'm losing it again. Thank you for your kind words."

"Really, it's nothing."

"It's not nothing, you've been kind to me. I'm grateful, really, I am. I'll be up with a tray for you in a few minutes."

*

Ten minutes later, as she drank her tea, puzzling over why the crescent moon shaped shortbread biscuits always tasted slightly different to the other standard designs that were on the plate before her, Alba found herself thinking of Andrew – Viscount, the 8th Lord Hartfield but to her simply Andrew – once more. It would have been nice, she supposed, had he been here. There was a lot, clearly, to tell him and she would have valued his take on the tragic events that had unfolded here overnight. 'Yes, it would have been good if he were here' she thought but he was not and she felt it.

As she then placed her teacup down on the octagonal table beside her and leaned back into the tapestried chair, she suddenly found herself thinking about all the other random stuff that there was to tell him, starting with the journey here on Wednesday. At the time it had been eventful and upsetting but, of course, everything which had happened since had made her almost forget about her journey here. Yes, Wednesday itself had been a hectic and a strange day in itself and that was before she had even got to Kingsbourne Manor. Alba knew that, had Andrew been there in the room at Kingsbourne Manor with her, she would have told him all about it.

CHAPTER 4

Little blue triangles

It was hardly an early departure but the journey, on paper at least, was meant to be less than four hours, nearer to three in fact. So, Alba had not rushed and believed she was still giving herself plenty of time to get to Kingsbourne Manor by late afternoon, early evening.

She had been a bit unsure what to wear for the journey. She had alternated between the formal-posh of an about knee length sundress, the purely practical comfortable option of shorts and a T-shirt and the compromise, sitting on the fence, middle of the road smart-casual possibility of nicely cut tapered trousers and a simple blouse. 'Did she dress for the journey, the country house she would be arriving at or select an outfit that could well disappoint on both counts?' she had reflected on during the course of her unrushed morning.

As she sat, shortly after lunch, at her kitchen table with her 'pre-departure cup of tea' in hand, she studied her road atlas. As she did so, the room she was in momentarily faded from view and she felt herself once more sitting by her late father prior to some journey he was planning. A much younger Alba – the child she had once been – was there by his side, having to add up the mileage as he called out the numbers marked on the atlas; numbers he got from the midway points between those little blue triangles sited at each town centre or major road junction. Alba felt once more the pressure she was under to tally the 'score' as quickly as her father would read out those seemingly random figures. The figures began small – two, two, one, five, two, and so on. They were those smaller numbers as he plotted their 'escape' from the more urban area where they lived. Then suddenly, she would get hit by bigger numbers – twelve, nine, seventeen, yes, seventeen always seemed to catch her out somehow – as the journey her father was organising had broken free of the urban sprawl and made its way on to the major 'A roads'. That would mean they were now out in the country far beyond their home town where the gaps between the little blue triangles grew in distance. Once more Alba felt the childlike anxiety of waiting to hear the next number her father would call and whether it would be seventeen.

That anxiety would still be there as her father asked her what the mileage was – as he placed his finger on the map at the route's end. Yet it would dissipate as he then praised her for getting it correct. Of course, sometimes he would suggest they calculate it again, as he, without ever saying it in so many words, told her she had tallied it wrong. It took Alba years to realise that he had always been adding it up himself at the same time and had never needed her help but that it was his way – one of his ways – of imparting learning to his young daughter.

As Alba's current kitchen came back into view and memories of her childhood kitchen table and family holidays in their turn faded, Alba once more felt the warmth of her father's praise as she – be it at the first or a subsequent attempt – offered up the correct milage.

That feeling of warmth was added to today not just by the mug of tea she was cradling – poured from her mustard yellow 'Denby' teapot, which sat off to her left on the table – but from the warm June sunshine which flooded her kitchen and fell across her shoulders.

Having refilled her mug, she glanced at the open road atlas once more. She knew the mileage to Kingsbourne both ways – either using the motorways whenever she could or sort of heading cross country, taking the 'A' and 'B' roads. The motorways offered speed, or at least the potential of it, and functionality. The latter offered, if not rustic *old England*, then at least a little bit more visual stimulation to the journey; for the 'A' and 'B' roads would loop her under Guildford, see her traverse the 'Hog's Back', head her towards Odiham, take her well above Winchester, lead her towards Andover and then into Wiltshire itself. Either way, she would incorporate at least a small section of the A303.

To Alba, the A303 was the 'Great Western Highway' and it offered a gateway to Somerset, Devon and ultimately that most enticing of counties, Cornwall; though Alba was well aware that some way before Cornwall it had become the less alluring A30. Yet the A303 took one west and that was its charm. Of course, whilst Alba was a loyalist to it, to others, many many others, that same road offered up nothing more than being stuck behind cars towing caravans at painfully slow speeds, delays past Stonehenge and the dispiriting faded glory of those once grand roadside coaching inns which dotted the route. To those others, the A303 was simply that most annoying of 'A' roads.

Yet, to Alba, she would always take that road over logic – and even over her own father's advice. For it offered her the romance of being westward bound and the juxtaposition of being on a busy arterial road yet at the same time having major oak trees present, there between her and the oncoming carriageway. Even the faded glory of those roadside coaching inns appealed to Alba, with their 'To Let' or 'For Sale' signs. She was also intrigued by their overgrown gardens and weed-infested car parks; areas littered with seemingly abandoned bits of agricultural machinery. Yes, each dying inn or hotel intrigued Alba and somehow, to her if to no one else, offered something to her journey even now. For each one she drove past, caused her to wonder what glories it once exuded, what glamourous guests might have once stayed there in the hotel's heyday and whether, just whether, that particular one might have been the inspiration for 'The Pelican Inn' in Warwick Deeping's *Sorrell and Son*. Yes, she was teased by each once grand inn and her musings and her sense of wonder about it would last just long enough until she passed another dying building and she lost herself in wondering what that one once offered those who lived, worked or stayed there on their way to somewhere else.

To Alba, the road also had the lure that 'The Jupiter Hotel' was somewhere beyond the end of it; that hotel, compared to the faded, dying inns and hotels dotted along the A303, was still very much in its prime. The 'Jupiter' was still a loved building, which drew in guests from far and wide and it would be many a year before its glory waned. However, this time, this journey, Alba would not get that far and the draw of 'The Jupiter' would have to wait.

This time it would simply be a very small section of the A303 road she would be driving – she would be on it only until she started to hit those road signs edged in red, to denote the military sites on and around Salisbury Plain. However, to Alba any journey that included a section, however short, of her favourite road, promised to be a good journey.

*

As Alba sat in her kitchen, her route decided upon, and as she once more chose to focus on the appeal of the open road rather than perhaps on what – or more pertinently who – it was that she was keen to leave behind or to ignore for a while longer, and with her mug finally empty, there was a knock at her front door.

Upon opening it, Alba was met with a smile and the outstretched arm of the local vicar.

"A copy of the parish magazine for you, Alba" said Reverend Quinn as he held out a copy of the June edition.

"June's?" quizzed Alba with a slight tilting of her head and the ever so slight raising of her eyebrows.

"Yes, June's," confirmed the reverend.

He looked at the woman before him. Part of him wanted to comment on how nice she looked. He would have described it as a kind of floaty summer dress that she was wearing. It had a curved neckline, which did not mirror the hemline, and a sort of ruffled extra bit of material which followed the neckline and up and over each shoulder. It had a soft floral motif as was not unusual for Alba. However, he stayed silent and simply continued to hold out the church newsletter.

"It's the 16th," stated Alba. "We're closer to July than the beginning of June; in fact, I've already had my July edition of my magazine from the Royal Horticultural Society. Seems to me the C of E is lacking the efficiency of the RHS."

"Well, er, what with the Curate being off and, er–" but the parish vicar fell silent unsure whether to return his arm to his side and no longer offer up the simple eight page magazine; a magazine which he himself had struggled to put together in order to offer the parish anything at all this month. It had been a struggle due to the absence of his curate and with the church secretary being on sick leave.

"I'm teasing you," Alba quickly added as she sensed his awkwardness. "Well, it is the 16th but I'm teasing you on everything else. Are you still without, oh, I forget their names."

"Yes. Samson is on a residential placement at Bible college and Tina, our secretary, is off for a period of time."

"Oh, yes, I remember hearing about Tina from someone. How is she?"

"Her treatment is ongoing and you can tell she's struggling. She's still making it along to some services and just her being there is a great witness. What's particularly lovely is that she's not embarrassed for others to go up and ask how she is. She's quite happy chatting in the church hall afterwards, even if she has to often sit down as the treatment is quite draining."

"Something you're all too familiar with, I assume, given–" yet

Alba's words died as she was unsure whether to mention the vicar's late wife.

"Yes," Matthew Quinn succinctly said. "Trials come in all of our lives, don't they? I guess I just didn't expect it so very soon in my marriage."

"No," Alba simply said.

For a moment neither said anything, until Matthew spoke once more, as he thought back:

"My wife was always comforted by something Peter said–"

"Peter, do I know a Peter? I don't think so; is he your church treasurer?" asked Alba.

"No, that's Richard. No, you don't know Peter any more than in one sense I do or my late wife did."

"You've lost me – you seemed to be inferring the pair of you knew this Peter."

"Did I? Sorry. I was just thinking of a verse from something the Apostle Peter wrote to the scattered church, a verse which very much brought comfort to her. It was the opening chapter of his first letter but, now, was it verse six or verse seven – blow me, I'll have to look it up when I'm back."

"OK," said Alba. However, not wishing to seem as if she was uninterested in his loss, added, "well, let me know which it is but don't rush back this afternoon with the answer because I won't be around and not just up at the Hall but away away."

"OK, I'll let you know. As I always say, though, be careful taking a single Bible verse out of context, especially as this letter of Peter's was written to believers so you, if I may say, might not read it in quite the same way. For another time, though, as yes, I hadn't forgotten, you're away for a few days."

"Within the hour, I hope," said Alba. "I would have asked you in otherwise but I'm just tidying the last few things away, closing windows and making up a flask for the journey. If I wasn't setting off shortly I'd have–"

"It's fine. I wasn't looking to stop. Just thought I'd bring you round a magazine now – as you so kindly have picked up on – I have finally put it together."

"I was teasing," stressed Alba.

"It's fine," the Reverend Quinn said reassuringly. "I thought you could have a copy to take away with you – you're off to Warwickshire for a few days if I remember correctly."

"Wiltshire," corrected Alba.

"Yes, you had said. Not a part of the country I know well beyond the obvious big stony thing."

With that, Matthew gestured with his hands – for by now he had placed the magazine down on the little stone ledge in Alba's wisteria covered porch. He gestured as if he were placing large pillars, columns or even mighty 'Lego' towers around him in a circular fashion, to invisibly recreate standing within a ring of sarsen stones.

"Oh, that big stony thing," teased Alba, grateful the Reverend Quinn was happy to lighten the mood of what had been a rather sombre few minutes as they had discussed his late wife. "I thought you might have been thinking of the Giant's Causeway."

"No, I'm not that daft. I know that's not in Wiltshire."

"Nor Warwickshire."

"Isn't it? Gosh, I do learn a lot when I come to your door."

Alba was conscious that he was still very much at her door, even now. She was also aware that she had not even stepped from her hall to join him in the front garden – for them both to move from under the arching branches of the shaggy wistaria – her treasured white *wisteria floribunda* – which grew up her porch. Yet she wanted to get away from her village and to be somewhere else for a while. Thus, she felt the need to stress her desire to get on.

"Yes, I'm off soon," she reiterated.

"Sorry, yes, you said and here I am holding you up. I just thought I'd see if I could catch you before you went; I saw your car so I thought I'd knock. Going by yourself or is–"

"No, just me."

"Oh, I'd have assumed Andrew might have needed a break as well. It has been a few months since his grandfather's funeral and I suspect he could do with some time away."

"Just me," repeated Alba succinctly.

"OK. I'd just assumed, if you're having a few days away in the country that, er, and together–"

"It's just me, alright," stated Alba, with an edge to her voice which was not lost on the vicar.

"All I was trying to say–" started Matthew but Alba would not let him finish.

"Look, it's me by myself. Andrew's busy, so I'm going alone." Then, with an anger which seemed to emerge from nowhere, Alba added:

"He's always blinking busy. Always tied up with letters, meetings, time up in London. It's not like it used to–"

With that, though, Alba caught her own tongue and fell silent.

"If you want to talk," offered up Matthew – leaving his comment as wide open as he could.

"No," said Alba bluntly.

*

The awkwardness of the moment was not lost on either of them; Alba trying to blind herself to her own hostile demeanour and the minister desperate not to depart from the woman opposite him with such an air between them. He offered up an 'arrow prayer' as he stood there – lifting the moment to above.

Then, suddenly, the awkwardness was broken by the sound of Alba's front gate going once more this Wednesday daytime.

"Hi Alba," called Sam. "I'm so pleased to have caught you in. I need a favour." As Sam took a further few steps down Alba's path, and as Alba wondered what it might be, Sam added, "Oh, hello Reverend, didn't see you there amongst all the leaves."

Samantha was now at the reverend's side. She observed Alba just for a moment then added:

"Blow me, Alba, the front of your home is looking like a right jungle. You look lovely, I might add – the angled hemline of your dress is *so* you – but this plant out here is rampant. It was lovely when in bloom last month; it was last month, wasn't it? Now though, it's all over the place."

"It's just the wisteria," offered back Alba. She was grateful to have some plant-related comment or question to focus on, compared to the pressure she was beginning to feel from Matthew. "It's just about due its summer prune."

"Summer prune?" queried the minister – himself grateful for an alternative topic. "That kind of suggests it gets more than one hacking back a year."

"Nothing in my garden gets hacked back."

The coldness in Alba's comment was evident to Sam. Sam now stood alongside the Reverend Matthew Quinn – the vicar of St Mary's, the village church – and amongst and within the bushiness of the climber; it was one which had over the years and with Alba's careful guiding hands, and before her the hands of the previous owner, entwined itself up and around her front porch and a good section of the front of the house. The somewhat curious look Sam offered back to Alba, prompted Alba to add, though this time in softer tones:

"If you prune plants as you're meant to you should never need to hack at any living thing. Wisteria, like most climbers and vines, is pretty prolific and it does put on a lot of growth each year. So, yes, Matthew, it needs pruning twice a year. In the summer, prune the new growth back to six buds and in the winter back to just two buds."

"That all sounds a bit complicated," suggested Sam. "I'd be forever getting confused; I wouldn't know what to do when."

To that, self-depreciating comment, both Alba and Matthew

smiled, for they both knew that Sam was organised, efficient and intelligent. Sam, still only in her early twenties, had simply been, when Alba first got to know her, a local girl who worked in the tearooms of the local stately home – Hillstone Hall – in between her days at catering college. Sam had all the culinary flair of her gifted mother but with an astute business brain as well. So, by now, just a few years on, Sam had become Hillstone Hall's catering and entertainment supremo. She was still very much a local girl but her worth had been quickly noted by Andrew. Even in the years before he succeeded his grandfather as Lord, he had ensured his grandfather, the 7th Lord Hartfield, had retained and then promoted Sam as the right vacancies arose.

Nonetheless, as Alba, Sam and Matthew stood at the front door, Alba played along with Sam's claim of ineptitude.

"You shouldn't put yourself down. It's simple really if you remember the tiny little saying of 'two shillings and sixpence' or even just 'two and six' – in the second month, prune to two buds and in the sixth month prune to six. Obviously, prune out any dead stuff as well but if you remember 'two and six' you can't go wrong."

"Can't we?" challenged Matthew on behalf of Alba's two visitors. "Do you want us to prune it whilst you're away?"

"I think it's best if…"

Yet Alba's full reply was smothered by Sam's question:

"Oh, are you away sometime soon? Not too soon, I hope. As I say, I need a favour like now-ish."

"Depends what it is," offered up Alba. "I'm hoping to set off in about forty-five minutes; I'm off to Wiltshire for a few days with–"

"With Andrew, good. As the favour I need is for a lift to the Hall. Mum can pick me up late tonight, once I've got everything ready for tomorrow, but I can't get there easily now, what with the things I've got to transport up there from home. That's because my car won't start but I really need to get there soonest and start prepping. So, on your way to collecting Andrew could you give me a lift?"

"Oh, please, why does everyone think I'm going away with Andrew?" With that, Alba's prickliness resurfaced.

"Well, I just assumed–"

"You assumed wrong."

"So did I," volunteered Matthew as a way of offering solidarity to Sam.

"But could you give me a lift on your way to seeing Andrew before you go? It would be really appreciated if you could."

"I'm not going via the Hall. I don't need to see Andrew to get his permission to have a few days away and he can cope without me fine. He seems to be doing that a lot these days."

"Things are obviously different for him now," offered up Sam.

"So everyone keeps reminding me but I am aware of that fact. It's affected me too," said Alba.

"If you want to have a chat sometime, just give me a shout," Sam warmly volunteered.

"No thank you."

"Oh, OK," said Sam – a slightly confused and somewhat hurt Sam. "Anyway, I had just hoped you could help me get up to work."

"I can't. I'm not going to the Hall, I'm not going that way out of the village and I really need to get on if I'm to make it to Kingsbourne before the worst of the rush hour."

"Sam," voiced Reverend Quinn. "I'll give you a lift. I can deliver the rest of these magazines another day. After all, as has been recently pointed out to me, they are already weeks late. Another hour or so, a day even, won't make a lot of difference."

The smile and word of thanks Sam gave Matthew was picked up on by Alba but in a negative way. Perhaps Alba did not really mean what she then said, perhaps she regretted saying it before it had even left her mouth, perhaps she knew she would before too long have to apologise to both of them for her tone but with Sam's smile and the Reverend's generosity, Alba said:

"Well, that's alright then. Everybody is happy. If you'll excuse me, I'll get on," and with that, with her copy of the parish magazine still on the stone ledge where Matthew had placed it, Alba stepped back into her hallway and shut the door.

*

A puzzled, almost pained, look from Sam prompted the minister to say, as he gestured for them to about turn:

"I sense things are more different up at the Hall than we previously thought."

As she secured the latch on Alba's gate, Sam said:

"Things were always going to be different, though, weren't they? I think Andrew is doing an excellent job and is coping remarkably well given he's not long lost his grandfather – wasn't expecting Alba's prickliness just then, though."

"Nor me when I knocked. She's struggling, you can tell."

"Yes, more than she realises but what can you do? There's only so many times I can offer to have a chat with her."

"I echo that but best we don't speculate further."

"No, exactly and I've got too much work to sort out at the Hall to dwell on Alba being out of sorts. Anyway, thanks for offering to take me yourself."

With that they made their way to the vicarage and specifically, the minister's car, in order that he could take Sam to her home to collect what she needed and then onto Hillstone Hall itself. His act of kindness did have one small unexpected happy outcome; for Sam's mother – Mrs Rowan – as she had been chatting to the reverend, as Sam had loaded her books, pots and sample menus into the minister's car, offered, due to having a free afternoon herself, to deliver the rest of the parish magazines for him.

*

Almost an hour later, with Sam duly unloaded at the Hall, Reverend Matthew Quinn drove back into the village. He passed 'The Sun and Moon' pub, 'Stapleton's' – the village shop – and then shortly after that drove past Alba's home. As he did so he observed Alba's car waiting to reverse out of her drive.

'When she is back I must tell her one of her rear brake lights isn't working', the minister said to himself. 'We want her safe on the roads'. With that, as he drove on to the vicarage, he offered up another of his brief 'arrow prayers' for Alba's safe travels.

CHAPTER 5

Wednesday: midday

Trying to calm herself down or to just find some *space* – even though of course the whole cottage was hers – Alba retreated into her back garden. Maybe just being outside was what she needed – to feel the sun's rays on her cheeks, to watch the dunnocks, the tits and the tree sparrows and to just be still for a moment. Her regular robin was also present. It had been hopping around Alba's wooden garden bench until her appearance had scared it off. Yet it quickly accepted her arrival and came down off the shed roof it had flown to and joined the dunnocks pecking at the ground beneath Alba's bird feeder.

She sat there no more than a few minutes but felt calmer for doing so. Now, though, she decided it was really time to depart. As she stood, she instinctively ran her hands down, down from the small of her back to her thighs, to smooth out her sundress. The fractionally damp feel, coupled with the slightly sludgy sensation she experienced as she rubbed the fingers of her right hand against her palm as she pulled her hand away from her dress, told her what she had just sat in before she looked at her hand itself.

'Oh, these blessed birds,' thought Alba as she realised that in her irritability, she had sat down in something a feathered creature larger than a robin had left.

Ten minutes later Alba came down the stairs into her hallway and was now attired in nothing more sophisticated than a pair of denim shorts and a white V-neck T-shirt; the dress in question had been rinsed out and left to air on a padded hanger on the back of her bathroom door. It was as she was in her hallway that her telephone rang.

*

On picking it up, Alba heard Eleanor's voice on the other end of the line:

"…"

"Last night you tried? What time?" asked Alba.

"…"

"Yes, well if it were around seven, I was in 'The Sun and Moon'."

"…"

"Yes, good guess, it's our village pub. I was with Helen; do you remember Helen?"

"…"

"You do. I'm impressed for she was always the quietest member of our little group. Anyway, she wanted to meet up for a quiet chat so we met there – which was a bit of a mistake because it was a Tuesday and Tuesday in 'The Sun and Moon' is pie night, not that we ate, we just met for a drink but the pub was busy and we could hardly hear ourselves speak."

"…"

"No, not that much of a shame as I didn't really want to chat about what Helen was trying to get me to open up about. I suppose she meant well by it but it wasn't the right time for me and–"

"…"

"No, don't worry about what Helen wanted to talk to me about.

I'm still good to come if that's what you're telephoning to check about. I am still wanted, am I? You're not calling me to say the thing's off or that you've found someone else to, er, be with you there? I mean, don't get me wrong, you're completely free to have got someone else, someone better than me – far better no doubt – but I'm setting off in a few minutes or at least was intending to, so if I'm not needed after all, you've caught me just in time."

"..."

"I am? OK, that's fine and, as I say, I'll be setting off in just a few moments so I'll see you later. What time, out of interest, will you be getting there?"

"..."

"You're there already?"

"..."

"But I thought–"

"..."

"A change? What's changed – has something happened?" enquired Alba, who could not quite work out the restrained energy that was now evident within the voice of Terry's sister.

"..."

"Sorry, did I hear you correctly? Say that again?" asked Alba.

"..."

"Engaged! You're engaged?"

"..."

"Well, yes, I know that means he's proposed to you but, well, er, I suppose what I should say is congratulations – yes, congratulations Eleanor. Wow. Gosh, er–"

"..."

"Yes, it is very exciting."

"..."

"Well, yes, of course the ring sounds exquisite – a deep red, you say?"

"..."

Minutes elapsed as Alba listened to the other woman's animated narrative surrounding the proposal. Alba was happy for the other's joy but, as Eleanor's energy levels and speed of talking rose once more, Alba felt she had to say something:

"Whoah, slow down a bit, please. I know you're excited – you're bound to be – but you've got to slow down, plus leave a bit to tell me in person. And, to be awfully practical for a moment, I really need to be setting off soon, very soon, if I'm to actually get to Kingsbourne. Plus, it would be nicer for you to tell me all about it face to face."

"…"

"No, don't apologise. As I say, you're bound to be excited and wanting to tell me everything. But leave some for later. You've told your parents, I assume. What about Terry?"

"…"

"Well, yes, it is a remote part of the world. I suppose your idea of a letter would reach him but any missive from you is hardly going to be delivered by second post tomorrow, is it? It could take weeks. Why not try calling him again?"

"…"

"Well, yes, if he's only just proposed then you haven't had a lot of time to get hold of everyone. Surely your own brother–"

"…"

It was quite a lengthy reply as to why Eleanor had not felt quite yet able to keep trying her own brother; to tell him that Dr John Sunday had proposed to her that morning, catching her, so to speak, off guard and that she had effortlessly said 'yes'. Eleanor added that John had decided to propose as he suddenly realised that he no longer wanted to refer to Eleanor as simply his girlfriend or partner when with his family but rather wanted her known as his fiancée.

"But you'll think about trying to get hold of Terry again, won't you?"

"…"

"Well, yes. Look, all that is purely as I see things from this end and I can't make the phone call for you. So, have a think. Do what you feel able to do and tell me about it once I get to you in a few hours. If I set off in the next few minutes, I'll be with you in good time and–"

"…"

"No, I've opted to take the scenic route, looping under Guildford, the 'Hog's Back', Odiham and then joining the M3 in time to pick up the beginning of the A303."

"…"

"No, I love it, the 'Great Western Highway' – well, that is what I call it – so, yes, I'll be going that way rather than dropping down to Kingsbourne from the M4 above. All being well, I'll see you in about three hours, maybe four."

"…"

"OK. Tell me later. Bye for now."

"…"

"Of course I want to see the ring. See you soon. Bye."

"…"

With that Alba replaced the receiver. She then went and double-checked she had emptied her teapot, that the kitchen door was locked and finally she picked up her chosen handbag for her time away, which had been on the hall table by the telephone. It was not a snazzy clutch purse nor a more conventional Monday to Friday nine to five type of black handbag. The one she had selected for her few days away was more informal than either of those styles. The one she had opted for was made of fine Italian leather, with a long thin strap and was rectangular in shape, being slightly deeper than it was wide. She subconsciously put her head and left arm through the strap and it naturally fell snug against her left hip.

*

She sat in her car on the drive and about to start. It was in that moment, when one might normally feel an excitement for the journey ahead, relief that the house was 'shut down' for the time away or simply tiredness, Alba felt a pang of guilt. Those normal pre-holiday feelings evaded her this time and instead she experienced guilt. Or, more accurately, she felt pangs of guilt. Layer upon layer of regret and awkwardness suddenly rose up from that strange place that seems to exist in one's body – that place which could never show up on an X-ray or be discernible during an operation and yet is somewhere between the stomach and the heart.

It was not a bloated feeling, having eaten too much lunch, nor a tightness of muscles in the chest, from having stretched too much when on a small step ladder and reaching into an apple tree to thin the fruit. Neither was it a feeling of queasiness from some prawns that really should have been eaten the day before you ate them. No, the feeling deep within Alba, which she suddenly knew was there and which she now felt, pained her; she sat silently in her car, about to embark on a curious few days away at an unknown manor house, with a deep discomfort within.

Yet it was a pain she ignored. She did not have time, she felt, to pop a note through the reverend's door, nor Sam's letterbox, nor give Helen, let alone Andrew, a quick call to apologise to any or all of them for her offish tone, her curtness and her unwillingness to see that her friends were reaching out to her.

Alba was not yet ready to acknowledge that she was struggling with the loss of Andrew's grandfather and to her adjustment to Andrew's new role. Consequently, she ignored her feelings and that voice deep within her which was trying to guide her on what the right thing to do was – perhaps some brief two-line notes, along the lines of *'Sorry, can we chat when I get back next week?'* or a quick telephone call. How long would all that really have taken? She could at least have stepped out of her car and gone and picked up the parish magazine which was exactly where Matthew Quinn had left it in her porch. Yet she chose not to and silenced that voice within. Having dismissed that inner saintly voice, she simply hoped – nothing more than a vague abstract hope – that she would have a good journey where nothing else would happen.

As she made to reverse out of her drive she paused as she saw the minister's car coming along the road. She could have sounded her horn for him to stop in order that she could at least speak to him but she chose not to. Rather she waited until he had passed and then, with a final repositioning of her sunglasses on her head, set off on her somewhat convoluted cross-country journey which made sense in her head even if her late father might well have rolled his eyes.

CHAPTER 6

Daylight enquiries

"So, you'll get it fixed at your earliest convenience?"

"Yes, officer," said Alba as she stood between her car and his in the lay-by, with her sunglasses hanging from the 'V' of her T-shirt's neckline.

*

To begin with, having seen the police car come up in her rear-view mirror, she was convinced the car behind was simply looking for an opportunity to get past her on its way to some incident or other. Then, after several occasions when the driver could have overtaken her but had chosen not to, Alba convinced herself he was there checking her speed, perhaps even her adherence to the Highway Code. Her speed she was generally not worried about, her compliance with said code of the highways she silently admitted to herself was a tad more 'iffy'. Did she, she found herself wondering, have to look in her passenger side mirror having just overtaken that cyclist and moved back in? Had she pulled out too soon at that roundabout? Alternatively, would she be castigated for not pulling out quickly enough at that same junction and thus be accused of holding traffic up? These and numerous other questions raced through her brain as still the police car followed her.

There it still sat, nestled behind her. Her driving was near faultless by now – not that she could think of a manoeuvre of hers that, prior to it nestling there, would have triggered the constable's attention. Also, she had – surely she had – abided by the textbook at the junctions which took her over the A3 and as she had filtered immaculately on to the stretch of dual carriageway known as the 'Hog's Back', that would be taking her on to Farnham.

And still the car followed her. Then finally *it* came – the flashing of his headlights and the thankfully brief peal of his siren. With the road signs she was now passing on her left, which indicated a lay-by, café and toilets were coming up within a few hundred yards, Alba gauged that that was where she was being invited – well, not invited, encouraged, no, not encouraged, directed more like – to stop.

That indeed proved to be the case, as the officer explained. He knew exactly where he wanted the driver in front of him to stop. There was nothing random about where they now were. He had chosen his moment to ask Alba to pull over; to leave the dual carriageway and park up in this substantial lay-by. A place where he could talk safely with her and where their stationary cars were not putting other road users at risk. He apologised for causing her any undue distress in following her and reassured her that her driving was of a more than acceptable standard. However, he wished to stop her for nothing more serious than a faulty rear brake light. He stressed car maintenance was as important as all the 'mirror, signal, manoeuvre' stuff and he had stopped her as much for her welfare as for everyone else's.

Alba was grateful it was for nothing more serious. Nonetheless, she still felt an embarrassment and a slight fear that anyone has when standing opposite a person in such a uniform. Alba was also conscious of the other people in the lay-by, including those in the café, sited at the far end of the lay-by, watching her.

People were watching her. Those nearby, fleetingly so, as they got into their cars, but those in the café itself were watching for longer, seeing the whole drama play itself out. Yet, those in the café, who were staring out of the windows at her, were not doing so because Alba herself was causing a 'scene' – for there was no *real* drama to be observed. Rather they watched for their own reasons.

Two individuals, tragically on adjacent tables, were each sitting there alone, lonely and simply bored and would have watched almost anything to take their minds off their own forlorn plight.

On another table there was a woman sitting there with her husband. The husband, to his wife's sadness if not surprise, was more interested in trying to engage the waitress in small talk than in interacting with his wife of several decades. The wife, in turn, was desperate to feel – or if not to feel, to at least observe – love's spark once more, so studied the people before her through the window. Her gaze settled on this roughly thirty-year-old woman and slightly older police officer. The sad, broken-hearted wife thus watched Alba and the constable in conversation. The wife was unable to hear anything said between them, yet she wished – almost yearned – for them to be long-lost lovers; lovers who had found one another once more through this chance encounter and that they would fall into each other's arms and all, if only for a moment, would seem well with the world once more.

Finally, in this list of casual observers of Alba and the police constable, there was an eighteen year old lad. He was fresh from having finished his sixth form studies, having completed his final A-Level paper just the afternoon before. He had that freedom which comes from having finished years and years of studious effort and had – with parental permission of course – borrowed the family car and taken himself out on the open road, to explore and to have fun. Of course, it had already proved to be a 'false dawn'. The *freedom*, which he had for years craved as he applied himself to his relentless school work, to his revision and then to the actual exams themselves was already proving to be an empty dream. The *freedom* that he had craved as he spent summers completing the Duke of Edinburgh's Award Scheme, attending Scout camps and helping at some local animal charity, and which he now had in its fullness, was already disappointing him. He sat in this café all alone, for his friends were still revising for their remaining exams, and he was already feeling suffocated by the carefree openness he was supposed to be enjoying. Slumped at his table, he was bored with the open road, unsure where to actually head to next and knew he was already missing the school library, his form group and the sound of the lunch bell. In his boredom, he simply watched this random policeman engage some woman, a woman dressed in denim shorts and a white T-shirt in conversation; a woman who reminded him, if not in clothing, then in facial appearance, of his Geography teacher.

Whatever their reasons, in their isolation they each watched, observed, dreamed almost, the scene before them. Alba felt them watching her. Unknowing why they so watched, Alba feared for the assumptions they were making about her and why she had been stopped and she fought the inner desire to go and speak to each and every one of them and say that she had been called in for nothing more sinister than a faulty rear bulb.

*

"And there's no ticket officer, no penalty fee I have to pay?" enquired Alba as she stood with the bare backs of her legs touching the side of her car. Mirroring the heat she felt from those observing eyes, she could feel the actual heat of the car against her skin; her shorts were definitely not short short but short enough for her flesh to directly feel the car's heat. Thankfully – but not without design – Alba had stopped her car in the shade of some mature ash trees which bordered the lay-by, meaning the heat she felt from leaning against her car was not compounded by having to stand in the full June sun as the policeman spoke to her.

"No. Don't worry yourself on that score," he replied. "No, this is just a friendly stop and a polite word of advice. However, you will get the light fixed at your earliest convenience, I trust?"

"Yes, officer. Well, I'm heading off to Wiltshire for a few days break but I'm sure I can find a local garage near to where I'm staying and get it fixed."

"Good," the constable's reply came. "Just because we're in the height of summer and we're all enjoying the sunshine, doesn't mean car maintenance isn't important. You only need one trip that you have to do at night or a summer storm to hit as you're driving to realise how useful and necessary all the car's lights are."

"Well, yes, officer. As I say, I'll find a local garage or mechanic near to where I'm staying and get it fixed."

"Thank you."

"Am I good to go, then?" With that, Alba removed her sunglasses from her top, unfolded their arms, placed them over her eyes and then repositioned them to sit on top of her head.

"Yes, fine by me – you're clean. Here's my card, with my name, Constable Day, collar number 7979, and contact details just in case you have to explain to a boss or an angry boyfriend why you're later than expected."

Sometime further on from now but not now – not in this moment, for Alba was still smarting from her not so long ago conversation with the Reverend Quinn and Sam – Alba would regret not saying anything back to the officer on that point. Later but not now, she would desperately have wished she had said something to the effect that *her* boyfriend was never angry. That Andrew would never question, challenge or think ill of her if she were unexpectedly late and that he would never – never ever – ask her for proof, for example, that she had been delayed by a well-meaning police constable. Yes, Andrew was busy at the moment – 'up to his eyes' busy – but that, that and absolutely nothing more, was all she could lay at *his* door. He was good to her and yet she was choosing to blind herself to it and she would for a while longer. The result of which was that she took the card the policeman gave her, silenced the voice in her head which told her to challenge the officer on what he had just generalised on, and meekly offered nothing by way of a challenge.

"Thank you," said Alba, as she unzipped the side pocket of her over-the-shoulder brown leather handbag and slid the card into it.

Yet the comment the grey haired officer made about being clean intrigued Alba and prompted her to query what he meant by that throwaway remark.

"Oh," said Constable Day as he removed his peaked cap, confirming for anyone who was interested, including those still watching from the café, that the grey was not just at his temples and around his ears but all encompassing, "you'll be amazed how many people in poorly maintained cars we stop. They are easy to pick out, you know, such as on rainy days when they're not using the wipers because they don't in fact work, dodgy brake lights are another obvious one, as are missing rear number plates. That sort of stuff. Or we notice that they've chosen not to wear a seat belt. All those little tell-tale signs just hint to us that just maybe they happen to be driving uninsured or untaxed cars or, dare I say it, cars which aren't legally theirs. All in all, a faulty rear light may actually shed a lot of light on things."

"But I'm good for tax and insurance," stressed Alba.

"Yes, I know. As I said, you're clean. I got the station to check your registration plate as soon as I fell in behind you the other side of the A3. So, I wasn't expecting this stop to throw up anything nasty, so to speak. However, having noticed your tail light not working, I thought I would stop you. You can never take a lax approach to road safety."

"I guess not, officer. You took a while to pull me over though."

"Well, yes, but I gambled you'd be coming this way and this is a good lay-by – nice and deep – to direct people into. Space too for colleagues to attend if I had had to call for back up."

"I can see that – we are standing a good way back from the traffic, aren't we? As for stopping me, well, it made me a bit nervous I can tell you, as you were sitting there unmoving behind me mile after mile; I've never been pulled over before. Actually, I was more than a bit nervous, I was a bit scared in fact and I've had a tense morning as it is. Still, if you've got my safety at heart, I understand now. I guess you've seen some terrible crashes not to be mindful of road safety."

"Truly horrible sights. I won't even begin–"

"No, please don't. Death, especially unexpected, violent death, is not nice, is it? I know. It leaves a graven image in your mind, doesn't it? And we struggle to let go of such images, don't we? I know that from experience."

This time it was the policeman who was intrigued by what the other had just said.

"Do you?" he enquired.

"Yes," said Alba succinctly.

The constable looked at her. He could suddenly sense that perhaps there was more depth to the woman standing before him than he had first given her credit for and he reprimanded himself for somehow assuming that this was only ever going to be a simple pulling over of someone about a failed rear light and that there would be absolutely nothing he would learn from the person before him. He was annoyed with himself for being lax and he wanted to know more. However, before he could formulate a comment, she effectively curtailed any further line of enquiry he might have pursued.

"As you will understand though, officer, my experiences equally are not ones I wish to just casually revisit. Definitely not for recounting at the side of the road, if I may say so."

"No, that's fine. I wasn't really prying." Then, trying to recover from his sudden feeling of being on the back foot, Constable Day added:

"Right, I'll go and have a word with the café's proprietress, now that I'm here. I can ask if she's had any more trouble from a group of lads that sometimes hang out here. Have a safe onward journey, Miss White."

"You know my name?"

"Yes, as I say, I got the station to check you out; I know your name, insurance details, and a few other details about you. As I say, though, all routine enquiries that I do on anyone I'm about to pull over."

"Well, yes, I suppose so. Well, thank you officer; thank you for taking the time to stop me."

"Just don't forget to get the bulb changed," said the officer as he started to make his way towards the café.

"No, promise," offered back Alba to the departing figure.

*

As he approached the café, Constable Day scared off some carrion crows. The birds had, up until that point, been pecking at some discarded sandwich crusts, half, perhaps nearer three-quarters, of an apple and the remnants of a pack of bacon flavoured 'Frazzles' crisps; all of which someone had simply thrown from their car window at the end of their time in the lay-by. Discarded because the driver felt it was too much effort to walk just the few yards to the litter bin.

The partly eaten shiny red apple, one that, in conjunction with the sandwich and the packet of crisps, had been part of some corner shop or petrol station's 'meal deal', had no doubt looked enticing on the shop's shelves, being such a deep red. Yet its soft texture clearly had instantly disappointed and the result was that the majority of the fruit had been dropped out of the car, to fall alongside the already discarded crusts and the not quite empty crisp packet. Had the person who had succumbed to the 'meal deal' been gifted with a more discerning mind than simply being lured by the colour or the waxy sheen, he might have enquired for the variety of the apple – after all, a 'Norfolk Royal' is nothing like a 'Newton Wonder' to bite into – but he had not and so the crows, until their dispersal by Constable Day, had pecked and fought over the apple and the rest of the detritus left in this lay-by.

*

Half an hour later, as he made his way back to his patrol car, having had a friendly conversation with the lady who ran the café, as well as just finding the time for an americano coffee and a beef and black pepper sausage sandwich – for this was a good roadside café and there was more than one reason why he felt this was a *very* suitable lay-by to direct people into – he found himself thinking again of the woman he had been speaking to about her broken rear brake light. He felt that the name 'Miss Alba White' was somehow familiar and he was suddenly grateful the station had also given him her address.

CHAPTER 7

Thankful to arrive

It can be the smell – or, perhaps put in a kinder way, the aroma – that one gets when walking into a village pub that instantly makes you feel at home. Naturally, if you are meeting friends, are a local – and so know the staff – or have read about it within some travel book or it has featured in an article in the weekend newspaper, you may feel at home as you enter it anyway, aromas aside.

For Alba, though, it was the aroma she experienced as she entered the 'Earl of Clarendon' which made her feel at home. Perhaps anywhere would have felt homely after the journey she had had. Not only had she been stopped by that police officer, there had then been the subsequent accident which she had not, thankfully, been in but which had brought the A303 road to a standstill for what seemed like an eternity, even if it had been less than an hour. After all that, she had then had the frustration of failing to find Kingsbourne Manor, despite the written notes she had made for herself. Anywhere Alba would have walked into at this moment, would have felt homely as she entered the premises but the aroma definitely helped.

She had been getting cross with herself, and more than frustrated with the journey, as she drove the last few miles down country lanes before finally coming – chancing more accurately – upon the village sign of 'Kingsbourne' and seeing the pub sign not long afterwards. She knew she needed to stop somewhere and not just to use the toilet. She needed to have a few minutes out of her car. She needed to have a drink and then either to consult her road atlas once more – this time, gratefully without the pressure of having a full bladder – or to ask for some local guidance for directions to the manor. Thus, the pub sign, when she saw it, had an instant allure and offered her the chance, if not of redemption for the day as a whole, then at least the chance of respite from the here and now.

As she entered the 'Earl of Clarendon', the warmth of the inside met her – not that it was a cold day, far from it and the glorious June day was effortlessly transforming itself into a fine evening. Nonetheless it was cooler than it had been earlier in the day, such as when she had stood against her car in the lay-by as the policeman spoke with her. Thus, the relative coolness, coupled with the pub's car park being to the side of the building and out of the early evening sun, meant the pub's subtle warmth, along with the array of pleasant smells, instantly began to revive Alba. Those aromas stemmed from the selection of craft beers being served at the bar, to the fresh roses which decorated each table, gathered from the pub's own beer garden, and finally, in no small part from the plate of food being literally carried past her as she entered – a towering burger in a brioche bap, secured by a wickedly long bamboo skewer, with sides of coleslaw, sweet potato fries and a not insignificant pot of barbecue sauce.

As she made her way towards the bar, clearly her face told the young barman what she was about to ask him. He spoke to her before she had even reached the bar itself.

"Toilets are through the door just to the side of the bar," he said as he pointed to his left, Alba's right. "Turn left and ladies are second door on the right; first door is into the kitchen."

"Thank you," said Alba.

*

A more composed woman re-emerged and on her return to the bar ordered herself a pineapple juice without ice.

The bar top itself was a highly polished brass one, with an equally polished width of copper trim running horizontally flush underneath it. The copper strip was a good eight to ten inches wide and, but for knowing you would leave fingerprints on it and so ruin its sheen, somehow lured you to touch it, to caress its beauty as you sat at the bar. The evenly spaced little matt black hooks, which were slightly lower than the bottom edge of the copper strip, which were there to hang a dog-lead on, a damp raincoat on an October evening or perhaps, for the more seasoned walkers, to hang one of those squarish transparent map cases – containing their precisely folded Ordnance Survey map – on, were less appealing to Alba, as she caught her left kneecap on one as she took her seat.

Once he had served her her drink, the barman spoke once more:

"We've got a few tables left if you're wanting an evening meal – you're fortunate tonight. If it were tomorrow night, well, the local archaeology group are having their annual dinner and all the tables are gone. On Friday night we've got tables left but there is a large booking from the big manor house but their presence will ruin it for everyone else, I'd say. Think they can lord it over us just because they come from the big house."

"Oh, is that–"

Yet the barman did not let Alba finish her question.

"Just because he owns it and is dripping with money, thinks he is now the village squire. So, better off you're wanting a meal tonight than tomorrow or Friday; tomorrow no bookings left, day after you just wouldn't want to be here with that snob from the manor and his party of cronies and hangers-on. Hope they all spill wine down their fancy shirts or expensive dresses. Wish dad had refused the booking but–"

"But it is a booking for eleven people, Eddie, and we'd be daft to refuse the booking. We don't have to like the man but the doctor is as welcome as the next customer, especially if it's a party of eleven," said a second, older, man behind the bar, who just happened to be the landlord and Eddie's father.

"But he's not welcome, dad. He's an outsider and you know it. Not welcome here, if you want my opinion, and, actually, half if not more of our regulars would agree with me. OK, I'll concede it's a good number to have for one booking but I reckon we'll lose more customers as a result of their coming. Him coming in here, throwing his money around and showing off, will stop our regulars eating in – they'll just see who's here and opt to eat at home or, if they have a meal, they won't stay for desserts and further drinks – puddings and liqueurs are where a lot of our profits come from, so you always tell me. Our regulars will just eat up and go after their mains. And why do you keep calling him a doctor? He's not you know! Sandy told me."

"Did she?" said the older man.

"Yeah, she did. Said he's just some bloke who's a teacher and–"

"Well, the cheque he gave me as a deposit gives him as a doctor; not that I wanted money from him as he's a local but he insisted."

"Is that–" Alba tried to enquire but Eddie was not about to let his father have the final word in the assessment of the person they were talking about.

"A local? My–"

"Eddie, watch your language. We've got a woman at the bar."

"Giving a cheque up front – pah! That's not him showing loyalty that's just him dangling his wealth beneath your nose, dad. Typical wealthy sn–"

"Eddie, be careful with what you're about to say," warned his father.

"Well, all I'll say is I wouldn't have taken the booking. Leave him and his fancy group to stew in their own juices up at the manor house."

"Well, I did take the booking, son. He's paid a deposit which, as I say, he didn't have to do. Plus, he said they'll be celebrating something. So, there should be a tidy little drinks bill to be had as well."

"Whatever. I'd say that's typical of him, though, coming in here and throwing his money around. Plus, by paying a deposit he's making sure you see his fancy title on his chequebook. It's all just pomp and it sickens me. And, as I say, why can't he have his food at his fancy manor house instead of coming here and lording it over us?"

"Look, Eddie," said the now slightly sterner sounding older man, "just drop it, will you? Just see whether the Miss at the bar wants a table or not. But, as for Friday night, it's a booking. The doctor didn't need, being a local, and, yes, take that look off your face, he is a local whether you like it or not, so he didn't need to pay a deposit. For villagers we operate – and you know it – on trust when we take table bookings but he wanted to pay some to show his commitment to us. All I will say is eleven for dinner seems a strange number, it's like someone has refused to come or someone has invited him or herself into a more conventional number. But eleven it is and that's a booking we're not going to turn away whatever you think about it. I know your job up there didn't work out as you wanted it to but that is no reason to constantly rubbish him. To me he's just a punter, like the next man or woman. So, please just let it go and, please ask the woman opposite you if she wants a table or not – she's looking like she could do with something more substantial than a fruit juice."

With that the older man took a step towards Alba and spoke to her directly:

"Sorry. You look tired and there you are listening to our village grumblings. Please be assured you're very welcome to the 'Earl of Clarendon'."

However, before he could add anything further, a bell chimed from the kitchen, indicating there were plates of food ready to be served.

"Ah, the bell – we live by the bell. If you'll excuse me, I'm hoping that's indicating the mains are ready for the group by the fireplace. I'll leave you in Eddie's capable hands."

Alba smiled an appreciative smile back as the owner of the pub made for the kitchen. She heard him whisper to Eddie, as he went behind his son and pause for a moment as he spoke, 'to drop the enmity towards those from the big house and be nice to the customer in front of him'. As the elder man departed, and as Eddie's face turned once more to the lady at the bar, Alba pretended not to have heard the quietly spoken but nonetheless clear request.

"Sorry about all that. It's just that there's this bloke–"

"It's fine," offered back Alba. "We can't like everyone."

"No, no we can't. Anyway, can I get you another drink and would you like a table?" asked Eddie.

"Another pineapple and I'll have a bag of crisps too – what flavours have you got?"

"Oh, all the usual ones, including prawn cocktail, but we also have 'Cornish sea salt', 'ham and mustard' and 'lamb and mint'."

"The sea salt, please," offered back Alba just as another man sat down next to Alba. The new arrival, evidently a local as he knew to miss the black hooks, spoke as he took his seat at the bar:

"Evening, Eddie. Pint of the usual please."

"With you in a mo, Ash. I'm just getting this lady her drink and stuff."

Once he had placed a glass before her and retrieved Alba's selected flavour of crisps from the cardboard box out of sight from beneath the bar, he asked once more whether she was looking to have a meal as well.

"No, but thank you. I'm meant to be eating with my friend when I arrive at where she is staying but it's been a difficult journey and I'm struggling to find the place; which is kind of surprising, given–"

"Not newly moved to the village, then?" interrupted Ash, the person now at Alba's side.

"No, just here for a few days to be with a friend."

"Oh, that's nice," commented Ash to Alba. He then added a 'cheers Eddie', as the man behind the bar placed a full pint glass before him.

"So," resumed Alba, "I'm sort of passing through but needed somewhere to stop for a few minutes and have a break. It's been a difficult journey and I'm now struggling to find where my friend is staying. Perhaps one of you two could help me, maybe."

"Difficult journey, you say?" said Ash.

"Well, yes. As I say, I can't find where my friend is staying and what with being stopped by the police en route and–"

"Hear that, Eddie? Stopped by the police! She's one of us. Here," Ash continued as he turned and spoke to Alba, "let me pay for that, you might not be from around here but if the police don't like you then you're fine by me."

With that, Ash placed a ten pound note on the bar, asked for a pack of peanuts and then told Eddie to keep the change.

"You really didn't need to do that, I'm quite happy to have paid," said Alba.

"Nah, my treat. If you've been causing the boys in blue a bit of hassle you deserve to have a drink bought for you. What did they stop you for? Hopefully something more than speeding – selling stuff, were you? They didn't find it, I trust? When they stop me, I hide it–"

"No, no, nothing like that. No, not at all," protested Alba, before the other could finish.

"Oh, shame. But, to be fair–" said Ash.

Ash, like Eddie, was probably mid-twenties and both had a slight staining to their fingernails. Not dirt, as such, and the hands were otherwise clean – perhaps more a bike oil, grease type of staining, than mud, cement or plastering dust. Ash had curly brown hair to Eddie's blond wavy hair and visibly had more tattoos on his body than the solitary one which was apparent on Eddie's right forearm.

Though Eddie only had one visible, it probably did entwine its way up his entire arm to his shoulder, and which depicted a sort of tribal weave – not flames working their way up his arm, nor Aztec in influence, rather more a pacific island type of motif. It suited Eddie, Alba felt, and just for a moment she was curious what the whole artwork looked like.

"…if you've been causing them a bit of stress, you're good with us," continued Ash.

"So, what did you do?" enquired Eddie. He then added, to the person to Alba's side:

"Ready salted or dry roasted?"

"Roasted ones, Eddie, mate." He then turned to Alba, in anticipation of her reply.

With the two men now waiting on her next comment, Alba somehow, fleetingly, curiously, wished that she could have said something more exciting, more dangerous, something darker even, than a faulty rear brake light. Perhaps, that desire to impress was due to her feeling welcomed into the 'Earl of Clarendon'. Or, maybe she was just more relaxed and carefree than she had been for most of the day, if not the last few weeks, and was enjoying the attentions of two slightly younger men waiting on her next words.

Nonetheless, she did not embellish her story; she simply told them what had happened.

*

"Hear that, Eddie," joked Ash. "Our new friend here–"

"Alba," said Alba.

"That's a delightful name," commented Eddie.

"Tha–" started Alba but Ash was not finished.

"Our new friend here – Alba – thinks *that's* being stopped by the police. Think we should tell her about that time we were in Melksham and stopped?"

"Ash, that was a few years ago and I'd rather not."

"Aww, come on Eddie, tell her why we were stopped."

"Ash, I'd rather not." Then, to change the subject, Eddie added: "Your glass is empty – another one?"

"Yeah, go on then, Eddie. Same again."

"Well, it was a bit frightening for me," offered up Alba. In saying that, Alba wished to keep the man at her side from pressurising the man behind the brass-topped bar, from having to reveal what no doubt was an embarrassing and probably juvenile episode from their joint past. Alba chose to 'sacrifice herself' before Ash to spare Eddie.

"Frightening! You're having a laugh, surely?"

"It was to me," pleaded Alba.

The genuineness in her voice was, if dismissed by Ash, detected by Eddie. Alba continued:

"I'd never been stopped before. Having a marked police car follow me for mile after mile, being directed to leave the road and then the public talking to, in front of all of those observing faces from the café at the other end of the lay-by, was frightening for me."

Maybe it was the sympathetic look emanating back from Eddie, maybe it was the latest waft of pleasing aromas from the food Eddie's father was carrying behind the backs of Alba and Ash – this time two still sizzling steaks – or maybe Alba had simply reached a point where she would have unburdened herself to anyone, that prompted Alba to further explain why she had found the experience of being spoken to by the grey haired police officer so unsettling.

"You see, I've come away for a few days to support a friend who's meeting her boyfriend's extended family for the first time and it's going to be an awkward few days. I've been asked to be there as neutral, as a sounding board, as a, well, to be truthful, I'm still not completely clear what I'm going there for. But I've given up a few days because I've been asked and I said I would."

"Right," acknowledged Eddie, to show he was listening.

"Then, just before I left home the friend – Eleanor, not that you know her or have ever met her before – telephoned me to say she'd just got engaged."

"Aww, how sweet," slightly mocked Ash, who had decided Alba was already telling a story he was no longer interested in.

"I'm obviously happy for her," continued Alba but she then paused before continuing. "Yes, I am happy for her, I suppose it just brought into focus my own struggles with the man I've been seeing. We've drifted apart you see."

"He'll regret that," said Eddie softly.

"I'm not sure; I'm more to blame, I think, as friends have tried to get me to see and I've upset them in the process. So, all in all, it's been a tough time. Then, today, just the journey here has been horrendous, what with getting followed and then pulled over by the police, sitting for an hour in stationary traffic on the A303 because of an accident – some wally trying to rejoin the road from one of the petrol stations and not judging the speed of the traffic he was merging into, well, that was the impression I got as the traffic officers finally reopened the outer lane and allowed the held traffic to finally get past."

"It happens; we see the results of road accidents a lot in our job, don't we Ash?" said Eddie. He spoke looking at Alba but his question was to the man opposite him. Yet at that moment Ash gulped another handful of dry roasted peanuts, allowing Alba to speak once more.

"Your jobs? But you work here?"

"Only some evenings – help dad out when he needs cover. He's asked me to work Friday evening but I wish I didn't have to as we have, as I've mentioned, that posh bloke coming in from the big house with his cronies and–"

"Is that–"

Yet Eddie did not let Alba finish her question as he wanted to offer to help Alba with something:

"But during the day we're garage mechanics, aren't we, Ash?"

"Yeah," confirmed Ash.

"So, tell you what, if you're staying locally and you've got a fault with the car, bring it in sometime and I'll sort it out. Ash is better with bikes and I focus on the cars. I'm happy to sort it out for you."

"That's very kind of you. Think you'll have the right bulb in stock, assuming it is just a faulty bulb?"

"What car you got?" asked Eddie.

Alba turned to the window in the wall off to her right; she pointed as she stated which car was hers.

"That one," confirmed Eddie. "I'm sure we'll have bulbs for that, they're pretty standard. Bring it in if you like. Although, actually, I've got the next two days off work, as I've promised dad I'll help him rebuild the shelves in the cellar, so Saturday would be convenient; you'll probably want the thing dealt with before you head home, so if you're still in Kingsbourne come Saturday, well, as I say, bring it in."

"Oh, yes, please. I'm staying until Tuesday and I really wouldn't know how to go about changing a bulb myself, I'm afraid to say. I really know nothing about cars," confessed Alba.

"Driving that thing," said Ash referring to the car Alba had indicated to the pair of them that was hers, "I believe you!"

"Look, Alba," said Eddie with a kindness, "bring it in at the weekend and I'll fix it for you."

"To be clear," inserted Ash, "whilst bikes are my thing – actually, Eddie, I've been working on a Yamaha Fazer 600 since you left this afternoon."

"Cor, don't see many of those having to be brought in, they're so reliable," reflected his business partner.

"Wouldn't have seen this one until its next service but for an idiotic driver of a skip lorry clipping it. The bike's owner said he'd left it carefully in a bay at the side of the road whilst he was in the chippie in Tidworth but that the skip driver was still able to hit it. Yet, what I'm trying to say is, Alba, whilst bikes are my specialism, I am more than capable of changing a bulb on a car, even that car out there! So, if Eddie begins to annoy you, bring it in for me to have a look at and I'll do it. Or, if you get it done on Saturday and it stops working by Sunday bring it in on Monday and I'll do it properly."

"Ash!" said an annoyed Eddie – whereupon he threw his damp tea towel at this friend and business partner.

"I'm humbled either of you want to help," said Alba. "I've only been in the pub a short while and you're already offering to help and I haven't even paid for my own drink. I'm grateful, really I am."

"It's fine," said Ash, as he threw the cloth back to his mate and indicated with his fingers he wanted a further drink. "Take it in at the weekend and Eddie will sort you out. And happy to buy you your drinks if you keep the police occupied from time to time. However, we will have to get you getting up to bigger things next time, such as–"

"Do you know where our garage is?" interrupted Eddie, keen to prevent the silliness and, no doubt, crudeness he knew was about to emanate from his friend's mouth.

"No, as I say, I'm only visiting. I'm staying with my friend when I find the place."

"Oh, OK. Anyway, here's the card for our garage – we're not technically in Kingsbourne itself; you've got to go through the village, get on the road to Southbourne and we're just on the sharp left bend once you've left the village. As the card says, we're 'Kingsbourne Cars and Motorbikes'. It's not a clever business name but it says what we do."

"Thank you," said Alba as she took the card from Eddie's hand, understanding now why it was stained as it was. It was not from working in 'The Earl of Clarendon' but rather – as she realised were Ash's – from days spent working with engines, changing tyres and repairing bodywork. She unzipped her handbag's side pocket and slid this further card in.

*

They chatted a further ten minutes – which involved Eddie answering Alba's questions about village life in Wiltshire, her comparing it to her own experiences on the Surrey-Sussex border where she was from, and Ash trying to impress on her his love of motorbikes – especially his latest pride and joy, a Yamaha XJR 1300 in racing green – and offering to take her out for a ride on it. Somewhere within those mingled conversations Eddie refused payment from Alba for a further soft drink and gifted her two packets of 'Cornish sea salt' crisps for her eventual journey home on Tuesday. Then, following Alba having made clear she did not want a further drink and upon her re-emergence from the ladies, Eddie reiterated the directions to the garage from several directions.

"Well," said Eddie, finally realising the mistake he was making, "it would make sense to tell you how to get to us from where you are staying, wouldn't it?"

"Uh-huh!" agreed Ash.

"So?" said Eddie to Alba.

"Kingsbourne Manor," Alba replied.

"Sorry, did you just say…"

Yet Eddie's words were lost within a spluttering of lager, air and peanuts as Ash half-choked. He was equally as shocked as his friend behind the bar was, at the revelation of where their new acquaintance was staying. Having finally cleared his airways, he turned and looked incredulously – as Eddie was doing – at Alba.

"Yes, Kingsbourne Manor. I've sort of been trying to enquire after the place since I got here," pleaded Alba.

"Not very well," said Ash. "Oh, bleeding–"

"Ash!" cut in Eddie and curtailing an almost certain string of expletives. "You know what dad says about foul language in his pub."

Yet any sense Alba may have had of Eddie being on her side quickly dissipated once she had reiterated that she was staying there to support her friend who had just got engaged to John Sunday.

"Doctor bleeding Sunday," repeated back Eddie. "I don't effing believe it. Hear that, Ash? She's only going to be staying at the flipping manor house up the road, with that snob who thinks he's a doctor."

"Yeah, I hear you, mate," concurred Ash. "She's strung us along all good and proper, hasn't she? There we were, thinking she was one of us, in our camp and all along she's a frigging spy! Makes me sick."

Eddie did not reply. Alba could see the disappointment, almost hurt on his face, and his silence she felt. She had felt welcomed here, the stress of the day had eased and she was appreciative that she was going to get help with her car. Yet, now, she felt all alone once more, the burdens of the day resurfaced and she did not know quite what to do other than leave – and still without directions for where she was struggling to find. She spoke as she placed her handbag's strap over her shoulder and retrieved her car key from the bag's main compartment:

"I'm sorry if you feel I've misled you, that wasn't my intention. We were having a pleasant chat and I was grateful you were offering to sort my car out, really I was."

"Pah!," offered back a dismissive Ash, who did not bother to turn round from the bar to look at the woman talking to the pair of them. "Whatever," he added. He then spoke to Eddie but it was clear his words were directed at Alba:

"Kept her loyalties hidden until I'd bought her a drink or two, didn't she, mate? Quite happy to take my money when it suited her, wasn't she? Bet you though she's rolling in dosh. Yeah, reckon she is – she's in with that snob at the big house, after all. He's spent millions I reckon doing it up and she's just one of his cronies. They'll all be dripping in cash and here I am, the poor bloke at the bar, who grafts hard all day, has oil under his fingernails and yet it's me, muggins here, buying her a drink. Pah! Makes me sick."

"Caught me out, too" was all Eddie could bring himself to say. He paused, then added, "Yeah, wasn't expecting her to drop that on us – staying at the manor and all."

"Minded to ask her for my money back if she's still here," said Ash. He knew Alba was still there – he could tell from both his friend's look and because he had not heard the pub door go. "What do you think, Eddie mate, shall I run after her and ask her to buy me a drink? Only fair, I'd say."

Having fumbled in her handbag, Alba stepped towards the bar and pushed some coins towards Ash.

"Here you are, I didn't mean anything–"

Yet Ash would not let her finish and dismissively pushed the money away from him with a force that saw two of the coins fall to the pub floor.

"I don't want your charity, your handouts, Miss. You can't buy me so keep your cash but don't go choking on it, mind you."

"I'm sorry," Alba quietly spoke. "I wasn't trying to mislead, I just never quite found the opportunity to explain where I'm meant to be staying and we were having a nice chat–"

"Oh, were we?" said Ash sarcastically.

"Well, *I* thought we were. Look, I'm sorry if I'm staying somewhere you don't approve of or with people you don't like. I've been asked to join a get together at the house to be a support to a friend. That's why I'm going, see? To be a support to someone; I've promised her I will go and so, with all due respect Ash and Eddie–"

At that, Alba paused and looked at both of them in turn, for by now Ash had turned to hear Alba's 'speech'. She then continued:

"I will be going because, whatever you two think about things for whatever reasons you may have, I have made someone a promise. It's as simple as that. So, yes, I will be staying at Kingsbourne Manor at the invitation of Dr Sunday–"

"Doctor?" questioned Eddie.

"Yes," answered Alba with a surging passion. "Not a medical doctor but his learning of medieval England is of such a level that it is at that standard. I believe he is breaking new ground in his papers on the poetry of Chaucer. The wife of–"

"Oi, hear that mate?" said Ash. "If I get brake fluid squirting up into my eyes in the morning, I now know I can go to the good doctor and he'll sort me out by reading me one of his blessed poems!"

Eddie nodded in agreement to his friend. Alba chose not to reply to that particular comment, instead she simply sought to conclude her summary of why and where she was going:

"I'll be at his house, as his guest, for a few days. I had been hoping one of you might be kind enough to give me directions to Kingsbourne Manor but probably best I leave it and I'll just go and sit in my car and look at my map once more and try and work it out for myself."

There was silence from the pair of them – there would be no offer of help. Not now. As a result, feeling she ought to ask for permission, Alba spoke directly to Eddie:

"Your father will let me sit in the car park for a few minutes, won't he, as I check my road atlas? I really wouldn't want to upset anyone else."

"Oh, for pity's sake," said Ash. "Don't try and play the 'poor little me' card on us. Look, I'll tell you, if only to get rid of you so you can join your posh friends up at the palace."

"Well, er, thank you," said Alba. "That would be kind."

"It's on the Quarrybourne road. So, turn right out of the pub's car park and, go into the centre of Kingsbourne itself, left at what was the post office. You'll see it as the sign is still up even though it has closed down. Go past two left turns – one's a cul-de-sac to some retirement bungalows, the next is just a farm access – and take the third. That's the Quarrybourne road. Go down that road until you see the village church. Kingsbourne is a bit of an elongated village so the church is a bit of a way down that road. Actually, you don't see the church itself from the road, it's set back you see and there are lots of yew trees screening it, but you see the memorial cross for those who died in the wars. So, once you've seen the memorial cross, you're about four hundred yards from the manor's entrance on the right. It's not obvious as the stone gate posts had to be removed when building materials for the manor were being delivered on some big lorries. So, to repeat, that's right out of car park, left at the old post office, then third left. Then, once you've seen the cross, start indicating and the turning is on your right. No need to indicate before you see the cross as you'll aggravate the drivers behind you and we've had enough aggravation from you for one evening, I'd say."

"Er, well, thank you," offered back Alba not wishing to challenge his assertions that she was the only one at fault, if indeed anyone was at fault.

"It's fine, if it gets you out of our hair. Just remember, the manor is quite a way down the road to Quarrybourne, its driveway isn't obvious, so stay on the road until you see the memorial cross. Only then start looking for the driveway on the right. Right, good, we're done."

With that Ash turned back towards the brass bar and his half-empty beer glass.

Having offered up a 'thank you' and having patted her left hip to remind herself she still had her handbag, Alba retreated from the 'Earl of Clarendon' and sought sanctuary in her car – a car, twenty minutes or so ago she was seeking sanctuary from.

Sunglasses positioned on her head, seat belt on, she turned her engine on and, with a check of the mirrors, manoeuvred so she was at the car park's exit, indicating right to head into Kingsbourne. She had to wait a while as the road was suddenly quite busy.

*

Back in Alba's home village, a completely different type of conversation was taking place at the front door to the vicarage:

"All delivered, Reverend."

"Thank you, Mrs Rowan. That was very kind of you. Did I print off enough copies for you?"

"Yes, even had a few spare but 'Stapleton's' were happy to have them on their counter – the assistant said people will read anything as they wait in the queue for the Post Office counter."

"Anything? What, even my parish magazine?" said Matthew in a self-depreciating tone.

"Oh, reverend, you do put yourself down, your little offerings each month are very good. We all think so," offered back Sam's mother.

"Not everyone," reflected the vicar. "I had taken a copy to Alba–"

"Oh, that's right, that's where you bumped into my Sam."

"Yes. However, Alba, for one, clearly doesn't think too much of my regular musings. For she deliberately left it out in her porch when I was with her earlier."

"Maybe she did but don't despair. She probably reads them more than you or even she thinks she does. They're good; people read stuff that's creatively written."

"Thank you, Mrs Rowan. That's kind of you to say."

"Think nothing of it, just saying it as it is. Actually, I especially liked your reflections on 'the Fall' a few months back."

*

Finally, the road she was looking to join cleared and Alba, still attempting to leave the pub's car park, found the car's biting point and readied herself to set off once again. However, at that moment there was a knock on her rear driver's side car window.

She assumed it was some disgruntled pedestrian wishing to stress that her car was straddling the pavement but she had to block the pavement so she had adequate visibility to make joining the road safe. Then there was a further knock but this time at *her* window.

Having heard the further knock, it was the tattoo she noticed first. Yet Alba was unsure whether a further barracking was coming from Eddie and so was reluctant to wind the window down. She did not feel she had really done anything wrong and anyway she was hardly the type of person to swagger into an unknown public house and boast about being invited to a house party in the big manor somewhere within – or as Ash had just explained – on the perimeters of the village. Alba felt she did not need to defend herself any more and so simply sat there unmoving and not wishing to make eye contact.

Eddie had other ideas and he went and stood in front of Alba's car, effectively in the road itself. He had the air of a man who was going to be unmoving until he got his way. His arms were resolutely folded, his stance was wide and secure and he did not flinch when several cars and even a small removal lorry went past him, each having to swerve in return to avoid him. Eddie was deaf to their subsequent horn blasts and blind to more than one offensive hand gesture.

Sensing the Rock of Gibraltar would probably be more likely to move before Eddie himself budged, Alba fearing for his welfare, as well as the safety of those travelling on the road itself, felt she had no option but to reverse back from the pub car park's exit and back into one of the parking bays.

Engine off, Alba stepped out of her car and confronted Eddie, who was now standing about level with her driver's side front wheel.

"What?" said Alba defiantly. "What?" she repeated. "I've apologised not that I think I really needed to. If you have an issue with John Sunday personally or with anyone who lives in the big manor house, that's for you to sort out. Don't take it out on me. If you hold grudges against those well off, so be it but don't you dare start judging me. You don't know me. I came into your pub because I needed a break from a difficult journey, I fancied a small, sweet tasting drink and, I will confess, because I needed to use the facilities. However, I bought – well, would have, bought – a drink and some crisps in return so, so to speak, I paid my way, meaning you can't, then, lay that one at my door. So, you can jolly well move further out of my way and let me get going."

Eddie was silent and still unmoving.

"Look," Alba added, "I'm grateful for the directions your mate gave me. If he feels I didn't thank him enough, well, he should be out here himself but I did thank him."

Yet still Eddie stood there, though now there was almost a half-smile on his face – definitely some expression that was a touch softer than a smirk.

"What?" repeated Alba. "Think I can't remember the directions he gave, that I'm just a silly girl, an outsider unable to remember a few simple instructions?"

"No," said Eddie. "I don't think that."

"Don't patronise me, Eddie mate," stated Alba. "It was right out of this car park here, once in the village it's left at the former post office, then third left, so I miss the bungalows and the farm access. The third left is the Quarrybourne road. I head down that road for a good while until I see the memorial cross to the fallen and then, what, why are you shaking your head, that's just as Ash said. Don't try and twist it or make me confused. I'm not confused – I remember the details you see. Helped me 'call a few people out' so to speak on more than one occasion, remembering the details, so stop shaking your head. I'm correct. And after the memorial cross, I indicate as the manor's entrance is just a few hundred yards further on; I indicate upon seeing the cross."

"No," offered up Eddie simply.

"No?" challenged Alba. "No to what? I'm pretty sharp on my lefts and rights."

"I have no doubt you are," said Eddie. "But you'll never find it, the manor house I mean, if you follow Ash's directions. Don't get me wrong, Kingsbourne Manor is on the Quarrybourne road and is not so far from the church and, as Ash rightly says, the church is hidden from the road, so the church can never be a landmark to look out for."

"So, I'm looking for the memorial cross, aren't I?" challenged Alba.

"No," stated Eddie calmly.

"No, what do you mean 'no'? Every village churchyard has a memorial cross to the village's dead sons – and occasionally daughters, I might add – from the two world wars. So, so long as the churchyard is in front of the church–"

"Which it is," acknowledged Eddie.

"Then I'll know when to indicate when I see the cross."

"But there is no cross, Alba," said Eddie. "Ash is playing a trick on you – we play it on lots of people who come into the pub and are looking for somewhere nearby. We tell them it's on the Quarrybourne road and they just have to look out for the memorial cross. They might be workmen looking for the manor itself, delivery drivers or amateur archaeologists looking for specific fields round about. Actually, we've got a group of them in tomorrow night for a dinner – I think I may have mentioned that earlier – so, no doubt Ash will play the same wind up on any of them who are new to the society and asking for directions. He's played it on you, no doubt because like me we get fed up with all the comings and goings from the manor; all the posh cars, the wealth and all the luvvy-duvvy talk we have to listen to in the pub from the handful of villagers fortunate enough to have employment up there. We get fed up with it, so–"

"So?" asked Alba.

"So, he played the same trick on you, like all those before you Ash has scammed. You would have kept driving down the Quarrybourne road looking for a cross that isn't there and end up finding yourself, before you know it, taken onto a stretch of dual carriageway that you can't get off for a good four or five miles until you're nearly at Marlborough. It's such an easy trick to play and is our way of having our little moments of revenge on people we've taken a dislike to – 'just keep driving until you see the cross' is, after all so innocently said and, as you yourself have just said, every village churchyard has one, doesn't it?"

"Well, yes," answered Alba. Yet she was not so confident as she had been when she first asserted her claim.

"Thankfully, we don't," said Eddie.

"You don't?"

"No, Kingsbourne doesn't and we're thankful for that fact. Yes, Kingsbourne is indeed thankful – doubly so, to be precise, for we have no cross."

"Vandalised, was it?" asked Alba. "Damaged in a storm?"

"No," offered back Eddie. "Kingsbourne never had one to begin with and, no, it's not because villagers couldn't agree on a design. Kingsbourne is thankful – doubly so, as I say – because we never needed to erect one. We are, as the saying goes, a doubly thankful village because–"

Here, though, Eddie paused for effect but for too long as it drove Alba to prompt him to continue:

"Because?"

"Because they all came back. It's not that we – as in the village of Kingsbourne – never saw soldiers, sailors or airmen go off to war. No, Kingsbourne saw a number of them go off to war but on both occasions they all – truly, all of them – came back."

"How interesting," said Alba.

"Interesting, yes, near unique would be another way of putting it. I think, from what my dad has said, there are about fifty 'thankful villages', where all those who went off to the Great War came home but only about a dozen villages can be said to be 'doubly thankful' because all those who went off in the years 1939 to 1945 also came back. Stocklinch over in Somerset is another," at which point Eddie gestured with an arm towards the lowering sun, "over that way, some distance, yes, Stocklinch is another of this small band of doubly thankful villages. Which all in all means–"

"There's no memorial cross. How interesting – I will tell my friend Matthew, the local vicar, about that when I get home, for I wonder whether he's aware of such places. We, as you will have realised, do indeed have a memorial cross in our village and every Remembrance Sunday the veterans, scouts, guides and local cadet forces lay their wreaths as the village pauses to recall the sacrifice. Yet, I'd never stopped to think there might be villages where such an annual event can't take place."

"Oh, don't get me wrong, we do remember, on the 11th November especially so, but it's out of thanks rather than out of recalling one's loss. Dad always made me attend the church service each year, as he was so conscious of his grandfathers and their fathers returning."

"How poignant," said Alba simply. Yet then a look of puzzlement came over her face and she asked:

"But why tell me? Why tell me there's no cross? You've kind of ruined yours and Ash's own trick on me. I, like the next weary, uncared for and unsuspecting traveller passing through would have fallen for it and ended up more lost than before and somewhere approaching Marlborough if not the other side of it. So, why come and tell me? Why not stand at the window and smirk at me as I drive off as, I wonder, whether those people in the café did at the lay-by that the policeman directed me into? Why the niceness, especially as I am trying to find the place you seem to despise most in life? I'm puzzled."

"I don't know, really."

"That's a bit weak," said Alba.

"Well, I collected your money, the money you offered Ash and which he turned down and knocked half of it on the floor in the process and thought I should offer it back to you," at which point Eddie stepped towards Alba and held out a handful of coins.

"Thank you," said Alba. "And?" she added, sensing Eddie had more to say.

"Well, er, I wanted to say, strangely, I'm still happy for you to bring your car into the garage on Saturday if that would help? I am, despite how we both treated you in the bar, willing to help fix the bulb. As you left, for once, I regretted who we'd played the trick on. I guess it's not your fault if you've been invited to the manor and, given you're struggling to find it, you clearly aren't a regular visitor to the manor and so you're probably not one of the doctor bloke's hangers on."

"He is a doctor, academically speaking, please remember that. He is a good man in my eyes whatever you may think and I am staying at the manor to be a support to a friend. It's not for me to say why she needs my support but she does and that's that as far as I'm concerned."

"Right you are," accepted Eddie. "For some reason, I'm not quite sure why, I realised as you left dad's pub, I didn't want you to be our next victim."

"I'm grateful. So, how do I find the manor or has the kindness already stopped?"

"No, willing to help. Ash's directions are good, well mostly save for the cross bit. That's why the deceit works, not because he's telling a big lie but because he's telling a little lie within an otherwise truthful story."

"Yes, I can see that now you've pointed it out to me. It reminds me of something Matthew, my friend – he's the vicar I was just mentioning about – wrote about recently."

"Which was?" asked Eddie.

"That, oh, how did he put it? That the serpent was able to deceive Eve in the garden of Eden not because it told her a whopper of a lie but because it distorted God's words ever so fractionally. Matthew's article said Eve would have been on her guard against a lie that was a 'biggie' but that her guard was down when it was a subtle distortion of the truth that was put before her."

"Well, I wouldn't call my mate, Ash, a serpent," said Eddie slightly taken aback.

"No, please don't think I was quite inferring that; I was simply saying how the deception – the leading someone astray – works better for it being a little lie. If I were not almost the victim, I'd be rather impressed with Ash's cunning."

"Well, you're not a victim. I've spared you that," said Eddie warmly.

"You have, thank you. But to get to the manor?"

"Oh, yes, abide by Ash's directions but forget looking for the church once you've turned into Quarrybourne road, 'cause you'll never see it as it is screened by some trees but I've measured it. It's – that's the turning into the manor, for the gateposts are indeed missing, taken down when lorries were delivering beams for the newly restored roofs – exactly two point two miles down the Quarryboure road once you've turned into it: two point two."

"Two point two, got it, thank you."

"My pleasure," said Eddie. "And you'll come and see me about the bulb – I'm happy to sort it for you."

"And you won't play any tricks on me," clarified Alba.

"Definitely not, promise," promised Eddie.

"OK, then," replied Alba. "As I say, I'm here to support my friend but if things are going smoothly come Saturday morning, I'll come along then. I've got your card so I'll find the garage. What time?"

"Oh, so long as it's morning, doesn't matter. Assuming it's just a bulb, it'll only be a little job."

*

'Assuming it's just a bulb' mused Alba as she watched her mileometer click a second mile since she had made the last turning. 'Yet assuming things can stop you from seeing the truth' she further thought and she well knew that to be true. However, she, too, did hope it would be nothing more than a bulb that needed replacing.

Then, as her car indicated a fifth of a further mile completed, she saw the entrance, shorn as it was of any gateposts or stone pillars. She indicated and then turned into the grand lime tree lined drive that would take her, as it took everyone visiting Kingsbourne Manor, to the house itself.

After the day, the journey and her time in the 'Earl of Clarendon' that Alba had had, and appropriate for the village she was in, she was thankful – almost doubly so – to have arrived at her destination.

Alba had arrived at Kingsbourne Manor.

CHAPTER 8

Wise old elephants

With hindsight, all anyone needed to have told Alba about locating Kingsbourne Manor, was 'once on the Quarrybourne road, look for the double line of mature lime trees'; not the citrus trees, these were Common Lime, Britain's tallest broad-leaved tree, *Tilia* x *europaea* she was seeking.

They were, after all, the only lime trees around – a previous incumbent of Kingsbourne Manor had conspired to have all the other lime trees in the village felled, such was his desire for the drive to his house to be a bold horticultural statement in its own right. Over time, though not without the occasional threat of eviction or the imposition of harsher terms to a villager's tenancy, the locals accepted the eccentricity of it all. As the centuries passed, villagers even took a pride that the only lime trees in the neighbourhood were the ones to be found at the Manor.

Thus, still to this day, and as Alba was now discovering, Kingsbourne Manor was approached along a long driveway and down each side of the drive were fully grown lime trees. They were evenly spaced but, owing to the gentle curves of the drive as it discretely descended towards the manor house itself, there were in total, for anyone who wished to count, three more limes on the right-hand side as you approached the house itself, compared to the left. The trees had been there for several hundred years – not as old as the original foundations to the manor, which dated to the thirteenth century, as Alba knew from Terry's letter to her, but definitely old enough to have been those planted when the manor was remodelled in the early eighteenth century – and were the ones, such was their owner's pride in them, which caused the felling of all the others. The now grand trees graced the approach to the house and, with their grey, aged, somewhat fissured bark, gave just a subtle hint to anyone on their way to the house, of two lines of wise old elephants, guiding you silently towards the property itself.

The drive was not as broad as the one up to Hillstone Hall nor were the vistas from it, as you went along it, as grand. In part, the lack of fine views was due to the fact that what one could see was regularly obscured by the trees themselves. Mostly, however, it was the result of the fact that Kingsbourne Manor was set somewhat more *within* the landscape rather than *on* the landscape as Hillstone had been.

Kingsbourne was not a house to be seen from far and wide. It was not but it was never meant to be, a Belvoir or Kenilworth Castle, projecting the power of a Duke or an Earl across the landscape. It was more, far more, an intimate property that nestled within the land it had been married to. It was, as Ightham Mote in Kent, Woolsthorpe Manor in Lincolnshire or Trerice in Cornwall were, designed to be part of the natural world around it rather than to dominate it. With the elegant drive dropping gently towards the house as you got closer to it, that sensation was more apparent still.

The aged elephants, as it were, escorted you all the way to the front of the manor house and then they gracefully curved round to each side, stopping as they grew level with the property itself. The broad gravel area before the house was where visitors and guests parked and – given the number of cars lined up – everyone else had evidently already arrived. Uniformly they had parked themselves in line at the edge of the gravel, in order to be under the branches of the limes and so shielded from the heat of the summer sun.

Logically, Alba should have added her car to one end of the row of neatly parked vehicles. Yet, just as she was about to swing in to her chosen end, she brought her car to a halt. She knew she did not wish to join this end nor indeed the other end. So, having undone her seatbelt, she got out of her car to see if there were somewhere else where she would be happier to park. She walked to the end of the line of cars nearer the house and then took a further few paces. It was at this spot she noticed the gravel area did not end altogether, here in front of the manor; for a gravel track went off from this broad forecourt-type area between the third and second to last lime trees.

Alba made her way between the two trees and beyond their canopy on the far side. There, Alba found herself in something more akin to the works area. It was where the staff parked, where a small tractor was, where tonne bags of recently delivered grey gravel had been unloaded by 'Ede and sons', the local builders' merchants. It was an area containing a wooden pallet with thirty-nine bags of compost on it. An area where there was also a substantial pile of York stone – stone to be used in the repair work that the property's ha-ha was scheduled to have done once this house gathering was over.

'This is more the type of place where I'd park,' thought Alba to herself. It was lacking the compost bays which Alba expected to also see here, as they had in the similar parking area where she parked at Hillstone Hall. Nor was there a hut for the gardeners to shelter in on wet days or simply to collapse in when it was lunchtime on a particularly hot August day. Yet, those differences aside, it was entirely where Alba felt comfortable leaving her car. Further, it meant she would not have to leave her car under a row of lime trees in the month of June.

Once she had parked, she made her way back to the manor's front door. She showed no interest in the row of parked cars behind her – one with a circle, divided into blue and white segments as a logo, one with a three-pointed star, some with shapes or imagery that Alba recognised even less than the others and one, the one Alba would have parked next to but for her deciding to park beyond the line of trees, with a lion motif on it. Vehicles duly ignored and, on having reached the front door, she rang the bell.

*

The housemaid who answered could not have been much older than eighteen or nineteen. She wore a simple black dress underneath a hessian apron. The dress was one without any white collars or cuffs, just black, understated, with an unimaginative neckline and sleeves to just beyond the elbows. It might have worked on someone else but, apart from fitting her, its simplicity did not suit the young woman who was wearing it.

"Good evening," said the housemaid as she deftly removed her apron and rolled it up in order that she could hold it in one hand without anything dangling. "Please come in. Welcome to Kingsbourne Manor. Did you find it alright, given the gate posts got taken down recently?"

"A local helped me with the last bit," said Alba succinctly.

"Oh, good. Well, would you like to meet the others? Some are in the gardens, Dr Sunday's brothers are playing snooker, I believe. Or would you rather I show you straight to your room?"

"That's very kind of you. You have rather assumed I'm staying and not just here to ask for a job or a local reporter looking for a story or—"

Alba left her comment open deliberately and, as the housemaid struggled for a reply, Alba retrieved her formal invite from her over-the-shoulder handbag.

Having seen Alba retrieve the card, the maid spoke:

"Oh, yes, er, you're right. I had assumed you were here to stay. I only started here last month and I'm still learning. I just guessed you were staying as well. I'm already so used to family members turning up, usually unannounced, and just barging their way in without seemingly even noticing me, I assume everyone who rings has a right to enter. It's been like it again today; it feels like I've been constantly answering the door when I've been trying to clean Dr Sunday's collection of gold candlesticks. I did at least know they were coming today but it's slowed me down with the main cleaning chore I've got to do."

"But that chore is done now, is it? You've just removed your apron," noted Alba.

"Oh, er, yes," replied the maid. "Just done the last few, thank goodness. Just done the ones that I had to bring down from the landing – they're all gleaming now. It took such a long time; I've been up and down to this front door more times than I care for."

With that, the young woman who had answered the door looked beyond Alba at the row of cars. She then continued – her frustrations tempting her to speak far too openly to the woman before her:

"They all just make me feel so small and insignificant – except for Connie. Connie is nice, she is and she notices me. Hugh pays me attention, too, but he just gives me the creeps and I rather wish he would just leave me alone."

"Well," began Alba, "like Connie, whoever she is, I'm more than happy to notice you. Thank you for coming to the door so promptly and, yes, I am here to stay for a few days."

With that, Alba passed her the invite from Dr Sunday, which *warmly requested the pleasure of Miss Alba White* to join him, Miss Eleanor Evans and his wider family from now until Tuesday.

"My invite," stated Alba.

"Oh, yes, thank you miss, er, Miss White. Very good, please do come in. May I help with your luggage?"

"No, it's fine. I'm happy to get the other pieces in a bit and it sounds like you've been busy enough as it is. Oh, I'm parked in the area through the trees, is that alright?"

"It's fine. Assume you're not blocking anyone but you could have parked out the front here along with the rest of the family."

"I'm not family, for one, and I wanted to avoid–"

"You're not? I assumed everyone coming for this get-together was family."

"Everyone else might be but I'm not. I'm a friend of Miss Evans."

"Oh, oh, right you are."

"I've never been here before," added Alba. "So, I will need you to show me where everything is – where my room is, for one."

"Yes, yes, of course. Let me…"

Yet her words were drowned out by the excited voice coming from behind her.

"Alba, you've made it! Thank goodness, I was beginning to get worried," said Eleanor and with that she came past the housemaid and embraced her. Embrace over, Eleanor spoke once more:

"Thank you, Sandy. No need to show Alba around, I'm more than happy to give her a guided tour; or would you like a drink first?"

"Ring, first, surely?" replied Alba.

"Ring?" answered a puzzled Eleanor.

"Ring," repeated Alba – whereupon she extended her left arm and wiggled her fingers. "Ring," she repeated.

"Oh, no, not yet," answered an embarrassed Eleanor. She then turned to Sandy and addressed her:

"Thank you, Sandy, I can take things from here. Would you mind making us up a tea tray to be served out in the garden in ten minutes?"

"No of course not, Miss. If I may, as you don't want it straight away, I'll just replace the stuff I've been cleaning and then make up a tray. Tea and coffee, will it be?"

"Have you taken to coffee, yet?" enquired Eleanor of her friend. "Or is it still just tea?"

"Oh, tea, please," offered back Alba. "Tea will be just lovely – out in the garden, too. Sounds idyllic."

"Just teas," voiced Eleanor to Sandy.

Once the maid had departed, and after a further embrace between Terry's sister and Alba – Terry's best friend – Eleanor spoke more freely to Alba:

"Well, it would be idyllic were it just you and me but with the rest of the family here, well, perhaps not so much. But we can't hide in our bedrooms the whole time, can we? So, we shall have tea outside."

"I agree; you are not to hide," said Alba. "That's why I'm here – well, in part at least. I mean, it's lovely to see you. It's been a while and you've clearly got lots to tell me but I'm here to support and tea out in the garden sounds a delightful way to begin, whoever else may be around. It will give us a chance to watch your new ring sparkle in the evening sunshine, too. Come on then, let's see it."

"No, I can't, not yet."

Alba's puzzled look prompted Eleanor to continue:

"He hasn't formally given it to me yet. I've seen it but I reckon he wants to surprise the family at Friday's meal. Don't get me wrong, he has proposed – went down on one knee and all and I said yes, oh yes, and the ring he offered me was, is, stunning – but he asked if it would be alright to present it to me publicly another time."

"Oh," simply offered back Alba.

"No, it's fine," said the other woman reassuringly. "John has proposed, that's all that matters. He knows and I know, so there's nothing to worry about."

"And I know," added Alba.

"Well, yes, I couldn't not tell my friend."

"But not the others?"

"They're not my friends."

"But–" began Alba; however, she was unsure how to finish her comment.

"They're not my friends – not even close. Let them be surprised on Fri…"

With that, though, Eleanor's further words were lost as someone rushed past them both, knocking Alba's wrist as she did so.

"Did I catch you?" Isabel said once she was part way across the gravel towards one of the cars in their neat line under the trees. "Didn't mean to," she added and which was said without even a glance towards the two women in the manor's doorway. "Looking for something, can't find it anywhere, have you seen my…"

This time it was Isabel's words which were lost to Alba as Isabel opened her car door – the one with interlocking circles as an emblem – and lent into it to search behind the driver's seat.

"Hardly an apology for barging past us," stated Eleanor to Alba. "There's always a drama wherever Isabel is concerned. It gets boring after a while, watching her make herself the centre of attention all the time. You alright? You're rubbing your wrist."

"It's fine. Isabel?" enquired Alba.

"Isabel Sunday, John's sister," answered Eleanor. "Whatever she can't find, won't be important. Come on, let me show you up to your room briefly and then we'll go and have tea on the lawn."

*

As they sat in their wicker chairs on the lawn, the evening June sun still warmed Alba as much as the tea revived her.

"I'll have to explore the garden later," stated Alba.

"Of course."

"I'm happy to meander, you won't have to escort me," added Alba.

"Don't be silly, it'll be lovely to show you it. Terry reminded me you're somewhat green-fingered but don't expect too much."

"I'm sure it's lovely."

"Well, don't expect *Chelsea*. Neither John nor myself are too focused on the garden at the moment – even if we knew what we were doing, which we don't. John's work at the university and the energy he's investing in the house itself is all he has time for and I was in the final throws of putting my doctorate together on the Shropshire socialist, William Langland, and how his poetry permeates politics today, so the garden is rather left to the outdoor staff to manage. There's not many of them and things had got a bit unkempt, save for the rose garden, so they're up against it. They even had to service their own machines for a while as the mechanic we had in to do them we had to dispense with as he, well, he, er, never mind. Thankfully, John has now got someone else to maintain them."

"The garden will be worth exploring, whatever you say about it, Eleanor," reassured Alba. "That said, I can see that the evergreen magnolia needs retying to the wall trellis on this side of the house just behind us. It's growing out from the wall far too much but I do like it when they're grown in a two-dimensional way against the wall of a manor house like this one. Almost stately even if in need of a bit of tender loving care. The wooden batons themselves looked pretty robust and secure as we walked past a moment ago so it might be just a case of replacing perished ties."

"I'll get John to mention it to the gardening team."

"I'm not being critical, just commenting," insisted Alba. "It's a fine tree and one that works being planted so close to a wall – you can hide a multitude of sins behind such a tree so close to the house!"

"The walls are all fine," insisted Eleanor. "John has had them all assessed as well as the trees in the ground – all from a health and safety point of view."

"Never a bad thing to get tree health assessed and you do have some impressive Horse Chestnut trees over there. Strange isn't it, how just a few weeks ago they would have been covered with their tall, erect candelabras, as their flowers came out. When you see them like that, in full bloom, you think they'll last for ages and then suddenly you glance up at them and all the flowers have faded. Things are so fleeting in the garden, don't you find?"

"I'm not sure I really noticed them in flower at all; as I say, my studies are somewhat occupying my time."

"But you'd have noticed surely, as John brought you here earlier in the year, whether their 'candelabras' consisted of the traditional white flowers or the slightly more unusual red?"

"Oh, Alba, you must think me a complete fool but I really couldn't say. I mean, I guess they were in blossom a while back but I really didn't pay much attention. White, I guess but maybe one or two were red – I really couldn't say."

"Never mind, Eleanor, it's not important. I should be able to work it out for myself when I wander over in that direction – the red horse chestnut, *Aesculus* x *carnea*, has a darker, smaller leaf compared to the other. Its red candelabras are beautiful."

"Are they?" offered back Eleanor.

"Yes." However, Alba chose not to press the horticultural study of the garden before them as it was evident from the tone of the other's last question that Eleanor was losing interest.

Into the sudden silence, Eleanor simply said:

"Well, so long as you don't get so distracted by them all that you fall over the ha-ha."

"I'll try not to." Alba then watched as a person came into view at the far end of the lawn. Having observed her for a minute, Alba said, "She seems rather troubled."

"That's May. She does, doesn't she," concurred Eleanor.

*

The two seated women watched the slightly theatrical approach of May as she drew closer to them. She was gesticulating with her hands and arms, as if she were reliving an argument she had just had with someone. Perhaps she was trying to rephrase her half of the exchange, in order that she could revisit the discussion with the other person at some future date, with a greater chance of 'winning'. The theatrical was somewhat added to by May's long, flowing bohemian-style copper-coloured sundress and 'Richmond' style felt hat which was angled on the back of her head. It was a luxurious looking hat – even from the distance Alba was observing it from – and with its broad brim and splay of game bird feathers tucked into the leather banding, it was a fine statement accessory. Yet, as the person got closer, Alba felt did not quite suit May. For starters, it should not, Alba believed, have been worn at such an angle. 'Just wear it properly' she thought as she observed the approaching person. 'Have the confidence or the maturity to treat it simply as a hat on your head rather than trying to *glam it up* by wearing it at such an accentuated angle. The hat carries itself, so to speak' Alba further thought.

Maybe Alba was being a bit too hard on the young woman approaching them and yet perhaps the hat did suit a slightly older woman's head. Or perhaps it did not quite suit May because it was rather at odds with her white 'tennis court' type shoes. Or perhaps the burgundy colour of the felt did not quite – at least to Alba's eye – work with the coppery dress. The hat, the dress, the shoes were all, Alba sensed, expensive items and yet worn together spoke of a slightly confused mind or, put fractionally kinder, sent out too many competing messages – country pursuits, carefree and flighty as well as sporty casual – which did not quite work when worn together. Of course, maybe Alba, now definitely into her thirties, was just the wrong side of twenty-nine to appreciate the look.

As May continued to approach them, Eleanor and Alba observed the young woman move her arm across her eyes, to wipe the tears away, and, as she got closer, could hear the conversation May was angrily having with herself. Yet, as she drew level with them on the lawn, May fell silent. She did not stop; she simply went into the house without a further word being said.

"It would seem crass to ask if she's alright," commented Alba to her friend. "But do you think we should go and check on her? Well, when I say 'we' that's probably you, I've only just turned up and I'm absolutely the outsider here."

"I hardly know her either," said Eleanor. "I might be John's fiancée

– not that they know that yet – but that doesn't make me responsible for everyone. Plus, she does have her parents here with her."

"Oh, good. That is reassuring to hear," stated Alba.

"You'd think," replied Eleanor somewhat cryptically.

The quizzical look she got back from Alba encouraged Eleanor to explain her comment:

"Hugh and Alice Sunday are May's parents. John is the eldest of three brothers, Hugh the youngest."

"And the middle one?" asked Alba, keen to get her head round the 'who's who' for her time here at Kingsbourne.

"Middle one is Anthony. He's married to Johanna."

"Right you are."

"But back to Hugh and Alice, May's parents. Hugh works in publishing, sees himself as a bit of an investigative journalist, and Alice is a solicitor. Think she does tax and estate planning type of solicitor work – I think. May's their only child and she's just back from a gap year travelling South America."

"What was she–"

"Oh, nothing," cut in Eleanor. "If you were about to ask was she doing anything worthwhile out there, I mean like Terry is doing out in Tashkent, then the answer is no. May was just on a long holiday. Machu Picchu, Copacabana beach, Christ the Redeemer, Cartagena."

"Cartagena? But isn't that in–"

"Columbia," clarified Eleanor. "Not the one on the Spanish coast."

"Oh, OK. Didn't make sense otherwise."

"No, it wouldn't."

"But her parents are here?" checked Alba, feeling someone should be checking on the unhappy figure who just went past them.

"They are but, oh, hold on," said Eleanor as a figure of an older woman came into view and followed the same route May had just taken towards the house. "That's Alice, May's mother, approaching."

Alice was striding towards the house. She was not walking,

strolling or ambling along on a warm June evening; she was most definitely striding and it did not take a genius to work out that she was pursuing her daughter.

The two seated women watched the other approach them. Unlike her daughter, Alice did stop and speak to Eleanor and Alba.

"I assume my spoilt daughter passed you a few moments ago," stated Alice.

"Yes," confirmed Eleanor. "She seemed somewhat upset."

"Upset?"

"Yes. But she didn't stop to speak to us."

"Upset," repeated Alice. "Upset, I don't think. Self-pity more like, with a bathtub full of fake tears thrown in as well I don't doubt."

"We couldn't say beyond she appeared to be wiping tears away as she passed us," replied Eleanor. "This is Alba, by the way, Alba White, a friend of mine who's come to join us for our few days here," added Eleanor, feeling despite the moment she ought to introduce Alba.

"Oh," expressed Alice to Eleanor. "I thought this was a family gathering. Well, that's what I was told. If I'd known we were allowed to bring outsiders, well, I'd have brought my secretary and he and I could have made some progress on the Probate for two rather complex estates we're acting for but I didn't bring him as I was told 'family only'."

Alice then added, as she spoke to Alba:

"Sorry, Miss White, don't take that the wrong way but I was told by John it was a family gathering – family," she pointedly said a second time. "Yet it would seem either not everyone got the memo or not everyone understood it. Nothing personal."

A quick dismissive look towards Eleanor was lost on neither Alba nor Eleanor.

"As I say, nothing personal."

"I think," offered back Eleanor, "that John meant for those with families, the whole family were welcome to come. Whereas I was allowed to bring a friend – a companion, if one wished to use a phrase from a time gone by. You, of course, have Hugh and May."

"A convenient redefinition to suit your own ends, it would seem. But, Eleanor, dear, it was really quite a simple rule – family only – and everyone else abided by it, didn't they? But you chose to be different with your clever word play. Eleanor, you young thing, you. You should take up law, you really should," said Alice sarcastically. "I'll just have to find you a position within my practice. You seem to be an absolute whizz on legal interpretation; the literal rule, the golden rule and the mischief rule and all that. *So* clever of you."

"I'm not bending the rules, Alice. That's as John explained to me. If you have an issue with John's guest list you will have to take it up with him."

"Hiding behind him, are we? Thought you, his latest flame, would eventually but not quite this quickly. Well, I'm surprised," challenged Alice.

"I'm not sheltering behind John," said Eleanor. "I don't understand–"

However, Alba, detecting a faint weakening, maybe a sudden nervousness in her friend, was keen to stop the exchange turning uglier. She therefore intervened:

"May," Alba simply said. She then added, "Do you think one of us should go in after her and check she's alright?"

"Oh, May," replied Alice Sunday unemotively. "Given you seem to care for her so much, would one of you two ladies like to go and check on her?"

The surprised, definitely 'caught off guard' looks Alice got back forced her to continue:

"No, didn't think so. Suppose it falls to me then, does it?"

"Well, you are her–" Eleanor started to say.

"Yes, as her long-burdened mother, I will go and check on her."

Alice, then, born out of years of frustration, maybe out of disappointment in what her daughter had, or more pertinently to Alice's mind at least, what she had not, achieved in life so far, or simply out of coldness, voiced her thoughts as to what was troubling

May. They were thoughts that would have been left best unsaid or at least not said to two women she probably held in equally low esteem as her own daughter. Although, perhaps, Alice opened up because, somewhere within her was a desire to speak down, to express her disillusionment with all the younger women she was now seemingly surrounded with, whilst staying at Kingsbourne Manor:

"Her long-burdened mother," Alice continued. "You put her through the best prep schools, board her at the best private establishments money can buy and look at her now. Achieving nothing with her life. At her age, I'd put myself through law school, secured my articles and was renting a flat in Pimlico. What's she done with the start we gave her? With the money we've invested in her? Nothing! A silly little job in the theatre company her aunt sometimes gets a role through and then somehow gets us to finance a year's travelling in the Americas in order that she 'write about finding herself'. Find herself? Utter rubbish; it's just put her off doing anything worthwhile with her life for even longer. And now, why is she upset, you ask, for you do seem to care so very very much, don't you?"

"She was in tears as she came past us," reiterated Alba.

"Crocodile tears, I assure you. They might work on her weak father but not on me. Her pathetic pleading of wanting us, well, me, to finance another trip for her, this time across Canada, ending up in British Columbia, specifically Vancouver Island, in order that she could develop her travel writing, well, she got short shrift from me. Told her it was about time she got a proper job and even if I wanted to help – which I don't – I couldn't because of what's going on with her father."

Yet the look Alice got from Alba forced the former to add:

"But yes, I'll go and check she is alright and isn't about to do anything daft. Children! Thank goodness I only ever had one. If you will excuse me," said Alice. However, she moved away before either of the other two could offer anything by way of a reply.

*

"Oh, my," said Alba simply, once she was absolutely sure Alice was within the manor house behind them and so out of earshot. "Oh my," she repeated.

"Oh my, indeed," concurred Eleanor. "Successful, high-flying, solicitor by day, nasty, unloving mother by night."

"Not that she probably did that much mothering of May in her formative years, if she had been sent off to boarding school," reflected Alba.

"Whether she did or not, a difficult mother to engage with, I'd say."

"I think I'd echo that," offered back Alba.

"And yet," observed Eleanor, "by the end of your stay here, you might regard Alice as one of the nice ones in John's family."

"Really? Well, I suppose Terry did hint it would be an interesting time here."

"I'm sure he did; even if he did so in his very polite and discrete way. Lengthy letter, was it? He was never one for brief missives."

"Quite long," agreed Alba.

"Thought as much. You might not hear from him for ages and then suddenly he hits you with some encyclopaedic correspondence."

"It was good to hear from him. Yes, it was; it had been too long."

"That sounds like my brother. Still, time is getting on. I really ought to take you in and get you something to eat. It's being set out as a buffet tonight. Nothing formal as people may be tired from their journeys."

"Me, for one," stated Alba.

"Exactly. So, let's go in and get you something to eat and then we can retire to our rooms and chalk off one day here at least."

"But it is lovely here," stressed Alba. "Just look at the garden and the view across those fields beyond the ha-ha. OK, the plants need a lot of work but the structure of the garden has survived; I can see that as my mind's eye reduces the overgrown shrubs and tidies the long borders. It *is* a lovely view and let's not wish our time away too much."

"Perhaps, Alba. For now, let's get you something to eat. You'll have to chance meeting John's other sister-in-law, Johanna. She's something else."

CHAPTER 9

Low life; high life

After a bowl of porridge topped with a sprinkling of sunflower seeds and two teaspoonfuls of homemade strawberry jam – not that the jam had been made here at the manor, rather it had been made by a woman in the village from whom Dr Sunday bought. The jam was delightful and, having succumbed to a third spoonful, Alba jotted down a note of the variety which usefully had been recorded on the jar's label and promised herself that she, too, would try growing 'Cambridge Late Pine'. As for the breakfast more generally, Dr Sunday was clearly employing a very able chef, for Alba could have also had a full English. Or kippers or smoked salmon. Then there were poached eggs on toasted muffins and even boiled eggs and soldiers. 'When had she last had them?' she wondered. Nonetheless, for today at least, Alba was entirely content with porridge.

Save for Sandy serving her, she ate alone. She had missed the early risers but was down before the remainder. Yet solitude was her preferred way of starting the day for it gave her time to think.

Breakfast over and with Eleanor still to make an appearance, Alba sought out the billiard room, having decided over breakfast that, if the room were empty, she would, never having tried it before, have a go at playing snooker.

Maybe the appeal of the game was how ordered the table looked at the beginning of any frame, with the fifteen gloriously red balls laid out in a perfect triangle. Then there were the accompanying seven other balls, all in their separate colours, all – well, save for the white – precisely set out on their designated spots. It was wonderfully symmetrical and it visually appealed to Alba. The green baize and the dark wood of the table itself, set on its legs of immense girth, further drew Alba in, with its tactile warmth.

Unfortunately, the appeal of the game was quickly lost on Alba when she actually tried playing it. A full size table was surprisingly large. Very quickly Alba realised she had never grasped just how hard, nor how accurately, she would have to strike the cue ball to get it to go the distance she wanted it to go. Then there was the issue of what she wanted it to do once it made contact with another ball. Many shots later and having finally got the red triangle to disperse somewhat, she at least was playing down the lower half of the table. Even then, despite not having to strike the white ball as hard as earlier and not having to calculate the angles over such big distances, the balls still did not do as she wanted. She did sink one red one but that was solely because it ricocheted off the ball she had mishit and went into one of the pockets she had not even been aiming for.

It was not that she was not enjoying trying her hand at the game and she definitely enjoyed the rub of the felt as she drew her hand along it in between shots. Also, the click of the balls as they struck one another – whether by design or by chance – was audibly endearing. Yet it was clear – abundantly so – that she had discovered another game she absolutely, definitely could not play. After a further few equally underwhelming attempts, she placed the beautifully tapered cue and the white cue ball against the table's top cushion and found peace in resetting the table; re-establishing the order of the red triangle and the perfectly positioned remaining other coloured balls.

Having placed the final ball on its spot beneath the fifteen reds,

Alba, with her back to the door she had come in through, walked up the length of the table to collect the cue in order to return it to the rack over on the right-hand side of the room. As she did so, she did not notice, nor hear, a man enter and silently observe her.

*

The rack was, as everything else in the Billiard Room, a beautifully crafted thing. There within the elegant frame, secured by discrete brass clips, were several other cues and rests of varying sizes. They stood there as if they were an archer's bow, a knight's rapier sword or a sharpshooter's slender rifle waiting silently for their owners to come and choose them; to effortlessly take them out of their securing clips and proceed with them out to the field of battle. To be used so expertly that they somehow became as one with the person wielding them, a tool deftly wielded by a master warrior.

Alba, in comparison, was no such skilled person of war or even of snooker. Where she had failed to wield the cue expertly over the green baize, she equally failed to successfully secure it back into its rack. At her second attempt, having collected the cue from the floor after the failed first time, she stretched up to the polished brass clip at the top of the rack to reassure herself the cue was correctly held in place at the top as well as at the bottom.

"Here let me help," said a voice right beside her. Instantly, a hand rested on Alba's hands, forcing them to remain motionless, and another hand deftly twisted the fitting a fraction more until a faint noise was heard – not so much a click, more an easing of a piece of metal into a groove it was designed to nestle within.

"Oh, er, thank you," said Alba.

"My pleasure," said the other as he lowered his arms and took half a step back from Alba. "I was watching you. Obviously, I didn't want to interfere – I'm sure you're a very independent woman – but I sensed the cue was going to fall a second time unless I worked the catch for you."

"You were watching me?"

"Only for a pleasant moment. Sorry, I'm Hugh by the way, John's brother."

He held out his hand as he asked a question.

"And you are?"

"Alba," she replied as she took his hand.

As he shook it, Alba felt he held her hand just a fraction too long and she definitely did not like the way his thumb seemed to momentarily move across the back of her hand.

"Alba? Sorry, you'll have to forgive me but I don't know you, do I? I wasn't aware other guests were staying. John had said–"

"Family only, yes I know," acknowledged Alba. "It was somewhat pointed out to me yesterday evening, shortly after I'd arrived by–"

"Alice, no doubt."

"Yes."

"My wife. Oh, so you're the attractive woman she was complaining about to me later in the evening, shortly before she took herself off to her bedroom."

"I doubt your wife would have so described me," stated Alba.

"My addition, then," confessed Hugh. "So, are you my nephew Henry's latest flame? You can't be. You're a bit too–"

"Old?" suggested Alba.

"Oh, my dear, absolutely not. Too refined, too graceful, just too delightful for him. Old, though, definitely not. Surely Henry hasn't caught *your* heart?"

"Given I've never met him, the answer is no."

"Oh good," responded Hugh. "There's still hope for me, then."

"I don't think so. Plus, your wife might have something to say about–"

"Alice? Never mind her," offered back Hugh.

Keen to free herself from a conversation she was beginning to feel more than a bit uncomfortable in, Alba changed the subject:

"I was just trying my hand at snooker. I'd never played before but it wasn't going very well. As a result, I'm calling it a day in here."

"Not going very well? Oh, my dear friend, we can't have that, can we?"

"Can't we?"

"No, absolutely not. We must teach you."

With that and before Alba could say no, Hugh had released the cue they had just secured in the rack. He felt the weight of it, tried to hold it level across the palm of his hand and then replaced it and selected another, slightly shorter, one.

"Right, here you are," he said as he handed it to her and directed her to the top of the table. "The balance of the first one didn't seem quite right as I held it. Now, with this better cue, place the white ball somewhere within the 'D' and then position yourself as if you're about to strike it."

"The 'D'?" queried Alba. "I assume you mean the half-moon, do you?"

"Never heard it called that before."

"Some people think more lunar thoughts than others, I suppose," said Alba. As she stood there, holding the cue vertical before her, as if it were a bamboo cane that she was about to sink into a vegetable bed for the beginnings of a runner bean frame, she thought of her dear friend Vaughan. She closed her eyes momentarily as a pang of sadness swept through her. 'Dear Vaughan,' she thought, 'I'm a little bit closer to my thousandth than I was when you left'.

"Place the cue ball somewhere in this space here," re-iterated Hugh, "and then take your stance."

"Really, we don't need to," said Alba. "I'm really not that bothered."

"No, come on, I insist. I'll have you playing in just a few minutes, trust me."

Alba did as she was asked. She placed the white ball between the green and the brown balls and took her stance.

"Ah, there's your first problem," said Hugh. "Your stance is all wrong; your feet are too close together. Here let me help."

With that, he stepped right behind Alba and with his hands on her waist, he put one of his legs between hers and with his foot forced her to move her right foot several inches.

"There you go, that's better," he said as he released his tight grip and took a step back and looked at her from behind as she was angled over the table. "Much better," he said. "Your stance was all wrong, much too narrow, feet need to be about shoulder-width apart. Surely, that feels better?"

"No," replied Alba. "I feel rather uncomfortable."

"That will go as you practice – you look much better. Right, draw your cue back as if you're about to strike the ball."

She did so.

"Ah, I see another problem. You're not taking it back smoothly. Hold it there, don't move and let me show you."

Again, Hugh stepped right behind Alba. She could feel his breath on her neck as he placed his left hand over her left hand, which was the one she had on the butt of the cue and thus was the one extended behind her.

"Right, let me guide you. You'll see how you keep the action smooth; not all jiggly as you've just done."

He proceeded to force her arm back and forth several times. His presence and his way of being there, right up tight, as if for a moment he was her exoskeleton, forced her to relinquish her independence of actions. She had to allow him to control her, to guide her arm back and forth, with one leg of his tucked tightly against one of hers and with his spare hand now on her right hip.

"See or should I say, feel the difference. What you're doing now is so much better," he insisted.

Whatever else Alba was thinking in that moment, she did have to concede that she could indeed feel – sense – a difference in how the cue, how her elbow, her wrist even, were moving more naturally, more as one and she did feel more set in her stance. She also felt incredibly invaded. She spoke, seeking to address that:

"Right. I accept I'm moving the cue differently. Do you mind stepping back and letting me have a go at striking the ball, please?"

She asked it as a question but was not about to take no as an answer.

"No, of course. More than happy to step back and watch you play."

Once he had moved back, and Alba had readied herself to take the shot, he added:

"Now, do it as we've just rehearsed. Take the cue as far back as I was helping you to; don't go and instantly revert to your old movement. Plus, remember not to stop the cue as you hit the ball. Your follow through is as important as what we've just been doing together; straight and smoothly she goes."

"OK."

"And keep your head down and watch the ball you're striking, not the red ones down the other end of the table. Watch the ball you're hitting: I'm watching everything else."

She took the shot.

*

"Brilliant," he said.

Indeed, it was rather a good shot. Not only did the cue ball make it to the triangle of reds but it caught them just on the point of the triangle, which sent half a dozen red balls out from the triangle but doing so without drawing all the energy from the white ball. The white ball was thus allowed to work its way off a couple of cushions and make its way half way back up the table, just past the blue.

"Excellent," said Hugh.

"Beginner's luck," offered back Alba.

"No chance. There's natural talent there, now you know a few of the basics. There's more I can teach you."

"You really don't need to."

"Don't be daft. It's my pleasure. Right, look at where the cue ball has come to rest."

"Yes, just there," said Alba, instinctively pointing at it with the cue stick that now, strangely, felt comfortable within the grip of her left hand. "I can easily reach it if I move around the table and stand half way down that side."

Alba moved to stand by one of the middle pockets.

"Why would you want to stand there? Look at how some of the reds have nicely split for you – can you see?"

Alba clearly could not.

"Look at the red one on its own near the bottom left pocket. That's your next shot."

"But I can't angle myself for that," replied an anxious Alba, worried for Hugh touching her once more.

"Well, not if you stand where you've just moved to," agreed Hugh as he stepped towards the rack that could have been made to take bows, rapiers or rifles but was simply holding an assortment of cues and rests of varying lengths and shapes.

"You need to be back at the top of the table, almost exactly where we were and you need to utilise this rest. I might have to show you how to hold both at the same time. We'll practice stroking the cue a few times through the rest. You'll pick it up, I have no doubt. With a bit of guidance, you'll crack it once more."

Uncomfortable for what – or more specifically who – she sensed was about to engulf her again, Alba instantly declined.

"You've done more than you should have, already," she stated. "You really have."

"No, dear me, no I haven't. Happy to do more. Come here, let me show you again."

"I'd rather, well, how shall I put it? Let me just say again, you've done too much already."

Then, knowing she had to stand up to the man in the room with her and address what had just happened, Alba added:

"Please don't ever touch me again, like you've just done."

"Like what?" came back the other, claiming innocence.

"You know full well. So, no, I don't want you to instruct me on the next shot. Why don't you show me how it's done and I'll watch you."

With that, she held out the cue.

In that moment, she realised that one of the things she now very much appreciated about the game of snooker was that, when sharing the same cue as someone else, especially an opponent one was uncomfortable in the presence of, the cue was of such a length that you did not have to stand particularly close to them and still be able to hand it over.

"You show me," she repeated.

He did so. She observed how he did not move the rest at all during the shot, that he did not frantically try to lift it or the cue away from the table the moment he had struck the cue ball – something she would have instinctively done – and she watched as the red ball in question disappeared into the pocket whilst the white ball moved into position onto the pink, which in turn would allow him to tackle another isolated red.

"Very good," she had to concede.

"Your turn," he offered.

"Thank you but no."

"Sure?" said a disappointed Hugh.

"Absolutely. It has been an eye-opener but I do feel I've had enough for today."

"We've only just started."

"It's been more than enough."

"That's a shame. Maybe I can lure you back later – this evening perhaps. We'll get the fire going and we'll be very cosy in here together; you under my careful tutelage, me observing once your body position is correct."

"A fire in June? I don't think so – there's hardly a cold front sweeping in across the country. You're aware just how warm it has been today and is forecast to be into the weekend? A fire, in here?"

"It would make things nice and warm, for sure. Still, if whatever you'll be wearing for dinner made you too warm in here later, I'm sure no one would mind if you unzipped the back of your dress a fraction to cool your neck."

"I really don't…"

However, Alba's further words were lost as the voice of a second man drowned her out. The person entered as he concluded what he was saying:

"Ah, you are in here, Hugh. Good show – fancy a game? I'd like to try and win back some of what I lost to you last night. Oh, sorry, you're playing already. No, hold on, you've only got one cue, though – you both playing or not? Sorry to interrupt if you are – hello," he added to Alba, "I don't think we've met. I'm Anthony."

"I'm Alba."

With that, Alba had to explain once more that she was not family, nor a girlfriend of someone else staying and was simply a friend of Eleanor. Alba then had to deal with the puzzlement, bordering on annoyance, of Dr Sunday's two brothers as they together worked out who actually was here for this family gathering at Kingsbourne Manor. Not wishing to give them the impression that they had driven her from the room, Alba had to endure listening to their gripes and complaints as to what their brother John was actually up to. As she sat on one of the leather benches which adorned one of the walls – and as she pretended to read a 'Country Life' magazine, specifically a feature on the gardens at Penshurst Place, which had been left on an occasional table nearby – she could hear Anthony describe his brother John in terms of being *primus inter pares*, of being first amongst equals. She heard them agree that, by being the eldest of the three brothers, John had an honorary position within the family but nothing more and that they were loath to allow him to wield any actual power. It was only with the sound of Eleanor's voice – as she spoke with Sandy in the wide hall – that Alba, bored from listening to their moans, was able to extract herself from the Billiard Room. She simply stated she needed to see her friend and left.

*

Had they chosen to carefully listen to the hushed conversation between Alba and Eleanor, two of the three people, along with John himself, who they would rather wish were not present at all, Anthony and Hugh would have heard Alba ask Eleanor to follow her upstairs and sign something she was about to go and write. They would have also heard Eleanor inform Alba that later in the day there was a walk to the clootie tree in the land beyond the manor's grounds.

They were not listening, however, for they were too wrapped up in their own ongoing conversation.

*

"Flipping heck, Hugh," said Anthony. "I knew this girl of John's was going to be here this visit, not that I like her, never have, having worked her way into our brother's life, but really, it now seems she's able to bring her own hangers on as well. Despite what she's just said, who really is that woman who's just left us? I'm not happy – not happy at all."

"I agree it's a bit odd. Would have been nice to have been told in advance. Our dear brother, though, does seem to keep his cards close to his chest."

"Too close – I wonder what he's really up to or got planned. Why has he brought us all together, I wonder? Bringing all his nearest and dearest together, like this, and then on top of it this outsider has been invited in. I'm suspicious; what do you think she's doing here? Journalist, like you? Another mature doctorate student he's got the hot's for, progressing through his women in a way Henry VIII would have? I mean, she's alright."

"Don't think she's a journalist as I don't recall her name. As for you describing her as alright! A bit more than alright I'd say. She wears a fine deep fragrance – I wonder what it is. It is somewhat alluring. Plus, there's a spirit within her, as well, which is arousing. Reckon she's a bit of a fighter, so it will be a hard-won victory. So, all in all, I'm rather taken with her; I'll have to orchestrate making sure I'm seated next to her each dinner time."

"Hugh! You never stop, do you?"

"Whilst there's still blood in these veins, why would I?"

"You're a leach. How are you going to make sure you get seated next to her at the dinner table?"

"Oh, I'll have a word with that young thing who's a maid here. I think I've got her hooked now, following my visits here since she's started. Making out I'm interested in her, smiling when she passes, hold the odd door open for her as she carries stuff round. Keeping myself close to her. She's easily mouldable and I think is bowled over that a brother of the all too absent owner of the manor has taken an interest in her. Being so timid, she'll be an easy victory; she just doesn't have the fight this Alba woman has."

"You're disgusting; you must be twice, perhaps three times, the maid's age," stated Anthony.

"A man can try. You reckon I should just focus on this stranger who's joined our family gathering?"

"At least you're a bit closer in age but, Hugh, really, what does Alice think of it all?"

"Alice? Who cares what Alice thinks and anyway, she's so wrapped up in her career, she wouldn't care even if she suspected."

"I wouldn't be so sure. Her career is still going well, is it?"

"Yes, usefully. Nice to have her salary to help me in my predicament."

"That not resolved yet?" asked Anthony.

"No."

"Oh. Anyway, to add to your woes, I'm here to try and win back what I lost to you last night – if you're up for a few frames."

"Always happy to take more money off my brother. I mean, why not just give it to me now and save yourself the time at the table?"

"Let's see, shall we? I almost beat you last night. It's your turn to break. In any case, we need time getting our heads together, trying to work out what our brother is up to. I don't like this Eleanor girl of his, even less so now, as she's clearly able to start shipping in friends of hers as and when the mood takes her. Blow, they'll be here all the time before long. Well, that or John deciding to bring more of his medieval cronies to visit or even, perish the thought, basing some of his university teaching here. I've got rather used to having a pretty free run of the house whilst big brother is off on another of his America tours or even just when he's based back at his Faculty during term time. Yes, I'm quite enjoying how things are all nicely arranged here. Plus, it allows Johanna and me to let her London home for periods of time. All in all, we need to work out what this Eleanor woman is up to, since change is not always a good thing."

"Why not just ask her yourself when we're all on this walk this afternoon?" replied Hugh.

"I don't think and surely you don't really either, that she'll open up just like that."

"Probably not but it's a long walk so there'll be time perhaps where you can catch her off guard."

After he had chalked his cue, Hugh added sarcastically:

"Wasn't it good of your Henry and Connie and my May to organise this walk for everyone? A walk with all our loved ones – how delightful!"

With that, Hugh placed the white cue ball within the table's 'D' and proceeded to break.

*

Half an hour later – by which time Anthony had lost the opening frame and was at the point of needing snookers in the next – Alba and Eleanor, having completed the task Alba knew she had to immediately fulfil, sought out the dining room in the hope that a pot of tea might be present and could be taken out to the garden. As they entered, there sitting before them was Dr Sunday himself.

He stood up as they entered.

"Ah, good morning, Eleanor dearest."

With that, he stepped around the table to meet his fiancée; they embraced and kissed.

Their first 'meeting' of the day over, Eleanor spoke as she moved away towards the sideboard to select two teacups:

"I'll let you two say 'hello' – you haven't met John since you got here, have you Alba?"

"No," Alba replied to the back of her friend's head. She then spoke to the person before her:

"Dr Sunday, it's so lovely to see you once again. Sorry to have missed you last night," and with that she held out her hand.

"Alba, my fault for not being around last night. I'm here now though and it's a delight to see you again. Please, though, no need to be so formal – in fact you'll offend me if you do. It's John. You are here as my dearest's friend and, I trust therefore, as my friend, too."

He stepped towards her and held out his arms slightly to his side and Alba reciprocated and they embraced.

Embrace over, John spoke once more:

"As I say, it's John, please. Find us alright, yesterday, did you?"

"The directions I'd written myself were a bit lacking but I got some guidance from someone in the village pub, which were spot on."

"The 'Earl of Clarendon'?"

"Yes."

"What did you think of it, the pub, I mean?"

"I'll take the teapot and some cups out onto the lawn – I'll leave you two chatting for a mo," cut in Eleanor.

"Seemed very nice – not so sure about the hooks under the bar," answered Alba to John's question once Eleanor had gone through the French doors. "They seemed to be positioned to ensure you catch your knee every time you cross your legs."

"But hooks aside?"

"Very nice. Food looked good and smelt good, fresh flowers on the tables and the soap dispensers in the toilets had soap and you can't say that for every pub."

"Good," said John. "Pleased you approve as we will be eating there tomorrow evening. They do do good food, I agree, and I'm keen to give them the business. Plus, it will give chef here an evening off which he'll appreciate as he's looking after us for the rest of our time here. I concede I'm not helping him much by my having such a late breakfast today. Still, tomorrow evening, as I say, we'll be at the 'Earl of Clarendon'."

"Yes, the barman's son said as much."

"Did he? Still, let me not keep you from joining my dearest out on the lawn. Once you've had your drink, I'll show you round the manor myself, if I may?"

"That would be lovely."

"Good, Eleanor will find me for you – it's nice to see my star pupil once again, Alba."

"Hey," called through Eleanor from outside, who was not sitting so far out in the garden that she could not hear the conversation from within, "I thought I was your star pupil."

"You are dearest," answered John once he had moved to the open doors and spoken out towards Eleanor. "You are – you absolutely are – but Alba was a different cohort and she studied a slightly different period to you, so I'm in no way comparing. You very much are *my* star."

He left the dining room and went and knelt by the seated Eleanor and took her hand and kissed it. 'My dearest' Alba heard him add 'you are not Anelida', a reference, if memory served Alba correctly, to one of Geoffrey Chaucer's poems.

"Oh, John, I'm teasing you. I know Alba was a gifted student and Terry always said she could easily have pursued an academic career, so I have no doubt she was a star in her own right. I'm just teasing you. Up you get, you over-dramatic thing and, yes, once Alba and I have had our tea, I'll bring her up to you. You'll be at your desk, I presume?"

Having confirmed that would be exactly where he could be found, he left the two friends to themselves.

*

"Here we are then, within the beating heart of my two worlds," said John to Alba who was now seated opposite him. As he spoke, he moved one hand across his wide desk and with the other, as much as anyone's elbow and shoulder joints would allow, did his best to gesture towards the bookcases behind him.

He was, as Alba understood, referring to the renovation of the manor and his work as an academic. It was of no surprise to Alba, having stood up and moved towards the bookshelves, that the shelves contained more than just books on architecture and local history journals. There were also copies of all the academic works which he undoubtedly had on his university bookshelves as well. As Alba ran her fingers along the spines of the books and as her eyes read the authors' names and the titles, she was instantly taken back to her student days – for she saw once more the works of Gower, Chaucer and Langland before her. There were books on those poets by people like Coulton and John's own published works and books covering the medieval period more broadly by the prominent historians, such as Weir, Feiling and Neillands.

"A fine collection you have," said Alba.

"Other than my own humble writings there is a wealth of material on those shelves, I agree."

"You could have fitted more books in if you hadn't given over one shelf for this picture to hang. It's a fine pencil drawing but you'll have to help me as to who it is. She's probably a Matilda or a Katherine – they nearly all were one or the other from that period."

"Or an Eleanor," suggested John.

"Oh, yes, how could I forget all the Eleanors – of Castile, of Aquitaine, of–"

"Of Provence," continued John. "The woman looking down on me as I sit at my desk is Eleanor of Provence, wife of Henry III. She's buried not so far from here, at Amesbury, although no one quite knows where exactly. She was far from a perfect person, definitely had an issue with Londoners, but she intrigues me."

"Maybe we all need some flaws," mused Alba.

"Perhaps. However, whatever yours are, Alba, they won't be as serious as those of the woman from Provence."

"Well, I seem to have upset and ignored a few people back home just before I came away, so they seem serious enough to me."

"I'm sure your academic recall will convince you you're not remotely in the same category as the woman from Provence. However, if you can't quite remember her failings now, I can fill you in perhaps on this afternoon's walk, which my nephew and nieces have orchestrated for us all to go on, but not now."

"I think you'd rather walk with your betrothed," commented Alba.

"You know?" said John in surprise.

"Yes. Don't worry, I haven't told anyone else but you could hardly expect Eleanor to keep it a secret from everyone. She is a young woman in love, after all."

"I hope she is in love but it wasn't to be announced until–"

"Until dinner tomorrow evening. I know, Eleanor told me. Rest assured, though, your secret is safe with me. She's told me but it is a secret that is not for me to destroy by retelling."

"Thank you."

Alba's attention was then caught by one of the ornaments on

the desk; a miniature of a seemingly sleeping knight. However, her admiration for that character from ages past was forgotten about when John added:

"If you will keep that secret until tomorrow evening then may I reward you by inviting you into another secret of mine. One not everyone in this house knows about."

With that, before Alba could answer, John, having stood up and turned round, pressed a small square section of wooden panelling to the lefthand side of the bookcases behind his desk and a small door swung out, allowing the golden daylight and the warmth of the morning to rush into the room.

"Care to step out with me, Miss White?" he said as he himself stepped through the previously unseen door.

*

If he had invited her to step through a wardrobe into a strange snow-ladened world, where the animals could talk and righteous battles needed to be fought, Alba would have only been fractionally more surprised than she was now. For she was indeed surprised; very much so. For, having stepped through the door as instructed, Alba found herself outside, out seemingly on top of the world. In that moment it did seem other-worldly. The contrast from the dark rich wood panelling, studious, cerebral and definitely Angevin-themed room, which she had just left behind, to the broad, sun-filled lofty openness she was now exposed to, could hardly have been greater.

Here then she now stood. She was next to Dr John Sunday, her highly respected former university lecturer. Next to the soon to be husband of her best friend's sister. Out on the roof of his beautifully restored country house; she was literally standing on Kingsbourne Manor. They were not technically on the very highest part of the building but they were still a good way up even if their height was not immediately apparent. Perhaps that was because the parapet masked the vertical drop, perhaps just being out here with John stopped her from considering how high they were or perhaps simply the surprise of being invited to step through a previously unnoticed door stopped her from looking directly down. Whatever the reason, it was not until later in her stay at Kingsbourne Manor did Alba truly grasp how high someone was when standing out here on the roof. It was a height from which it would be fatal to fall.

"I'm speechless," said Alba.

"That's allowed. So long as you're not scared? It is perfectly safe."

"No, no, not scared."

"Good," said a relieved John. "Just to be clear, though, we are standing on a lead-covered solid oak roof. The wooden joists were sourced from Leicestershire, the parapet is newly repointed and certified secure and any unsteadiness you may feel as you walk about out here – and by all means feel free to do so – is because there is enough of a slope to the roof to allow the rain water to drain towards the gulley at the base of the parapet."

"That's all reassuring to hear," agreed Alba. "Don't worry, though, my motionless is the result of my surprise having still not quite ebbed away rather than due to me being scared."

"Right you are," offered back John.

Silence fell between them. It was a silence born out of the beauty of the moment – of the gentle rolling landscape drifting off before them, of the broad, blue sky above, occupied by a single Red Kite effortlessly gliding through its domain – which kept them from talking.

Eventually, Alba did speak:

"It's just beautiful – out here, up above everything."

"It is, isn't it? But please don't think I've brought you out here to show off."

"No, not at all; I never thought that was your style."

"No, indeed not," agreed John. "Quality, yes. Thoroughness, absolutely; beauty, of course but brashness? Never. I just thought you might appreciate it. Eleanor was telling me earlier you're a bit of a country girl at heart, so I thought you might enjoy seeing the landscape from up here."

"It is stunningly beautiful. As for being described as a 'country girl', if by that you are expecting tweed skirts, going off on shooting weekends and a penchant for being driven around in big fancy cars, you will be disappointed" stated Alba. "Whereas if you perceive me in terms of 'outdoorsy', green-fingered and passionate for nature, you will be much closer to knowing me," reflected Alba.

"As I suspected. I might add that I know you were a true loss to the world of academia – I wish I had been able to persuade you to stay on to pursue a doctorate but alas I could not."

"No," agreed Alba softly. With that she fell silent once more as she wondered what Eddie, as he served at the 'Earl of Clarendon' or assisted Ash as he worked on a bike's water pump, would say about her having once considered pursuing a doctorate and whether he would be more likely or not to come to her for assistance following an accident at work.

"Well, however you view yourself," resumed John, "I thought from what my love told me, you would appreciate the view from up here."

"Oh, absolutely – it's just captivating. Bring me out a chair, one high enough to see over the parapet, and bring me a cup of tea and I could sit out here all morning."

"It's even more mesmerising at night time. Eleanor and I have been out here as the sun has set, lying on blankets, watching the stars come out, seeking out the shooting stars and watching the bats emerge and perform their strangely angular and jolting flight."

"I think the daytime appeals to me more," replied Alba. "I can just lose myself in this view. It's not the greatest view, as in distance seen, I mean, for the land rises up around us, doesn't it? But it's a view that will not have changed for centuries – perhaps there's now less chimney smoke coming up from the out of sight villages that must be nestling in the folds of the landscape before us. But that aside, it's unchanged, surely?"

"Yes, the view will not have changed much. The addition of the ha-ha was a beautiful way of the previous owner not to break the view – that is why so many great houses had them."

They stood out there admiring the country before them, not saying too much and simply enjoying the peace and calmness away from the majority of those also currently staying at the manor over these few days. Eventually, needing to get some papers read before joining everyone else on the afternoon's walk, John took them back inside the manor – where knights slept, queens looked down on them and Anthony was more in debt to his younger brother than he was the evening before.

CHAPTER 10

May I walk with you

They convened by the front door of the manor but it was only after the predictable flurry of last-minute change of minds by several of those gathered – swapping hats, deciding to take or not take a shoulder bag, topping up a water bottle, waiting for Sandy to bring something in a tub for Eleanor – that everyone was ready finally to go. It was a frustrated May who finally announced the walk was underway and led the group off across the gravel and between the two lines of wise old elephants.

Wishing not to be viewed by the group as unable to leave Eleanor's side but also to allow Eleanor the space to walk with John, Alba set off at her own pace. She hoped she would end up with someone to walk alongside, for she still had many of John's family to get to know, and, so long as it was not Hugh, she was curious as to whom she might end up with.

Quite quickly, before they were past the first half dozen lime trees, Alba found herself out in front, walking with May.

*

"Am I allowed to walk with you?" asked Alba.

"Feel free," replied the younger woman. "At least now we're walking – it's the insufferable waiting as everyone else faffs around that does my head in. Travelling has taught me to be organised from the get-go; I find other people's 'shall I take this?', 'maybe I'll change my shoes', 'where did I leave my whatever?', just so infuriating."

After a pause, May vented an 'Aarggh!' and shook her arms out in an attempt to ease the tension within.

Fifty yards further on, when May seemed calmer, Alba spoke once more:

"I'm Alba. You're May, if I've got that right."

"Yes, I'm May and mum told me about you over lunch – a friend of Uncle John's girlfriend, I gather. Mum is puzzled why you're here but I told her it wasn't her business and to get over it."

"Er, thanks."

"Doesn't bother me why we've all been brought together. Maybe Uncle John is about to announce that, having virtually done the property up, and despite all his promises to the contrary, he's selling up. Realises what the house is now worth and has decided to sell it for another small fortune."

"Another," offered back Alba. Alba was keen to explore Terry's understanding, that John, alone of the four siblings, had inherited a sizeable fortune from a bachelor uncle, who had made his money mining.

"Oh, yes," replied May. "Another. Left a packet by his uncle who had made his fortune out in Africa. Can't tell you how much it annoyed dad, aunt Isabel and uncle Anthony and, of course mum and aunt Johanna, that they didn't get an equal share. They were all livid. Mum pored over the will, looking for a loophole – she's a solicitor, in case you didn't know."

"I gathered, yesterday," said Alba.

"Right. Mum absolutely went through it, looking for grounds to challenge it. Reckon she got half her practice to work on it as well but alas for her, without success."

Alba said nothing, feeling it was not for her to pass judgment on someone else's last will and testament; more so as she was not even part of this fractious family.

"You didn't comment," observed May. "Thought you might have gone for the easy, weak, comment of 'shame it wasn't shared out equally'. You're quite right, though, not to give an opinion."

"I hardly know the family but that's not to say I don't have a view."

"Perhaps you do, perhaps you don't. Either way, I said to mum it was none of her or dad's business. Great uncle Leonard could do with his money whatever he wanted. Don't understand why mum got so angry about it; it was never her money to begin with. Of course, had she been able to get her hands on some or all of it, she'd have used it to expand her law firm in an attempt to be recognised within legal circles; she's desperate to get elected onto the Law Society Council for starters."

"You really don't have to share this all with me," Alba stressed. "I'm quite happy, walking along in the shadow of the limes and enjoying the countryside. We seem to have set a good pace – we've left the others behind already."

"We'll stop when we get to the end of the drive and let the others catch up. We can wait on the other side of the road having crossed. When we're one group again we can set off once more and head along the farm track. Normally, I'd be walking with Henry but he busted his knee a while back surfing and he's still not up to speed. It's making him pretty grumpy!"

With that, May laughed at her cousin's misfortune.

Ignoring the laugh, Alba said:

"Oh, hence the walking pole he's using. I wasn't sure if that was just for show or not."

"Don't get me wrong, good old Henry, he's alright. Suppose I shouldn't really laugh about it. Yet, he is a bit of a show off – hard to be a surfer and not care how you look to others – but his pole is, this time, to keep some of the weight off his knee. I do find it funny, though, that he managed to bust his knee, not actually surfing but as he carried his board across the sand and managed to get caught out by a trench some children had dug around their sandcastle."

"Was he sure it was a sandcastle and not a sand-fort?" said Alba.

"A what?"

"Never mind – that was more of a musing to myself. Sorry, you were saying Henry fell into a hole in the sand."

"Yes. Nor was it a very big one. I promise you that he won't share that bit with you if he tells you about his surfing injury."

"No?"

"No – dear old Henry, he'll be too embarrassed."

With that, May laughed once more at her cousin's misfortune before continuing:

"As for sharing my thoughts on uncle John's inheritance, guess I'm a bit like mum in this regard, in that I'm quite happy to give voice to what I'm thinking irrespective of who's listening."

"But not like her in others?" mused Alba.

"Definitely not," stated May, as the two women came to a halt at the end – or was it the beginning – of the drive.

They crossed the road in order that they could rest against a large concrete block a farmer had deliberately placed across the start of the farm track. Placed in order to prevent both off-road enthusiasts 'green laning' and caravans being taken onto his land. Enjoying the shadow afforded by a wayfaring tree behind them, they waited for those still making their way through the lime trees.

"That said, were mum to inherit some of it, perhaps she would be a bit more willing to forward some of it to me. I'm looking to travel across Canada as soon as I can get some funds together. I'm aiming to travel east to west, ending up on Vancouver Island but I need the money to go."

"Canada?" mused Alba.

"Yes, I know it's not quite so 'new worldly' as South America but if I start off from Prince Edward Island, travel up to just some of the many Nunavut islands and finish at Vancouver Island, it will be more challenging – and thus more readable – than it sounds. If I can go off 'grid' so to speak and meet, stay even, with those living in isolated communities, it will be worth writing about and I'll conclude with some musings on the Mowachaht people from Vancouver Island itself. Communities throughout Canada where, still today, there is a subsistence existence; where law and order, justice, punishment, if you like, is handed out by the dominant members of the tribe or community – irrespective of whether Canadian authorities proper, approve or not. That is the Canada I want to discover."

"Sounds interesting."

"Oh, it is and people will want to read about my travels. I got a few articles published after my last trip – in travel magazines mostly but one thing I wrote about Rio actually got referred to in a TV documentary. Didn't make me any money but it was exciting to be quoted."

"I can imagine."

"So, when I can get travelling again – I'm itching to go I can tell you – I'll be submitting what I write to the TV channels as well. Now though, I just need to get the cash to go."

"Ah," acknowledged Alba. "That is so often the stumbling block: money."

"Yes," agreed May before falling into a period of silence.

"Water?" asked Alba, offering the other her bottle.

May declined the offer, saying she had some in her bag but was saving it for later. Duly, the others joined them on this side of the main road.

*

After a pause long enough to infuriate May once again, the group set off once more. Alba and May, out front immediately, resumed their conversation.

"I like your strappy dress," said May randomly. "I'd have worn it without the T-shirt underneath myself. It's a very soft yellow."

"Thank you and yes; and I like the slightly puckered effect of the material. It's a bit different I think."

"A bit retro, I agree," said May. She then, having stooped to feel the dress against Alba's thigh, a manoeuvre which caused both of them to break their stride, added, "Oh, yes, the rippling effect is quite tactile. Myself, I opted for simplicity for this walk – denim shorts and a country shirt."

"As I can see – plus a hat. If I can say without offending, I preferred the one you wore yesterday but that one would have been too grand for today's look. The straw hat you're wearing, with its ribbons, goes much better."

"Yeah, yeah," agreed May. "The ribbons are an extra touch for today."

Once over a stile that took them both over a dried out stream and into the next field, Alba asked:

"Where is this walk taking us? I understand you, Henry and Connie suggested it."

"It was mostly me who suggested it. I wanted us all to go to help Henry; we're bound for the 'Clootie Tree'."

"Clootie? I thought I was pretty good with my trees," offered up Alba. "Beech, hornbeam, maple. Varieties of horse chestnuts, the hazards of limes in the summertime, the wayfaring tree we were in the shade of just now, even what a 'Verdun Oak' is but a clootie tree is a new one for me. Some new cultivar, is it? Some specimen you brought back from your South American travels and have planted on your uncle John's estate?"

"No, nothing of the sort," replied May. "It's not a variety of tree – it's a holy tree."

"A what?"

"A special tree – Kingbourne's sacred tree. It grows by the source of the Bourne – clootie trees are often found besides a source of water, be it a stream, a well or a spring."

"Right," said a still puzzled Alba.

"You see, in times gone by, villagers round about believed in the healing properties of a tree associated with the rising and falling of the Bourne itself."

"The tree has some medicinal element, does it? What variety is it?"

"Oh, I don't know but people don't come and harvest its leaves and boil them up. It's the tree itself which is sacred; people come and perform healing rituals by it – symbolised by leaving strips of cloth or ribbons tied to its branches."

"Oh," said an uncomfortable Alba.

Yet Alba's unease was lost on May who was in her element.

"I got to witness a lot of village rituals in Peru and Bolivia. When I got back from my travels I read up on ancient rituals in this country and learnt about clootie trees; I was amazed to find one so near to uncle John's home."

"And what happens when we all get to the tree?" asked Alba.

"We will hold hands, then I'll pour some water onto the ribbons which are currently tied round my hat and then we'll tie them to the tree. We can pray for healing for Henry's knee from the spirit in the wood."

"Er, right. And if we don't want to hold hands and all that?" asked Alba.

"Why wouldn't you want Henry's leg to get better?" challenged May. "It's a perfectly safe thing to do and Henry might feel better. Everyone has got to do it or it might not work."

"Well," answered Alba, as she moved a foot further away from the woman she had, up until that moment been comfortably walking alongside, "I'm not part of this family for one."

"That doesn't matter, even if mum doesn't like you being here. I want the energy from the whole group."

"And I'm not sure what my friend the Reverend Quinn would make of it all. I think he'd advise me to stay–"

"Some church man got you under his thumb, has he? Surely, you don't believe all that God stuff, do you? It's so condemning and enslaving – where's the freedom and the peace we're all seeking? I want something that is fresh and different, ancient, even. The solstice festivals, ley lines and clootie trees – they are where I see freedom and healing. Not in church, I can tell you."

"On that last point, Matthew, he's the reverend, would say you don't go into church, for the people are the church, you only ever go into a building where the church meet."

"Silly semantics!" decried May.

"It seems an important distinction for my friend."

"Whatever. I'm under no one's control. I want to do what I want to do – to live my life, my way. What harm can that do – holding hands, asking a spirit for healing, tying ribbons on a tree? I'm finding myself within this stuff and I, for one, will be coming back on Monday of next week to sit by the tree at sunrise."

"Why Monday?"

"Summer solstice."

"Oh, yes. The twenty-first," said Alba.

*

As they came upon a sizeable section of oak tree, which had come down in a storm and lay at the side of the last field before the woods they were clearly heading for, they paused as May shook out a stone which had got into her sandal from the sun-baked path. Then, just yards further on, they were out of the heat of the afternoon as they entered the woodland. The two women remained on the defined path; one which generally followed a slight dip in the ground to their right and which was the dried out Bourne.

Noticing Alba looking at the dried bed of the tiny, at times hard to make out, stream, May said:

"In speaking with locals, it comes up in the winter, wet springs but very rarely in the summer; this summer especially so. So?"

"Pardon?" asked Alba.

"So, will you be joining us or not? Got over your silly reservations yet? Broken free of the shackles your minister friend has placed round your mind? Moved beyond what I see as boring? Will you be one of us as we hang our ribbons? What harm can a bit of engaging with the spirit world do?"

Then, before Alba could answer, May announced:

"Ah, here we are – the sacred 'Clootie Tree'. What a sight."

Alba simply saw a hawthorn tree, bedecked with ribbons, strips of cloth and flags. Some of the materials seemed recently hung but the majority were faded, rotting bits of whatever they had once been. To Alba at least, the beauty of the hawthorn, with its deeply lobed green leaves and scaly bark, was lost under the tokens left by humans searching for healing, spiritualism or ritual.

May, with arms outstretched as if she were welcoming a distinguished guest, walked round the tree twice. She paused to untangle a couple of ribbons – ones she herself had tied to the tree on an earlier visit – and then walked round it a third and fourth time. Alba, in contrast, removed her sunhat, took a sip of water from her bottle and simply observed the other's behaviour.

Once the rest of the group had joined them, May started her speech. With that, as Henry made his way to the front, Alba, and to her relief Eleanor, moved to the back of the group. The two of them quietly moved further away and retraced their steps out of the wood altogether. Once back at the farmer's field adjoining the wood, they sat on the sizeable section of the oak tree which they had not long before passed.

"That wasn't for me," stated Eleanor.

"Nor me. It's hard to explain why but I just sensed Matthew

would be disappointed if I had taken part. Pleasant walk otherwise," offered back Alba. "If we wait here for the others to rejoin us, it will look like we haven't abandoned them altogether."

"And sadly, looks are important to this family. I just wished John hadn't joined in; I'll have to speak with him about that."

With that, and until the others rejoined them, the two friends enjoyed the June sun, the sound of a tractor in some distant field and the succulent sweetness of a punnet of strawberries. Fruit which Eleanor had asked for from Sandy prior to the walk setting off and which Sandy had diligently packed to ensure the berries, which were being taken on a walk, remained more than a battered and mulched-up mess.

As they sat there, a Kite hovered above the field before them, circling some prey it had just spotted.

CHAPTER 11

Empires

On the walk back, Alba felt even more of an outsider than before. Eleanor had resumed her place at John's side but Alba walked alone. She had started off, as before, walking alongside May but the other, through her silence and body language had made it clear she was no longer interested in talking with Alba.

As Alba's pace slowed, others from the group came alongside her but they too blanked her and moved past her. Finally, she found herself at the rear with Henry and Connie. Alba opted to deal with the 'elephant in the room' there and then:

"I'm happy to drop further back if you'd prefer; given I didn't partake in your ribbon tying ceremony."

"No need for that," said Connie. "We don't mind you walking with us and making up a slow three at the rear, do we Henry?"

"Doesn't bother me either way," responded Connie's brother indifferently.

"Oh, don't be so grumpy H," said Connie. She then turned to speak to Alba. "His knee is giving him a bit of gyp. He says he needs to walk on it though, otherwise he thinks it will seize up altogether. I'm not so sure but he insisted on coming."

"Had to get out of that boring old house, no matter what, even if this walk kills me" stated Henry. "How long are we having to stay at this accursed manor?"

"You know full well," stated Connie in an almost matronly manner. "You know we are here until Tuesday."

"Tuesday! Oh, how the blazes am I going to survive until then? It's just so dull."

With that Henry stopped and looked around him.

"I'm stopping due to a shooting pain which just went up my leg. However, since we've stopped, look, just look," he stated as he gestured with the arm that was not holding his walking pole.

"At what?" asked his sister.

Equally, Alba was at a loss as to what they were meant to be picking out.

"At that," decried Henry. "That!"

"What? There's nothing there," stated Connie.

"Exactly. Exactly," voiced an almost triumphant Henry. "Nothing, absolutely nothing. There's just nothing there – it's just dull. So unbelievably dull. There's no colour, no movement, no focal point. There's no action, no energy, no danger, if you like. It's just boring; deathly boring. Someone dying out in the field before us would give it more life!"

"Oh, Henry, that's a horrible thought. As for it being quiet here, you can't live on your adrenaline all the time, surely?" said Connie.

"But it's so mind numbingly dull here, isn't it? I mean, just look at the view before us – it offers absolutely nothing. No movement, no intoxicating mix of sun lotion, salt and drying out wetsuits to fill your nostrils. Just boring, dull countryside offering nothing but a numbing of the senses. If only something would happen here!"

With that, Henry bent down, picked up a midsize uneven stone and proceeded to angrily throw it into the farmer's field before them.

'That won't do the combine or the plough much good if either of them catch it,' thought Alba to herself.

"What do you think, Alba? It is Alba, isn't it?" asked Connie.

"Yes."

"Thought that's what dad said. So? What do you think? Is my dear brother correct in his assessment of the view before us?"

"It feels like it's not for me to say," answered Alba.

"Oh, please, don't tell me you like it. There's nothing there," challenged Henry.

"I accept beauty is in the eye of the beholder but, since you ask, I see–"

With that, Alba paused and marvelled for just a moment at all she could observe with all of her senses.

"Well, come on then – what do you see?" challenged an angry Henry.

"I see," Alba said, "oak trees which have stood here for centuries. Trees which have felt the footsteps of those coming out to sow and harvest, felt the passing of carts and horses and now suffer the weight of the modern tractor and combine on their roots. I see a landscape which offers up a thousand different greens, browns and yellows, with the odd patch of purple haze thrown in – colours emanating from the myriad of hedgerows, crops and trees. I can hear the bustle of a pair of pigeons behind us in an ivy-clad hawthorn tree. I can feel the warmth of the English countryside envelop us and wonder what the kite flying above us has now spotted in this field before us. And I can smell summer."

"Oh, what a load of cobblers," said Henry. "But you're one of uncle John's medievalists, aren't you?"

"I did study under him for a time," acknowledged Alba.

"Thought so, another dullard. Suppose you're going to quote some ridiculous poetry now as well, are you?"

"Excuse me!" responded Alba. "You asked for my thoughts and I shared them with you. If you don't agree, that's no reason to be rude."

"I'm not being rude. If you think what we're looking at is anything other than boring you have no spark, no zing, no soul."

"Oh, Henry, do be quiet. Alba is uncle John's guest and she's allowed to disagree with you. It's obvious you're missing the sea and this injury has set back your plans for your fledgling surf school. I just think–"

What Connie did further think was of no interest to Henry, for with that he set off by himself, walking in a noticeably awkward way. The two women could hear him grumbling to himself and watched him whack his walking pole into the hedgerow beside him a couple of times, causing a blackbird to fly out in panic, giving a shrill as it fled.

*

"You'll have to excuse H," said Connie.

"He would rather be somewhere else, it would seem."

"Oh yes," agreed Connie. "He was all set up to open his surf centre – the lease on the building was all signed off and he'd got it fitted out at some expense; looks good though, I'll give him that. Staff were in place for the season and then he goes and gets his leg busted as a campervan reverses out of a space just as he's walking behind it through a beachside car park. Poor Henry. He's been in a lot of pain, though he's done well to do today's walk, though that might be something to do with May's persistence. Plus, he has a lot of financial worry as the business struggled at the beginning of the season as he wasn't able to be present. Staff were making mistakes and a lot of people had to be refunded, some staff left as there were clashes of personalities, which Henry, had he been there more, could have sorted out. More generally, it seems to be one of those businesses which needed the energy, enthusiasm and simple driving force of its founder being there in person. Sadly, without H being there it has too soon lost its way."

"Unfortunate," agreed Alba. Then, trying to be positive, or more accurately sympathetic to the other's plight, Alba added:

"Good of him to come to Kingsbourne for this week. Surprised he hasn't given his excuses and put his business venture first."

"Perhaps. However, there was a bit of a three-line whip for us all to be here for this gathering. That said, three-line whip or not, none of us would want to miss being here if we knew the others were turning up. Not sure what uncle John has up his sleeve. Obviously, his latest, even younger, girlfriend is here as well but that's not a surprise as we all knew about her already – he's hardly likely to have brought us here to announce he's proposed to her."

"You don't think?" mused Alba. She hoped she had got her tone just right – inquisitive, as anyone who was a friend of Eleanor would be, but convincingly unknowing.

"No, definitely not. Uncle John seems to get through his flames quite quickly, though I accept this Eleanor woman has stayed around longer than some. However, uncle John is a bit too tight with his money to suddenly announce he's marrying."

"Tight? He must have spent a fortune on the manor."

"Oh, yes, indeed. Don't get me wrong there but there's a difference between living an extravagant lifestyle and investing. The rest of the family live life according to the former mindset – you only need to study the line of cars everyone has turned up in, all neatly parked under the trees at the front of the house – whereas uncle John lives his life with the latter approach."

"A new roof is not cheap on a terrace house, one on Kingsbourne Manor must be substantial. Then there's the reinstating of the ha-ha, employing the grounds team and so on."

"I agree he's spending; a bucketful no doubt. Yet, it's all wise investment. In time, when he comes to sell, he'll have recouped all he's put in and some. His brothers and sister might spend but they spend on the here and now, on things that deteriorate – holidays, cars, cars which are expensive but hardly destined to be classics, school fees on children who would rather be lying on a surfboard, travelling the world or like myself just muddling through private school without great success."

"Eleanor told me you were off to Oxford."

"Only to do PPE – politics, philosophy and economics. I'm hardly going to change the world with that."

"You've done well to get in, whatever the subject or your views on it."

"You don't think uncle John had anything to do with that? You're naïve if you think he didn't."

Alba remained silent as Connie continued:

"Forget about me," she said as she ran her hands through her long brown hair, gathering it together as she did so and bringing it down the right side of her neck so that it now rested against her chest. "All I'm saying is uncle John is just like the rest of the family – we're all cut from the same cloth. Obsessed with money and building up our own empires. Naturally he's drawing on his academic interests but they simply showed him an investment opportunity that others had missed – either because they didn't have uncle John's eye for the early medieval period or because they lacked the money behind them which uncle John has, following his inheritance from great uncle Leonard. Once the manor is up and running as a going concern, it will be on the market for sure. So, all in all, I don't see where Eleanor fits into all that. The best – do I mean best? Perhaps 'strongest' would be a better word; the strongest empires if you like are those governed, ruled, by a single person. Eleanor would be both a distraction and a drain. That might sound uncaring, it's not meant to be as I think Eleanor, of all of uncle's girlfriends of late, is by far the nicest. I'm just saying it as it is."

"Meaning?"

"Meaning whatever uncle John has brought us all here for is not to suddenly announce marriage plans."

"OK. Yet, and I'm very aware I'm an outsider in all this–"

"As I'm sure everyone is making you feel since the moment you stepped through the front door to the manor."

"Well–"

"Oh, don't be embarrassed to say it – it's abundantly clear. May's just gone off in a huff as you did not partake in her little ceremony and Henry is now grumpy with you as well as with the rest of the world. As for the generation above, I heard aunty Alice have a good moan about you over breakfast, mum and dad haven't even spoken to you as far as I know and I won't tell you what the others think about you or their thoughts on the reason you are here."

"Eleanor asked me to come," said Alba simply.

"I have no doubt; she probably wanted your support against all of us."

"That's not what she said."

"No? Yet that's the real reason, I'm sure, whatever she may have said. Look, don't feel awkward; we're a nasty family – all of us are – we're all driven by money or power or both. For one, it's her legal career, another it's her acting career. Henry is desperate to make something of his surfing venture and May wants to travel the world and build a literary empire of followers who hang off her every word. As for mum and dad, well, that's another story and so on and so on."

"You're being kind to me and Sandy the maid is nice," offered up Alba, searching for needles in a haystack.

"Hmm, don't you think she's such a slight figure? At times, you hardly notice she's around."

"I agree she's quite a petite thing and her outfit definitely doesn't do anything for her. It's not a bad black dress, far from it, but it's not her. Its simplicity, I feel, would work better on a fuller, more curvaceous figure. It would, if I may say, look good on you."

"Why, thank you," responded Connie – whereupon she stopped, turned to Alba and performed such a theatrical curtsy that it was more suited to one having been performed by her aunt Isabel on stage.

The two women remained well to the rear of the rest of the group and, by the time they had crossed the road and were back walking in the shade of the limes, they had lost sight of everyone else.

"You're puzzling over something," said Connie. "Aren't you?"

"I'm not sure if puzzling is quite right; curious, yes, and it seems odd."

"What's odd?"

"I wasn't expecting such a character assassination of your uncle John. Dr Sunday, that's as I properly know him, was, is still I'm sure, a fine university lecturer and clearly learned. He put his students at ease, encouraged their research and always had a freshness about him. We all highly regarded him. Your description doesn't quite fit the person I know."

"Doesn't it?" queried Connie.

"Not to me," said Alba.

"Look," said Connie, as she linked arms with Alba, suggesting an innocence which belied what she then said, "I haven't said he was or is a bad university lecturer, have I? He's clearly good at his job – he wouldn't be on the lecture circuit in America if he wasn't. Yet, that doesn't make him a nice person when the doors are closed and you're just left with the man so to speak. He's empire driven like the rest of the family; aunty Alice is an exceptionally good solicitor and, if ever you want legal advice, go to her, but she will sacrifice friends and family for the sake of her career. Uncle Hugh had a good career in the world of journalism until an allegation was made against him."

"Really?"

"Yes, he's been suspended until it has been investigated, though, no doubt, he's trying to buy the complainant off. Then there's mum. She's pretty high up in the charity world – I won't bore you with which one but she's at the level where corporate fundraising, media presence and lobbying government seems to be more important to her than actually helping the people the charity was originally set up to support all those years ago. She'll stress over what to wear to work and what bigwig she'll be next meeting but no longer care for meeting the needs of those the charity is meant to be caring for; you see, for mum, the charity itself and her place at the top of it has become the charity's *raison d'etre*. Mum is the driving force behind that as she wants her own empire as well, tired as she was of living in dad's dying shadow."

"Your dad?" asked Alba.

"Oh, dad's almost broke now. He'll be having to declare bankruptcy soon – thought he could emulate his uncle Leonard but the countries of southern Africa have moved on. There was potential, or was it just hope, at the beginning but over the years his money sank into the mines faster than he was digging anything up. Mum is scared she's going to be brought down with him and lose what she has built up as I was just describing. You know, sometimes I think mum only stays with him in the hope of some future inheritance coming his way. They definitely don't seem very happy together any more – thankfully, I've been out of it for most of the time, having been away at boarding school, and soon enough I'll be off to Oxford."

"Oh dear, that does all seem depressing. Why didn't – though this is a somewhat forward question but since you are being so open about your family, I will ask – your great uncle Leonard leave his money equally to his nephews and niece, to help them all out? Make John, Anthony, Hugh and Isabel all beneficiaries, rather than, as he did, leave everything solely to John? If, to use your phrase, they are all cut from the same cloth, why not treat them the same? Why pick one out?"

"Sensible question to ask – don't think dad, aunty Isabel and uncle Hugh haven't gone over that question a thousand times. Aunty Alice, no doubt, officially on uncle Hugh's behalf but obviously for her own benefit too, will have got most of her office working on challenging the will in an attempt for a share of the inheritance. Yet, it was watertight and uncle John got the lot. I guess, great uncle Leonard saw in his nephew John what was missing in the others."

"Which was?" asked Alba.

"Just that drive – a drive to turn a large pot of money into a bigger pot. Not to be content with what he received but to use it, to build the empire further. Not necessarily in mining; great uncle Leonard was taking his money out of the mines when he died, as he saw the market, the labour pressures and the politics of the region changing. Changes which dad couldn't or perhaps wasn't willing to see – dad, wanting to emulate his uncle Leonard, succumbed to the romance of Africa, 'the dust on his shoes' and all that and failed to grasp the plain economics."

"I see."

"And Leonard, I reckon, simply saw in his nephew John that the money he, Leonard, had spent a lifetime accumulating wasn't going to be squandered; be it lost due to dad's poor business decisions, Isabel pumping it into second-rate theatrical productions simply in order to get her name up in lights or to uncle Hugh, who has been sued by people he's worked with one too many times. Plus, John has the other advantage over his brothers, at least as great uncle Leonard undoubtedly saw it, that he has no wife to walk off with half his money a year after the inheritance came his way."

"That is a rather sexist, cynical and definitely stereotypical comment," observed Alba.

"I didn't say it wasn't. I'm just taking you into the mind of Leonard – as I say, we're not a nice family."

"And yet, despite talking down your entire family as we've walked, the fact remains you've all come here to spend the week together. That's rather sweet. Could you be making too much of people's character flaws? There are few perfect families after all. It is nice your parents and aunts and uncles have decided to bring you and your cousin together, to have family time. Or perhaps, you've all got together simply to see and acknowledge the progress John is making in his restoration of the manor itself. Your time here could be viewed in a positive light, couldn't it?"

"Oh, bless your innocence, Miss White," said Connie. By now the pair of them were back on the gravel area before the main house. There was a sparkle in Connie's brown eyes as she continued:

"My dear new confidante, you are too naïve, you really are. We haven't gathered to be a family, to support one another and reminisce about happy Christmases from times gone by. We are here because uncle John has summoned us all here. With his wealth, we are all, whether we like it or not, in the palm of his hand. If he invites us here, we come. OK, mum and dad are spending a lot of time here as it is, as they are renting out their London home in a desperate attempt to put off the bankruptcy a while longer but we are here because here is where the money is. We would all rather like some of it for ourselves – we are drawn to it as wasps are to a jam sandwich. Plus, none of us would not come when we know the others are turning up, for we are all desperate, that's including us cousins, to keep an eye on each other; none of us can allow another to get ahead, to become a favourite of John's. We all have our own empires we are trying to build. Nor can we just allow an outsider – the latest one being Eleanor – to come in and usurp us."

"I might be your elder by a few years but you seem to have a worldliness that has passed me by," reflected Alba.

"You grow up fast in this family; you have to or you fall by the wayside."

With that, and as the hall gong chimed once telling everyone there was half an hour until afternoon tea would be served, they made their way back into Kingsbourne Manor.

*

As she entered, for the first time in months, Alba missed Hillstone Hall. She should have preferred Kingsbourne, the way it nestled in the landscape, the intimacy within the manor's tighter corridors, that it was in every way less 'stately' than Hillstone and yet, she found herself missing Hillstone Hall. Despite being grander, for it was, after all, the seat of a Viscount, and lacking a family beyond Andrew himself, she missed its homeliness, its warmth and she missed Andrew. For all

Kingsbourne had offered her so far, save Sandy's timid welcome and Dr Sunday's revelation of that fine rooftop view, was angst, distrust and spiritualism and she still had not met all the family.

That, though, was about to change.

CHAPTER 12

Gemstones to Germiston

It was never a grand garden party. There was no large marquee, no array of waiters and waitresses topping up cups or glasses or walking around offering small sandwiches filled with salmon, cheese and cucumber or beef and horseradish sauce. No random occasional tables dotted about the lawns with littles pots of black and green olives on them, each tiny fruit skewered with a little wooden cocktail stick. There was no larger table at one end of the marquee with a selection of cakes – Victoria sponge, black forest gateau and carrot cake. No jazz band near the rose garden, playing Miles Davis, Louis Armstrong and, of course, Sinatra. No glitzy array of guests, where the wealthy, the titled and the currently famous, mixed. Nor was there a charity raffle where one could win a ride in a hot air balloon, a 'Fortnum and Mason' hamper or two tickets to a 'Calcutta Cup' rugby union match.

It was simply tea, set out in the dining room, for the Sunday family and John's two guests, Eleanor and Alba. It was no swish affair. However, the garden was inviting on such an afternoon, there was a choice of homemade cakes and, with the French doors open, people naturally took their drinks and plates out into the garden.

It could have been as nice as some much grander affair. Or it could have been better for being more relaxed and intimate; it could have been. Yet, the Sunday family would, collectively, ensure it would not be. For now, though, Alba sat quietly with an empty chair to each side of her, cake fork in hand and enjoyed both the view beyond the ha-ha and the lemon drizzle cake.

*

Thankfully not before she had finished her cake, Henry came and sat beside her in one of the two free chairs. He placed one leg up on the footstool and knocked the empty plate, which Alba had just placed on it, onto the grass. She instinctively leant across and retrieved it and placed it down to her left, beside her chair before it got trodden on.

"Connie has told me to come and apologise for earlier."

"That would be appreciated if you did."

"So, there we go. Good. Right, that's that done. I'll go and grab myself a glass of something."

With that, Henry, wincing as he did so and almost catching Alba with his stick as he manoeuvred it about himself, was up and departed without a further word.

Quietness returned until it was this time broken by the sound of two Chinook helicopters flying overhead, the distinctive 'whump-whump' sound of their twin engines being, if not unpleasant, then definitely loud.

"They'll be dropping paratroopers over Salisbury Plain, no doubt," said Anthony as he came and stood by her side. "If it happens when you're out driving towards Everleigh and Upavon it can be both dramatic and disconcerting. I'm Anthony, by the way, in case you've forgotten."

"Thank you but I do remember from this morning when we spoke in the billiard room."

"Yes, of course. Seems a while ago."

He duly sat himself down in the chair so recently occupied by his son Henry and gazed up at the receding sight of the two helicopters with their tail ramps open. Alba, by contrast, studied the man who was now beside her.

He had retained a full head of dark brown hair and sported what to him was 'designer stubble' but to Alba, being a child of her father, was simply an unshaven look. Nonetheless, with his designer Polo Ralph Lauren shirt, chino trousers and chunky brown leather belt, he presented as younger than his fifty plus years might have suggested.

"Ah, there you are," said a third person who was approaching the two seated people from behind.

Recognising his wife's voice, Anthony turned apprehensively and spoke in an almost childlike way to Johanna:

"I had literally just sat down; we were watching the chinooks – the helicopters."

"Whatever. John is looking for you. Says he wants a word indoors if you can spare him some time."

"Now?"

"Of course, now. John's hardly going to be looking for you in the hope he can speak with you tonight, the day after tomorrow or a month next Tuesday. Clearly now. Use some common sense, Anthony."

"Yes, dear," answered a sheepish and self-conscious husband.

With that, having offered his apologies to Alba, he got up and headed into the dining room which he had not so long ago ventured out from.

In his place, Johanna sat herself down.

*

"I'll join you," she said as she rearranged the cushioned backrest, in order that she could sit more upright than the somewhat slouched position which Anthony had taken.

"That would be nice," replied Alba, unsure whether it would be or not. "I'm Alba, a friend of Eleanor."

"A student of John as well, I gather," said Johanna. "I've been doing my homework on you; decided now though I ought to speak to you in person. Form my own opinion."

"If you need to. So, yes, a former student but that's incidental; I'm here as Eleanor invited me."

"That was decent of her. Thinks she's lady of the manor already, does she?"

"I don't think so. I'm sure no one, least of all Eleanor, is trying to put the family out. I just think she and John thought she'd enjoy having an old university friend here with her for these few days."

"Did they? How wonderfully good of them both to think of themselves. Yet, a rather strange way to host a family get-together and make a family announcement."

"Family announcement?" queried Alba.

"Surely," stated Johanna. "John wouldn't just gather us all here for a summer retreat, to do some pleasant walks, play some garden games like Kubb and have a meal at the village pub together. That might be the itinerary as John has told me but that's not *why* we're here. No, mark my words there's something he has got lined up to tell us. My guess is he's been offered some post at an American university and is upping sticks and moving out there indefinitely."

"That will be a shame to lose your brother-in-law," said Alba kindly.

"Will be a shame to lose this place."

"You think he'd sell up rather than mothball it for the duration of his time out there? Sell rather than consider leasing it? Nor ask the family to manage it for him?"

"Definitely sell," stated Johanna. "He likes to keep things simple. He's an ordered man, likes things to be tidy. Overseeing this place whilst over there, just wouldn't be him. No, this place will be on the market soon enough if not already. It's now structurally sound and the interior is virtually there. Work still has to be done on some of the outbuildings, the ha-ha needs an overhaul and the grounds team need to pull their fingers out with regards to the garden."

"I think, given how small the garden team are, they are doing a good job," responded Alba, well aware of the back-breaking work needed to manage a garden of this size, particularly one that had 'got away from' the previous owners. She was not about to allow fellow horticulturalists, whether she knew them or not, to be dismissed or criticised unfairly.

"This was a neglected garden," continued Alba. "It takes a lot of work just to…"

Yet Alba was instantly spoken over by Johanna:

"Oh, spare me the sob story of manual labour being hard work. They have ride-on mowers for cutting the lawns, log splitters, a little tractor and trailer for moving heavy stuff around and all the power tools they could ever possibly want. It's easy and I've told John as much; I'm also convinced he's paying them too much."

"Easy?" reflected back Alba. "Pruning the roses is done by hand and you're constantly bent over doing it. Tying in the climbers is a delicate affair where you're constantly stretching, the herb garden looks good but that can only be achieved through deft, intricate hands-on work and there's no power tool yet invented that will bring a long border back – that is born out of month after month of hard graft. I think the grounds team are worth their salt and some."

"Oh, don't tell me your another socialist. What do you know about looking after a garden of this size?"

Alba wanted to pass a simple comment back, along the lines of either 'Ever been to Hillstone Hall?' or 'Have you done anything to help in this garden?' but she did not. Instead, remembering she was here to support Eleanor and to be Terry's 'eyes and ears', Alba opted for discretion even if that was not quite being herself. She wanted to lance the boil of arrogance and lack of compassion she felt Johanna was emitting but chose to play a cleverer game.

"Your London garden must look glorious at this time of year," said Alba calmly.

"Well, it's not too bad. I had to be strict with the gardener we had, who came once a week. We have several large pots in the front you know that needed looking after. The back is part paved and there are lots of evergreen shrubs; now though Anthony is having to look after the garden as we couldn't afford to keep the gardener."

"You help him, surely. What are your favourite jobs out there?"

"Me? I don't think that type of work is quite me. Anthony is responsible. In any case, it's his fault we had to dispense with the gardener. Odd sort of bloke, he was, if you ask me. He kept trying to explain what he was doing, how plants grew and 'npk' percentages, whatever they were and so on. He would talk to me, would you believe it, as if he were my equal. Plus, do you know, he had the audacity to ask for a pay rise once. The bare cheek of the man. So, in a way, I was not sorry to lose him but it was embarrassing explaining to our neighbours our plight. If only Anthony–"

With that though, Johanna fell silent. She looked down and stared at the rings on her fingers. She twisted her wedding ring, 'unscrewing' it from her finger and then studied it in the palm of her hand. As she put it back on, Alba spoke.

"That's a beautiful engagement ring."

"Thank you; they're sapphires and opals. The former come from Tanzania; shame they didn't come from one of Anthony's mines but not a lot has annoyingly."

Alba observed Johanna rotate her wedding ring several times and slide it off her finger once more. As she studied her, Alba wondered what the other woman was really thinking and why she had dressed up so much, simply for drinks on the lawn. For, unlike Alba, who was still wearing the dress and T-shirt combination she had had on for the earlier walk, Johanna had changed into a full-length white and royal blue dress, the cut of which revealed an almost embarrassing amount of cleavage. It was a dress, Alba felt, which was definitely more suited to some official social function than where she was now. Once she had again finished toying with her jewellery, Johanna continued:

"You fall for a man who owns a string of African mines and think what an exciting, exotic, dangerous even, adventure you are about to embark upon. However, it's been one long disappointment; year after year of desperately trying to keep ourselves financially afloat. We just can no longer keep up repayments to those people who loaned him the money all those years ago – loans he had annoyingly negotiated before I ever got on the scene. Alongside which, slowly, one by one, he's shutting down and selling off the mines. What a shambles and there I was trying to raise children in the midst of that failure; children who didn't appreciate the sacrifices I made for them and now, now I tell you, I can't even afford to keep our gardener on, as strange as he was."

Johanna lent down and retrieved her cup but had to pour the contents away as a bluebottle fly had landed in it; which prompted another wave of disgust to wash across her face. She then continued recounting her life:

"Henry thinks he'll make something of his surf school but, just like his father's enterprises, it will fail. I had higher hopes for Connie but she underachieved for the schooling we put her through. I concede she is still waiting on her results but I'm not optimistic. It's just so frustrating and unrewarding – where's my happiness in all this? Don't I, me, myself – the Johanna I used to be – have a right to be happy? Yet, I'm not and haven't been for a long, long time and now I don't even have a gardener to look after our London place."

"That's OK, though, if Anthony is doing it."

"Well, he was but we've let the house as a way to try and raise a bit of income. We're staying here at the manor for a bit. I just doubt the tenants will keep the outside looking as nice as the bloke we had in, did."

"I thought you didn't like the gardener you had."

"Well, he knew his stuff. It's just one thing after another with my family. Anthony's mining company, Henry asking for financial backing for his beach enterprise and then with his injury on top, it's just one thing after another. I've had my fill of it."

"You don't have to tell me all this," said Alba.

"Oh, I know. I don't know who you are or why you are really here with us but I've gone beyond caring. Everyone else in the family knows what's going on, so why not you? I stopped being embarrassed a while ago and if I didn't have my job and the opportunity to live here for a while I would, well, I don't know."

"Don't be too hard on Anthony," suggested Alba.

"Why not? Everything is his fault as I see it."

"For one," suggested Alba, "it can't have been easy being in the shadow of a successful uncle and, on a personal level, for each year you kept the mine company going, it was another year of employment, of income for your workforce. Some workers must have been thankful for that."

"Thankful. You really don't understand, do you? They would frequently go on strike, complaining about their working conditions or low pay. It was a nightmare. So, yes, I can be hard on Anthony; it could have been a success if he'd tried harder, been stricter with his foremen and got them working their teams harder. We might have had some financial security in our lives but no. As you just saw when he vacated this seat a moment ago, he's a timid, pathetic creature."

For a third time, as she sat there, Johanna took her ring off and studied it. She spoke once more – effectively addressing the gold circle which she now held between her fingers:

"Why, oh why, couldn't some of Leonard's money come this way – my way. Why is my life as it is? It could be so much more. Aren't I entitled to some happiness? If one more thing–"

Her voice, at that point, tailed off and her sentence went unfinished.

Alba was unsure how to respond beyond the tried and tested formula of asking whether the other would like another drink, to compensate for the one that got poured away. Johanna's request for coffee led Alba to head back to the dining room.

*

Stepping back into the dining room, Alba hoped to once more enjoy the peace and solitude of the room which she had experienced over her bowl of porridge that morning. Instead, she witnessed a heated exchange between John and Anthony; one which had clearly been going on since Anthony had vacated his seat next to Alba out on the lawn.

"…so you've just got to reconsider," pleaded Anthony.

"As I've already said," replied John, "I have plans for this place and whilst giving you free run of it for a few months hasn't put me out personally or got in the way of the building work too much, the time has come for you to move back to your London home."

"This isn't fair."

"Brother, I would say that I have been completely fair. You've been living here rent free for a while now. Johanna, too. I mention her separately given you are in two bedrooms and virtually eating apart from one another and all that is causing double work for my house team – Sandy was almost too embarrassed to mention it when I sat down with her and asked her how she had settled into the role and whether her workload was fair. As I say, I almost had to force it out of her. She was clearly feeling awkward about raising it but she was right to do so. I hadn't realised she was basically doing two jobs with regards to looking after you two. Thank goodness it hadn't been over the winter months when you'd both be expecting fires lit in your bedrooms and the other rooms you were separately using around the manor."

"But John–"

"Look, I'm sorry Anthony. Sorry, too, that things are clearly a bit, how shall I put it, not quite right between the two of you, but it doesn't change–"

"Oh, come on John, what am I going to say to Johanna? You know we've rented out our London home. We can't just move back in with the tenants."

"I didn't know you were letting it for such a period; you never shared that with me. However, even if you had, it doesn't, it can't change what I've just asked of you. I'm sorry."

"But you haven't even told me why!" exclaimed Anthony.

His fraught voice was obvious to John and also to Alba – for she was still at the French doors. She had remained because she had promised Johanna a hot drink and aware, that if she returned empty handed, and had to explain that was because her husband was having a disagreement with John, meaning the drinks table was inaccessible, it probably would not help Johanna's current state of mind.

"I'm so sorry to interrupt," said Alba. "May I disturb for a moment just to get Johanna a drink that I've promised her?"

"Yes, of course, Alba. The doors were open for a reason and family and guests are welcome in here. There's as much tea and cake as you need; homemade biscuits have appeared as well now. Make yourself at home, please."

"Welcome here! Be at home!" threw back Anthony. "You're having a laugh, brother. A jolly good laugh at my expense! Darn you – what the blazes is Johanna going to say to me?"

With that, John placed his cup down on the central long table and went over and opened an inner door. Having done so, he turned and spoke to his brother:

"Anthony, I had hoped this was going to be a simple, less contentious discussion than it has been–"

"Expecting me to say 'yes, brother dearest, I can move out tonight', were you?"

"Anthony, don't be daft. That is not what I've said. However, clearly we need to talk further."

"Perhaps if you'd explain the reason–"

"As I've said, for the time being, I am not prepared to say exactly why but let us vacate the dining room, so others – Alba for one – can make use of it. Let us continue this discussion up in my study out of everyone else's way."

John then spoke to Alba:

"The room is yours. Kind of you to be looking after some of the others – please, as I've said, make yourself at home. If you need anything, ring for Sandy and she will assist you."

"So, this Alba you want to be at home! Your Eleanor girl too, of course. What about your real family, John? Eh? What about us?"

John in reply, simply held the door to the hall open and gestured for his brother to follow him through.

The door closed behind them as John followed his brother out and their subsequent conversation was lost to Alba's ears. She, in turn, stepped over to where the drinks and cakes were laid out against the right-hand wall from where she had entered, in order to get Anthony's wife the drink she had promised her.

*

Drinks poured and with some ginger nut biscuits balanced on each saucer, Alba was about to pick the cups up when a voice next to her startled her.

"Any tea left in the pot or shall I ring for another one? Do you reckon I should chance one of those swell cookies, too?"

It was not what was said that startled Alba. Nor that it was Isabel who had spoken – even though Alba had not yet properly spoken with her since her arrival. It was the accent the words were spoken in, which caught Alba off guard. Alba left the cups on the sideboard and turned to Isabel. Alba tried to hide her confusion and puzzlement as she did so but failed; of the two women standing side by side, Isabel was clearly the better actress.

"I'm practising," said a somewhat deflated Isabel.

"Practising?"

"Yes, working on my accent."

"Oh, sorry, yes," said Alba. "That's what caught me out. I wasn't expecting a South African accent."

"It's Australian," stated Isabel sharply.

"Oh, yes," lied Alba. "That's what I meant to say."

"Right, good," said Isabel, her feathers slightly less ruffled. "Practising, you say. For what?"

"My next starring role. I'm in a touring production of 'The Wootton Wives'. I'm the leading lady."

"How exciting."

"I'm playing Catherine Wootton."

"Right," said Alba. "Yet, I must concede it's not a play I'm familiar with."

Having said that, Alba feared another ruffling of the prima donna's feathers and some sharp retort. Thankfully, on this occasion it was fine.

"No, you wouldn't have. It's a new production by that excellent playwright Tony Verdie."

"Oh, I have heard of him. Didn't he write, well, actually can we take these drinks out into the garden, I've promised Johanna a coffee and it'll be cold if I don't get it to her soonish. But I'd be really interested to hear about this new play."

"'The Wootton Wives'," reiterated Isabel.

"Yes, yes, I hadn't forgotten. Come and join us and tell us, for I'm sure we would both like to hear about it."

"Would you?" said an almost surprised Isabel, back. Her surprise was evident in her voice, for the forced accent was gone and a genuine, pleasant voice voiced those two words.

"Of course. Grab a drink if you want and come and join us."

With that Alba went out. Isabel, unused to genuine interest, in her excitement, splashed milk on the sideboard as she rushed making herself a drink, keen as she was to catch up with Alba. She then needed a second saucer as she overfilled her cup with tea. Finally, in her haste, she failed to remember to take her handbag, for it dropped down the left-hand side of the unit and out of sight when she hastily mopped up the mess she had created.

*

"You've done what?" said an annoyed Johanna as she took the coffee cup from Alba.

"Asked Isabel to join us," said Alba. "I thought it would be nice to hear about her new play."

"You naïve fool," stated Johanna bluntly.

"Pardon?"

"Naïve fool, I'm afraid to say. Yet again you're demonstrating you're an outsider here. If you knew anything about Isabel, you would know never to ask my *dearest* sister-in-law about her performances. We won't be able to shut her up; we could be here for hours!"

"Well," said Alba, "I wanted to hear; you don't have to stay when she joins us."

"I won't be."

Yet before Johanna could depart, Isabel appeared before them and, using the accent she was trying to perfect for her upcoming play, asked:

"May I join you two? My, isn't the view before us mighty fine? Aren't the Downs just so green at this time of year? So different to Taree."

With that she sat in the third seat. As she did so, Alba, speaking to puzzled looking Johanna, said:

"It's Australian – she's rehearsing it for the play."

"Yes, my latest starring role," Isabel said excitedly.

"In?" said Johanna feigning interest.

"'The Wootton Wives'."

"It's a new play, I've just been told," added Alba. "By Tony Verdie."

"I'm helping to finance it, too," said Isabel. "It's not cheap, you know, putting on a touring production but I'm trying it once again. We've now got all the venues booked; we just need to get enough tickets sold to start to recoup our outgoings. It will be a success, I'm just sure of it. Tony is such a good writer and this time, he says, he's written about one of his passions, racing. So, it's bound to be a success."

"A play about motorcars and pit lanes. How dreadfully dull," said Johanna.

"No, it's about horses; horse racing."

"Oh," said an almost equally disinterested Johanna.

"Oh, sister-in-law, you are so dismissive of anything that doesn't involve you."

"That's not true."

"Yes, it is true. Maybe I'm about to overshadow you and your glitzy charity work and be in the next big thing. We could be taking it to the West End if we get some good reviews."

"If, if; sounds like a big 'if' to me," stated Johanna coldly. "And you'll need people to actually come and see it. Maybe one or two will, maybe you'll even get the odd review out of them. However, be prepared for whatever they write to be as critical as the last one I read about one of your plays – *cardboard* was a word they used, if I recall correctly."

"That was about the set," protested Isabel.

"Odd. I rather took it to be a description of one of the actresses in the performance. Can you remember who they were talking about, Isabel? No? Oh well, it doesn't matter."

Alba saw the anger and the hurt in Isabel's eyes.

"Oh, you're so bitchy when you're on the back foot. You're just jealous of my probable success," challenged Isabel finally.

"Isabel, dearest. If you become a successful actress, I will come and watch you. I will take a box at the Prince Edward theatre in London. I will throw flowers at your feet as the curtain comes down but until then, I fear this will be another flop that will not make its full run."

With that, Johanna placed her half empty cup down on the grass, stood up and confronted both women.

"What took you so long to bring me just one cup of coffee? Don't bother answering. As for my charity work, Isabel, it is vitally important."

"Which leading charity, is it again, I forget, for there are so many doing the same thing, I find," responded Isabel.

"You know full well."

"It's just slipped out of my mind, sorry. My head must be so full of the lines I'm having to learn."

"Oh, you learn your lines, do you? I had wondered."

"Funny, aren't you. We've got our full dress rehearsal in a couple of weeks. Talking of dresses, you trying out that dress you are in for the next big fund-raising dinner, are you? You'll get a few blokes interested in the charity, or should I say in you, if you wear that thing!"

"How dare you. This is an Italian label!"

With that, Johanna walked away. Had Alba watched her, she would have observed Johanna twist and rearrange her hair in a way that mirrored how her daughter Connie had done hers on the earlier walk, for Johanna wished to make the cut of her dress obvious for all to see.

*

"That was heated," said Alba.

"It was standard for Johanna."

Then, whereas Alba might have taken hours, days even, to reflect on such a hostile exchange and how she could, or should, have conducted herself better, perhaps been more compassionate to the other's point of view, Isabel simply dismissed it from her mind and started to tell Alba all about her forthcoming play.

"Yes, it's about horse racing in its broadest terms but it's a story about love, loss and how people reminisce at the end of their lives."

"You did say but who are you playing?"

"Catherine Wootton. She was the first wife of Richard Wootton – he was a famous horse trainer at the beginning of the twentieth century."

"Not something I know a lot about," said Alba.

"Nor me until Tony sent me the script and then took me out to dinner and told me about it and asked whether I'd like to come on board."

"Right."

"The twist, if you like, is that the play is set at the end of Richard's life. Well, maybe not twist but it's the 'hook', so to speak, to get the audience interested from the very beginning. By setting it at the end of Richard's life, Tony has captured that moment of reflection so brilliantly. He's done it by having Richard's first wife, Catherine – that's me – appear to him in a dream. No, not a dream, in a vision; yes, that would be a better way of putting it, I appear to him in a vision. Yes, yes, Catherine appears in a series of visions in the weeks before he dies and it's their conversations with one another; of lost love, about their children and the 'what might have beens'."

"How interesting."

"Exactly," said an excited – excitable – Isabel, still reeling from having someone show her some interest. "Catherine died in childbirth in 1909, yes, I'm sure it was 1909, with their fifth child. They had moved from Australia, to South Africa, back to Australia and then in 1906 came to England. Richard – I know all this, as I say, as Tony has drilled it into me – was already a successful horse trainer. He'd won the Metropolitan Handicap in Aus in 1902 and the Gemiston Handicap in Turffontein, South Africa, in 1903, before setting up his training school in Epsom. He and Catherine had two sons, Frank and Stanley, both of whom went on to be successful jockeys and trainers, two daughters and then she dies in childbirth giving birth to another son."

"Oh, how sad."

"Yes. And that's what makes this play. It's not about horse racing *per se*, it's about love, loss and what ifs – the things you ponder in the late evening of your life. Would Richard have become champion trainer had his first wife lived – which he did in 1913. Would Frank and Stanley have had the careers – been the men they went on to be – had their mother lived. What life might Richard's second wife have had, had Catherine lived. It's all so, oh, it's hard to stay calm describing it all. You know, well no, of course you won't, but the scene stealer is when Frances, that's Richard's second wife, comes on stage as Richard is there holding my hand and – well, I won't tell you as you will have to come and watch it."

"Oh, yes, please," said Alba.

Irrespective of whether Alba felt Isabel was dismissive of John's staff, whether Isabel should speak in kinder words to her brothers' wives or whether Isabel should get someone to properly teach her the right accent, Alba did genuinely think it sounded a play she would like to watch. Plus, she knew Tony Verdie was a gifted writer – hearing the script, even if not the performance of it, would be worth the ticket price.

"You'll have to let me know when the tour comes my way."

"Of course. You're where exactly?"

"East of here. Down on the Surrey-Sussex border."

"Oh. Well, I think the nearest we hope to get is Guildford."

"That's not that far – I'm looking forward to it already."

"I just hope we can get the money to come in to cover the cost of booking all these theatres. The set, too, is quite expensive, given what we've got planned."

"Really?"

"Oh, yes. We've got to take the audience from Victorian Australia to the Surrey Downs in Edwardian times, via an ocean-going liner and South Africa. We've also got to portray the horrors of the Great War and somehow recreate the Derby from 1913."

"Gosh, that's more than a repositioning of a couple of chairs, refilling a glass of pretend sherry and a change of clothing."

"Yes. It's a bit of a worry but it's got to work. It's just got to succeed. I'm so excited for this play – I really do think this time it could be when I'm discovered. We've just got to have the opportunity of a full run. It just has to work. Otherwise, it could get a bit embarrassing if I have to ask John to help me out again."

Alba reached over and took the two biscuits from the saucer of Johanna's abandoned cup of coffee and offered one of them to Isabel. Isabel offered a 'thank you, my good woman' in a southern hemispherian accent – though quite where south of the Equator it derived from was anyone's guess. That apart, for the next few moments, Alba and Isabel gazed into the view before them and, in their imagination they could both see a field of racehorses, with the riders in their brightly coloured racing silks, come galloping towards them. They each saw them clear the ha-ha effortlessly, come ever onwards towards them and then to suddenly wash over them and go beyond them, racing into the very manor itself through the open doors and windows.

CHAPTER 13

Kubb

"Well, that was a miserable game," stated Johanna as they stepped in from the garden.

"We enjoyed playing it in the past," stated John reflectively. "I thought we might again."

"Did you? Did you really?" retorted Johanna with a real anger in her voice.

"Yes. However, with, no, never mind."

"With what John, with what, may I ask?"

"Just drop it Johanna, please. I had hoped it might be enjoyable once more but it clearly wasn't to be," replied John.

He moved across the dining room and poured himself a glass of chilled homemade lemonade – this time made by John's chef rather than the lady in the village who did the jams.

"I am taking my drink to my study before I say something I might regret. I have a paper to finish," he stated.

He might have held his tongue but he was unable to refrain from slamming the door behind him as he left.

The other participants, who had followed John and Johanna

into the dining room this Friday morning, remained silent. Had it been a cooler day, maybe with some cloud cover, perhaps a breeze or simply just earlier in the year, then probably everyone else would have dispersed sooner. However, today was another hot day, with a June sun burning down from a clear sky, and so everyone was in need of a cold drink, probably two. Necessity kept them together.

"As I say, that was a bloody miserable game," persisted Johanna. "Nice of him to bang the door as he goes off to sulk in his little den."

"We used to enjoy Kubb," said Anthony. "John was right there."

"Did we, Anthony, did we?"

"I thought we did," he offered back weakly.

"Well, you're wrong, hubby dear. As you've been on so many things. You're lucky we got put on the same team this morning, otherwise I might have been throwing my wooden batons at your ankles instead of at your team's posts."

She turned to face the wall and poured herself a drink. Having finished it, she slammed her glass down on the table and then headed to the same inner door John had exited just a few moments before. Before she exited, she turned once more to her husband and virtually screamed at him:

"And why the blazes didn't you stand up to your 'Lord-of-the-manor' brother yesterday afternoon, Anthony? Why didn't you? He's basically evicting us and you did bloody nothing."

"As I tried to explain—"

Yet his wife shut the door behind her before Anthony could add anything further; she did not need to bang it shut, closing it on her husband as he was mid-sentence was deafening in its own quiet way. Anthony reached for a dining chair just behind him and slumped into it. His son, Henry, having poured two drinks, took his father one and then went and sat by himself outside, on the paved area before the lawn began, rubbing his knee as he made his way out. An audible 'what a stupid game, that was' could be heard from him as he went. Eleanor, who had been the fourth person on Henry's team along with his parents, also took this opportunity to head up to her room once she had a drink in hand.

Alba, willing to wait to last to help herself to a lemonade, observed Anthony as he sat there, sipping at his glass. He was not, to Alba's mind, simply embarrassed. It was closer to being broken; he had a look of a person suffering from shell-shock, if that were a description one was allowed to use for someone who had not fought in battle. Had Connie not also been in the room, Alba wondered how Anthony would have otherwise coped. Thankfully, Connie went and sat with her father, placing her hand on his on the table, where his had been resting beside his glass.

"A lemonade, for you, Alba," stated Hugh.

"Er, thank you," she said.

"You look hot," he added. "Would you like me to hold an ice cube to the back of your neck? Quite happy to; I'll hold your hair out of the way and just keep the cube there gently so you can cool down."

"No. No thank you," she clearly stated, whereupon she moved away from him and sat herself on the far side of the table, in order that it was between her and him.

*

"So, you're being thrown out of the manor, are you brother? Oh, deary dear me. Whatever have you been getting up to?"

There was a smirk on Hugh's face as he spoke – not that Anthony saw it as he, Anthony, was looking at his half empty glass of lemonade. Hugh, enjoying his brother's torment, continued:

"You kept that to yourself."

"John only told me yesterday."

"Did he. Nice of John to have us all here so we can witness your distress. So, what was it?"

"What was what?"

"What made him serve you notice. Hand in the till, was that it?"

"I beg your pardon?"

"Helping yourself to a little bit of our favourite brother's money, were we? Found his cheque book lying around and thought you'd sign a couple on his behalf – payable to yourself and seemingly, to any bank clerk studying it, signed by John. Yet, signed by little old Anthony no less!"

"How dare you – take that back! What will Connie think?"

"Oh, I'm not sure what she'll make of it; let's ask her! Niece, dearest," Hugh continued but now addressing Connie, "What do you think of your papa helping himself to a little of uncle John's money? Can't say we should blame him too much – he needs it after all, doesn't he?"

"Father wouldn't steal," stated Connie.

"No, perhaps not. Yet, it's not really stealing, is it Anthony? After all, you would have been simply taking a small bit of what uncle Leonard should have shared out to all of us in the first place. So, brother, don't be embarrassed by just a couple of cheques; John's hardly going to miss the odd five thousand pounds. Reckon you could have risked a bit more – I would have if I'd been you – but you probably didn't have the guts."

"Ignore him, father," said Connie, who was still at her father's side. "He's teasing you." Then to her uncle, she added:

"You are teasing him, aren't you uncle Hugh?"

"Why, of course, yes – unless you did dip your hand in, brother."

"I did not," said an irritated Anthony.

"No, no you didn't. Well, if you say so. What was it then? Were you being a bit too friendly with the staff? Hmm, wonder if that was it. That new girl, have you been–"

"Hugh!" said Anthony as he stood up and faced his brother. "There are women in the room."

"Have I touched a nerve, brother? That is interesting. I had wondered whether she was your type or not."

"Type? Type; may I remind you I am married to Johanna."

"But for how much longer, I wonder. Plus, does being married prevent you from, well, you know? How about we summon the maid in and see how she responds to you, shall we? Let me just ring the bell here and see how quickly she comes running to you."

With that, Hugh pulled the bell cord.

"Uncle Hugh, you're being repulsive, please stop it," said Connie. Alba was grateful something had been said for she, too, was feeling extremely uncomfortable and was about to challenge what Hugh was saying herself.

"Am I, Connie? I'm sorry," said Hugh unconvincingly. "I will remind you, however, that your parents are being thrown out of the manor for something. You need to ask yourself what it is your father did, if it wasn't being a bit too familiar with one of the staff. If he didn't take any money and didn't, well, you can imagine what with that new girl, you need to ask yourself what he did do to earn an early departure."

"Nothing," protested Anthony. "Nothing, John didn't tell me why. He simply has asked myself and Johanna to move back to our London home."

"Ah! Now we're getting somewhere," stated Hugh, with even more swagger in his voice. "So, there is a reason but John's not telling you yet. Clever, I like his style. Maybe he's telling Johanna in his study now, at this very moment. What do you reckon? Maybe in her anger, she's gone to confront him and she's learning a few truths from John about her dear husband."

"I haven't done anything," insisted Anthony.

"Whilst I might believe that about your running of your mining business, as for your time here, well, I'm not so sure. Anyway, I've had my drink, so I will leave you, brother, and these good people around you to try and work out what it is you have in fact done. I've summonsed the staff; so, if the new maid appears, the rest of you can watch the body language between the pair of them."

Hugh made for the door just as Sandy was coming in to the

dining room. Rather than stepping back to allow her to enter, Hugh made his way out as she came in, brushing himself past her.

"His behaviour is disgusting," announced Alba.

She was unable to contain her abhorrence any longer. Certain Hugh was not about to reappear, Alba went over where Sandy was now standing and spoke to her direct.

"Are you OK? Did he–"

"I'm fine, miss."

"Really?" said an unconvinced Alba. "We all saw what just happened."

"I'm fine. Please don't make anything of it. Nothing really happened."

Alba looked at Sandy. She almost wanted the maid to retract her words and say things were very much not fine with regard to Hugh's conduct towards her. Sandy, though, stood there resolute and simply enquired as to why the bell had been rung.

"My brother Hugh rang it for reasons known only to him; put it down to him being annoying," informed Anthony.

"Oh, right you are. Well, given I'm here, I might as well, if it is alright with you all, collect the dirty glasses and check on things. Would you like me to bring you anything else if I'm returning with some clean glasses?"

"Some more lemonade," requested Henry – who suddenly had reappeared.

"And a ginger nut biscuit or two, please," asked Alba. "If there are any left from yesterday. They were rather moreish."

"I'll see what I can find," said Sandy.

"Bring my drink out to me in the garden," stated Henry and said without so much as a please or a thank you.

"Yes, sir," said Sandy but Henry had already gone.

"Oh, dad, uncle Hugh does talk a lot of rubbish," said Connie.

"He does but the fact remains, in all his foulness, that uncle John has asked your mother and myself to move back to London."

"He must have explained why," said Connie.

"No. No, he didn't, which doesn't help; makes it all so odd."

"But you can't move back, father. You've rented it out."

"Yes, I know, blast it," he replied angrily. However, he immediately added, "Sorry, Connie, dear. I shouldn't have let my frustrations out when speaking with you."

"That's alright. You've got a lot on your mind."

"Yes. Yes, I have. Still, if you'll excuse me, I think I'll take a walk by myself. I need to be alone."

Once he, too, had left the room, just Connie and Alba remained – and Sandy, who at that moment, having been tidying around the unit to the side where the drinks were laid out, announced with a touch of surprise:

"Oh, there's a strap sticking out down the side of the unit, between it and the tapestry."

She bent down and pulled on the strap. In doing so, she retrieved a handbag. As she stood up, she asked Connie and Alba whether it belonged to either of them.

"Not mine," offered up Alba.

"Likewise," said Connie. "But I do recognise it – think it's aunty Isabel's. She was looking for it after dinner last night, out in the garden."

Connie moved round the table to take it from the maid. Having passed it over and confirmed she would bring the lemonade and hopefully some biscuits, Sandy departed.

"Have you realised that you can never have a pleasant quiet drink here?" asked Connie, as they both sat back down at the table, to wait upon Sandy's return.

"I'm beginning to learn that."

"Not surprised. We're a pretty intense family to be amongst."

Alba opted not to voice her agreement with Connie's last comment. Instead, Alba reflected on the game the eight of them had just been playing:

"Anyway, well played out there. You've got a good throwing arm. Thought we were going to lose at one stage but you then took out the field kubbs in their half so they had to throw from their baseline once again."

"Thank you. Well done, you too, for keeping everyone out there until it had at least finished. Probably helped that an outsider acted as adjudicator-come-judge, even though you were playing as well. Mum would have enjoyed it more had she been on the winning side."

"Oh dear."

"That's one difference between her and dad. Dad is happy playing; mum is only happy when winning."

They chatted some more until the drinks and Alba's hoped for biscuits were brought in by Sandy; Sandy then went and took Henry his drink outdoors. Connie and Alba, at Alba's suggestion, then followed her out, to go and look at the rose garden for starters but in the broad hope of encountering Isabel.

*

They did not find her in the rose nor the parterre garden. As they wandered round the house, they did observe Anthony and Alice in conversation near to where Alba's car was parked. However, it was just as Alba and Connie came out from the gravel track, between the third and second to last lime trees, at the front of the house, that they saw Isabel at her car.

"Aunty," called out Connie. "Aunty."

Isabel ceased leaning into her car and turned round to where the voice was coming from.

"Ah, Connie. Was that you calling me? I had my head in the car."

"Yes. Yes, it was me. I have your – I think it is yours – handbag. Is it yours?"

The two walked over to where Isabel was still standing and she eagerly took it from them.

"Yes, it is. Where was it? I was just looking for it in my car. It's been missing since yesterday. I was getting desperate – even looking in my car even though I didn't go out in it yesterday. That's how desperate I was getting. Where did you find it?"

"I didn't," said Connie.

"You didn't? You had it all the time, then? I might have expected Henry, definitely May, to play such a nasty trick but you, Connie, well, I am disappointed."

"No, aunty."

"No?"

"Sandy found it. She discovered it in the dining room just now; it was down the side of some furniture, tucked between it and a tapestry."

"Oh, did she? Did you catch her having a look in it before she handed it over? Is anything missing? Wouldn't put it past–"

"Aunty Isabel," stressed Connie, "Sandy found it whilst tidying up. We were there, she couldn't have looked in. She handed it over as soon as she found it."

"Sure on that? I wouldn't put it past someone like that – got kicked out of uni so I heard – to be swift of eye and swifter with hand and help herself to a little something that doesn't belong to her. Deftness becomes such a person in opportune moments. Everything had better be here; everything!"

"Oh, aunty. You are so untrusting of people. She passed it over the moment she announced she had found it and I've been guarding it ever since. Nothing can have gone."

"That had better be the case."

With that Isabel opened the handbag and spoke as she started to check the contents:

"Where are they? They had better be in here still. Wish Anthony hadn't–"

Alba and Connie simply watched as Isabel got more flustered. Suddenly, she turned back to her car and tipped the contents of the bag onto her driver's seat.

"They're not here. They aren't here. What the blazes am I going to say to your dad?"

It was not quite a question that Alba felt Isabel wanted an answer to – it was spoken, Alba felt, more in panicked concern than as a proper question. As if to prove that assessment, Isabel continued her increasingly troubled monologue:

"They've just got to be here. Where else was I meant to keep them? There's no safe in my room and Anthony could hardly keep them with him. They just have to be–"

However, whatever she was searching for, were not there and she turned once more to her niece and Alba. Her worry was evident.

"What's missing?" asked Alba.

"Might something have dropped under the car seat as you emptied the contents out?" asked Connie almost simultaneously.

"Nothing dropped," said Isabel.

"Well, can I look anyway?" suggested Connie.

A nod from Isabel allowed Connie to kneel by the car and run her hand down the side of the driver's seat and underneath. She even lifted the plush car mat and then arched over to repeat her actions under the front passenger seat.

"Would you like to tell us what has gone?" asked Alba again. "If only so Connie knows quite what she is searching for."

"Anthony said I wasn't to tell anyone but if that thieving petite housemaid of John's has taken them, I'll have to tell people they're now missing, I suppose."

"Taken what?"

"A pair of diamond earrings."

"Oh."

"A pair of chandelier style diamond earrings in a blush pink, suede pouch."

"Were you hoping to wear them at tonight's dinner? For it seems to me, this gathering is hingeing around the meal John has organised," offered up Alba.

"At the meal in some ghastly pub in the village? I really don't think so!"

"It's not ghastly," said Alba. "I called in there on my way here on Wednesday for directions. The food smelt and looked good and the staff were friendly. Eddie, the landlord's son—"

"Oh, spare me please. You're already on first name terms with the publican's son, how common! Flirting with some young bloke who works the bar, were we? I had thought you had a bit more class about you than that but I must have been mistaken. Still, if you think some village watering hole is where a lady wears the finest jewellery, it can't say much for either your choice of eating establishments or the quality of your jewellery."

Whatever warmth or sympathy Alba had felt towards Isabel yesterday, as she had enquired after the other's acting career and her upcoming role in 'The Wootton Wives', it evaporated with what Isabel had just said to her. Alba felt her grandmother's rings on her right hand and a righteous anger burned within her.

"Excuse me," challenged Alba. She realised she was finding it increasingly hard to remain polite and civil towards the vast majority of the Sunday family; Terry had warned her but she was beginning to realise she had massively downplayed his warnings.

"'Excuse me' what?" snapped back Isabel. "If you think a woman wears diamond earrings, earrings of the quality and the value that were in my handbag, to a public drinking establishment, you've either got no class or are simply deluded. We will be eating in the pub in the village! It'll be ghastly; I'm an actress and yet John expects me to spend my time in a place full of locals. Locals who do boring normal everyday jobs. Do I need to remind you, I'm an actress? Yet I will have to mix with the likes of delivery drivers, shop assistants and goodness knows what."

"Perhaps mechanics," added Alba sarcastically. "People who work on motorbikes and cars and who get oil and grease underneath their fingernails."

"Exactly," said Isabel, thinking Alba was now agreeing with all she had just said. Isabel was mistaken in that view as Alba was quick to make clear.

"Look," Alba said bluntly, "I am a guest here and you are clearly a bit stressed if something has gone missing—"

"If! Of course they've gone. A pair of pearl and marquise-shaped diamond chandelier earrings, in a discrete little bag, have gone. No, more than gone, they have been taken from my handbag."

"They're not under the seats in the car," confirmed Connie as she stood up.

"So, they are gone," continued Alba. "However, I would ask you to stop being rude to me as you deal with that fact. And, I might add, 'The Earl of Clarendon' is a good pub from what I saw of it when I called in on Wednesday. The food might not be 'Michelin Star' quality but it smelt lovely, looked great and they definitely weren't scrimping on their portion sizes."

Isabel said nothing. Alba had hoped for an apology but was now realising that saying sorry was not something members of the Sunday family were capable of doing. Alba, in her annoyance, continued:

"And, yes, I'm on first name terms with the guy in his mid-twenties who works behind the bar. He was very helpful. Good looking, too, I might add. I could hardly not notice; I hadn't previously thought tattoos could be attractive."

"Tattoos, really!"

"Yes. Well, the one he had. So, yes, he's attractive. Anyway, that's beside the point. He was helpful as he gave me directions to get to the manor. That said, I am kind of now wishing he hadn't bothered; for if I had never found this place, I'd have been spared all this rudeness. Finally, I might add, it's the villagers, those who frequent a pub on a weekday evening, people who put a little bit of their hard-earned spare change in the pot on the bar, for the local air ambulance or the RNLI, who are the very same people who you are desperate to have come and see your latest performance; so don't make out you are above them. Tony Verdie's writing might be excellent but you're no longer selling it to me."

In her disgust at how she had been spoken to, Alba turned her back on Isabel and took herself into the manor. As she did so, Alba promised herself that later, when they were all at the 'Earl of Clarendon', she would demonstratively engage with the staff who served her. She would also make a point of talking with the locals at the bar and make it generally clear she was entirely comfortable with and genuinely enthused about a pub meal on a Friday night – especially one in the 'Earl of Clarendon'.

And she would get to see Eddie again.

CHAPTER 14

First-fruits

"Oh, hello Sandy," said Alba as she stepped from her car.

Alba had just parked in the pub car park and, as she lifted up her sunglasses so they sat on the top of her head, saw the maid exit the pub.

"Miss, you're here much earlier than you need to be. The table booking is not for another hour. I was just here checking on the arrangements on behalf of Dr Sunday. You are unexpectedly early; you've got time to go back to the manor and relax for half an hour and still make it back in time."

"Thank you. You do seem to be looking out for me during my time here but I'm deliberately early. I fancied a quiet drink, you see."

"But miss, I can get you a drink up at the manor; there's time."

"You are kind but I fancied a *quiet* drink you see. As good as the food and drinks are at the house, nor could I fault the service, let's just say the atmosphere is not completely to my liking. I reckoned I could guarantee a quiet drink here."

"Right you are, miss."

"Alba, please."

"Miss, that is sweet of you but, if you don't mind, I'll keep it formal. It's simpler that way and it means I won't be expected to address certain other guests by their first names as well."

Alba reckoned she knew who the young maid had most in mind; Alba was thus comfortable to keep things formal between herself and the maid.

"So, are things in order?"

"Pardon, miss."

"You said you were here to check on arrangements for tonight – it's all going ahead, is it? Any changes to the menu? Or would you recommend I slip down to the village and treat myself to a cod and chips instead?"

Before Sandy could answer, the door to the pub opened and Eddie appeared. He did not notice Alba initially. In part, that was because Sandy was between Alba and himself but in part it was due to that strange human ability to be blind to things, people even, because you are not expecting them to be there; sometimes the human mind only registers what it hopes to see.

"Ah, you're still here. I really don't think–"

Eddie cut himself short, when movement beyond Sandy – as Alba readjusted her smoke-grey, slightly oval, sunglasses – told him someone else was present.

"Alba," he said in surprise. "You're here but you're–"

"Not due for another fifty-five minutes, I know. I've come for a quiet drink by myself and away from the others but you are not," and with that, she moved her sunglasses down to sit on the end of her nose, to give the impression of being a schoolmistress who was looking over her glasses in order to be strict with her charges, "not," she repeated, "to tell them I said that. Is that clear?"

They both got the humour of the moment. For Sandy, for the reason just re-established, her answer of 'yes, miss' came naturally enough. For Eddie, however, it was a slightly more stilted response even though he, too, said 'yes, miss'.

"Good. I'll go and sit in your beer garden. Eddie, when you've finished discussing with Sandy whatever it is you came out to say to her, may I have a—"

"A pineapple juice."

"You remember?"

"Of course. I'll bring it out to you in a couple of minutes."

"I'll be at whichever free table has the best view."

"In that case you'll want the table nearest to where we are currently standing. If you sit with your back to where you've just parked, you'll get a fine view. The tables further into the beer garden, where the ground drops away, might be quieter as they're further away from the road and the car park but they don't allow you to see over the hedge to the farmland beyond," said Eddie.

"I'll be at the nearest table, as you suggest," said Alba, knowing she could trust him.

As the other two went back into the pub, Alba entered the beer garden. She located the table and, with her experience of a couple of days ago still fresh in her mind, carefully checked the seat before she sat down.

A few minutes later, Sandy brought out Alba's drink and a packet of 'Cornish sea salt' crisps. Sandy told Alba the crisps were with the compliments of Eddie but if she did not want to eat them now, in light of the meal she was to have here later, she could just leave them in her car on her way into the pub when she was up to joining the rest of the party. With that, Sandy said goodbye and said she was heading back to the manor.

*

It was a truly beautiful early evening. Being June, the sun was far from setting but it was lowering in the sky and the shadows were just beginning to lengthen and light was becoming softer in tone. She was grateful she had trusted Eddie's guidance once again, for she was afforded a fine view from where she was sitting.

As she sipped at her drink, she could make out a church steeple in the distance. She was fairly certain it was not Kingsbourne's church – it was too far away for that – but her orientation was not that good for her to be certain whether it was Southbourne's or Quarrybourne's church. It did not really matter, it might even have been another village altogether, and not knowing, or was it not needing to know, rather added to the loveliness of the view.

In one of the nearer fields, Alba then spent several minutes watching a herd of brown cows, slowly make their way across the field to a newly opened gate. They were possibly South Devons but they were not quite near enough for Alba to be certain. Once the cows had moved out of sight, she enjoyed the busyness of a number of tree sparrows darting in and out of the hedging which surrounded the beer garden and she, in turn, studied the solitary oak leaf which an overhanging tree had decided to earlier drop onto the table at which she was now sitting; dropped as if to remind anyone who sat beneath its branches that, despite their stillness and silence, the plants themselves were very much contributing to the view before them in the way they framed a scene or provided a habitat for the wildlife. Had at that moment some 'Painted Lady' butterflies come and settled themselves on a clump of thistles growing out of the hedge just off to her right, it would not have surprised Alba. The perfection before her – born out of its simplicity – started to make her think that all the ugliness and nastiness she had been experiencing these past two days could only, after all, have been in her head. She felt that somehow she had dreamt it all up; for could such pettiness and self-interest really exist just a few miles up the road from where she was now sitting?

As a result, as she sat there alone, alone apart from Eddie coming once to check all was OK with her, she started to convince herself that perhaps the family's mood would be lighter, less intense this evening, for they were, after all, out in public and therefore on show. Furthermore, they were coming to a traditional English pub at the end of a warm summer's day and surely that would raise anyone's spirits, would it not?

*

Alba heard John and Eleanor arrive first. She wondered whether Eleanor would come over and say 'hello' – Alba had informed her friend she would be getting to the pub early. However, Eleanor did not. Yet, Alba was not surprised, for Eleanor would surely be beside herself with excitement, holding John's arm ever so tightly, for in just a few minutes or, at least, at some stage during the evening meal, John had said he was going to propose to her in front of his whole family. Why would Eleanor leave John's side for a moment and come and talk to Alba? Why would Eleanor have eyes for anything other than the man she had arrived with? Their conversation, though, was not quite of two love birds:

"So, what are you going to do?" said Eleanor.

"Nothing. Isabel's my sister but that doesn't give her the right to have access to the maid's room. Even if the maid has borrowed something and not given it back, I won't allow Isabel to take the master key from my study and just let herself in. Whatever Sandy has borrowed, Isabel will have to ask her nicely to return it. What else can I do?"

"It's not going to ruin…"

With that, though, their voices were lost to Alba as John and his Eleanor entered the 'Earl of Clarendon'.

Alba next heard Henry and May turn up. To start with, Alba could hear May saying she did not find his joke funny and Henry claiming, as he undoubtedly had during the car journey itself, complete innocence of what she was alleging he had done. Then their conversation moved onto May puzzling over why Connie had wanted to drive herself, instead of coming with the two of them, and Henry's response that he had not bothered to ask and, anyway, that he was more interested in whether this pub had any craft beers.

A further car pulled in but no one opened a door to get out. There was no music blaring from inside and no mechanical noise as the driver, were he or she sitting in a convertible, waited for the roof to unfold itself and secure itself in place. There was simply silence.

Alba was telling herself not to turn round. Of course, the person who had just pulled in might well be a local or, as Alba herself did on Wednesday, someone stopping to check their directions before heading off again. However, eleven of them were due for dinner here this evening and Alba had decided to wait until she had identified at least nine of the party to have arrived before she went in to join them. Including Alba herself, five of them definitely were already here; she did not expect to have long to wait. Duly, another car entered the car park.

*

"Right, let's get this over with," said Johanna.

"Well, try not to ruin it for Henry's and Connie's sake at least," suggested Anthony.

"What are you talking about?" snapped back his wife. "I'm not going to ruin anything. It's–"

"Johanna, look, all I'm trying to say, to ask, is–"

Alba, as she overheard their conversation, sensed they were conversing over the roof of their car.

"Is what? Do I need to remind you, yet again, I'm not the one throwing others out of their home."

However, with a further car door opening, as Isabel stepped from the next car along, Johanna did not get to add to her statement.

"Ah, Anthony," exclaimed Isabel in seeming surprise. "Anthony, so glad I just caught you. Could you do me a small favour? Or you, Johanna, if you know anything about lights on a car's dashboard?"

"You know I don't!" Johanna crossly answered. "I guess Anthony can help you but does it really have to be done now?"

"Well, I'd rather–"

"Oh, whatever. Anthony go and help your sister – clearly the thing just can't wait another moment. I will go in and at least get myself a drink. I trust John will be paying, having brought us out here and forcing us to go through with this silly charade of his. He's got something up his sleeve but what he's planning on announcing in a seedy village pub is beyond me; would he really choose here to announce, oh, never mind, your sister is giving me one of her looks. I know I'm not wanted yet again."

"Don't be silly, dear," said Anthony.

"Exactly," added Isabel. "I'm just keen to have someone look at it before the meal. I want to know I can drive back safely and not worry about it over the meal itself."

"Yes, of course, how foolish of me to read anything else into your facial expression. It must be me once again getting all confused; you are such a great actress after all."

"I am rather, not that you'll admit it," retorted Isabel. Then, ignoring Johanna's continued presence, said to Anthony, "Can you please have a look? There's a yellow light that's just come on, it's a sort of squiggly line with a, oh, I can't really describe it. Can you come and have a look?"

"Go and do as you've been bidden. I'll go and get a glass of the best red this establishment can offer – John had better be paying."

A brief moment later, Alba heard Johanna call back, from the door of the pub:

"Don't you dare get oil on your fancy shirt if you end up lifting the bonnet."

"The engine is in the boot of Isabel's car, actually," said a strangely emboldened Anthony.

"You know what I mean; don't try and be funny with me. Not tonight. It's going to be awful enough as it is – all this forced niceness."

Having said her bit, the sound of the pub door went and Johanna's involvement in the exchange ended.

"How do you put up with her?" quizzed Isabel of her brother. "Never mind," she instantly added, "she's gone for the moment, thank goodness. Still, we better sit in the car and at least pretend I have something wrong with the car. Knowing her, she'll be peering out the window to keep an eye on you. I don't know why you don't leave her."

"What's this all about, Isabel? Is there a problem or not?"

"There's a big problem. Look, just sit in, will you. We've got a major thing to worry about – you think you had problems before but they've been taken."

"What have?"

"Just get in, will you."

The sound of two car doors going brought silence once more to the car park and the beer garden which adjoined it.

*

Emboldened by the silence, a pair of sparrows flitted out of the hedge, settled on an empty picnic table for a moment, pecked at something wedged between the strips of wood and then, on the sound of another car pulling in, darted back to where they had emerged from.

Doors opening and closing were followed by the sound of Hugh's voice:

"You do look stunning, Alice, dear. You really do."

"What are you after? Whatever it is, it still stands that as soon as this meal is over I'm heading back to the house. I have a pile of stuff to work through if the practice is serious about expanding in the next six months. My worry is the sums just don't add up but we just have to expand."

"Oh, you worry about things too much," suggested Hugh.

"Someone has to in this marriage."

"Really? So, this is the pub he's been promising us; what do you make of it?"

"It's a public house – what do you expect me to make of it? Why on earth has he brought us out here? What is the game he's playing?"

"Who cares. You should learn to relax a little, Alice."

"Relax? With the pressures of work and what you are currently putting me through?"

"That thing?"

"Yes – that thing!" confirmed Alice.

"Oh, don't worry yourself on that. I'm not worried. It'll blow over; she'll withdraw her allegation before too long, I'm sure of it."

"She had better. I'm not falling if you fall."

"It'll pass."

"Make sure it does. That aside, it still stands I'm heading back as soon as I've finished eating. If John plans to take us on somewhere or has some silly surprise up his sleeve, tough. I've got far too much work to get through – I've lost too much time as it is with this ridiculous meeting up of your family. If only it could all end tonight and we could all go back to our normal lives elsewhere."

Alice paused for a moment before adding:

"Well, when I say elsewhere, your brother, Anthony and his self-righteous wife will stay on as long as they can at the manor even though they've been given their marching orders."

"You're happy they've been asked to leave?" queried Hugh.

"Absolutely, as I know you are. Yet, whereas you are enjoying their plight, in terms of some childlike amusement at someone else's distress—"

"Amusement? Absolutely, my dear! There are, after all, two types of good fortune in life; good fortune for oneself and witnessing misfortune befalling somebody else. Another person falling off a bike is always funny, I say; Anthony getting his notice to quit is funny."

"You are such a kid, Hugh. You really are. Whereas, you'd have chucked Anthony and Johanna out of Kingsbourne Manor just for a laugh, I'd have got rid of them a long time ago but for a grown-up reason."

"A grown-up reason! How fancy – tell, what might that be?"

"You're such a fool. You play all your silly games, flirt with anything that moves yet miss the obvious. Can't you see what Anthony and, more probably, Johanna are up to? Possession, not that I should need to remind you, is nine tenths of the law. If something were to befall John, you do realise they'll be so much harder to shift from the manor if they can claim residency, even more so if they can miraculously provide some kind of written – forged no doubt – proof of the arrangements of their stay including some peppercorn rent. Whatever share you, we, might have got from John were he to get hit by a bus, would inevitably be much reduced if we have to prize your brother and his wife out of Kingsbourne via the courts. John, thankfully, has done the sensible thing at long last in kicking them out."

"Alice, you're stressing too much, as usual. Let's get inside for a drink and learn why John has brought us all here."

"A drink, yes, just the one though, for, as I say, I'm leaving the moment I've eaten."

*

Once Hugh and Alice had vacated the car park, Anthony and Isabel stepped out of her car; too wrapped up in their own situation they had missed everything Alice and Hugh had just said; Alba, by contrast, had heard it all without trying.

"So, as soon as you can leave, you must get yourself back to the manor and keep looking," reiterated Anthony for the nth time.

"But I have looked! You're not hearing me."

"I mean, you've got to get into the maid's room. If she's taken them as you say, she's stashed them somewhere. She hasn't had time to get out and meet someone she can pass them on to; she's been around the manor all afternoon and then I heard John give her more stuff to do concerning tonight. What, though, I don't know and don't care but she can't have found the time to offload the stones to someone so they must still be at the manor."

"How am I going to get into her room, though? John won't even give me the key. The staff have all got the evening off – they'll each be in their rooms or their communal sitting room, meaning I can't just walk up to their floor and start poking around looking for a blush pink suede pouch containing a pair of earrings worth tens of thousands of pounds."

"You've told John!"

"No, don't worry yourself on that score. I simply said the maid had borrowed something and I needed it back. I was wonderfully vague and unflustered about it as I asked – I am an actress, after all – but still John refused. He stated the staff had their rights. So much for being his sister – sometimes I think he favours the staff over his family."

"Yes, I agree but thank goodness he doesn't know. Annoying we can't easily get into the maid's room. Frustrating but let's turn that problem to our favour – concerning the maid, let's bank on the fact that, if she's sharp enough to recognise the earrings are valuable enough to risk her employment and even her liberty if caught, she might be canny enough to know not to stash them in her own room. That would be too obvious. If there's more of a brain to her than I first thought – silly of me not to be more wary of her moving around the house as her job allows – she'll have found somewhere clever to hide them in one of the communal rooms. Of course, we might have to search her room as a last resort, meaning we might need to get ourselves into her room, whatever John might think about it. Communal rooms first though."

"OK but where should I start? I might not have much time before the others leave the pub after this ridiculous meal John has arranged for us. There are numerous rooms it could be."

"I know. I know," repeated Anthony. "Start with the dining room. The room where she *discovered* your handbag. Why, oh why, didn't you notice you'd misplaced it the night before? I mean–"

"Anthony, drop it. I've said I'm sorry."

"Sorry!"

"Yes, sorry. I had a lot on my mind and this interloper Alba woman, was showing an interest in my upcoming play. I'm playing Catherine–"

"Isabel, I know who you're jolly well playing. You've told me often enough!" said an exasperated Anthony.

"If I have, you've never showed any interest. Whereas this outsider Alba, Eleanor's friend, was showing real interest, so I got all excited in telling her about the play, the pressures of putting it on and in my excitement, I misplaced my bag. It's easily done."

"Easily done? I'd entrusted you with tens of thousands of pounds worth of gemstones and you misplaced it because someone asked you about your acting. Oh, help me please! You're a fool."

"I'm not and it was an accident; do you want my help later or not, brother dear?"

"I need your help. What on earth is Johanna going to say to me if she gets wind of what I've done; that I've made out that we're broke, on the verge of bankruptcy and yet I've got stashed away a pair of earrings that on the right day and with the right buyer could be worth up to one hundred thousand pounds."

"A hundred? You said about fifty to sixty."

"Yes, I was trying not to put the wind up you too much and, naïvely, thought you'd look after them whatever their value."

"I did, well, I did until that maid took them from my handbag. Don't look at me like that, Anthony, where was I supposed to keep them hidden but in my bag? We don't have safes in our bedrooms at the manor and I doubt my car insurance would cover me leaving them in the glove box. Plus, I'm still puzzled; Johanna has always said your mines never gave up anything of real value."

"They haven't, except for what I entrusted to you. The mines produced just enough small, lower grade stones to keep them open as going concerns and, with enough just enough coming out, financial backers would invest in the hope of something big being unearthed."

"And they have!"

"Yes. But I wasn't going to tell my backers that – nor my wife – the first-fruits were always going to be mine. Johanna will divorce me soon enough; originally, she was holding on in the hope of some of Leonard's money coming my way, then it's been waiting on the mines to offer something. Now, though, she's given up on both and thinks she can do better without me. She'll be off when she thinks the cards are as much in her favour as they will get. So, all in all, I was never sharing the first-fruits, when they came, with her. It's why no one, no one bar you and me can know about them – otherwise I'm ruined."

"So, you want me to start in the dining room when I get back?"

"Yes. The dining room first but, hold on, what do we really know about this Alba person? Could she be in on it? Might she be the maid's courier – the maid's means to get the gems out of the property? What do we really know about her, in fact, either of them? Nothing. Be that as it may, search the communal rooms first. I hope neither of them would risk storing the stones in their own bedrooms. We're looking for somewhere discrete but easily accessible."

"Might we be looking for something like a priest's hole?" suggested Isabel.

"Perhaps. I've definitely thought of that. If there is, I haven't yet found one; I've been looking since I've been staying at the manor. There could well be one and, if there is, I reckon John's got some of Leonard's first-fruits stashed in it. Reckon Leonard was far richer than even he let on."

"Oh, how exciting. It really is. You know, I should ask Tony Verdie to turn this all into a play or a book – stolen jewels, hidey-holes, mysterious guest, it's got it all. If it were a book he did, gosh, well, I could be the voice of the audio book. I can see him now, fountain pen in hand, sitting in his study, scribbling away at a script. What might he call it? How about '*The maid sparkles*'? Any good? Doesn't matter, Tony will come up with a brilliant title. How thrilling this all is!"

"Isabel, for crying out loud! Stay in the real world – this is not thrilling, it's a flaming nightmare. We have, just have to get them back. Look, let's just get ourselves in, so we can eat. Then you can chase back and start searching. I'll join you when I can. If, by way of some miracle, you do come across a priest's hole and it's empty, don't give up. I've heard rumours that often there'd be another one hidden directly behind it; the people who built them, gambled that the people hunting for treasure or, more accurately, the priest, would give up if they found one but it was empty. They'd assume the prize had flown and never think to tap the boards at the back of the hole and listen to whether they were getting a further hollow sound. Don't, just please don't, get distracted or despondent if you come across an empty space, keep looking. For now, let's just get this sham of a happy family meal over, shall we?"

*

Alba had counted nine go in and felt she too should now show her face. No one had noticed her sitting there – it was not quite a case of hiding in plain sight, though there was a hint of that, it was that no one was looking for her. They were not expecting her to be there and were clearly – had not each of them made it abundantly obvious – wrapped up in their own worlds and fears. They were never going to notice the nice things in life as they pulled into the 'Earl of Clarendon', be it the view beyond the beer garden, the wildlife darting around the picnic tables or even a solitary figure enjoying a quiet drink.

As she stepped from the garden to the car park, a further vehicle, driven by Connie, pulled in. Alba opted to wait for her so they could enter together.

"Hi, Alba. All by yourself? Thought you'd have turned up with Eleanor and John, otherwise I'd have happily given you a lift."

"That's kind, Connie but I've been here enjoying a drink by myself in the garden." With that, Alba wiggled the empty glass in her left hand. "Actually, can you put these in your car and we can share them another day?" With that, Alba threw the packet of 'Cornish sea salt' crisps to Connie.

With the crisps on the passenger seat of Connie's car, Alba informed her that everyone else had already arrived.

"Why didn't they invite you in to join them?" asked Connie.

"Too caught up in their own problems to notice little me," suggested Alba.

"Well, I've noticed you. Shall we go in together and get jointly told off for being last?"

"OK. Nothing wrong back at the manor, I trust, what with you being last here and all that?" asked Alba.

"Oh, no. Everything is fine – you know how you can get wrapped up in things and suddenly the time has flown by. I like your outfit, by the way; being a billowy skirt, I didn't notice the splits in it until you threw me the crisps. All in all, you're looking wonderfully summery and nicely relaxed."

"Thank you. We'll see how long that will last as we join the others."

"Do you think Aunt Isabel has calmed down yet in order that she can enjoy this meal or didn't you notice?" pondered Connie.

"I heard her talking to your dad as they entered the pub. It did not sound as if the missing items have been found."

"Oh dear. Father will be beside himself and as for mum, I think—"

"I don't think your mum knows," cut in Alba.

"She must. Why would father keep it from her?"

"Maybe to spare her the stress of them being missing," said Alba innocently, wishing to spare Connie, for now at least, from the impending doom that her parent's marriage was about to experience. "Perhaps he's hoping he and Isabel can find them and your mum need never know."

"That's typical of father, wanting to spare his family his worries. So, we won't mention we know, then?"

"Best not to," agreed Alba. "Leave it to your dad or your aunt Isabel to mention it."

"Should we offer to help them look for it, after the meal, I mean? You and I could head back early and help."

"I'm not sure your aunt has let on to your dad that we know something is missing. Maybe she's simply forgotten that fact or maybe she, like your dad, is keeping that bit of the story from him to save him additional anxiety."

"Why would father knowing I know, cause him worry?" pondered Connie.

"I sense your dad just wants to keep it between himself and Isabel for the time being; if he knows his plight has gone beyond the two of them, it'll stress him more than he probably needs right now."

"Poor father," said Connie. "He's such a martyr. Well, I can always head back early and just look by myself, couldn't I?"

"I guess, unless," but with that, Alba paused as they were about to enter the pub door.

"Unless what?" asked Connie.

"No, nothing. Not for me to say," said Alba.

"Come on," insisted Connie, aware Alba had thought of something.

"I'd rather not. It's an unkind thought and I wish it hadn't just crept into my head."

"Alba! I insist. So long as you're not about to accuse me of taking the jewellery, then, if it might help father and aunty, I'd like to hear it. If you know where someone has hidden them, whether it's for a joke or not, please tell me."

"I'd prefer not to. It's not fair."

"You must tell though." With that Connie placed an almost matriarchal hand on Alba's left forearm and then added, "You must."

"I, we in fact, have assumed they are missing," said Alba.

"Pardon?"

"We have made a careless assumption, haven't we? The diamond earrings are missing because–"

Yet Alba left her sentence unfinished, wondering if Connie could see things as she, Alba, now could.

"Because aunt Isabel couldn't find them in her handbag."

"Says your aunt Isabel," stated Alba.

"Yes," said a puzzled Connie.

"But don't you see? I accept it is not a nice thing to suggest. But neither of us looked in her handbag, did we?"

"Er, no."

"Exactly. You looked under her car seat, I asked her what was missing but we never checked the very bag itself – assuming that's where she was hiding them for your dad in the first place. It's a horrible assertion I'm making and I'm sorry for that. However, being an outsider to your family perhaps helps at this moment, as I can be detached from the relationship ties. Look, if the earrings are as valuable as I gather, that's a lot of temptation for Anthony to put in someone's way. More so, when that someone is worried for an upcoming play she's starring in, fearful of a short run and already concerned for the revenue from ticket sales. What if she succumbed? A hundred thousand pounds is a lot of money."

"A hundred!" exclaimed Connie.

"Yes," conceded Alba. "That's what your dad just admitted to your aunt Isabel as they walked in. A hundred thousand pounds. That could keep a touring production going for a bit, couldn't it? Remember, too, your aunt is an actress – even she could feign surprise, shock and panic as she took her bag from you and exclaimed 'where have they gone, they must be here'. We weren't expecting her to be acting in that moment but she could have been. So easy, too, to blame the innocent new housemaid; a maid who your uncle John has employed out of sympathy as she had to leave university early. Maybe the earrings were in the handbag and Isabel carefully caught them in her hand as she, in seeming panic, tipped the rest of the contents dramatically onto the car seat. Or, perhaps, they were always stored in her bedroom or a hiding place somewhere else – there must be a few loose stones in the ha-ha for a start that would shield a small pink pouch. If your aunt Isabel deliberately 'lost' her handbag, in order that it could be returned to her, and, with an audience before her, she could proclaim a theft had occurred in dramatic fashion."

"The devious whatsit!" exclaimed Connie.

"To be clear, it's an unfair allegation to make. I have neither proof nor is your aunt here to defend herself. What I am saying, is that it is possible the earrings have not been taken in the way and by the person we had assumed."

"Aunt Isabel! Maybe you're a better actress than we all thought; you played the innocent party oh so very well." With that Connie gave a low whistle, almost in admiration. "What a clever aunt, I have. Oh my!"

"I'm just saying–" started Alba.

"Yes, I know, it's possible but not proven. Still, oh my, gosh! Come on let's join the others for the meal. I think I'm going to enjoy it after all. I'm going to watch aunt Isabel very closely; we'll be ready if she trips herself up, so to speak. If she does, we can wink at each other but I won't say anything for now, partly to spare father and partly as I'd rather chose my moment to confront my devious aunt."

Connie promptly held the door to the 'Earl of Clarendon' open and said:

"Come on Alba, grub's up. This is going to be a meal to remember."

With that, the tenth and the eleventh members of the group joined the others and they all sat down for the meal John Sunday had planned for a long time.

CHAPTER 15

A time for grace?

Assured that the ingredients, save the fish, were locally sourced and that the eggs were free range, Alba opted for the salad nicoise. Once they had been served, she was almost caught out when everyone simply just started eating; she was now so used, from her meals in 'The Sun and Moon' pub in her home village, in the company of Matthew the vicar, to someone, admittedly that someone was always Matthew, saying 'Grace' to begin the meal, that just eating seemed slightly wrong. Alba did not give thanks as such but the Reverend Quinn, had he been an invisible observer, would have noticed that Alba did pause before eating and he would have nodded ever so slightly to himself and allowed himself the faintest of faint smiles.

*

The conversation within Dr Sunday's group of eleven was amicable. The loveliness of the food helped; the size of Henry's fish and chips even brought a momentary smile to his face. It also helped that John had made it clear that he was paying. The polished brass bar counter had also impressed everyone as they had each in turn entered and Eddie's father, the landlord, had ensured they were seated at a spacious, out of the way, table – meaning people were not constantly walking past them, nor were those at the table banging elbows as they tried to eat. It was a nice meal; Henry had been speaking to his aunt Alice about employment law, Connie was picking Alba's brains about university life and Eleanor just looked excited.

As a member of staff cleared the plates away and prior to the arrival of the dessert boards, Alba excused herself from the group to use the facilities. As she passed the bar on her re-emergence she paused to speak to Eddie, who was stood behind it processing a tray of glasses that had just come out of the dishwasher.

"The food was lovely," said Alba. "Please thank the chef from me."

"Will do," replied Eddie with a smile.

"No Ash, tonight?" enquired Alba.

"His girlfriend has dragged him along to the pictures – think they're seeing 'The Day After Tomorrow'. Have you seen it?"

"No."

"Nor me," said Eddie. "Would like to see it but the person I really want to go with can't get the time off work. I mean, it's good she's in a job but I haven't seen her much for the last year or so and it would be nice to have an evening out together. Never mind, Ash will tell me the plot and the ending in the morning as we work in the garage, even if I ask him not to say anything about it. So, all in all, there won't be much point seeing the film after that."

"You still OK for me to bring my car along in the morning?" asked Alba. "I'm sure Eleanor can cope without me for an hour or two."

"Eleanor? Am I meant to know her?" enquired Eddie.

"No, not really. Nonetheless, Eleanor," said Alba as she turned and discretely pointed, "is the woman my age sitting to the right of Dr Sunday. You know who he is as you have a bit of a thing against him, don't you?"

"Yes, Alba. I know who you mean. The first one to turn up this evening, came in and made it clear to all the staff he was paying the bill for everyone in his party at the end of the evening. Big show off, making it obvious how wealthy he is. Had he tried to make the booking with me, I'd have told him to sling his hook – for all I care he could have his meal at 'The Plough' in Quarrybourne."

"Because?" asked Alba.

"Because it's all TV screens, fruit machines and they can't keep a chef for more than a few months. Dr flipping Sunday would fit right in with all that crassness, glare and mediocre food. What right does he have to come in here and show off his family and wave his wallet around? I'd like to tell him to–"

"Eddie," said Alba kindly, "try and see it as him being generous. I think there is a reason he wants to treat everyone tonight; let him have his moment."

"I get you're trying to see the good in everyone, Alba. However, I don't like him. He's come into our village, thinks he's Lord of the manor and that he can buy his way into our hearts. I don't care for him and I will not allow him to lord it over me. I am my own man. If this were my pub, I wouldn't have him in but it's dad's so, in that respect alone, I do as I'm told. However, with regards to your good doctor Sunday, however, I am my own man and have no time for him."

"Oh, Eddie, I fear it's eating away at you. Try to let it go or it will be the undoing of you. Returning to Eleanor, though, the woman I'm trying to point out to you, well, she is the person to the right of him as you look."

"Right, I know who you mean now," confirmed Eddie.

"So, she's Eleanor and I've known her for a few years; she's the friend I've come to support that I was telling you about on Wednesday. I'm sure, though, she can cope for an hour or two if I come on my own and get my brake light replaced, if you're still willing to help me in the morning."

"Said I'd help," stated Eddie.

"Good. After all, she has John, that's Dr Sunday to you, who's her boyfriend to keep her company."

"Boyfriend!" exclaimed Eddie. "She must be half his age."

"Well, I accept she's a few years younger than me and I'm–"

"Oh, yes and how old are you?" probed Hugh, who suddenly appeared at Alba's side.

"I really don't think that's any of your business," said Alba.

"Aw, come now, Alba. Don't tease me, like this. We've been having a nice meal together."

"There's been eleven of us and you are three seats away from me," stressed Alba, keen to reinforce the distance between them in every sense.

"My loss," said Hugh. "Duty bound to sit next to Alice, I'm afraid, but I'm sure I'd have had more fun down at your end of the table."

"It would have been different had you been seated nearer," acknowledged Alba.

"Yes. Yes, indeed. We would have had a great time," responded Hugh, deliberately misinterpreting what Alba had inferred. "I'm surprised we weren't next to each other – I did ask that new maid of John's to try and arrange things so that we were."

"Really?" said a disgusted Alba. "I think it was right she, if she had any influence at all, sat you next to your wife." Then to Eddie, Alba said, "Eddie, could you take this man's drinks order to allow him to get back to enjoying his wife's company?"

"Alba, that's very kind of you but, really, I'm happy to chat some more. My wife doesn't want anything else to drink. One is her limit which is so dull and boring if you ask me. I said to her I was coming to order another drink for myself but that was a ruse to come and talk to you. I saw you leave the table and thought I'd catch you on your return – Alice will hardly notice I've gone. Actually, now I'm standing right by you once again, I really would like to know what fragrance it is you're wearing. You were wearing it this morning when I was teaching you snooker. I'm finding it somewhat alluring; I must admit. If you would tell me, I can get some for my wife, which will allow me to think of you whenever she wears it."

"Oh, my. You never stop do you?" said an annoyed and uncomfortable Alba. "I'm going back to the table. Eddie," she added to the man behind the bar, "I'll catch you later."

With a nod from Eddie, Alba turned from the bar and made to rejoin the others. Yet, before she had taken two steps, Hugh called out:

"Well, at least tell me your age. You were going to tell this barman, here, so you must be OK with at least sharing that fact about yourself. Please," pleaded Hugh.

"You'd like to know my age?" said Alba as she turned round to speak to Hugh.

An excited look was quickly extinguished when Alba simply said:

"I'm two years past being bean straw and winter forage."

"You've lost me," said a disappointed Hugh.

"Good. Of course, if you had read 'The Merchant's Tale', you would understand," said Alba.

She did not turn back to answer his further childlike pleadings to learn her age.

*

Once everyone was once more at the table and desserts had been ordered – dairy ice-cream for Alba, consisting of one scoop of honeycomb and two of raspberry ripple – John tapped his glass to get people's attention. Attention gained, he stood up and spoke:

"Thank you for coming tonight. I hope you will agree with me that what we've so far had has been excellent. Also, I think it is important that we can support local businesses where we can."

It was probably only Alba who, on that comment by John, heard a hushed 'Pah!' coming from someone standing behind the highly polished bar. However, Alba did not turn round to confirm it was Eddie for she was too interested in watching the excitement build in Eleanor's face.

"Thank you, also, for coming to spend a few days with us here at Kingsbourne. The village was old in the time of Henry III and its origins lie in the Heptarchy. That I have found a home here, well, I am indeed fortunate."

"Thankful?" suggested Alba.

"Yes, Alba. Quite right – you sound like a local. It would be more fitting to say I am thankful to have my home here. It is a lovely village set within some glorious countryside. I'm looking forward to doing the walk I have planned for tomorrow afternoon to Ludgershall Castle. As you should all realise, Henry III is a particular favourite of mine. He was a rarity from medieval times, being a King of England to die in his own bed of natural causes – and Ludgershall was one of his favourite hunting lodges. To have found my own 'lodge' so to speak, so close to his, is thrilling for me."

John paused and took a sip of his wine before continuing:

"What is equally thrilling for me is to have, as King Henry III had, my own Eleanor beside me."

With that he placed his hand on her shoulder, squeezed it a fraction and then continued once more:

"So, I have gathered you all here over these few days – and now brought you here tonight – to inform you I have asked Eleanor to marry me."

As he paused, feeling Eleanor's hand rest on top of his, which was still on her shoulder, he somehow assumed at least one of his siblings would congratulate them both, that a sister-in-law might say something nice to Eleanor directly or one of his nieces or nephew might simply raise a glass and say 'cheers, Uncle John and Els'. However, whilst he was right his announcement would generate a response, he was totally unprepared for the reaction he got.

"Sorry, brother, you've done what?" exclaimed Anthony.

"You can't have asked her, surely?" stated Alice. "It's a joke, you're playing on us. It must be a joke; she's not wearing a ring for starters."

"But he says he has, Alice dearest," said Hugh. "So, ring or not, perhaps you need to be asking yourself what my elder brother could possibly see in a woman less than half his age."

With that, Hugh finished his wine and mockingly held up the empty glass, as if making a toast.

"Uncle Hugh!" exclaimed Connie.

"Connie, no need to take that tone with me, your favourite uncle. I've only voiced what you are all already thinking – what does a moth-eaten tired university lecturer see in a young, research student with a size eight figure. It's what we've all been thinking from the day we each first met her."

"Hugh, how dare you!" said John, angrily. "Take that back."

"What? Retract a truthful statement? Curious way for an academic by profession to manage a little disagreement. To start denying truth! My, my, what will your employers think?"

"Hugh! Take it back. I insist you apologise," snapped John.

By now, Eleanor had retracted her hand from on top of John's. As she did so, she looked to Alba and Alba saw her face full of sadness and self-consciousness; in that brief moment, Alba knew Terry had been right to write to her and ask her to accompany Eleanor over these few days. Alba then looked to Hugh, for he had fallen silent. However, it was not out of embarrassment rather out of defiance. He took a sip from his wife's glass of wine and then stared his brother out.

May sat there wishing she had brought a notebook in order that she could jot down her impressions of the moment to work into some future article about 'travelling home for family get togethers' or some such topic. In a similar vein, Isabel was studying her brothers' facial expressions in the hope she could 'learn' them for future roles and Henry simply shoved his chair back, screeching it against the wooden floor, in order to stretch out his leg.

"I rather fancy that I won't. You see, John, I have been accused of many things in my time–"

"I am aware of that. The latest is still outstanding I understand."

"It is but thank you for sharing that in front of everyone. However, she will withdraw her statement – they always do."

"They?" challenged Eleanor. "Please don't clump all the poor women you've harassed over the years as some impersonal collective."

"Oh, spare me," snapped Hugh. "Not one allegation has ever progressed; each time, the claimant has backed down when my solicitors get involved."

"Because they're suddenly intimidated by all the fancy legal wording. They know they can't risk raking up legal fees, losing their positions or what little savings they have. I have no doubt your victims are all somewhat isolated, poor, vulnerable even, women," said an angry Eleanor.

"There have been no victims," threw back Hugh. "You have just slandered me in front of a good number of people. I think you ought to apologise otherwise you might be getting a letter from my solicitor – actually, you might get one even if you do throw yourself at my feet."

"Hugh!" said a reddening John. "She will do no such thing. Would you please be quiet and stop embarrassing us all."

"Me? Embarrassing us? I somewhat think you and the little miss to your side are embarrassing us – you think you're living out some medieval romance when you've in fact hoodwinked another of your students. My solicitor will be writing to her I am inclined to think."

"I'm not scared," said a defiant Eleanor. "Must help having a wife in the legal profession to cover your back."

"Don't bring me into this," stated Alice. "I've told you I'm a tax and estate planning expert. That is nothing to do with defamation law but you're still all in a muddle about it. Probably best you stick your head back into some sixteenth century literature and leave the real world to us."

"Sixteenth century is Tudor. My specialism, if *you'd* listened to me over the breakfasts we shared the last couple of days, is late thirteenth through to early fifteenth. Plus, I know enough about the modern world to–"

"To latch onto your university lecturer and then stay limpet-like attached when you got wind of his wealth," suggested Johanna wickedly. "After all, what does a young woman see in a teacher over twice her age once she's done her degree and elicited the marks she needed for her First? Surely, it could not be anything to do with the fact of his sizeable inheritance from a mysterious uncle of his? A mysterious figure, who sunk mines in the dusty African soil and found a treasure trove of gemstones; jewels that perhaps never officially passed through customs or were declared to the Exchequer on his death."

She had held her own to this point but Eleanor's strength, energy or will now gave way; the emotion of it all was just too much. It was meant to have been her happiest moment of this long weekend but it had become the worst and it broke her. In tears, she fled from the table and rushed into the toilets to weep.

Sensing a weakness in John's armour, Alice, for she could tell John was uncertain whether to go and console his supposed fiancée or stand his ground before his siblings, challenged him on his marriage announcement.

"John, before you rush to her side, I am puzzled by something."

"Which is what?" said a worried and drained John. He sat down at the table, for he himself was emotionally shattered and felt his legs suddenly waver underneath him.

"You've made this grand gesture announcing your engagement, in this pub here this evening," started Alice.

"Surely it would have been grander back at the manor itself?" offered up Isabel. "The dining room could have been all beautifully decked out, the candles lit, soft music playing, away from the villagers – that's how I would have staged it. Theatrically, so much better."

"Well, for some reason he chose the village pub," contributed Johanna.

"Indeed. Yet the central component was missing. You didn't go down on one knee and present her a ring, which I find rather odd," said Alice.

"I had already done that," stated John.

"Yet, she's not wearing anything on her ring finger, as I have already mentioned. Have you proposed or not? You see, I just can't quite make it out. Is this all a sham? Are the two of you playing some wicked little game on us all?"

"It's not April 1st, John, old boy – got your dates wrong, I think," sniped Hugh.

"This is not a joke, I assure you," said John.

"And yet there's no ring," challenged Alice. "Or at least not one that you're willing to have seen in public or in front of your family."

"What's your point?" said a bemused John – he finished the wine from his glass as he waited on Alice's reply.

"Her point," said Anthony, "as Johanna has just hinted at, is that she is wondering, as we all are, why you've kept the jewels from us. Perhaps you have given her a ring; if you have it's clearly not one you're willing to publicly advertise, is it? One you inherited from uncle Leonard, was it? Or one you have had made up from a bag of gems he left you; gems that Her Majesty's Tax Office never knew about? Bit of a tax dodger, are we?"

"I completely agree," added Alice. "I'd quite like to have a little look through uncle Leonard's papers once again now I know what I'm looking for; I always felt there was something missing but never quite could gauge what. Finding a specific piece of a jigsaw from within the box of pieces is just so much easier when you have the surrounding bits done. Just so much easier when you know exactly what you are looking for. I had assumed we were looking for something within the documentation on which to challenge the settlement. Now, I see we should have been looking *without*. Now I know what my team are looking for, we'll find it. I only employ the brightest legal minds. You're finished, I reckon."

"There always did seem to be too much money sloshing around. Money which you were able to throw at this rebuilding project of yours," reflected Anthony. "Trying to 'wash' the money, were you? Find a semi-derelict country house, renovate it with 'dirty' money, sell it for a tidy profit, pocket the 'clean' cash and then take some teaching post out in the States; Johanna had a hunch you were heading stateside. Now it is suddenly clear why. Hoped the tax office wouldn't pursue you out there, did you? Hope they wouldn't bother if ever they suspected or learnt uncle Leonard's papers were not quite as he or you said?"

"This is preposterous!" exploded John. "I am a respected academic. My paper on the 'Gawain Poet' was–"

"Irrelevant," announced Johanna. "Unconnected to the discussion in hand. You might be a good school teacher."

"I'm head of my Faculty, as you well know!"

"But that's not important to what we're discussing here, is it? Everyone has their price, I say. You sold out your family to the temptation of wealth, didn't you? Kept stuff hidden from the rest of the family; hoarded everything for yourself. Untold riches I imagine must be quite alluring. Alice," Johanna continued, though now addressing her sister-in-law, "you might also want to get a handwriting expert to check the authenticity of uncle Leonard's signature on the will itself. After all, why should John stop at just keeping the gemstones from us? If he were that conniving towards his dear family, he probably forged the will itself, in his desire to take everything."

"Oh, absolutely; no stone will go unturned. I admit handwriting and asset investigation are not quite my firm's specialisms but I think I know who we need to get hold of to help us. He's a private investigator."

"Really?" said Isabel. "How exciting – a spy!"

"No, Isabel, you're getting carried away again. However, John," said Alice directly to him, "I am told he is accomplished in what he does. I heard about him through 'Chatteris, Corby and Lane', they're a Bristol based firm of solicitors. I met one of their partners at a conference in London recently and she was telling me about a case they had dealt with a year or so ago. Through the work of this private investigator, whom they brought in to help, they found a missing heir to a big Cornish estate. When I'm back in the office next week, I will ask my secretary to speak to 'Chatteris, Corby and Lane' to get the investigator's name. We'll see if he can help – she did tell me his name but it has slipped my mind."

If Alice had shown Alba a moment's niceness over the last few days and if, in helping Alice it would not have undermined John and thereby Eleanor, Alba would have happily, would have willingly, given Alice Daniel Jones' name and number there and then. After all, his business card, which he had given her when they had met at 'The Jupiter Hotel', was still in her handbag. However, Alice had not shown such, indeed any, niceness and Alba was here to support Eleanor and by default John. Consequently, Alba stayed silent, keeping that card, so to speak, to her chest. She promised herself, though, she would give Daniel a call herself once back home and have a chat with him – everything else aside, it would be nice to catch up with him.

Unaware of Alba's sudden extra level of interest in what was unfolding before them all in this recessed area of the 'Earl of Clarendon', John responded to Johanna and Alice's accusations:

"This is laughable. The will is genuine and there are no jewels stashed away behind a fake wall or in a false bottom of a golf bag."

"In that case, may we see the ring?" asked Henry and which triggered a snigger from his cousin May.

"You will see no such thing, young Henry! Do not make demands of me. Now all I wish for is to be with Eleanor. However, I would imagine she is in the toilets, meaning I cannot go to her. Alba, would you be so kind as to check on her and bring her back to the manor when she has composed herself and is up to it. For myself, I am driving myself home now. I cannot stay a moment longer."

John then addressed everyone else:

"Anthony, Isabel, Hugh and your families, I had expected more from you. I had assumed loyalty. Had assumed affection. If you could have managed neither of those, surely you could have displayed common grace tonight but, alas, no. It would seem your love of money, of your jobs, of fame that you think you already have or are entitled to, has destroyed the family we once were. If you can find it within yourselves to apologise to myself and Eleanor – for all I have will be hers upon our marriage – that will be a start in moving forward. However, I will not come and find you to start that conversation. I trust you will come and find us tomorrow. Goodnight."

As John stepped away from the table, he turned to speak to just one person within the group:

"Alba, thank you. I entrust her into your care."

With that, Dr John Sunday stepped outside; venturing into the setting sun of a midsummer evening.

*

With almost theatrical timing, eleven desserts were at that moment served.

"Well," said Henry, "that was a laugh. Who wants a cheese board which I believe is now going spare? Alba, would you like to take someone's fruit salad into the ladies' toilets now you're responsible for miss goody-two-shoes? What a laugh! So, do we really think there's a treasure chest stashed away somewhere? There's been so much building work going on at his place, it would be hard to know where to start looking for a false wall."

"Well, someone can have my pudding, too. I'm heading back to see if uncle John is alright. I didn't say anything unkind," stated Connie.

As Henry dolloped his sister's ice-cream onto his chocolate

brownie, Isabel pushed her dessert into the middle of the table and announced her prompt departure:

"I sense we will all be asked to leave at some stage tomorrow. If that is the case, there is stuff I need to gather together; probably should have a bit of a rummage around in case anything has dropped down out of sight. Good evening – it has been a most theatrical evening, hasn't it?"

"I'll follow along with you," Anthony instantly added. "Johanna, you stay and enjoy your pudding. No need to rush, really no need. You can catch a lift with one of the others."

"Anthony, what's going on? What's the rush?"

"Nothing dear, nothing. Just thought I'd help sis look for her bits – show John we can look out for each other whatever he might think. As I say, take your time."

"Well, I'm heading off too, as it is," said Alice. "I told Hugh as we parked, I'd be heading back as soon as the meal was over. I'm not really bothered about the dessert – strawberry cheesecake, hardly original. I have a pile of papers to wade through. At the beginning of the evening, it felt a bit frustrating having to give up a summer's evening – even one in dreary Wiltshire – to work on the stuff brought from the office. Now, though, I'll sail through it in light of what we've revealed tonight. We'll be on the phone to that Bristol firm first thing, Monday. Hugh, you coming?"

"No, it's fine dear. You head off. I'll catch a lift with one of the others; Alba, perhaps."

"I don't think so," stated Alba. "Nor would Eleanor wish you to accompany us."

At that moment, having observed so many guests leave – not just stepping outside for a cigarette but literally driving away – Eddie came over to check if everything was alright.

"Oh, it's fine," exclaimed Hugh.

"Er, OK. Well, as I'm here may I gather a few empty glasses and wipe a few mats in case people return."

"As you please," said Hugh. Hugh then spoke to those still seated at the table:

"So, I can't get a lift with Miss White. So, that leaves just my dear daughter, May. You're taking Henry, I assume. You can hardly leave him to hobble all the way back to the manor all by himself, can you? Room for your old dad?"

"I need a lift, too," stated Johanna. "Don't know why Anthony rushed off as he did. I shall be having words with him when I get back if he hasn't shut himself away in his bedroom as usual."

"Well, I'm going now," announced May. "Can't have Connie sucking up to uncle John all by herself, can we?"

"Well, I could stay," mused May's father. "Perhaps, when you get back, you could ask that young maid to come and pick me up. She seems to do what I ask. If she's off duty, it'll be nice to see her in something different to that black dress she has to wear – it's not that exciting, after all."

"Dad!" said an embarrassed May.

"Oh, sorry, dear. Your dad overstepped the mark, did he?"

"I'm going to the car. If you want a lift, you'd better come by the time I've helped Henry angle himself into the passenger seat. Coming aunty Johanna?"

"Yes, May," replied Johanna. "Barman," she added.

"Yes," responded Eddie.

"Given you're still here and as strange an evening as this has been for us, that was a nice fruit salad I've just had. Strawberries were especially succulent."

"Right you are, thank you for the compliment. I'll mention it to our supplier."

With that, May, Henry and Johanna left. Remaining now were just Alba and Hugh, as well as Eddie for he was now suddenly confronted with tidying additional empty seats. Hugh casually ignored the publican's son as he, Hugh, turned once more to Alba.

"So, Miss White. What is a man to do?"

"I beg your pardon."

"I'm in such a quandary. Do I fall at your feet and beg you to reconsider giving me a lift?" As he spoke, he reached for Connie's glass of unfinished wine.

"Please don't. It will get you nowhere, I promise you," replied Alba.

"Well, in that case, it's being driven back by my daughter or shall I insist that young maid comes to my rescue?"

"She has a name, you know. She's not just a thing," stated Alba.

"She's a thing, a young thing, to me. Shall I ask her to rescue me? To arrive in her casual attire, furnish a man in distress with a hip flask of brandy and we can then drive slowly back to the manor, perhaps pulling in somewhere. I have her round my little finger, you know; have her at my beck and call. She will do my bidding, that petite little slip of a girl."

"I think," said Alba standing up in disgust, "you have had too much to drink and that you should go back with your daughter. You are being unpleasant, to say the least."

"Am I? I am *so* sorry."

"You're not," stated Alba. "Please go."

"Alright," announced Hugh, sounding strangely undefeated. "I shall go, as you insist. I might be able to catch the maid on my return to the manor. Have a brandy with her, there. Delightful. Well, goodnight, Miss White it has been quite an evening."

*

As Hugh left, just Alba remained. She resumed her seat and was grateful it was now just her and Eddie. Sitting amongst a multitude of untouched or half-eaten desserts, she shook her head in bewilderment and sadness. It had been horrific; just what had Terry brought her into. She tried, desperately, to think of some positive, something good within all the bad.

"At least one of them paid a compliment about the fruit salad," said Alba to Eddie. "Didn't think she had it in her."

"She did. However, you will notice, when you look down this end of the table, she didn't finish it. That means she couldn't have thought that much of it. Plus, I knew it was a ruse to distract me."

"A ruse? Ruse from what?" asked an intrigued Alba.

"Ah, Alba, my new friend – sorry, may I call you that?"

"Yes, Eddie, that would be nice."

"Ta. A ruse, as I say."

"From?" said Alba.

"From not picking up the bill."

"I'm not getting your point."

"Alba, you clearly don't work in hospitality, so let me explain. When you arrived on Wednesday, calling in here as you couldn't find Kingsbourne Manor, you told Ash and myself you'd been invited as a guest to support your friend."

"Yes, who's crying her eyes out in the toilets. I really must go to her in a minute."

"Yes. I'll explain quickly. So, you weren't ever the one to pay the bill, were you?"

"No."

"Whilst Mr Sunday–"

"Doctor," corrected Alba.

"Alright, as we're friends now, Doctor Sunday was meant to be paying but he scarpered pretty quickly. Most of the others quickly followed him out, leaving just three of you. There was no way that obnoxious oaf, who had clearly had way too much to drink, was in any fit state to settle up. Concerning him, I'm quite worried for my Sandy's welfare with him around. Someone should be with her; they really should."

"I'll check on her once I'm back but what was the ruse?"

"So, the only person, of the three of you who remained at the end, who could have paid was the lady who gave a compliment about the dessert she had. Yet, she just said it to try and distract me and get out of the pub before I asked her to pick up the bill for eleven mains, eleven desserts, coffees and teas and all the alcohol everyone was having – and they were all going for the best wines. I knew what she was doing, being all nice, thinking she was getting my guard down and then heading out pronto."

"So, why didn't you challenge her?"

"Simple; I know where Dr Sunday lives. I'll make sure he pays and if he doesn't, well, I made copies of the keys for his ride-on mowers he's brought to us at the garage for servicing over the months. If he refuses to pay, well, I'll just pop along and drive one of those away. I could easily sell it on, even though that's not what I do any more. I'm straight now."

"Promise," said Alba meaningfully.

"Scout's honour – unless the good Doctor doesn't pay. So, the lady can have her false and empty praise. I knew what she was up to and saw through her shallowness all too easily."

"How insightful. Now though, I must go and check on Eleanor."

As Alba made for the toilets, Eddie spoke after her. In his words, Alba could hear his concern:

"You will check on the maid, Sandy, for me, won't you Alba, once you're back at the big house?"

"Girl Guide's honour," called back Alba as she disappeared through the door to the side of the bar, to get to the toilets.

*

"Eleanor, you in here?" called Alba as she opened the door.

CHAPTER 16

Every picture tells a story

She was not.

Nor, with Eddie's assistance, for she got him to enter first, was Eleanor in the men's toilets.

As the two of them returned to the table where the group had just been sitting, whatever else Alba, Terry, even Sam or the Reverend Quinn, might have expected her stay at Kingsbourne Manor to throw up, investigating the gentlemen's toilets on a Friday night with the landlord's son in some rural public house, would not have been top of her or anyone's list.

The male toilets were everything she imagined, indeed feared, they would be – a tap had been left running, used paper towels seemed to be everywhere but the waste bin and the amount of liquid soap from the wall-mounted dispenser that lay around the sinks indicated a unique male inability to co-ordinate one's hands so that one was under the gadget as the other pressed the button. Eddie's comment that the toilets were not in too bad a way left her reeling.

As they returned to the table, Eddie assured her that the trapdoor to the cellar had not been open at all through the evening – 'never is on a Friday', he stated – and, given Eleanor had arrived at the 'Earl of

Clarendon' with John, there was no vehicle of hers in the car park she could have sought solace in.

"What a waste," said Eddie as he looked at all the food that lay before them on the table. "It's probably one of the hardest things about this industry, seeing the amount of uneaten food that has to get thrown away. What makes looking at that table even worse is none of it has so far been paid for. Neither dad nor you, Alba, believed me when I said I knew their type but I feel vindicated now. Told you, didn't I?"

"Eddie, be that as it may—"

"Reckon the piece of cheesecake and the brownies are salvageable. Not to resell, let me be completely clear on that, but I'll offer them to Mr and Mrs Singh. Dad says they've had a tough few weeks due to Mr Singh's health but as they've made it out this Friday night, well, I'll go over and offer them what I think is still more than edible – entire desserts completely untouched, what waste!"

"But where is Eleanor, Eddie? Are there footpaths she's taken to walk back to the manor?"

"Not direct. Footpaths, plenty, but not that would naturally take you back there. I know the route I'd take cross-country if I had to walk it but I've lived around here all my life and know the lie of the land. I doubt your Eleanor would be so confident – that's not me having a go at her, I'm just saying it as it is."

"Yes, I understand. Could she have gone off, not caring which way she went? She was in a state as she left the table. Perhaps, after composing herself in the toilets, she just set off for anywhere as 'anywhere' wasn't here. Oh, my, all of Wiltshire to search!"

"It might feel that and yet, if your friend is as ordered as you clearly are—"

"What makes you say that?" said a curious Alba.

"For one, as we've been sitting here, you've turned the three beer mats round so they're readable to those sitting in the respective seats. Plus, I did notice – not that I was spying – when you first sat down to eat this evening you rearranged your cutlery. Given I had laid the table perfectly there remained something wrong with it as far as you were concerned but I still can't figure out what."

"I'll tell you another time. However, your point is, if Eleanor is as ordered as myself, she'd had gone off walking in what direction?"

"If she went out the back door to the pub and thus into the beer garden, there are two easily visible green footpath signs. One is pointing straight across the pub car park, directing people to cross the road and head up by the side of the village school."

"Which she wouldn't have taken as that would have taken her past the window where John's family were just sitting and so many of them would have seen her."

"Precisely," confirmed Eddie. "So, if she fled in tears from those who had upset her in the group, she would not, even in her distress, have chosen to have fled right in front of their noses. She'd have taken the other path. That one leads through the beer garden itself, down to the hedge at the bottom, across the small stream on the other side, which you get over by way of two wooden railway sleepers, and then diagonally across the farmland beyond, heading generally towards Haxton Farm. Not that she was wanting to get to the farm, just she wanted to get away from the cause of her upset. So, all in all, if she is as ordered as you in her thinking, and she's gone anywhere on foot, she'd have gone that way."

"And I was facing the window from the table and I didn't see her. So, let's go the other way. I'm not quite dressed for traversing the countryside but needs must. Sorry," Alba suddenly added. "I'm assuming you were coming as well. You really don't have to – you're working here after all."

"It's fine. Most of the food for the other diners is out and I can tidy later. Plus, if we can find her, it means you can get back to the manor sooner and check on Sandy's welfare."

"Yes, good point. Good of you to remember her. Shall we go then?"

"I'll meet you in the beer garden in two minutes," said Eddie. "Let me just take these desserts over to Mr Singh and his wife and check they're good for everything and then I'll join you out in the garden."

"Sounds like a plan. I'll see you out there and then we'll begin our search."

*

It proved to be the quickest manhunt imaginable. It was over before Eddie had even appeared; in fact, it was over the moment Alba stepped outside. For there, at the garden table, the one where the ground has dropped most, down towards the hedge which had the little stream on the other side of it, was Eleanor. She was seated on the far side of the table. Her legs were stretched out towards the hedge and her back was to the pub itself. Her elbows were behind her, resting on the top of the table, forming two sort of triangles if viewed side on. They were taking her weight and the whole of her, as a result, was sort of on a forty-five degree plane to the table. Her head was angled upwards and her eyes were wide open. She seemed to be simply staring skywards, watching a kite perform its graceful circles and glides as it honed in on its latest prey.

Alba walked down to her friend.

Alba paused at the side of the table and looked at her unmoving friend, who seemed fixated with the evening sky above them and the still circling bird of prey. Her hunt for her friend was over and Alba did all that she could do at that moment.

She went and sat down beside her.

*

"Hello, you," said Alba. "You had me worried for a moment."

"Hi, Alba. Did I? Sorry about that. When I came out of the

ladies' I could still hear some of John's family talking so I headed out here. It's so peaceful here, isn't it? Away from the road, away from the comings and goings in the car park, away from–"

"The view is better up at the other end of the beer garden – being higher up enables you to see over the hedge."

"Perhaps. If you're looking skyward, does it matter? Just look up, will you? Doesn't the sky just take you away with its expanse, its colours and it allows one to dream, doesn't it? Well, I think it does. That bird isn't dreaming, though, is it? It's spotted its meal for tonight and will swoop soon enough. Ironically, despite all that has happened tonight, I did enjoy my meal here. It is a good pub; shame my pudding got wasted."

"I think Eddie, the landlord's son, is going to be offering the untouched desserts to some of the pub's regulars."

"Oh, that's nice of him," offered back Eleanor casually. "Shame to see stuff go to waste. You OK?"

"Er, yes. Can I just say, though, you seem a lot calmer than I was expecting. Are you really alright – might you be in shock? You seem almost detached from what has just happened. Could you have had some kind of blackout in the toilets causing you to forget what's unfolded?"

As Eleanor sat herself upright and turned to her friend, Eddie appeared at their side.

"Oh, you found her. Good."

"Yes," concurred Alba. "Easiest bit of detective work I've ever done. Reckon she came out for some fresh air and lost track of time."

"Right you are. Good. Pleased it's that simple. If you'll excuse me, I'll head back in and get on."

"Of course," agreed Alba. "Thanks for coming out, we might have been searching for ages and still you came out to help. That is kind of you."

"My pleasure – after all, Alba, you've been here twice in three days, which means you're almost more of a regular than Ash is!"

"Well, thanks again. Hopefully one day I will come in and have a full meal, without a scene and where a girl can enjoy her pudding."

"Promise?" challenged Eddie.

"Promise," agreed Alba. "Girl Guide's honour."

"Perhaps, when you do, I could introduce you to, no, never mind," said Eddie.

"To?" enquired Alba.

"Never mind. What I will say, though, is that Mr and Mrs Singh were very grateful for Dr Sunday's generosity."

"Well, that is something good to come out of this evening," agreed Alba.

"Cheeky blighter, though," said Eddie. "He said he'd like it even more if he could have an extra scoop of ice-cream with it, given the one on the plate had virtually melted. Cheeky chap! Fine by me, that is what I say. In fact, I gave him two scoops and a hazelnut wafer for his audacity."

"That was kind of you."

"Not really, Alba. I've added it to Dr Sunday's bill – it's no skin off my nose."

With that, Eddie threw his hands up before him as if to visually say 'my responsibility here is now over' and headed back into the pub.

*

"I must say," resumed Alba to her friend once Eddie had gone, "you are much, just so much calmer than I was expecting. Are you sure you're not in shock?"

"No, I'm fine," insisted Eleanor.

"Really?"

"Really. I'm good. Don't you see?"

"See, see what?" asked Alba.

"See that the worst is now over. I accept I fled from the table in tears. I was truly distraught – they were all so unkind and malicious. Couldn't one of them have said congratulations? Couldn't one of them have turned to the barman and asked for a bottle of champagne and some glasses? But no. They couldn't and I fled."

"You looked so upset," agreed Alba.

"Yes, yes I was. However, as I sat in the toilets, I realised the worst of it was now over. It suddenly felt like a refiner's fire had swept through the group tonight. The dross has been burnt off, or will be come this time tomorrow once they've all packed up and gone. John won't let them stay with things left as they are. You've seen how unkind and self-centred they all are – not one of them will come and apologise. So, as I say, come tomorrow the impurity within John's family will be gone from Kingsbourne. Yes, it was horrible to go through – I realised that as I was in the ladies' – but, to mix metaphors, the boil has been lanced. It's over."

Eleanor paused and then simply added:

"It's over. Tomorrow will be a good day. John and I have the rest of our lives before us and that begins tomorrow."

With that, Eleanor smiled a smile of contentment, of peace and one which reflected a certainty of the life that she believed lay before her.

"Come on then," suggested Alba. "Let's get you back to the manor. I reckon everyone else will have scurried off to bed, so we can slip in, make our way to our bedrooms and tomorrow will be better."

"I'd prefer not to chance bumping into them. Let's sit here for a while."

They did. Conversation ranged from how long Terry might be in Uzbekistan for, Eleanor's post-doctorate plans and Alba's desire, despite her love of the countryside, to 'do' London properly at some stage – to take a few days, staying in a hotel up there and exploring it at all hours of the day and night and just spending time being in the capital.

Even having to wait an extra couple of hours, as a breakdown van came to their assistance to replace a punctured tyre, which they only noticed once they made their way to Alba's car in the pub car park, did not dampen Eleanor's mood. Alba was impressed how quickly Eleanor had turned an upsetting episode into such a positive situation; two mugs of hot chocolate and some shortbread biscuits – thankfully none that were crescent moon shaped – supplied in Eddie's absence by his father, once he had heard of their plight upon their going in to ask to use his telephone, had, of course, also helped maintain a positive outlook.

*

It was thus rather late as they returned to Kingsbourne Manor. Only a couple of lights were still on and the building had an air of itself being at rest – both women hoped John's wider family would themselves be sleeping or at least have retired to their respective bedrooms. They both knew Eleanor would not wish for another confrontation with them, be it in the dining room, the billiard room or even up on the long landing as they made their way to their bedrooms.

Alba parked, as originally, beyond the row of lime trees, where the staff tended to park. Equally, as before, Alba, as they made their way to the front door, ignored studying the row of cars parked, parked slightly less neatly this time, under the lime trees in front of the house.

The two of them made their way in quietly. They passed Sandy on the stairs as they were going up. Sandy said they had startled her as she had assumed all the guests had retired for the night. Having apologised and explained the reason for their lateness, Alba checked Sandy was alright. Alba made a point of asking whether any of the guests on their return had caused her, Sandy, any distress, especially given, so Alba informed the maid, that one or two of them had clearly had too much to drink during the evening meal. With Sandy assuring her she was completely alright, Alba and Eleanor continued their way up.

"I guess you'll be wanting to see John now we're back," said Alba to Eleanor once the maid had made her way downstairs.

"It's late," replied Eleanor. "I'll leave John be. Think I'll just head to my room. He will be lost within his books at this time of night – he always seems to be brightest in the darkest hours. He'll be back in academic mode and probably the better for it after tonight's unpleasantness. He'll know I'm alright as no one has come banging on his door. I'll see him in the morning; plus, I'm tired."

As they made their way along the Long Gallery, they passed the large tapestry – a convincing replica of one believed, according to records held by the museum in Salisbury, to have once hung at Kingsbourne Manor – and several aged cracked oil paintings.

"The paintings are originals," confirmed Eleanor. "John's been buying them up at local auctions in Marlborough and Devizes and from an antiques shop in Hungerford."

"They look the part," said Alba. "Know who they are?"

"No," conceded Eleanor. "At least not yet. Once things are more settled – which I sense they will be from tomorrow – we'll have more time to start researching them. John might well bring in one of his fellow academics to help in that regard, possibly even utilising a post-grad student to undertake some research. We'll also get them professionally cleaned, which won't be cheap but let's not say anything more about money and how John spends it tonight, shall we?"

"No, let's not. The pictures do look good; they give a certain *gravitas* to this wonderfully grand long landing. This one here," said Alba as she paused by one in particular, "I particularly like; it's a simple composition of an elderly man sitting at a wooden table, with a bowl containing a few morsels of food before him, gazing out of the window. You can sense he's reflecting on a life lived outdoors, working the land, bringing food to his family's table in all weathers. The little cameo picture on the mantlepiece behind him, you assume was his wife, don't you? Then there's the evening light coming through the window, casting its long shadows as it does so. That reinforces the sensation that time, be it a day, a marriage, a life, is drawing to a close. I just love it – I mean, just look at his weathered hands. Artists in those days really knew how to paint, didn't they?"

"Yes. This, though, is my favourite," said Eleanor, as she turned to one of the pictures on the other wall. It hung above a medieval looking dark oak side table, upon which was a candlestick. The lit red candle added its own flickering glow to the painting above.

Alba turned to look at a picture of a young woman, standing upright but with her back against the trunk of a willow tree, holding a letter to her chest. Her long flowing auburn hair was being caught by the breeze and the artist had added flecks of mud around the hem of her satin dress.

"You just know, she's run out of her parent's home once she'd got the morning mail and taken herself off into the woods to read her lover's letter alone. There, in secret, she would have absorbed each and every word and yet I can't quite make out if the letter has caused her heartbreak or joy."

"No, the painter has cleverly hidden her face with a low branch from another tree and her hair, caught by the wind, covers part of her face as well. Very clever; it leaves you wondering, doesn't it? You wish it is good news she's just read but you fear she's just learnt that he's fallen in some far away battle."

"She's holding a lock of his hair; do you see that, too?" said Eleanor. "Sent as a token of his unending love or cut from his broken body as he lay lifeless in some foreign land having fought and died for King and Country. This flickering candlelight adds something, too."

"It's the not knowing that holds you, isn't it?" said Alba. "Still, it's late, we're both tired and given you seem more than OK, despite all that's happened this evening, I'm heading to bed myself. Plus, I'm planning on getting up early and taking my car to the local garage to get the rear lights sorted out."

"Oh, that's right – you had mentioned it."

"Eddie, the publican's son, is a mechanic during the day and said he'd have a look at it for me."

"Oh, I knew he was a mechanic. John said he used to service the garden machinery here. However, John didn't feel Eddie was quite right for him. Apparently, Eddie didn't like being given instructions from someone new to the village – John ended up giving the work to a guy from Quarrybourne instead. Anyway, as for the morning, that's fine. Head off and get it sorted – John never doubted Eddie's ability as a mechanic, I think they just had a clash of personalities. I'll see you mid-morning, all being well."

"Good night then."

"Night Alba and thanks for putting up with all this tonight, today and basically the whole time you've been here."

"It's fine. I'm pleased I've been here to support you. Still, as you say, tomorrow is a new day."

"Oh, very much so," said Eleanor, as she stood by her bedroom door. She flicked the landing lights switch to plunge the upstairs into near darkness, save for the solitary candle illuminating the image above it, of a woman clutching her lover's letter.

CHAPTER 17

'Croft and Sons'

"Morning, Eddie," said Alba.

This Saturday promised to be another glorious summer's day. The sky was clear and Alba could feel the warmth of the sun on her arms, even at this time of the morning. Her arms were bare for she was wearing a sleeveless polka dot navy blue dress – which had white circles slightly smaller than mid-size against a dark background. It finished just above the knee and had a pencil thin leather belt in matching blue. It was a delightful summer look but it was one Alba instantly regretted wearing the moment she stepped from her car on the garage forecourt; it was not, if indeed anything was, the outfit to get oil on and there was no way either Eddie or Ash would have anything to try and remove a stain beyond, literally, spit and polish.

Eddie was unaware of her arrival, despite Alba's call, preoccupied as he was with washing a car to one side of the main forecourt. His not knowing she was there made Alba feel even more ill at ease, for she feared for the spray from his hose soaking her. Or, even if it did not directly soak her, she feared she might be splashed with oily water from the ground, were Eddie to suddenly sense someone had turned up and instinctively turn round with the hose still on and spray anywhere and everywhere before him. To get his attention, she opted to retreat to the far side of her car and sounded her horn to inform him the garage had a customer.

*

The garage was as one sees dotted every now and then throughout the countryside on the outskirts of many a British village. In a time gone by it had sold petrol – indeed, two of the original pumps were still in situ on the forecourt. There was once a time when it was the beating heart of the village's foray into the world of the combustion engine. It was a place where Mr Sykes would fill up the new family car each and every Saturday morning. It was where Mrs Hart, whose husband, despite no one quite knowing how he had made his money during the war years, would bring her burnt orange, vinyl-roofed Ford Corsair to have its tyres and oil checked on the last Thursday of every month and where Mr Rawlins would bring his grocer's delivery van religiously every Monday afternoon to top up the tank to ensure he could undertake the week's rounds.

It would have been almost as much part of village life as the butchers, bakers and Post Office once were. For a time, when people felt wealthier or succumbed to post-war advertising, which made everyone believe they would be happier if only they had their own motorcar and stopped relying on the always reliable and sociable bus service, the village garage-come-petrol station was there for everyone. The garage was part of things and people would trust the mechanics who worked there. They would know its little shop would sell them useful car accessories, such as a small dustpan and brush to keep in the boot in order that they could sweep out the footwells from time to time. Equally, they would accept the price of a gallon of petrol at the pump, never caring whether it might be cheaper somewhere else because *this* garage was *their* garage.

Then, as with first the greengrocers, then the bakers or butchers and more recently village Post Offices, the garages themselves started to close down. People stopped valuing them. They stopped buying their children their first cars from the choice of second-hand cars it had on its forecourt in front of the pumps. Then people went elsewhere for the fuel itself, succumbing to the fluorescent strip lights and swishing glass doors of petrol garages, with their 'Little Chef' type restaurants attached, on the newly opened bypass or dual carriageway.

Thus, as far as the village of Kingsbourne was concerned, what had once been 'Croft and Sons', the village garage and petrol station, which was on the sharp bend of the Southbourne road on your way out of Kingsbourne, was now no more. It used to sell fuel to all who stopped by but its pumps had been drained a long time ago. Its mechanics – one of whom had been RAF groundcrew, working on Short Sunderlands, and another who had somehow got a summer internment at the Maranello factory in Italy one year in the mid-sixties – had been made redundant and they had moved away from the village; mechanics who used to lift the bonnet of Mrs Hart's car every month, mechanics who offered MOTs at a moment's notice to help forgetful people like Mr Sykes out, who had forgotten to book it in and yet was about to take his family on holiday to Ilfracombe the next day, and mechanics who would, in between everything else, happily sell little dustpan and brushes, as well as coloured elasticated straps with their black hooked ends, to help Mr Rawlins keep his grocer's van clean and secure. The straps were needed because of the increasingly unreliable rear door handles on his van. 'Croft and Sons' had ceased trading a long time ago because people had just stopped coming.

The plot had then sat vacant for decades. It was a scar on the face of the village, an ever-present reminder to the current villagers of the fickleness and disloyalty that their predecessors had shown towards Mr Croft and his family. It was a different, coarser, type of scar to the site of the greengrocers, which was now simply a house whose front door opened directly onto the pavement, but another scar nonetheless.

Then, though far from taking the site back to its former glory, two local lads, Eddie and Ash, took out a lease on the site with the support of a south Wiltshire charity, which sought to support local business startups. Eddie and Ash were boys who their teachers had not got too overly excited by from an academic point of view. However, to be fair to the teachers at the 'Edward Hyde School', the modern comprehensive secondary school in Tidworth, neither Eddie nor Ash had ever got too excited over William Golding, the 'Eastern Question' or french feminine pronouns. Yet here they were, opening their first business together and trying to put something back into village life that an appreciation of 'Lord of the Flies' never could. Perhaps, to be fair to at least one of their former teachers – a certain Mr Bellamy, their design and technology teacher – he at least had felt they could do something with their skills if only they could keep themselves away from their petty offending and sudden angry, tempestuous outbursts when challenged by someone in a position of authority over them.

So, the site of 'Croft and Sons', if not back to its heyday of the nineteen fifties and sixties, was alive once more, and now the location of 'Kingsbourne Cars and Motorbikes'. It remained far from being the beating heart of the village but it had a pulse, even if a tiny one. It offered something and it was where Alba was now standing this Saturday morning trying to get Eddie's attention if not the attention of his hosepipe.

*

She sounded her horn a second time and on this occasion Eddie heard.

Alba was wise to have stood back for he did send water squirting wildly as he turned round. As he dropped the gushing hose to the ground and left the large oval-shaped sponge on the roof of the car he had just been cleaning, he gestured he would go and turn the water off before meeting her inside. Alba nodded her understanding and gingerly made her way to the little reception area, stepping between the puddles in her strappy low-heeled sandals.

"Good morning," said Alba as Eddie came into the room from the rear door.

"Hi, Alba," he replied. "You've come!"

"Of course!" she offered back. "Why wouldn't I – we agreed I would, didn't we?"

"Well, yes but things are, no, never mind. So, it was, er–"

"A bulb needing looking at. You alright, you seem a bit distracted?"

"No, no, I'm fine. Sorry, I sort of had my head somewhere else as I was washing my car."

"You didn't tell me you did a car cleaning and valeting service as well," teased Alba. "Did I have to book for that or can I request it now that I'm here? You did say you'd clean and polish my car as well, didn't you?"

"I most definitely did not! Plus, I wouldn't want to wash the mud and grime off your car as I reckon they're the only things holding it together!"

"Hey, you!" said Alba with a smile on her face. "It's not *that* bad! I won't hear a bad thing said against my car."

Eddie stepped round from behind the small reception desk and went to the door that Alba had just come through and held it open for her. As he did so he added:

"Let's have a look at it, then. I'll give the windows a wipe down if they're smeary but let's have a look at the lights first. Front or rear, was it?"

"Rear brake light, I was told. At least, that's what the police officer said."

"If you sit back in and start the engine and put your foot on the brake pedal, I can check. Just the one bulb we think?"

"That's all the guy said, having stopped me. However, I'm happy to wait – if you want to finish washing that other car first, I really don't mind. It's nice to get away from the manor for a bit."

"Is it? Why what's happened?"

"Nothing," said Alba. "Nothing's happened today, I just mean nice to get away from yesterday's arguments and nastiness. No, I got up early this morning and had left before anyone else surfaced."

"Oh, OK. Right. As for the other car, that's mine; I can finish washing it later."

As they made their way across the forecourt, Ash turned up on his Yamaha XJR 1300, prompting Eddie and Alba to pause as they watched him sweep in. Once the sound of the bike's engine had died, Eddie spoke to Alba:

"His new love of his life. Know anything about bikes?"

"Even less than cars," conceded Alba.

"Oh, my. Still, and I'm not being unkind in saying this, we need people like you to keep us in business. If everyone knew how to change a bulb, we'd lose a chunk of the fledgling customer base we're building up."

"That's fine, I'm not upset. Cars were just something no one ever taught me about. I am paying, too. I want to be clear on that. You're not going to treat me as you did in the pub on Wednesday when I turned up. I'm paying my way today; you're running a business here."

"Right you are. In you get then and start up; we'll check the indicators too, whilst we're about it."

*

It was just the one bulb that had gone and which was swiftly replaced by Eddie. Having cleaned her windscreen and also got her to open the bonnet and check her oil and screen wash levels, the latter of which he judged needed topping up, they returned to the reception area where Ash was sorting through a tray full of keys. It was no straightforward task, for some were loose, some keys were on rings with numerous other keys attached, be they shed keys, locker keys or even house keys and some of the things on the tray were in little cloth bags of varying colours, ranging from black, dull green, pink, all the way through to the garish luminous yellow. That was because some owners of vehicles were very particular and made it clear that they did not want other people's keys scratching their favourite keyring, be it a keyring with their football team badge on, the matching crest for the make of car or motorcycle in question or some cartoon character their young child had given them one Father's Day – a hastily bought present at a quarter to five on the Saturday afternoon before the 'great' day, when the child's mother had suddenly remembered she had not got the husband anything for their young child to give his or her dad and had rushed down to the shops whilst the dad was listening to the football results come in.

"Morning, Ash. Wasn't expecting you in today," said Eddie.

"No but no worries. Having been told it was ready, a guy wanted to collect his bike so he could ride it at Castle Combe tomorrow. Plus, he said his friend, who'd be dropping him off here, wanted to have a look at the motorbikes we have for sale. Friend wants to get one again since his wife left him, apparently. So, I thought – all due respect and that, mate – I'd come in and talk machines to him rather than you."

"Makes sense. I accept I can't bring them alive in a sales pitch like you can."

"True and, if memory serves me correctly, you had a big job on this morning, didn't you? Someone bringing in a car with a dodgy rear light – mate, that might keep you busy till we shut later this afternoon!"

"You–"

With that, Eddie, in much the same way as he had done in the 'Earl of Clarendon' with a damp tea towel, threw the damp rag at his friend, the rag which had just wiped Alba's front and rear windscreens.

"Good of you to come in, really," continued Eddie once Ash had thrown it back at him. "Makes sense, for you're better at bikes than I am. Another sale this month would be a bonus. Which one do you think he might want?"

"Well, I doubt he's going to be after the Fireblade, as much as we need to sell that one. I wouldn't be happy selling it to him even if he wanted it. If this guy hasn't been riding for a bit, even if his licence allows, I wouldn't want him getting straight onto a Fireblade; too much, too soon. From what was said on the phone, I'm hoping they'll be looking at the Tiger or the grey BMW."

"Selling either would help," stated Eddie.

"So?" asked Ash, though now addressing Alba.

"So?" she offered back puzzled by the question. She tried to offer up more of a whimsical look than a dismissive one. She was aware that their last conversation had involved Ash snubbing her, giving her false information and generally being unpleasant but she hoped to move beyond how things had started off between them. Alba hoped Eddie may have built her up in Ash's eyes or at least persuaded him to be less hostile.

"So," said Ash, "do you think he's sorted your car out? I'm happy to have a look myself if you have your doubts. He's good for inflating tyres and working out how to pop a bonnet but technical stuff like rear bulbs, well–"

With that, Ash inhaled deeply and slowly before continuing:

"Well, as I say, that's big boys' stuff!"

"He's done it," said Alba assuredly, giving Eddie her full vote of confidence.

"Hmm, we'll see. Bring it in on Monday if it's not working and I'll have a look at it."

"Mate, I am still here!" pointed out Eddie. "I can hear what you are saying about your business partner – soon to be ex-business partner at the rate you're going on."

"Alright, Eddie. I'll reel it in. You been washing your car again? My, you really are testing your skills this morning, aren't you!"

"Ash! You said–"

"OK, OK, I'll reel my tongue in. You only did it yesterday morning, that's all."

"Yeah but it was all covered in sticky little spots this morning – like someone had sprinkled a bag of sugar over it and then sprayed water over the car. Wasn't you last night was it, when I was working at the pub?"

"Surely it wouldn't have been Ash," contributed Alba. She was hoping she had gauged the mood between all three of them – particularly that Eddie's friend had mellowed towards her – as she offered up her opinion. "Not Ash," she continued, "he's not the type of person to play a nasty little trick on someone when they're not expecting it, is he, Eddie?"

Alba was making out she was speaking to Eddie but she was looking at Ash and there was a twinkle in her eyes and a slight smile in the left-hand corner of her mouth as she did so – and Ash knew that she knew that she herself had once been his victim.

"Thankfully though, Ash doesn't play such japes," teased Alba one last time – putting a noticeable emphasis on 'thankfully' as she did so.

Ash was suddenly feeling a bit defensive and Eddie looked at him suspiciously.

"No, nothing to do with me," Ash insisted. "I was at the pictures last night, wasn't I? Went to see 'The Day After Tomorrow', didn't I?"

"Did you? Or perhaps you went to the Co-op in Pewsey and bought a small bag of sugar."

"I went to the cinema, I tell you."

"Film any good?" asked Eddie.

"Lots of people walking about in the snow and burning books to keep warm – yeah, it was alright."

"Did they survive? Quest fulfilled and did the hero get his girl? You might as well spoil it for me now as later tonight when we're in the pub drinking," conceded Eddie.

"Don't know, mate. Fell asleep before the end. Couldn't tell you what happened after the bonfire scene."

"Snow and naked flames," reflected Alba. "Hard to imagine anyone needing a fire in this weather – it's going to be another hot day."

As is the way when someone mentions the weather, even in a tad dishevelled, rough and ready round the edges, little garage on the outskirts of a Wiltshire village, those inside looked out of the window to assess the weather for themselves.

"Yup, another hot one," agreed Eddie.

As they were looking out, a grey Vauxhall Vectra pulled onto the forecourt and two men got out.

"Ah, reckon that's the guy come to collect his bike," said Ash, as he finally found the bunch of keys that he wanted from the tray which he had been rummaging through on and off all this time. "Why do we allow customers to keep their keys in these silly little brightly coloured bags? I've had to look in half of them to find the one I want; can't we give the bags back to people when they hand us their keys? We'll discuss it later in the pub, hopefully. Now though, I'll go and bring his bike round to the front."

*

"Right, how much do I owe you?" said Alba when it was just the two of them once more.

"It's fine," said Eddie. "Bulbs are pretty cheap."

"No, I insist. Plus, it must have been getting on for half an hour of your time. Then there's a bottle of screen wash and I'll buy a couple of spare bulbs for the rear lights, which I can keep in the glove box. Whilst you tot it all up, I'll go and look at your motorcycles and pretend I'm another interested punter and make these guys think they've got competition. No scrimping on my bill, I'm paying my way – only when I've been properly billed will I let you continue cleaning the stickiness off your car," reiterated Alba as she stepped to the door.

"If you insist. Our bikes for sale are all round the far side – we can't leave them out the front any more as we've had blokes stop in vans, literally lift them into the back of their vehicles and drive off before we can stop them."

"OK."

"And, Alba, if you want to look like you know your bikes–"

"Yes?" said a grateful Alba.

"Don't go twisting the throttle; that's what children and those who know nothing about bikes would do. Definitely don't say something like 'Gosh, that one looks fast'. Please don't try and tilt one off its stand – they are heavier than they look. Plus, to be absolutely clear, no, none of them come with the option of a sidecar and–"

"Yes?" said Alba, sensing a silly bit of 'advice' was coming her way.

"Handlebars are at the front end."

"That's an end with a wheel, is it?" queried Alba, which led to Eddie slapping a hand to his own face in despair.

Once he had lowered his hand and saw the charming smile of Alba coming back at him – knowing she was giving as good as she got – he said, in all seriousness:

"If you want to help, crouch down at the rear end of one or two of them and let the other punters see you feel the exhausts – someone who knows about buying bikes wants it to be cold, which it will be, I might add. Then be on the side of the bike where the chain is and be seen to be having a look at that as much as you can. Then, if you feel the others are losing interest in whichever machine Ash is trying to sell them, ask, during a dip in their conversation, if Ash could let you have a look at that particular bike's service and MOT history once he became free. None of that is being really dishonest."

"No, just making them think they have competition. I'm onto it – and no cutting corners with my bill or your car will stay sticky well into next week."

A nod from Eddie was the confirmation she needed.

"Good," she said. "Right, let's go and help Ash make a sale."

CHAPTER 18

Saturday brunch

Upon her return, the other guests were finally up.

A late brunch had always been Dr Sunday's plan – as well as giving his cook the previous night off, he was treating him to a late start this morning. However, in light of events from yesterday evening, a brunch turned out to be a fortuitous meal to have organised for everyone. It had given John's family – given they were not about to apologise to him or suddenly warm to Eleanor's appearance in his life – time to gather their things, put their main cases in their cars and, bar their coats and handbags, be ready to leave once they had eaten.

Unaware of the tensions and how things had turned out, the small kitchen team, had produced the full works – fresh fruit salad, eggs, poached or scrambled, sausages, chipolata and the slightly spicier Cumberland, Portobello mushrooms, fried bread, bacon and, with a nod to those who craved American fare, hash browns and baked beans. It was laid out on side tables within silver servers, alongside sweet pastries, yogurts and cereals, and the family were able to help themselves. Sandy was around to oversee things and to ensure nothing completely ran out.

Neither John nor Eleanor was in attendance. No one expected

them to be nor looked disappointed that they were not. Those present were grateful the whole family were not together for this final meal. However, in John and Eleanor's absence, they were instead accompanied by the 'elephant in the room'. They all knew it was there but, so far, they had avoided it; they neither wished to see it nor hear about it and spoke to one another as if it were not there.

The food being so good did also help them to ignore the invisible creature in the room. The bacon was salty to just the right extent and the fat was wonderfully crispy. The scrambled eggs were just so much better than one could achieve at home even though you could not work out quite what the chef had done differently and even the prunes had a caramelised taste to them that had proved a wonderful surprise to those who had felt they ought to start with something healthy.

Yet, it was not just the quality of the food that allowed those gathered to ignore the animal in the room. Given those eating had made their decision to pack up and go, rather than stay and resolve things, also meant they simply did not care for the said elephant; it is, after all, always easier to ignore something one does not care for. Equally, on another level, they could ignore it because everyone else was ignoring it as well; a collective lie is so much easier to absorb.

That, then, was how brunch was conducted. Of course, it would only take one person to 'speak its name' and the quiet, disconcertingly serene dining room would change in an instant.

*

"Morning, Sandy," said Alba, as she was about to enter the dining room and as Sandy was exiting with an empty silver platter. "Anything left for me? I've just got back from the village garage – I needed something done on my car."

"Morning, Miss. You been to–"

"'Kingsbourne Cars and Motorbikes'. Not the most imaginative title in the world but as I drove back I couldn't think of anything better. All I could come up with was 'Ash and Ed's' but you just know the locals would refer to it as 'A shed of a place' and that would be so much worse. So, best I stay away from a career in marketing and leave them to name their own business. If my lights work now, well, that's all I want, not some fancy business name."

"You've been to see Eddie? This morning?" asked Sandy.

"Ash was there, too. He wanted to meet someone who was interested in buying a bike."

"And everything was, er—"

"Fine. Don't worry," said Alba quietly. "Whatever tensions you may have picked up here this morning, that wasn't down to the pub meal we had. Neither was it down to Eddie's ability to serve nor Ash's behaviour at the bar, bad-mouthing those who stay in big country houses. In fact, Ash wasn't there at the pub at all last night; apparently, he was at the 'flicks' but was so tired he fell asleep during the film. At least he now can't ruin the ending for Eddie! All that said, whatever tensions you have detected here this morning is down to some family truths being shared over the meal rather than a run-in with the locals."

"Oh, right you are Miss. There has been a sort of silent, unspoken, tension. It's also been a bit puzzling watching everyone put their bags in their cars – it's as if people have packed up to leave but everyone is meant to be staying until Wednesday."

"I think," said Alba, "Dr Sunday will be giving you an update. Clearly, he hasn't already."

"No, Miss. He hasn't appeared this morning; not yet."

"He will and things will be explained, I'm sure. As for right now, I'm peckish but it looks like you're clearing away? Is brunch over? If it is, could I at least trouble you for a banana and a pot of tea."

"No, no. You're fine. There's still plenty set out and I'm just about to refill this with more sausages. If there's anything else you think is missing, please let me know."

"Right you are. I'm glad I'm not too late as I suddenly fancy a hearty breakfast."

"Must be all the petrol fumes and talk of speed that you got at the garage that's given you an appetite," suggested Sandy.

"Perhaps – that and the sweet smell of success in releasing a tiger into the Wiltshire countryside."

"Pardon," said Sandy.

"Don't worry. Right, breakfast time."

*

As Alba took her food to an empty space down at one end of the table, Connie smiled at her and said 'good morning', Hugh studied her for far longer than she was comfortable with and Johanna had a look of someone who desperately wanted this to be *her* gathering, *her* dining room and that people were breaking bread with *her*, rather than eating out of John's hand.

As Alba returned to where everything was laid out, to make herself a cup of tea, Anthony and Isabel were talking as quietly as they could at the other end of the lengthy side tables; quiet enough so those at the dining table itself could not hear but audible to Alba as she came into ear shot. If Anthony was not getting quite so desperate, perhaps he would have been more cautious as to whether he continued his conversation with Isabel but panic was beginning to take hold of him.

"I can't believe you still haven't found them; why were you so careless?"

"But I wasn't, not really and, as I've already told you, I've looked everywhere. I just can't find them. What more do you want me to do, brother?"

"But I'm leaving with Johanna in the next hour, you just have to give them back to me. They're my nest egg which she doesn't know anything about – if I delay us leaving, I'll have to tell her why and I'm not going to do that."

"But I don't have them. I can't give you what I don't have."

"Oh, blazes. You just have to find them – look everywhere again."

There was only so long Alba could drag out making herself a pot of tea so, before her presence became awkward, she took herself back to the table and marvelled at the texture of the scrambled eggs.

"Is the walk to the castle still planned for later?" enquired Alba of Connie.

"It might be," called down Hugh. "However, I doubt you'll have many people doing it. We've decided to head home after brunch, haven't we, dear?" He had turned to look at Alice as he spoke his last three words.

"Yes," she succinctly said.

"Feel we've outstayed our welcome," suggested Hugh. "Think John would prefer us to go."

"So he can be with that little limpet that has attached herself to him without us getting in his way," added Alice. "Why he brought us all here, I really don't know," she continued, once more giving voice to opinions she might have been better off leaving unsaid. "To show off? To tease us? To get one 'happy' family photograph of us all together so he can have it on his wall at whatever American university he sneaks off to; a picture so he can convince himself he has left a loving family behind? Who knows, who cares?"

"He must be going abroad," voiced Johanna.

Alba sensed that Johanna and Alice had drawn closer together during their time here. Alba felt the realisation that they might be able to bring John down and get their hands on an inheritance that they had always desired had brought them closer – that ancient adage *my enemy's enemy is my friend* seemed to apply to these sisters-in-law.

"The long arm of the law or, to be more accurate and which will be of more interest to us, the reach of Her Majesty's Revenue and Customs will find him wherever he flees to," said Alice.

"I'm departing the manor, too," added May. "I mean, I could stay as I've got my own car after all but since everyone else seems to be going, I don't want to be rattling around this big old house basically by myself. You're still going, aren't you Henry?"

"Yep. Connie's going to drop me at Reading and I can get a train direct to Penzance. So relieved everyone has seen sense and is departing early; I just couldn't last another day here as there's just nothing to do."

"I accept," observed Alba, "with a painful leg the English countryside might seem slightly less appealing but–"

"There's no 'but'," insisted Henry. "Busted leg or not, there is just nothing to do here. It's just all so boring."

Alba opted not to challenge him on his dismissive take on the landscape that lay out there beyond the manor's immediate gardens; she turned to look at it out of the dining room windows and the open doors behind her. When they had been on the walk to the clootie tree on Thursday, she had tried to encourage Henry to see the beauty which she could see then and which she could see now beyond the dining room. Yet, she had failed on Thursday and was in no doubt she would be wasting her breath if she tried again.

"So, you're heading off, too?" asked Alba of Connie, once she, Alba, had turned back to the table.

"Suppose so. I knew H wanted to get away and if I'm going to drive him to Reading for a train I might as well head home myself. There's stuff I could be getting on with."

"Really? All your studies are finished and uni is months away," said Alba.

"I guess but–"

"If you'll all excuse me," cut in Isabel, addressing everyone as she stood up. "I must just gather a few more things before I myself head off. A couple of extra days speaking with the theatres and pouring over the script will be useful. Before I leave, though, if anyone comes across a little suede bag of mine and its contents, which I seem to have misplaced, let me know."

"What have you lost?" asked Hugh.

Alba and Connie both saw Isabel flash a quick worried look to Anthony.

"Oh, er, she was telling me earlier," Anthony quickly offered up. "Some costume jewellery, wasn't it, sister dear? Some, er, fake earrings kept in a pink pouch type bag; you were practising wearing them, weren't you?"

"What on earth?" commented Alice. "Who in their right mind needs to practice wearing a pair of earrings?"

"Well, er, you see, they're quite cumbersome and I was, er, just getting used to the weight of them. Just wearing them around my bedroom, you know."

"So, you won't recognise them," added Anthony. "But if you come across any missing jewellery, please let Isabel know, would you?"

"Oh, this is getting silly," reflected Johanna. "First, Eleanor's missing engagement ring—"

"That's not missing," insisted Alice. "John and Eleanor have just refused to show it."

"If they are engaged. Who knows with uncle John," mused Henry.

"Oh, who cares. Unaccounted for engagement rings, now missing fake earrings," said Johanna. "It's all getting a bit silly."

"Well, if you see anything – anything – please let Isabel know," stressed Anthony a further time.

"Of course. Surely, though," reflected Alice, "if you were wearing them in your room and nowhere else, that's where they'll be. I might be a tax expert as opposed to a leading criminal barrister but surely you should be looking in your room."

"I have," snapped back a frustrated Isabel. "I have but they are not there."

"Perhaps they got caught up in something she was wearing and they dropped somewhere else round the house. Just keep your eyes open, will you, please?" said Anthony.

"Alright, dear," sighed Johanna. "Why are you so worried over Isabel's lost props?"

"Nothing, no reason. Just looking out for my sister, that's all," pleaded Anthony. "That's what we do in this family, isn't it?"

"Not if you're John, it would seem," stated Alice coldly. "Soon enough, though, we will have rectified that, I hope. I will enjoy bringing him and that little miss down."

"I see neither of them have dared to show their faces this morning," said Hugh.

As if to prove Hugh wrong on that point, it was at that exact moment that Eleanor chose to enter the dining room.

"Good morning, everyone," announced Eleanor breezily. "Hope you all slept well and are enjoying your brunch. Don't worry, I'm not stopping – just getting some fruit, a spoonful of sunflower seeds and yogurt to eat out in the garden. It's such a glorious day, isn't it?" Then to just her friend, she added:

"Hi, Alba, I'll catch you in a bit when you're finished."

A confident Eleanor exited the room through the open dining room doors and out into the manor gardens, leaving everyone seated, save for Alba, caught off guard by her flighty-carefree demeanour.

"Well," Isabel said once Eleanor had left, "I must be getting my stuff together and one final rummage and all that."

"That costume jewellery won't find itself," teased Hugh.

"Let us know if you–" started Anthony but he never finished his sentence for a woman's scream suddenly filled both the room and the ears of everyone present. It was not a 'woe is me' plea. Neither was it the sound of mild panic nor a yelp of surprise. It was a scream; a full bloodied, heart stopping cry of despair.

Then it came again. Perhaps this time it was for longer – it definitely seemed longer – and everyone who heard it sensed that this time the person, whose anguish they could hear, was screaming through their hands; hands now raised to their face to shield themselves from whatever scene they had encountered. A scene which spoke an untold horror.

CHAPTER 19

Back to the beginning

Alba stood up from the tapestry-covered chair she had been sitting in; suddenly it seemed as if she had been in it a long time. Here in her bedroom at Kingsbourne Manor, she felt she needed to stand for all that had been happening these past few days had almost become like a dream.

She looked out through the stone mullioned window once again. Terry's letter was on the floor to the side of the chair and on the octagonal table was her empty teacup and a plate devoid of the shortbread biscuits which Sandy had brought her.

Of course, it was not a dream, far from it. It was only all too real.

Once they had heard Eleanor's scream that second time, they had all rushed from the dining room to where she was outside. They found her slumped on the grey gravel beside her fiancé's crumpled body and they all, as one, stood there in shocked silence.

It was during that time that Alba had been struck by the height from which he, Dr John Sunday, had fallen. She had decided it was a greater drop when viewed from down on the ground than it had looked from up there. She had been up there, after all; it was only on Thursday morning when he had invited her to step out onto the lead covered roof and they had stood side by side marvelling at the view.

*

As Alba looked out of the window in her manor bedroom, she recalled how the path's grey gravel cut into her knees as she knelt beside Eleanor and tried to comfort the other in her distress. Then she remembered Anthony covering John's body with his jacket. After that, Anthony's daughter Connie had brought out the snooker table covering and laid it over John's body.

In the solitude of her manor bedroom, Alba reflected that even in those moments by his lifeless body, the family tensions did not take long to surface. Once Eleanor, in her distress, had claimed the family had driven him to it, Anthony, Hugh but mostly Isabel, accused Eleanor of working her way into John's life and Eleanor herself upsetting things.

Alba still felt it was right that at that point, she herself had calmed the situation by asking everyone else to move away and leave Eleanor to grieve in relative peace. Thankfully they had acceded to Alba's request and they left only Eleanor and Alba to just sit by John's shrouded body.

How long they had sat there, Alba still was not entirely sure. They had sat there until the emergency services arrived and chaperoned the two of them back into the dining room. It was right that Alba had stayed by Eleanor's side the whole time for, once they were back in the room where they had only just been eating brunch, Eleanor was in such a state she could not even open the bottle of water by herself and Alba had to do it for her.

Then, once Eleanor had had some water and Alba, herself, a cup of lukewarm but stewed tea, Alba escorted Eleanor upstairs to Eleanor's bedroom to rest; to rest until she, Eleanor, was ready for Alba to call Eleanor's parents to tell them the awful thing that had just happened.

Alba reflected how that walk to the other's bedroom had naturally taken them along the same landing which they had so happily walked just the evening before. The evening before, when they had been carefree, had seen them commenting on the tapestry and the aged cracked oil paintings which hung along the walls. It was, after all, a joyful Eleanor whom Alba was in the company of – for had not John just announced to his family that he had asked Eleanor to be his wife? Eleanor had been happy, for she could, could she not, despite or even because of the family's hostile reaction, anticipate a happy life with John for years and years?

They had walked the corridor together then and again just now – how one saw it differently, on those two occasions, depending on what life had just thrown at you. The evening before, Eleanor had drawn Alba's attention to one painting in particular, Eleanor's favourite. That one was of a woman holding a letter to her chest; a woman leaning against a tree, as the breeze caught her hair and covered her face. It was a painting that was somehow made even more intriguing for it had been illuminated by the flickering of a red candle which was lit on the wooden table underneath the picture.

In contrast, today, just half an hour or so ago, as she and Eleanor had walked the long corridor once again, they had noticed neither the paintings, the tapestry nor even what was left of the much-reduced candle. The melted wax had congealed down and around the candlestick itself, almost sealing it to the piece of furniture on which it sat. They had seen nothing. Alba had simply taken Eleanor back to her room and then sought rest herself in her own bedroom.

*

However, it was not real rest Alba had got. Rather, Alba had sat, still in her polka dot navy blue dress, in the chair by the stone mullioned window and read Terry's letter again. She had tried to get her head around all that Terry had written and all that had just happened;

Terry's claim that things would be better if she, Alba, were here for Eleanor seemed pitifully misguided.

Then, letter re-read and to break the intensity of the moment, Alba had rung for Sandy to bring her a fresh cup of tea. Yet that had simply led to Alba spending time comforting the young maid, who was visibly and understandably shaken by events.

Once the maid had departed and as Alba drank the tea and ate the shortbread biscuits, Alba found herself reflecting on all that had happened since she had left home on Wednesday. She recalled how she had left home being wilfully blind to the cloud that hung over her and Andrew. She remembered a last minute change of outfit and, more importantly, that she probably had been rude to Matthew and Sam on her doorstep. She recollected how she had been stopped by a police officer and brought in to a large lay-by near that café. She gave a faint smile to herself as she recalled how her journey here had taken her by way of the 'Earl of Clarendon' and how she would have been the victim of Ash's trick but for Eddie's kindly intervention. Finally, Alba's mind took her through the meeting of each of John's wider family.

So, here Alba was at Kingsbourne and she was alone. However, whether she had left her home village under a cloud or not, she suddenly wanted Andrew to be there beside her. To have him to talk to and just to be there with her. However, he was not and Alba had to decide what to do next, alone.

*

Then quite suddenly it came to her.

Terry had asked her to come and watch out for his sister and Alba saw that task had not ended with what had just happened. Indeed, perhaps now, was where that task actually began. For, if John had not jumped, had *something else* befallen him, might not Eleanor's life now also be at risk?

Yet, that was a big 'if'. Everyone had just stood around his crumpled body and spoken as though he had jumped – taken himself to his death out of the distress he felt over his wider family and to spare Eleanor from a life blighted by Anthony, Hugh and Isabel, John's brothers and sister. Marred by Johanna and Alice, his brother's wives and by the sniping and general apathy emanating from his nephew and nieces.

He had jumped, had he not? That was how everyone, Alba included, had just viewed it; even the emergency services had treated it as a suicide from the moment they were in attendance and they were the experts.

Yet, as she looked out of the stone mullioned window, she decided that for her at least there was something about Dr Sunday jumping to his death that just did not quite sit right. Something did not sit comfortably in her mind. Dr John Sunday, Alba had always felt, from her time knowing him as one of her university tutors and even over these last few days, was an orderly man. Things had their place – one only had to see his study here at Kingsbourne to grasp that about his character – and even Sandy the maid had just described him as a tidy person, one who did not like things scattered about. Dr Sunday liked things to be in their rightful place.

It was hardly a scientific assessment. It was not something one would step into the witness box in a criminal court and claim with gusto 'it didn't happen like that because…'. Yet, to Alba it was not within his character to take his life in such a way. That was not the man she knew – was it not just so untidy?

CHAPTER 20

Trunk call

Once she had checked on Eleanor, who assured Alba she would be fine and all she wanted to do was to sit on her bed, with her knees pulled up before her, and be alone, Alba took herself out of the manor house.

She found herself wandering along the main drive back up towards the road. The manor gardens would have been her preferred place to go and lose herself in – to wander between the clipped box hedging, to imagine the lost grandeur of the long borders, even to sit with her legs dangling over the ha-ha and marvel at the countryside beyond. However, although the emergency services had now left and there was nothing remaining to be seen, it just did not feel right to go and amble over the paths where she had not so long ago been sitting beside Dr Sunday's shroud-covered body.

So, inevitably, she had gone out the front. She did not need anything from her car and so the logical direction to walk was along the lime tree drive. She had no particular desire to walk that way and she definitively did not fancy going to find the clootie tree again. Nonetheless, she made her way along the drive, heading for the road. She decided she would, in the shade of the limes, walk to the wayfaring tree, which was on the other side of the main road, and then turn round. It was simply somewhere, when anywhere would do, to walk to before heading back.

It was an uneventful walk, yet it was marred by her sense that she had missed a number of things during the course of her time here at Kingsbourne Manor; things which had not seemed important at the time but, with the benefit of hindsight, probably were and yet she had let them slide by her. Missed, Alba felt in part, due to the constant crabbiness of John's family, sometimes between themselves but at other times directed towards Alba herself. She also felt she had missed things because she, Alba, had been made to feel constantly on edge, especially by Hugh. Then there was the family's hostility towards Eleanor, which had not helped either.

"No," Alba suddenly said out loud to herself. "No, no excuses."

With that, she pulled herself up and stopped – as if she were a jockey, pulling on the reins and bringing her mount to a halt. Having stopped, she, for no particular reason, looked around her – she had not sensed she was being followed and indeed she was alone. Somehow, though, almost instinctively she glanced around; perhaps it was to 'take stock' or maybe it was simply to 'see the lie of the land'. Either way, seeing she was truly alone, she took herself off to her left and went and rested against one of the limes and, with the early afternoon shadows the trees were casting, falling off to her right, looked out across the farmland.

She did not see the landscape as she would normally *see* it. This time she saw as little of it as Henry might have. This was because she was cross with herself – cross enough to reprimand herself:

"It's no excuse," she said to no one but herself, "to say people, events, even the atmosphere, have been distracting me. I should have been concentrating – isn't that, after all, why Terry wanted me here? Things have been going on and I've missed them. I've been careless, sloppy even. I simply have to up my game if I am to be of any use to Eleanor."

As Alba leaned against the tree, a faint, soft, warm breeze caught some of her hair. As she stood there, she decided she almost certainly could not have prevented whatever happened to Dr Sunday from befalling him – that would be taking her self-chastisement too far. Yet, she felt something had happened to him; she was, now, most certain of that. He had not jumped to his death to spare his bride-to-be from his unhappy and ungrateful family. Nor had he jumped over allegations of forging a will. If he had been intent on taking his life – which she did not think was part of his character – he would not have jumped. Another party was surely involved, and this was what she realised she was berating herself over; not that she had failed to prevent John's death but that she was completely unsure as to who else was involved and why.

"But someone has to be. Or indeed, some people," stated Alba.

As for why, she decided there were almost too many reasons why. Too many people were not unhappy John was dead. Too many people were standing to benefit from his sudden demise. 'Who, within the family, did not now stand to gain?' Alba asked herself. 'Even Connie gained if it kept her parents financially afloat and together for the time being. Plus, with the amount of money blowing around or, perhaps more accurately, that people believed to be blowing around, who could say whether it might prompt the nicest of people to do the nastiest of things? Goodness me,' Alba further thought, 'if he'd been found slumped at his study desk with eight knives protruding from his back, it would not have been a surprise. Indeed, was it not Connie who had described the family as all cut from the same cloth?'

As she stood, lost in her own thoughts, nothing visibly changed, beyond the early afternoon shadows becoming imperceptibly longer. Alba pushed her shoulders against the tree behind her and stretched out her back. If only these wise old elephants – as she regarded these lime trees which edged the drive to Kingsbourne Manor – could impart their wisdom and guide her in her thinking. However, they were still and silent; for the momentary breeze had dropped and there was nothing to even ripple their leaves. The limes went about their role without a word. They were living, breathing organisms and they hosted, within their branches, a whole ecosystem of birds and insects, from the majestic birds of prey down to the smallest of aphids feeding off the leaf sap. In their glorious silence, the trees left Alba to her own thoughts.

*

In time, Alba headed back to the manor.

As she came towards the front of the house, Anthony and Isabel were at their respective cars, with small suitcases, a briefcase and a make-up box on the gravel between them. They were once more in conversation with one another but they both were noticeably less tense than earlier over brunch; Isabel was definitely calmer than yesterday when Alba and Connie had presented her with the missing handbag, here beside her car. The relative composure of the two people before her gave Alba the confidence to speak to them as she came near.

"Afternoon. I wish you both a safe trip after the terrible, awful thing that happened here last night."

"Oh, neither of us is going," stated Anthony.

"But all your luggage is around you," observed Alba.

"Being unloaded," stated Anthony succinctly.

"We had both packed earlier. Clearly, over brunch you'll have gathered none of us had the desire to remain a moment longer. However, with John's suicide, it seems right we actually stay on for a bit. I think we could all do with some time to relax and unwind. So, we're taking our luggage back inside," said Anthony's sister.

'Relax and unwind' Alba felt was hardly the thing to say after finding your brother's body just a few hours before – something to do after a busy day at work or upon completion of a task you had not been looking forward to but as a way to describe a period of grieving, seemed somehow wrong. At least that was how Alba regarded it. However, as she had now learnt, the Sunday family were different. Alba opted to switch tack and asked:

"If you're talking of being able to relax, you must have found them?"

"Pardon?" said Anthony suddenly back on edge.

"The diamond earrings."

"Oh, Isabel's costume jewellery, you mean?" asserted Anthony.

To Alba though, his eyes betrayed the lie he was trying to maintain. As Alba studied him, she found herself agreeing, as much as she disliked his wife, with Johanna's assessment of her husband; of being a weak, rather timid man.

"No," Alba said with certainty. "The diamond ones. The ones you entrusted to Isabel – have you found them, then? Where were they, if I'm allowed to ask?"

"Sorry, Miss White, you seem all confused. As I said over brunch, Isabel was looking for some stage props which she had mislaid and–"

"Oh, Anthony. Let it go," interrupted his sister. "She was here with Connie when they gave me back my handbag that that thieving maid had rummaged through. Miss White knows what has gone, as does Connie."

"You said my daughter had handed back your handbag; you didn't say anything about this outsider also knowing! Who else knows? Who? Have you told anyone else? What if Johanna gets wind of all this? Isabel, what if this woman opposite us has been telling all and sundry?"

"Look, brother I haven't told anyone else. She was with Connie when they gave me my bag back; I couldn't do anything about that, could I?"

"And," added Alba, keen for her name not to be tarnished, "I haven't mentioned it to anyone else, either. So, I suggest you calm down and stop throwing out these wild accusations. Four of us know some valuable diamonds are missing – the two of you, myself and Connie. Just us four."

"And the maid who took them," added Isabel.

"If Sandy took them," corrected Alba, keen for no one, present or not, to be slandered.

"Of course she took them!" asserted Isabel. "I haven't lost them. I simply misplaced my handbag; it was found by the maid and my earrings are now gone. She put her hand in it no doubt, took them and then passed the bag itself to Connie. Thereafter, Connie passed it to me, here by my car."

"They are not lost," added Anthony. "Despite my innocent comments over brunch – they never just got lost. The pesky maid took them. We just have to find where she's hidden them. I haven't seen her leave the manor myself since Isabel told me the items were missing but of course we were all getting ready and then were at that farcical pub meal last night. So, maybe she did have an opportunity to slip out and move them on to someone. However, if she's an opportunistic thief – rather than a serial shoplifter or professional pickpocket – she's hardly going to have a handler to pass them over to straight away, is she? She'll have pocketed them on the spur of the moment, when having a rummage in sis's handbag, and now doesn't know what to do with them."

"So, she'll have stashed them somewhere," continued Isabel. "We just have to work out where she's hiding them – where does one cleverly hide a little material pouch no bigger than a match box?"

"You are assuming she took them," repeated Alba.

However, before either could reply, May strode across the gravel making her way to her own car. Her presence brought a halt to Anthony's and Isabel's accusations.

"Hello auntie and uncle," said May. She then acknowledged Alba's presence in less kindly tones:

"Oh, you're still here, are you?"

Alba chose not to reply but stayed for a moment longer as she was curious to hear May's reply to her uncle Anthony's question of whether May had decided to still go or stay on longer at the manor.

"No, I'll still head off later today. I'll go and chat with Henry for a bit before I go but I've places to go, people to see, you know. I'd prefer to be with like-minded people as I celebrate the summer solstice. Please don't get me wrong, what happened to uncle John is sad but I can't change what he did, can I? Mum and dad are now staying a day or two longer – dad will be down shortly to unpack his car as it seems you are both doing – but as for me, I'll still head off. Life goes on, doesn't it?"

With that, May unlocked her car and sat in her driver's seat to sort out the music she would listen to on her drive away from the manor. As she did so, Anthony and Isabel collected their final pieces of luggage from their cars.

Just as Alba was about to move away, the relative quietness was broken by a cry of despair emanating from May's car. All those present – Alba, Anthony and Isabel – watched as an irritated May stepped from her car, looked angrily at her uncle and then addressed him:

"Look at what he has done to my car again; just look at it!"

"At what?" asked Anthony.

"I can't see anything," added Isabel.

Nor could Alba, though she did wonder whether May had a flat tyre or a scratch on the side of the car that was out of view.

"Just look at it," May repeated. "Oh, he can be so, just so annoying at times!"

"Who?" enquired Anthony – still no wiser on anything.

"Henry, of course," snapped May. "Who do you think? Just because he hasn't come by car but by good old fashioned British Rail doesn't give him the right to play silly tricks with my car. Why does he think he has the right to play the fool? Really, though, that is no reason to do what he's clearly done. To do it once was bad enough but he's gone and done it again over my windscreen and he knows I'm out of screen wash; I told him as much when I drove him to the pub for last night's meal. Maybe he thought it was funny the first time – though he claimed no knowledge of what I told him off for – but to do it again, so soon, it's so, arrgghhh! He's just so irritating at times – why does he have to be the court jester? Ahh, I can't stand him at times. I love him as a cousin but, arrgh, he can be so childish at times. Today is hardly the day for silly tricks but that hasn't stopped dear Henry! Blast him. Do you think one of the gardeners will clean it off for me? I haven't got anything to clean it with, have I? I don't clean cars – I'm a traveller and a writer. I don't do menial work. Where's someone to clean it off? Uncle, go and find someone for me."

"Sorry, May, what has Henry done? I can't see anything amiss," said Anthony.

"Hurrmp," voiced May and the others noticed she suddenly had a knowing look about her. "Bet he hasn't just done my car again. He's probably done the lot of them."

May then proceeded to move from the far side of her car to study the windscreens of Isabel's and then Anthony's vehicles. 'Yep, yours as well,' they heard her say. She then walked the length of the whole line of expensive cars and the others observed her nodding with each one she passed. Once she had got to the far end, she returned and then studied her car once more, slowly shaking her head as she did so.

"It's my whole blessed car he's done. I thought it was just the windscreen but when you look properly, it's the whole flipping lot; windows, roof, bonnet, doors, headlights too, no doubt. So subtle but when you notice it, so annoying. I'd told him I was out of screen wash and yet he couldn't resist doing it again."

"What's he done, May?" asked Anthony once more as he came over and studied her car with her.

"Sit in and look out, uncle," said May.

As he did so, taking May's key in the process, Alba, in her curiosity, came nearer and stood right beside Isabel. Anthony then turned May's windscreen wipers on to clear what she was complaining about, which prompted an irritated response from her:

"No, uncle, don't do that! That has only made it worse – you've just smeared the whole windscreen now. As I keep saying, I'm out of the wash stuff which you need to clear it with. Henry, flipping Henry, knew that and he's gone and done it again. Uncle, go and get someone to come and clean it off; Henry ought to but I'll kick him if I see him again this afternoon."

"I still don't know what he's supposed to have done," said Isabel to Alba.

Alba stepped towards the nearest car in the line; cars that were all neatly parked under the lime trees at the front of the house. Alba studied it for a moment before returning to Isabel's side.

"I do," said Alba to the other woman. "Interesting, rather interesting. The rest of you, if I may be so blunt, in your fancy cars didn't notice or care to notice what has befallen them. As you set off for the 'Earl of Clarendon' last night, you each, no doubt, unconsciously used your wash-wipe facility and dealt with it, in terms of the windscreen at least. For May, though, if she's not able to clean the car's windscreen as she drives, I can understand her frustration."

Then, with an insight that perhaps only came from an encounter she had not so long ago had with a certain Officer Day, Alba added:

"It is important to always keep your car completely road worthy – even in the balmy month of June. That includes staying on top of the little things like brake lights working, having a foot pump in the boot and your engine fluids topped up. Yes, it would be wisest for her to clean her windows before she sets off; good visibility should never be taken for granted, especially if Anthony has now made it worse by smearing the windscreen."

"Just what has Henry done?" asked an irritated Isabel – for she was feeling left out as she still did not know what her nephew was alleged to have done.

"Henry?" reflected Alba. "He hasn't done anything."

"How do you know? May says he has; you're making no sense Miss White," asserted Isabel, as her irritation grew.

She then moved away from Alba's side and approached the other two. As she did so, Isabel asked May what it was Henry had done to all their cars.

"Oh, aunty, it's so annoying. It's like he has thrown sherbet powder over our cars. Perhaps he sprinkled sugar, does it matter what the substance was? Then with a water pistol or something he's sprayed the car to make it all turn into little spots of stickiness. Come and look up close and then look out from your driver's seat of your car and you'll realise he's done the same to yours as well. It's childlike on one level but when he knows I can't clean my windscreen..."

Alba, though, did not hear what May continued to say to her aunt and uncle. Alba chose instead to head back into the manor. As she entered, Alba wondered why May was so incapable of getting a sponge or a cloth and a bowl of water and cleaning her own car. Alba then thought, whilst trying not to feel too self-righteous, how sensible she had been to park where she had, beyond the others and where the work vehicles got put.

However, as she entered the manor, any air of insightfulness and foresightedness she felt was instantly shattered as Hugh approached her in the Hall.

CHAPTER 21

Let sleeping knights lie

"Ah, Miss White, how lovely to see you. I was just on my way to bring our luggage back in. We're staying on for a day or two; would be awfully insensitive to depart now, wouldn't it?"

Alba opted not to point out that his own daughter had decided to leave – Alba's silence allowed Hugh to continue:

"And you're still here; marvellous. You are staying as well, aren't you?" he enquired.

"I'm here for as long as Eleanor needs me, which I reckon will be until her parents arrive. I will be calling them shortly."

"Good, good," voiced Hugh. "Kind of you to care for her. Obviously, we are all looking out for her in her time of loss; we can all empathise as we've all lost someone we cared very deeply for. Of course, if you're feeling lonely yourself later, or sad, I'm happy to be there for you as well. We must stick together, mustn't we?"

"I'll be fine," stated Alba. "If you'll excuse me, I'll go and check on my friend."

To the departing figure, Hugh said:

"Well, if you want a caring arm round your shoulder, just come and…"

However, by then Alba was halfway up the stairs and not listening.

*

Eleanor stated she was fine to be left alone a while longer – Sandy had brought her a hot drink and a plate full of sandwiches, biscuits and fruit on a tray. Eleanor doubted she would eat any of it and they would all end up being left on the tray, which she would leave in the corridor for the maid to collect. Eleanor did add that probably Alba ought to make contact with her, Eleanor's, parents and inform them of what had happened. Further, if they could come to be with her, perhaps from the following day, that would be comforting.

*

Once Alba had spoken with Mr and Mrs Evans, she secured some further sandwiches for herself from Sandy – the roast chicken and stuffing, within the malted bread, were moreish had they not been so filling. Once eaten, Alba found herself once more drifting towards the billiard room.

The silence coming from the room told Alba it was 'safe' to enter. As much as she remained disgusted by him, Alba was curious to see if she could remember anything Hugh had, amongst all his unpleasantness, taught her with regards to playing the game itself.

She selected the slightly shorter cue, the one she had used last of all, placed the cue ball in the half-moon and took her stance – remembering to have the width of stance that she had, in a very intrusive way, been shown to take. She worked the cue smoothly, in the way she had also been unpleasantly shown, and struck the cue ball as she had been instructed.

Once again, whilst hardly a shot a professional would accept, the white ball did travel down the far end, strike the edge of the triangle of reds and make it almost as far back as the pink. Alba played for several more minutes and was thrilled to sink her first red – especially so, given it was the red she was aiming at and that it went into the pocket she intended. She almost, a while after that, made a break of eight. However, the black oscillated between the cushions at the very opening of the pocket and failed to drop.

Alba was far from in the 'zone' but the table, unlike on her first attempt a couple of days before, no longer felt oversized nor alien to her. The cue felt nicely balanced in her hand, whether she was playing a shot or simply walking the length of the table, and she could see angles and potential shots that she would have been blind to originally.

Then, even though she had sunk a further few individual reds and was 'progressing' through the frame, she had the urge to reset the whole table and break off again. She rested her cue – and somehow it did feel as if it were *her* cue and woe betide anyone coming in to the billiard room and taking it from her – upright against the fireplace and proceeded to arrange the twenty-two coloured balls accordingly.

In her moment of placing the final ball – for no significant reason the green – Anthony and Hugh entered.

"Ah, excellent, Miss White. You've got it all set up for a new frame. Just finishing, were you?" enquired Anthony.

"Or just beginning?" said Hugh, hopefully. "If you are, may we join you? Yes, yes, I know three is an odd number but given I keep thrashing my dear brother–"

"That's a bit extreme," decried Anthony.

"Brother, dear," stated Hugh, "when did you last get a frame off me? It's embarrassing how much money I'm taking off you – it really is. Money you haven't got and yet each time you still insist on playing for stakes."

"This time," said Anthony, "I'll beat you; I'm sure of it."

"You won't unless Miss White is willing to even things up," suggested Hugh.

He looked hopefully, expectantly at Alba, desperate for her to say yes. However, she stayed silent – which forced Anthony to enquire as to what his brother had in mind.

"I'll partner Miss White," suggested Hugh. "Miss White and myself against you, Anthony. Up for it? She and I will play alternative shots but I fear we will still beat you."

"I am far from flattered to be used as your handicap," stated Alba from where she was standing at the top end of the table.

"Miss White," replied Hugh as he approached her along the length of the table, "I am offended that you think I would *use* you. We would be partners. Equals, a team, joined at the hip. We, of course, would need to plan our shots and conspire together in hushed, close, intimate, conversation to keep Anthony from knowing our scheming. So, Miss White, would you care to enter the arena with me, to take battle to Anthony Sunday? We will, of course, share the winnings we will take from him."

"I think–" began Alba.

However, Hugh immediately interrupted:

"Oh, please don't worry about taking money from him even if he claims poverty at any given moment. I accept he has a wife who is soon to leave him, a son who's business is teetering and a daughter he now will be financially helping as she progresses through Oxford of all places but don't believe his claims–"

"Hugh!" protested his brother weakly.

Oblivious to the protest, Hugh continued:

"Of being cash strapped. That he might be currently but, Miss White, we need not fear taking money off him, not now. For Anthony is surely about to inherit a sizeable fortune from John. After all, John wasn't going to leave any to me; he reckoned I'd see it taken from me through some civil claim from one of these false accusations I keep enduring. Nor would John leave it to Isabel, believing it would simply be sunk into some second-rate theatre production. Remind me, what is the latest one Isabel has lost her head over? I can't remember, something like 'Woolly Jumpers', was it? No, that wasn't it – maybe the 'Butter Knives'?"

"That's not right," said Anthony, opting to join in his brother's rubbishing of their sister. "I think it was 'The Wooden Woman'."

"Very good, so apt," said Hugh with an unkind smirk. "Now why would someone cast our dear sister in the lead role about a wooden actress? I just can't possibly imagine."

"It was 'The Wootton Wives'," stated Alba, wishing, whether Isabel suddenly ventured into the billiard room or not, to bring an end to their unkindness.

"Oh yes," acknowledged Hugh. "Thank you; good of you to correct us. So?"

Alba just studied Hugh as he took a step closer but remained silent.

"So?" he repeated. "Will you be partnering me and sharing in the resultant untold riches we will comfortably take from my dear brother?"

"I think," said Alba with complete certainty in her voice, "I will leave you two to play without me. I will take my leave."

To reiterate her point, Alba moved away from both the table and Hugh and went to the fireplace to retrieve her cue in order that she could return it to the rack.

"I'll just put this back in the rack," she added. "Then you'll have the full armoury to choose from; I'll just clip it back in but," she said directly to Hugh, "absolutely no need to help me this time with the brass fittings. I have mastered them so you are not, as you see it, to assist me – clear?"

"Sadly, all too clear," conceded Hugh. "Still, if you want to have a frame later, perhaps?"

"I won't," replied Alba.

Once the cue was in the rack and Alba was making her way out of the room via the far side of the snooker table, the side furthest away from Hugh, the brothers went to select one each. They did, to Alba's strange relief, both ignore *her* one, the one Alba had just returned, and opted for two others instead.

"My turn to break," said Anthony.

Alba, to her surprise, turned to watch – 'just the opening shot,' she thought to herself. 'I'll stay just to see him break off.'

To Alba's hidden delight, Anthony's shot was poor. Whilst the white ball did strike the reds, which split, the cue ball stayed down the far end of the table amongst half a dozen newly released red balls. The white ball, even Alba felt, should have made its way further back up the table – up beyond the blue at least – to make Hugh have to think whether to play defensively or go for a riskier long pot. However, where Anthony had left the white, nestled amongst several spaced out reds, he had given Hugh numerous potable shots; red to black, red to the replaced black, red to the pink and those were shots and angles even Alba could now see. Alba reckoned for Hugh though, he could, as a good chess player also could, see several 'moves' beyond that. Before Alba had even left the room, indeed before Hugh had even come to the table, Alba knew Anthony had already lost his money he had wagered on that frame.

"Bloody cue," said an exasperated Anthony, as he stood up and looked at what he had left for Hugh to seize on, on the table.

"Aw, come now brother, a good workman never blames his tools."

"Well, I will," declared Anthony. "This cue is rubbish. The weight is all wrong – the butt is, oh, never mind. I'm changing before I play another shot with this piece of trash."

"Brother, for all I care, you can choose a different cue for every shot you play but this frame is very much mine now."

Hugh then turned to Alba who was still watching and spoke to her:

"See, Miss White. You should have joined me, you really should. Can you not see your prize money slipping through your very fingers as you stand there? You could have been quids in but you spurned my invitation. What a shame – for you and for me."

As the word 'me' came from his lips he bent over the table, paused for barely a moment to gauge his angles and then proceeded to sink his first red and leave the cue ball neatly on the black.

"Such a shame," he repeated but he made no further eye contact with Alba; his back was to her as she turned and departed the billiard room.

*

As she made her way to the top of the stairs, she encountered Alice and Johanna in conversation as they exited John's study.

As they left his private domain, Alba noticed they had both changed from the very casual attire they had been in over brunch – clothes relaxed enough for their respective journeys home – into more 'statement' outfits as they tested out their new positions within the family and amongst the manor's small group of staff. Johanna was wearing camel-coloured trousers, which went just short of her ankles. The trousers had a somewhat flouncy belt, in matching material, and which she had tied in a large bow to the front, just off-centre. She wore them with a sleeveless, antique white, top. Alice, by contrast, was more conservatively dressed in dark, tight-fitting trousers, and a light blue businesslike shirt with white buttons and white undersides to her cuffs.

Their conversation stopped as they noticed Alba.

"Ah, Miss White," said Alice. "I see you have opted to stay on, despite the tragedy – remaining as Eleanor's loyal friend. How kind – though of course we, John's actual family, are all here for her; you really do not need to stay if you don't want to remain. We can support Eleanor; she was, after all, so nearly one of us."

"So nearly," echoed Johanna. "Yet it would seem she was not destined to be part of the Sunday family, after all. Poor Eleanor."

"Yes, poor Eleanor," repeated Alice. "We haven't seen her since she discovered John's body. Er, how is she?"

"Broken, as you would expect," stated Alba. "Distraught and wishing to be alone; alone that is apart from myself checking on her every hour or so and Sandy taking in a steady supply of hot drinks and food on trays – food which Eleanor unsurprisingly leaves outside her room seemingly untouched. Could we expect her to be acting any different? How would you two feel if it were not John's body we had earlier discovered but someone else's; someone even closer to one of you?"

Alba was aware she was pushing the boundary of acceptable conversation on a day of such tragedy. However, she was curious – indeed most intrigued – as to how the two women opposite her would respond.

"I'd be heartbroken for May, had it been Hugh. She is very fond of her father," said Alice.

"Not a question I need to consider with regards to Anthony," reflected Johanna. "He wouldn't have had the guts to jump. For all John's greed and failings, at least he had the courage to step off the roof; whereas Anthony, well, my husband has no backbone. The only way he'd fall to his death would be if I were to push him. However," she added, after seeing the look on Alba's face, "I am not making a joke of what has happened today. It has been most upsetting; I suppose I'm just saying my husband would not have done what John felt the need to do. Of course, we will all miss John very much."

"I guess," said Alba, trying desperately not to sound sarcastic, even though that was exactly what she was being, "you two, sitting at his desk or browsing the bookshelves in his study, was your way of staying close to him in these painful moments when your grief is so raw."

"Well," Johanna responded, "we are all, in light of events, staying on at the manor for a few days. We are choosing to process our grief here to begin with and as one family."

"In his study itself, it would seem for some of you," observed Alba.

"Yes, in his study, Miss White. I'm not quite sure what you are inferring," challenged Alice.

"Nothing," stated Alba.

"But you are, aren't you?" said Johanna. "If you think we're up to no good, feel free to go in and have a look. Actually, we insist; that way you will be reassured that we haven't been ripping up floorboards, ransacking his collection of old books or taking a knife to the back of his leather chair in our quest for missing jewels."

Johanna moved back to the door to John's study and with a movement of her right hand, ushered Alba into the study – Johanna spoke as she did so:

"But, of course, you don't have to come in; I guess it's a matter of trust."

"Your choice, Miss White," said Alice. "Feel free to go in and prove we've been up to no good if you really think that is what two grieving relatives have been up to so soon after John's body was found."

Alba studied them both, looked into the study beyond the two women and decided to call their bluff; she entered the study. Alice and then Johanna followed Alba in.

"As you can see, Miss White, everything is intact. Your fears that we had burnt his books, damaged his furniture or pulled the panelling off the walls can be allayed," said Johanna as all three of them stood in the centre of the room.

For a moment Alba was silent and still. Alba deliberately chose neither to respond nor wander around the room. She was not seeking a verbal confrontation nor to be rushed as she made observations of things before her.

In time, she moved over to the bookshelves and once more, as she had done when she had been in there with Dr Sunday, she ran her fingers along the spines of the books. She stopped a couple of times; once her finger rested on one of John's own books and once on a book by the historian Alison Weir. It was obvious to Alba – almost embarrassingly too obvious – that someone, since John had last been in here, had lifted the books off the shelves, and in bundles of three, four, six or however many books, depending on how many they could grab at a time, had placed them on the floor or the desk. With their search of the bare shelving units completed, that someone had then swiftly replaced the books on the shelves. Alba felt that someone was almost certainly one or both of the women behind her. However, they had not put the books back in the same order. Books by Weir and Feiling were now on the same shelf as John's books on architecture and the works of Chaucer were now in between local history journals.

"Did you find what you were looking for?" asked Alba as she withdrew her hand from where it had been on the spine of 'The Canterbury Tales'.

"Pardon?" challenged Alice.

"Did you find what you came in for?" repeated Alba, as she turned to confront the other two. "It's just so amateurish. Successful in your fields you might be but really, this is childish."

Alice and Johanna looked at her in stunned silence.

"Look," continued Alba as she turned once more to the bookshelves. "If you're searching behind books, be it looking for missing engagement rings or confidential documents, at least put the books back in the order you took them off. You might have left it tidy to the untrained eye but there is no way John would keep Chaucer alongside these books – John would have the works of Geoffrey Chaucer alongside William Langland and Gower. At least, that was as he had them when I was in here on Thursday."

Alba duly rearranged where 'The Canterbury Tales' sat on the shelves – she wanted to rearrange many more but had to accept now was not the time. Nonetheless, she made a point of doing just one – and that one simply had to be Chaucer.

"Then, if you're making space on his desk as well," continued Alba, "as you undoubtedly laid out papers from his desk drawers, you must replace all the ornaments on his desk once you have put all of John's papers away. All of them, as opposed to leaving one on the windowsill as you have done, with his figurine of a sleeping knight.

Not just any sleeping knight, I might add, but a miniature of the stone effigy of Sir William Marshall which resides in the Temple Church in London. Sir William – the Earl Marshall as he was known – was loyal to the Crown and served four successive Kings; Henry II, Richard I, John and Henry III. He was one of the few, the very few, who could give Sir Winston Churchill a run for his money as the greatest Britain ever to have lived. As I say, your poking around in here was amateurish."

Confidently, Alba then proceeded to collect the stone miniature and return it to John's desk.

"Good job," said Alba to Alice, "that you're a tax and estate planning expert – as you angrily pointed out to Eleanor during our pub meal last night. I don't think you are suited to the world of criminal law."

"Alright, alright, miss know-it-all," said an embarrassed Alice. "We've been in and have had a look. We never technically said we hadn't, to be clear. May I remind you; you are a visitor here – to be blunt, no more than a friend of a friend. We are family. It is entirely appropriate we have come into John's study to search for things; papers need to be found when all is said and done. There is a time for mourning and there is a time for action, isn't that the saying?"

*

Alba knew that was a misquote. 'How odd,' thought Alba 'that saying had now come up twice in recent months'. Poignantly Alba remembered the funeral she had not so long ago been at; the service for Andrew's grandfather, Edward Chapman, the seventh Lord Hartfield. The Reverend Matthew Quinn had spoken on a passage from Ecclesiastes. Alba could remember the words he had read – still, maybe that was born out of Matthew always telling her never to take his word for what the good book said. It was, he always told her, for her to check it out for herself. Thus, after the funeral, Alba had gone home and checked out chapter three, verses one to eight and specifically verse four – the verse he had spoken most on. Verse four of that Old Testament book, Alba recalled, said there was a time for mourning and a time for dancing and not, as Alice had just claimed, a time for mourning and a time for work.

Alba recalled the minister had spoken on that passage because, apparently, Andrew's grandfather had danced in his youth. Indeed, it was his dancing at one of the many Balls in the Music Room at Hillstone Hall, his family home, which had caught the eye of a certain young Jane Trerose, and they were married shortly thereafter. Jane, of course, was Andrew's grandmother, and, to anyone other than Andrew, was more formally known as Lady Jane Hartfield.

It was a fine sermon Matthew had given. It had explored the fullness of a person's life and how God appoints different times for different experiences but that it was not wrong to remember the good times even during the bad times.

*

"It is correct," continued Alice – drawing Alba out of her private recollections as she did so – "that Johanna and I have been in here searching. As tragic as today's events have been, some of us need to keep our heads. It is entirely appropriate for us to be looking for a will, for insurance documents, for his address book."

"What happens," added Johanna, desperate to make herself sound all businesslike and professional, "if one of the staff suffers an injury this afternoon – who's responsible? What if there's a fire – have you thought of that? Or what if some of the garden machinery gets stolen tonight? Who now is the owner? Would we be allowed to contact the police to report a theft? So, who cares if we haven't put the blessed 'Cambridge Tales' back in the correct spot?"

"'The Canterbury Tales'", corrected Alba. "Chaucer's writings about a group of pilgrims travelling from Southwark to Thomas

Becket's shrine in Canterbury are hardly going to be called the 'Cambridge Tales'."

"Who cares what some dusty old book is called," snapped back Johanna and sounding, to Alba at least, just like her son Henry. "We – Alice and myself – need to know who is running Kingsbourne Manor now. Who, figuratively speaking, holds the keys. That is neither ghoulish nor wrong – there is an estate to be managed here. Simply sitting on her bed, as Eleanor is undoubtedly doing, is not helping anyone."

"Of course, Eleanor is in her bedroom," stated Alba. "Her husband to be has just died and it seems to me that you have conveniently already forgotten it was Eleanor who found his body. That she isn't running the length of the long landing screaming at the top of her voice is testament to her strength of character. Do you really expect her to be doing anything other than sitting by herself, weeping?"

"Weeping, perhaps," challenged back Alice. "Weeping over the fact that she will shortly be asked to leave the manor and leave this family. Why John ever fell for that creature, I'll never know but we will be shot of her soon."

"I am sorry," said Alba to them both. "I must leave you two. My friend is mourning the love of her life and all you care about is evicting her and finding the jewellery that you all believe John has got stashed away somewhere. You have no heart, no compassion and, on a practical and unimportant level, I doubt your amateurish attempts at searching will prove fruitful. Dr Sunday had a brilliant mind; so, if he has hidden anything from you, you will never find it. He was too clever for the lot of you. As I say, he had a first-rate mind; as does Eleanor. That is what they saw in each other. Their ages, or the difference in them which everyone else saw, didn't matter to them. Their minds were one and they would have been perfect for one another. Sadly, that can never now be proven to the lot of you."

As Alba reached the door to leave John's study, she turned and added to Johanna and Alice:

"I will be staying at the manor for as long as Eleanor needs and wants me. May I remind you, until you lay your hands on a will and can prove otherwise, it is entirely possible Eleanor is already the owner of Kingsbourne Manor. John may well have re-written his will once he had decided to ask her to marry him."

"Marry her?" challenged Alice. "A sham announcement during a meal in the village pub is hardly proof of anything."

"Nor was Eleanor proudly showing off any engagement ring – it must have been a sham," added Johanna.

"But if it wasn't, then jewellery is missing," stressed Alice. "A ring for starters and probably, given John's reaction to our accusations last night, plenty of other gemstones, too."

"Well, in your searching, don't forget to keep an eye out for Isabel's missing costume jewellery," said Alba. "Just *so* many things have gone astray, haven't they? Isabel would be rather pleased to have her props back."

"Well, of course, we will look for them. We are a family and we look out for one another; we stick together. We just have to work out where some jewels have been hidden and where others have been lost," responded Johanna.

"I will leave you to your searching and pondering on where your late brother-in-law would hide them and where your sister-in-law's earrings, in a small blush pink suede pouch, could have ended up."

With that Alba did depart – shutting the door on the two women as she did so.

*

Back on the long landing, Alba made her way along it towards Eleanor's bedroom. Alba went past the wall-hung tapestry and past the picture of the elderly man still sitting at his table, still gazing out of his window. She stopped and looked at Eleanor's favourite picture, which hung above the oak side table; a table on which rested a gold candlestick, one now covered in the melted wax from a burnt down red candle. She lost herself in the picture for a moment – a picture of a woman holding her lover's letter – and then Alba looked back at her favourite. She then reflected on the length of the landing itself, looked back towards the staircase and then once more at the tapestry, the furniture and then back to the candlestick itself. With its burnt down candle, it was as if it were trying to tell her that her time was up. She looked at the set wax which now coated it; it was as if it were conveying everything was now set in its new place and that if only she could see it, all would be illuminated.

'He did not jump,' mused Alba to herself. 'So, who was here with him after the pub meal? Where would she, Alba, hide one lot, maybe two lots, of valuable gemstones? One lot perhaps were hidden, stashed if you like, in haste, one lot – if there were a second lot – were cleverly hidden as the person had time to think it through.'

She looked at the picture once more, she picked at the red wax on the candlestick before her and then turned to go and knock on Eleanor's bedroom door. As she raised her hand, she glanced down at the tray Eleanor had left outside; a tray with an empty teacup and a plate of uneaten sandwiches, shortbread biscuits and an untouched apple and banana.

Alba bent down and selected a biscuit with a crest of a lion on it. As she did so, she stared at the things before her and she suddenly realised she knew where the diamond earrings were.

Mirroring how Eleanor was perhaps sitting in the room the other side of the door in front of her, Alba sat down on the floor, with her back against the wall, and pulled her knees up before her and wrapped her arms around them. 'If,' she thought, 'the earrings were where she now believed she had seen them, that connected two people in a way she had not really connected them before. If the other person were involved, how could she place that person at the scene? If only she could shed light on things.' In that moment, Alba felt she had as much chance of shedding light on things as the empty candlestick above her.

She studied the biscuit she had selected – why did the biscuits with the lions on them taste better than the crescent moon shaped ones? She further wondered whether she could glean any wisdom from the lion she held before her or, indeed, any wisdom from all those elephants outside – as she regarded the lime trees which graced the drive as being. She needed wisdom from somewhere. She needed to see something. 'No, not *see*', she thought, 'that was not what she meant. She needed to *connect* something. After all, had she not seen it all the time she had been here? From the moment from when she was thankful to arrive, had she not seen it all along? She just had to connect it with what else she now knew.'

Then she did.

She sighed – a long, sad sigh. She did not want it to be so but that is what the truth was now telling her. She sighed again.

Alba slowly, almost reluctantly got up. She knew she needed someone's help. Not just someone but a person she was not particularly fond of. However, she knew that person would have to be called on for her to establish what had happened to Dr Sunday.

She went – slowly, almost reluctantly – and knocked on the door in question.

CHAPTER 22

Alba has a novel idea

"Well, I wouldn't have noticed that the books had been put back in a different order," admitted the Reverend Matthew Quinn. "The shelves undoubtedly were regularly dusted – he had a number of house staff after all – so it wasn't that you noticed where a line of dust stopped or started. My shelves here at the vicarage are covered in dust, meaning if someone had come in and rearranged the books in my study, the dust might have been a tell-tale sign, but in Dr Sunday's study you actually noticed the arrangements of the books themselves. Alba, you really are one for detail."

"I'd have noticed the ornament being in a different place," claimed Sam. "I mean, if I'd been there over those few days and if he'd invited me into his study once I'd got to the manor, as he did with you, and I'd been chatting with him over his desk, I think, no, I'm sure I'd have noticed such an interesting ornament being somewhere else when 'invited' in by, er–"

"Alice and Johanna," offered up Alba to Samantha Rowan.

"Thanks, yes, that was their names – John's two sisters-in-law," said Sam.

"Me, too," insisted Matthew. "I'd have missed the books being all higgledy-piggledy but I'd have noticed the sleeping knight being out of place."

Andrew also nodded – indicating he was judging his own observational skills to be on a par with the minister's and Sam's.

"But please don't think I'm showing off in describing that bit of the story," insisted Alba. "I'm relaying how it was; how I saw it, that's all."

"No, no, Alba. Please don't worry yourself, I know that's not you – not your style at all," insisted Andrew.

With that, he took her left hand from her lap and pulled it up to his mouth and tenderly kissed the back of her hand before replacing it in her lap.

"You have an eye for detail."

"I guess but for me it was easy. I'd studied under Dr Sunday. I *knew* those books; whereas if I were, if I may use your home as an example Matthew, trying to establish if someone had been rummaging around your vicarage study, well, I wouldn't be able to tell if your Bible commentaries were put back in the correct order or not. Genesis over on the left, I'd assume, but after that I wouldn't know if Samuel came before or after Isaiah and then isn't there a Saul in the Old Testament and one in the New? And as for where the Psalms go, well, I give up! One version I've now got has them at the end and the one you gave me Matthew has them sort of in the middle. It's all so confusing."

"It is," agreed Matthew. "That the books are not in chronological order either, really doesn't help some people. For example, Job is placed after Esther but, if you had them in pure historical order, Job arguably should come before Joshua and probably part way through Genesis itself."

"As I say, confusing. Anyway, what I'm saying is," said Alba, returning to her original point, "that for me, John's books were easy to spot as being hastily replaced. Perhaps Alice and Johanna shoved them back onto the shelves as they heard me coming up the stairs

– suddenly desperate to make the room look untouched. I readily admit, however, that had John's academic interests been something so completely different to my own, well, perhaps I wouldn't have picked up on the fact that Alice and Johanna had been searching the bookshelves. I'd have noticed the sleeping knight, though. For sure."

"I think we all would," suggested Sam – which generated agreeing nods from the men in the room as well.

*

"Shall I make a fresh pot?" asked Matthew.

"Please," said Sam on behalf of all of them.

"Right you are. Now, I'm not one for home baking but I can offer some biscuits, if you'd like? Sorry, I should have brought some out to begin with. I've got shortbread and, I think, some oat crumbles and no doubt a pack of digestives."

"All, sorry, I mean most. Any bar the digestives for me, please," said Alba.

"Fair enough. The digestives tend to be for when Neale pops round for a chat; it's always good to see him."

"Oh, that reminds me," said Sam, "mum sent me here with a batch of her millionaire's shortbread. Sorry, I almost forgot; they're in my bag in the hall."

"Well, that trumps my humble offerings," admitted Matthew.

"The biscuits would have been nice," insisted Sam.

"But Mrs Rowan's homemade millionaire's shortbread–" started Andrew.

"Yes, yes, I totally agree," said Matthew.

"I'll get them whilst you're making the tea, reverend" suggested Sam – thrilled and humbled in equal measure that the others still valued her mother's baking prowess.

As the two of them departed, Andrew took Alba's hand once more and just held it as it rested on her lap. As they sat there together, in the lounge of the vicarage, they enjoyed – Alba especially so in light of her recent experience at Kingsbourne Manor – the peace of the moment. She valued it was just the two of them, comfortable by one another's side, and bothered by nothing more than the antics of a male blackbird on the parched lawn of the vicarage in its futile attempts to find a worm.

*

Alba had been home since Sunday afternoon. There were others now looking after Eleanor and Alba's duty was done. She had initially wondered whether to stay until the Monday but, as much as the food at the manor itself or as she could have enjoyed at the 'Earl of Clarendon' might have enticed her to stay another night, she wanted to get home.

Her desire to get home was driven by her awareness that there were people she needed to apologise to in her village and she knew that she had to do that in person; she wanted to return home as soon as things had been tied up at the manor and once they were, she did. Thankfully, her journey home had been as uneventful as the trip to Kingsbourne had been incident filled. There had been no last minute change of clothing due to a bird related incident, no 'quiet chat' with an officer of the law – a chat under the watchful eye of a random collection of passing motorists – and no village pub, where the locals played tricks on unsuspecting visitors. She had simply, apart from a fifteen minute break at Fleet services on the M3, driven home.

As she had sat at those motorway services, she was aware that, perhaps for the first time, she was keen to get home. Normally, she would sit there – in her car or at a table amongst the pine trees – sad to have left the west country behind her. Sad to have departed Cornwall and missing 'The Jupiter Hotel'. However, this time, she knew she just wanted to get home – actually, not home exactly but to Hillstone Hall and specifically to Andrew. To Alba, he was simply

Andrew, to those who did not know him, he was Andrew Chapman, 8th Lord Hartfield, Viscount and owner of Hillstone Hall.

She was not going to fall at his feet and prostrate herself. Nor were they going to fall into each other's arms and swamp one another with kisses – it was not a 'Hollywood' ending she was planning and, more significantly, it was just not her style. However, she was hoping to see Andrew; to apologise for how she had been treating him and to ask him not to give up on her.

Thankfully, he had been at home. He was neither out on the estate nor up in London at the request of someone in the Foreign and Commonwealth Office and he was delighted to see her. He had not even let her get past an initial apology before he said no more needed saying by her. He said he knew things would be different between them after his grandfather's death and he was neither offended nor disillusioned by the fact that their lives were now different. Andrew had even added that, if anything, he thought Alba was being too hard on herself and that he himself had wondered if he should have invested the time in her that she deserved. Not, he added, that she *needed* his attention, he knew she was too independent a woman for that, rather just making himself a bit more available to her.

They simply – after Andrew had wiped a solitary tear from Alba's right cheek – agreed to talk just a little bit more, to take time to walk the estate together when something needed checking on and even, from time to time, to make it along to the cricket on the village green on a Saturday afternoon and partake in one of Mrs Rowan's gloriously British afternoon teas; after all, and putting everything else aside, was not one of her Victoria sponge cakes to die for?

As they talked, Andrew had not even let Alba finish her apology concerning how bad she felt when she had not defended Andrew, on the occasion of her having been stopped by Constable Day on her way to Kingsbourne Manor. Alba was aware she had not stood up for his name; not defended Andrew when the policeman had suggested her boyfriend might get angry were she to be late meeting him or were she to have to admit to him she had been stopped by the police on the way. However, Andrew reassured Alba that there was nothing to apologise for; he believed that the policeman's generalisations were, even if unhelpful, not aimed at him, Andrew.

All in all, by the time Alba had made it to her own front door, a door lost behind the unpruned wisteria, a wave of exhaustion swept over her. She was tired from the journey but more so from her actual time away. She was also emotionally drained – albeit in a relieved, peaceful way – from her time with Andrew. A further wave swept over her as she put the key in the door and then as she made herself a pot of tea. She left it to brew in her mustard-yellow 'Denby' teapot but it went undrunk. It sat there untouched on her kitchen table; for she had gone up to her bedroom to open the sash window – to let some of the heat from the past few days out – and, having chosen to lie on her bed for just a moment whilst the tea brewed, promptly fell into a deep sleep.

*

"Right, here we are," announced the Reverend Matthew Quinn, as he re-entered the lounge of the vicarage.

Sam followed with an impressively piled up plate of her mother's famous home-made biscuits.

"Are those all for us?" asked Alba.

"We don't have to eat them all," commented Sam.

"But we might," conceded Matthew. "So," he continued as he sat himself down, reaching for his first piece of millionaire's shortbread as he did so, "one of them – Alice or Johanna – or both of them even, had pushed John off the roof the night before? Pushed him off in their anger that he had deprived them of an inheritance or in a desperate act as they frantically searched for a hidden hoard of jewels; jewels they now believed he had stashed somewhere within the manor. I imagine they confronted him once they were back from the pub, er, what was it called again?"

"The 'Earl of Clarendon'," said Alba.

"Right, yes. So, they confronted him once back at the manor, in a desire to take their share of an inheritance they believed was rightfully theirs. I guess they rushed into his study, found him out on that section of roof where he enjoyed marvelling at the night sky and there was a heated argument between them all. Then, when he maintained there were no such jewels or when he simply told them to go, they, in their anger, pushed him over – perhaps with a cry of 'if we can't have them, nor can you'."

"It's possible," agreed Alba.

"So was the fact he himself jumped out of heartbreak or loathing at the family he was bringing Eleanor into," said Andrew. "He could have taken his own life."

"Yes. To begin with, I felt he could have. I mean by that, that before I could prove otherwise, it was entirely possible he had ended his own life. In those first few hours after we discovered his body–"

"After Eleanor discovered his body," corrected Sam.

"Yes," agreed Alba. "We'll make a detective of you yet, Sam! In those first few hours, then, I was trying to tell myself it was a tragic suicide and I should not be trying to see a mystery or foul play in the comings and goings at Kingsbourne Manor."

"But ultimately you did," observed Andrew – as he reached and took his first piece of the shortbread. "What made you change your mind?"

"Well, I had no proof," said Alba. "I just felt, no not felt, knew he was not the type of man to end his life or, even if he were, to end it in that way. It was just too untidy and unordered. I know that's hardly scientific but I just couldn't shake my conviction that foul play was in fact behind his death."

"So, Alice and Johanna, or just one of them, pushed him as they frantically searched for his wealth – almost unimaginable wealth for one of those two women. For Alice, desperate as she was to build up her solicitor's practice and start moving in bigger legal circles, and for Johanna, keen to have the money to finance the lifestyle she desperately wanted but which her husband's African mines were no longer, if indeed they had ever been, financing," proposed Matthew.

"It was a theory I considered," said Alba. "Plausible, given their presence in John's study so soon after his death. I think they 'invited' me into the study, once I'd got to the top of the stairs, due to their self-confidence in their own abilities or, maybe as a poker player does, of calling my bluff. I don't think they thought I, as an outsider and as everyone had been making clear during my entire time there, would actually go in. Nor had they contemplated that I would then unmask their desperate attempts to find some gemstones. Catching them in the act, so to speak, did make me think they were involved."

Alba paused in order that she could take a bite of the 'queen of biscuits' which Andrew had placed on a small plate between the two of them.

"Just delightful," said Alba a moment later.

"Mum's good, isn't she?" said Sam.

"Absolutely. Still, back to Alice and Johanna," continued Alba, "could John's death have been a desperate act, driven by greed? Yet, that was a motive which applied to the whole family; no doubt the others were rummaging around as well in other parts of the house."

"All cut from the same cloth – wasn't that how one of the family themselves described them all?" said Matthew.

"Yes, it was. Connie made that observation to me as we walked back from the clootie tree. She–"

"May I just interrupt and say how pleased I was – relieved even – you didn't get involved in that pagan ritual," said Matthew softly.

Despite the softness of his voice, all those who heard him knew the seriousness of his words.

"It didn't feel comfortable and I didn't think you would have approved, Matthew," said Alba. "Still, back to what I was saying. Yes, they, to use the phrase, are all cut from the same cloth. Alice and Johanna, we've just considered. Hugh was involved in one too many litigations and civil court cases not to need greater financial security. Anthony was desperate to keep his mining company afloat–"

"Isabel had her acting career," contributed Andrew.

"Exactly," confirmed Alba. "Henry his newly opened surf school and May her travel writing. Or was it just travelling; I never was quite sure. If she were so passionate about the writing side of things, I found it odd she never showed me anything she had ever written. Yes, I did find that odd."

"And Connie?" asked Sam.

"Ah, yes, dear sweet Connie," considered Alba. "She was the enigma in all this – I never could quite work out who she was, so to speak. Young, definitely – she was only nineteen after all – yet, worldly wise and, as she also said, had grown up in a very disjointed and dysfunctional family. Yet, I never could deduce whether she was a good apple amongst a tray of bad ones or just one that looked good on the outside but was already rotting from the core out. So, her phrases, which she would throw out, such as 'cut from the same cloth' or 'empire building', I just never could decide what or how much was behind such comments, in terms of applying to her. Did she just enjoy the charade of making herself out to be as corrupted as the rest of them or was she just so ultra confident in her corrupted nature that she was baiting me by hiding in plain sight?"

"And then, and this is something I'm curious about," continued Andrew, "there is how Connie always seemed to be present at the critical moments."

"*Exactly,*" agreed Alba. She was happy for Andrew to continue whilst she took a sip of tea.

"She was, as you've told us, the one Sandy passed Isabel's handbag to. Connie took it once she, Sandy that is, had found it down the side of the piece of furniture in the dining room; meaning Connie had access to where the diamond earrings had been or still were being kept. Then, it was Connie who handed over the bag to her aunt when you encountered her by her car. What's to say Connie, rather than the maid, was the person who dipped a hand in the bag? Everyone in the house seemed to be of the opinion that the manor and everything in it was awash with hidden jewels – why not have a rummage in your aunt's bag as well? Put your hand in as you ever so nicely call out – 'Aunty, dear, we've found your missing handbag'."

"Yes," agreed Alba. "If she were a skilled pickpocket or even a good amateur card-sharp, she could easily have put a hand in without me noticing as we walked round the manor gardens. Equally, I wondered whether Connie, if she hadn't taken the earrings prior to giving her aunt her bag back, on hearing her aunt's anguished comments over missing jewels and seen her aunt tip the bag's contents over the car seat, found them as she, Connie, rummaged in her aunt's footwell and temptation consumed her in that moment of finding them and she slipped them into a pocket of her own before she stood up and announced 'sorry aunt, can't find them there either'. It's entirely possible, you see."

"Plus," continued Andrew, "it was Connie who brought out the covering from the snooker table to cover her uncle John's body. As she knelt and dutifully tucked it around the lifeless form, saying something like 'let's cover him up, you don't want to be staring at him now', maybe she was trying to take something from – or trying to return something to – his pockets. I just thought it was odd that she made a point of being around his body even though you, Alba, had asked everyone else to leave."

"Yes," agreed Alba. "Even in that initial moment of the tragedy, I thought, despite the seemingly kindness of the gesture, something was not quite right. Yes, Connie was ever present at the critical moments, wasn't she?"

"And she turned up by herself to the pub for the meal on the Friday evening, didn't she?" said Sam. "I wonder why?"

"I was conscious of that, too. So, it could so easily have been her; everyone had an opportunity to bump John off on Friday night, and that included Connie. I accept I could never quite discover a definitive motive for her but the amount of money the family believed to be sloshing around, would surely have tempted all but the noblest of people. I think," added Alba reflectively, "if I were writing a novel about what happened at Kingsbourne Manor, I would have Connie as my murderess – dear sweet young thing, hiding in the open, befriending the outsider and yet always present at the key moments with a warm smile on her face and kind words on her lips. Yes, I'd have her as my guilty party; the reader or the audience would be thrown at the end of the book or the play, that's for sure."

*

"But it wasn't her, or was it?" asked Sam.

"Well, I've given you all an account of my time away in Wiltshire. It was an intense time there, not helped by the fact that, on top of everything else, I was feeling guilty as to how I'd spoken or treated you all in the weeks and days before I left."

"You've already apologised," said Matthew. "To each of us. Please know we've already forgiven you as we undoubtedly did in the moment you, how shall I put it, snapped at us. It's fine – please let it go and stop beating yourself up over it. It's not an issue."

"Exactly," agreed Sam. "But gosh, reverend, I thought you were about to give us a mini sermon then! Maybe the line from the Lord's prayer – 'forgive us as we forgive' – or perhaps, now what was it that mum said you'd preached on recently? Something like, er, don't let the sun set on, er—"

"Very good, Sam, I am impressed. You're quoting Paul's letter to the Ephesians – he's the Saul of the New Testament, Alba, after he'd had a name change to Paul. He says in chapter four, verse twenty six 'In your anger do not sin: do not let the sun go down while you are still angry.' I am impressed, Sam; it looks like you've just given the rest of us a thought for the day."

"Well," said an embarrassed Sam, "be impressed with mum, not me; I'm just relaying what mum has stuck on our kitchen fridge – she's decided it's going to be her verse for the next few weeks. So, I see it every morning, noon and night! I can hardly fail to remember it."

"So, let any guilt, go, Alba," reiterated Andrew. "It's gone, done, dusted, OK?"

Alba nodded – it was an embarrassed, soft nod of her head but she felt a weight lift from her as she did so.

"Good," said Andrew simply. "Right, back to what you were saying, that you've given us an account of your time away."

"Right, yes. I've given you a narrative, if you like, of my time in Kingsbourne. Some of you are now thinking Connie was involved. I have neither assented to nor rejected that assessment because I'm curious you haven't picked up on one or two other things that happened there or that I have described. Gosh," said Alba with a big smile on her face, "there's one thing I feel I've mentioned a dozen times and not one of you have said 'oh, hold on a minute, could that be significant?'. So, if it is Connie – but I'm not saying aye or nay to her as the guilty party for the moment – I want you to conclude it's her for the right reasons. As I keep saying, everyone had motive, everyone had opportunity but I'm hoping you can, with all I've relayed to you, establish who it was by making the right connections. I know who it was, to be clear. I've seen, if you like, where the fingerprints were left. I accept you haven't but I've given you all you need and I will answer all your questions and explain anything you ask about the goings on at Kingsbourne Manor. I'm not trying to string you along for the sake of it."

"No, no. We get that," said Andrew. "I'm rather enjoying the puzzle."

"And our time together," added Matthew. "Another piece of millionaire's shortbread, Andrew?"

"Absolutely," replied Andrew, as he reached across to what the vicar was holding out to him.

"Hold on," said Matthew as he placed the plate down. "We've

spoken of the books and the ornament but what of the picture! You kept mentioning the picture in Dr Sunday's study."

"Yes, yes," added Sam. "A drawing; a pencil drawing, wasn't it? A framed image of a Queen, didn't you say, Alba?"

*

"Very good," said Alba. "Henry III's queen, to be precise; Eleanor of Provence. Devoted to her husband and Edward I was their son."

"Tell us you had a look behind the picture, Alba!" insisted Andrew. "If not, I think I'll drive straight over to Wiltshire myself to take a peek. A woman's face staring down on him but looking down on him from behind. Behind! If he were so taken with the beauty of the picture, because he liked the artist or admired the Queen herself, wouldn't he have had it in front of him, not behind? A picture he never really gets to look at, because it was out of his eyeline – out of sight apart from when you walk to your desk – can't be that brilliant a picture, can it? Plus, given he was a man surrounded by his books, from when you first described his study, I felt it was odd that he'd removed two or three shelves to have nothing more than a picture in the space. So, did you have a glance behind it? Please tell us you did!"

Alba nodded.

"Thank goodness," added Matthew, "otherwise I think we were all about to make our way to Kingsbourne."

"And?" prompted Sam.

"A little wooden door."

"A door!" said an excited Sam.

"A cubby hole, if you like," said Alba. "Neither a priest's hole nor a safe, just a little discrete cupboard, the small door being no more than, say, ten inches by twelve. I sensed it would have been where previous owners might have kept their favourite book."

"Maybe a book of the psalms or some daily devotional. Given the age of Kingsbourne Manor, I'm imagining something akin to Anne Boleyn's 'Book of Hours'?" suggested Matthew.

"Perhaps. Or a diary – something treasured by the owner, cherished if you like, but without real material value. So, no need for a safe to keep such an item or items in but a secure space so you knew where whatever it was, was. Well done for picking up on the possibility that there was something behind the picture," said Alba.

"I was rather hoping there'd be a will or something," reflected Andrew.

"Or a bag of sparkling jewels," suggested Sam. "There could have been, though, couldn't there? Maybe Alice and Johanna got there before you had a look and took the valuable stuff out."

"Perhaps but I sense not. I mean, I'm sure they had a look but when I looked later in the day, the little space was filled with a draft of Dr Sunday's next book, that he was shortly to publish. He was using the space as previous owners of the manor had used it – to store something of importance to him but without value to someone rummaging around, someone up to no good. The jewels weren't there, though."

"There were jewels, then!" decried Sam. "I knew it!"

"Oh, yes – there were jewels; plenty of them. You've still all got to find the missing earrings, haven't you! To be clear, they were the real deal. Despite Anthony's feeble protestations at one stage that they were his sister's stage props – nothing more than costume jewellery – they were genuine diamonds. When I found them, gosh, they were something like you'd see in a jeweller's shop in London's Old Bond Street. When you held them up, the light just sparkled through them and there were plenty of good sized stones in each piece. With hindsight, and this is the only thing that impressed me about Anthony, was that he wasn't more agitated and panicked by their going missing than he was," said Alba. "They were stunning and unbelievably expensive; I'm amazed he kept himself together at all."

"He wouldn't have taken them himself," surmised Andrew. "I

can't see any logic in 'stealing' from himself. They weren't insured – he couldn't insure them if they were 'secret' from Johanna, his wife. Kept from her as he didn't want to lose half their value when she divorced him – a split which everyone around the manor seemed to believe would not have been too long in coming. So, they were his nest egg but uninsurable and for that reason I can't, just can't, see Anthony being behind their disappearance."

"Correct," agreed Alba.

"So, then comes Isabel," continued Andrew. "She consistently said it was the maid but Connie thought Isabel herself could have kept them. However, if we're now doubting Connie's integrity, I fear I'm about to go round in circles – blow, I'm not sure if I know anything any more!"

"What we do know," said Sam, "is that Alba just said she found them; not that she came across them rather that she *found* them. That, to me, at least suggests someone had hidden them as opposed to the possibility that they'd just dropped onto a carpet and got overlooked. If they were hidden, someone deliberately took them but I'm stuck, as Andrew is stuck, as to who took them."

"Perhaps you'd do better to focus on working out where I found them. If you can do that, you'll massively narrow it and the whole tragedy, down. Where would you hide a small blush pink, suede pouch? I have told you, I might point out, as I described my time away; I have most definitely described my having seen them *after* they were taken."

Yet Andrew, Sam and Matthew looked blankly at each other and then back to Alba. Eventually, Matthew said he would go and make a third pot of tea and would return shortly.

*

Upon the minister's reappearance and as he placed the tea tray down, Alba, not wishing to string the others along any further, simply said:

"Useful things trays, aren't they? It is always curious what people keep on them. Equally, who hasn't played that Christmas game where a tray full of items is brought out, you get to observe it for a few seconds and then it's covered up and you have to remember what's on it? We've all played it."

"Er, yes," came their collective reply.

"So, a tray, you see, is plenty big enough to leave a small, material bag on, don't you think? Now, of course, a bag no bigger than an audio cassette, arguably a bit bigger than a matchbox, would be entirely obvious if it were there all by itself. You'd remember it – you'd never play the Christmas game with one solitary item on the tray, would you? Yet, the game works because the tray is cluttered; one item becomes almost invisible when nestled amongst numerous other items. Even more so when it's there amongst similar sized bags and other bits and bobs on the tray. Thus, a small pink cloth bag would be easily missed – even when it was the only one that colour present – when nestled amongst others which were black, dull greens and one or two luminous yellow. What was one random pink bag amongst the variety of colours?"

"A tray in the dining room? There were serving platters in there but you never described trays as such," mused Matthew.

"There'd have been trays in the kitchen," stated Sam.

"No doubt," agreed Alba. "However, I've never described the kitchen to you, so they weren't in there. To help you out, only the pink pouch had diamond earrings in, the other small bags in the tray had car keys in or locking wheel nuts and, as I originally described, some items in the tray were simply keys on keyrings or entirely loose keys."

"Car keys," said a surprised Sam. "A tray by the manor's front door, where everyone left their keys, perhaps?"

"No," said Andrew, with a knowing smile having worked it out. "Firstly, I doubt the Sunday family would trust one another with their expensive vehicles; meaning they would not leave their keys on a collective tray in the hall or lobby area. Secondly, I think we'll find that Alba found the missing little pink bag in the tray in the reception-come-shop area of 'Kingsbourne Cars and Motorbikes'. There was a tray in there, wasn't there Alba? You described it to us, didn't you? How on the Saturday morning, before Dr Sunday's body was discovered, you took your car to the village garage to have your brake light replaced. Once Eddie had done it, you said you returned to the reception area to pay your bill and Ash was in there – in there sorting through a tray of keys and little pouched bags, bags we all assumed contained further car keys or the other half of people's locking wheel nuts. You did describe it to us and we all ignored its significance, didn't we?"

"Yes," agreed Alba. "As I did originally, I might add. Why think there was anything else in one of those seemingly random bags. It was simply the village garage. People take their cars or motorbikes in to be serviced and have their MOT tests done. Equally, Eddie and Ash have a few cars and bikes for sale, so there are always a good number of keys lying there, as in any village garage. At 'Kingsbourne Cars and Motorbikes', it was that they were lying around in a tidy way, in a tray in the garage reception area. No doubt, each evening, they dutifully put the whole thing in a locked cabinet. Why would anyone think to look for an unimaginably expensive pair of diamond earrings in such a place? They were a young start-up business, one that literally put grease under their fingernails. They serviced your run-of the-mill cars and had a few second-hand models for sale. They were hardly trading top of the range luxury cars, were they? A few old 'Fords', 'Vauxhalls' and a 'Toyota' for sale and four or five bikes – including a Fireblade."

Three blank faces stared back at her.

"It's a motorbike," explained Alba. "The one I liked the look of."

Alba was about to add that she liked it because it looked fast. However, she remembered that that was the type of comment Eddie advised her not to come out with if she wished to develop her knowledge of bikes. Thus, Alba simply added:

"But you'd need to be an experienced rider to have one of those. Anyway, the jewels were perfectly safe in the tray in the garage's reception area; safe until the person who had them could work out what to do with them, longer term. Who would think to look in such a place?"

"Not me," said Sam – which generated consenting nods from Andrew and Matthew.

"Nor me," added Alba. "At least not until I worked out where they were. Once I had, I went back to the garage late Saturday afternoon. Thankfully I got back just before they closed and I found the earrings as I waited in the reception area whilst I got Eddie to sort out my brake light."

"But Eddie had done it that morning," insisted Andrew. "In the morning – before the body was discovered – and he no doubt checked your brake light worked before you left the garage. It would have been working, I'm sure of it."

"Yes, it was," agreed Alba. "He's a good mechanic and it was no trouble for him to sort it out."

"So, why go back in the afternoon? Why ask him to replace it again if it were working?" puzzled Matthew.

"It wasn't working when I took it back – I made sure of that," stated Alba. "I needed a fault with my car, in order that I had an excuse to take it back and insist – in a grumpy tone, a tone I realise I can 'do' at times – they sort it out there and then whilst I waited in the reception area by myself. I needed to keep the mechanics out of the way whilst I had a rummage in the reception area, you see."

"Not really," said Matthew.

"Who did you get to deliberately tamper with your car?" asked Andrew. "You don't know a thing about them, meaning it couldn't have been you by yourself. In that moment you needed an ally. So, who?"

"Yet neither of the mechanics, er–" started Sam.

"Eddie and Ash," confirmed Alba.

"Yes, Eddie and Ash," acknowledged Sam. "Neither of them had been at the manor during your time there."

"Ah," expressed Alba. "That's not strictly true."

"But you never mentioned seeing them," said Andrew. "Bit naughty of you to hold that back from us and still expect us to work everything out."

"I haven't held anything back," insisted Alba.

"I know," said Andrew. "I was only teasing but that doesn't mean I'm not puzzled."

"To be clear," insisted Alba, "I didn't see either Eddie or Ash at the manor, either. However, I realised one of them had been there – as you could have worked out, for I've told you numerous times what gave him away."

"So, one of them went to the manor that Friday night to murder Dr Sunday," continued Andrew.

"No," said Alba.

"No?" questioned Andrew.

"No," confirmed Alba. "Neither Eddie nor Ash went to the manor to murder Dr Sunday for the earrings."

"Well," reflected Andrew, "I mean, that sort of makes sense. For the earrings weren't Dr Sunday's and they had gone missing before Friday evening. If I'm correct, I'm not aware Dr Sunday even knew anything about Anthony's missing jewels. Now, if Isabel or Anthony had been found dead, that would make more sense."

"Nothing makes sense," added Sam. "I feel I'm getting more confused!"

"Not a lot was making sense to me, either," agreed Alba. "Probably best I explain. Explain how an incredibly expensive pair of earrings came to be in the village garage, why I got someone to tamper with my own car–"

"Who?" asked Matthew.

"Henry," stated Alba.

"Henry! But he was rude to you, offish and the person who played tricks on people," said Sam.

"I thought that was Ash who played tricks," said Andrew. "Wasn't he the one sprinkling bags of sugar over Eddie's car and May's car? Though what links May and Ash is beyond me, other than being similar in age – at least I think they're of similar age. Did May take the diamonds, pass them to Ash and then he came back greedy for more wealth? Yet, if they're a pair of jewel thieves, why was he going round annoying people by covering their vehicles in sugar and then soaking them to make it all sticky?"

"He didn't – no one did," said Alba. "No one had been to the shops in Pewsey or raided the kitchen at the manor to steal a bag of sugar. No trick – be it by Henry or Ash – had been played on anyone during my time there that involved a bag of sugar. How do I know? Let's just say some wise old elephants told me."

CHAPTER 23

Like manna from heaven

"An elephant?" asked Matthew.

"A herd of them," stated Alba.

"Have you had too much summer sun?" asked Sam.

"No and I'm also completely *compos mentis*," insisted Alba.

"So, you're telling us, numerous cars were covered in some sticky substance – a substance I reckon must be sugar as, for the life of me, I can't think what else it would be – and yet it wasn't there as a result of a trick someone played," summarised Matthew.

"How does sugar just fall out of the sky?" questioned Sam.

"Well, I know," said Andrew, "towards the end of the second world war in Europe, Bomber Command carried out 'Operation Manna'. Grandad–"

With that, though, Andrew fell silent and looked away from the others into a far corner of the vicarage lounge. No one rushed him; their unfolding conversation had brought him back to his recent family bereavement and they knew he needed a moment to compose himself.

"Sorry–" started Andrew.

"Don't be daft," said Alba.

This time, it was she who took his hand and held it.

"If you want to talk some more about him, please do," offered Matthew.

"It's fine. I mean, I'm fine," insisted Andrew.

"Well, the vicarage door is always open, if you wanted a chat another time," said Matthew.

"Thank you," said Andrew. "Perhaps. Anyway, where was I?"

"Operation Manna," said Alba.

"Ah, yes. Grandad told me about that – his work in military intelligence touched on that episode. He told me how information was coming through to the allies that the Dutch civilians in the still German controlled areas of the western part of the Netherlands were starving – starving, not just hungry but genuinely without food. As a result, even though the war was still going on, the Royal Air Force's Bomber Command flew mercy flights and dropped several thousand tonnes of food supplies to the Dutch."

"How fascinating; an entirely appropriate name for the operation, too," reflected Matthew.

"Well, yes," agreed Andrew. "And it must have been surreal for the RAF ground crews to be filling the bomb bays of Avro Lancasters with food parcels rather than explosives. Grandad said there must have been a few poignant smiles amongst those hard-working ground crews. Probably a few ironic smiles, as well, given the fact that the four thousand pound bombs that they had been loading into the bays for months, no doubt years, were colloquially called *cookies*; it must have seemed bizarre to actually be loading biscuits into the planes' bomb bays. So, biscuits, tea, flour, a whole variety of foodstuffs, including, perhaps, the odd small bag of sugar. That was Operation Manna but back to the present day; are we finding ourselves saying that some random aircraft flew over Kingsbourne – both the manor and the village garage – and was depositing open bags of sugar onto people's cars. If that's what we're claiming happened, I think the summer sun has got to us rather than to Alba. Yet, I can't see how else such a substance got onto people's vehicles. More than that, I can't see what the significance of it is. Yet it must be significant, though, for it was something Alba realised was the key to unravelling the mystery."

He then turned and spoke, not to everyone but to Alba. He addressed her on behalf of himself, Sam and Matthew as he said:

"Please tell us."

Three expectant pairs of eyes concentrated on Alba.

"It wasn't sugar but you're right, Andrew, that it did fall from above," said Alba.

"You're kidding! A plane – perhaps a light aircraft – was depositing a sticky liquid," said Andrew.

"You mentioned watching birds of prey circling overhead," added Matthew, "but not people in planes dropping stuff from above. If they were dropping stuff, I guess it's possible to hit a car parked by the village garage but I'm surprised they were able to land whatever substance it was on the line of cars parked at the manor; impressed, actually, because you have kept describing them as being parked under the trees all the time. That said, maybe impressed is not the right word because I'm not quite sure who we're talking about or what they were actually doing; still amazed that they got enough of the stuff on the cars to repeatedly annoy May."

"Did you get it on your car, Alba?" asked Sam suddenly. "Did you? I ask because it's suddenly struck me that you told us that you didn't park with the others at the manor; you said you parked beyond the trees that graced the drive and then bordered the front of the house. You told us you left your car where the works vehicles were stored and where garden supplies, such as stone for the restoration of the ha-ha were stockpiled; that's where your vehicle was, wasn't it? You didn't just park it there to be different, to make it clear you were not family or even because that's where you felt at 'home', so to speak, from your days as a volunteer gardener at Hillstone Hall – parking with the workers, as it were. You parked where you did at Kingsbourne Manor – beyond the trees – because you knew something was going to happen to the other cars, didn't you?"

"How could you foresee a light aircraft dropping a gloopy liquid from above? That's almost miraculous!" said Matthew.

"Oh, Sam and Matthew, you're so very very close," said Alba. "To be clear there was no aircraft involved. There was neither the Lancaster from the Battle of Britain Memorial Flight – practising for an air show that wanted to mark the sixtieth anniversary of Operation Manna – nor a light aircraft from the nearby airfield of Thruxton engaged in some silly stunt. Sam, though, you're absolutely right; I deliberately parked away from everyone else. That was because I did not want to get it all over my car as well."

"You knew what was going to happen, then? From the moment you turned up on the Wednesday, you knew!" said Andrew – conveying both his own confusion and how impressed with Alba he was.

"Of course," she replied. "I like my little car – whatever Eddie thought about it. Why would I park under a row of common lime trees in summer? It just leaves your car covered in those tiny sticky patches – the ones May found so frustrating. To be fair to the trees themselves – those wise old elephants – it's not their doing, as such. It's not tree sap they are weeping through wounds in the bark – we're not talking Canadian maples, here – nor trees blighted by bacterial canker. Rather what is going on, as it does with every common lime tree at this time of year, is that tiny insects, little aphids, are feeding off the leaves and the partly digested leaf sap drips onto whatever is below. For all their wealth, hoped-for wealth and prestigious careers, not one of the Sunday family knew to avoid parking under the lime trees. For me though, I would always look for somewhere else to leave my car – parking in the works area at Kingsbourne Manor was entirely logical for me as I know my trees. It wasn't that I was trying to stand apart or present myself as an 'outsider' – I tried so hard to engage with John's family whilst I was there. It was simply I didn't want to have to wash my car once I got home. Why park under a lime in June when you can park thirty yards away? I did try to explain to Sandy, the maid, when I first arrived – explain why I had parked apart from the others – but then Eleanor appeared and the conversation went in a different direction."

"Sap from the leaves!" reflected Andrew. "Well, I'll be–"

"It's the aphids which are the issue," insisted Alba. "Not that I'd advocate spraying the trees – I'd prefer sap to chemicals falling onto my car – but, for me at least, something easily avoided."

"So, that explains why May was annoyed. Yet, what's the relevance of Eddie's car suffering the same fate? Other than this being an interesting gardeners' question and answer session, what's the connection to Eddie's car and, more fundamentally, to Dr Sunday falling off the roof of his manor?" asked Matthew.

"Exactly!" replied Alba. "Exactly. Everyone staying at the manor had an opportunity to push him off his own roof and yet, in that moment on Saturday afternoon as I listened to May complaining about the tricks she was convinced Henry had been playing on her during their time at the manor–"

"Tricks he always denied, you said," added Andrew.

"Yes, because he hadn't played any, had he? It was where the cars were parked, nothing more, nothing less. Still, as I listened to May's assertions that her cousin was up to his childish tricks, I realised that not only was May slandering Henry's name but, more significantly, it placed another vehicle at the manor. It placed Eddie's car at Kingsbourne Manor."

"Assuming it was the same thing that had happened to his car – the leaf sap and aphids and all that – doesn't that simply tell us, that he, like me, I might add, doesn't know his trees very well," mused Matthew. "We can deduce he also parked under a lime tree but I don't see how you can be any more precise than that – specifically, how you can place him precisely at the manor?"

"To be pedantic, your honour," said Alba, feigning a courtly air, "I have stated it places his car at the manor."

"How?" asked Andrew. "There are lime trees all over the country. We've got several in the village and plenty on the estate here. It doesn't place his car at one particular spot on a given day, does it!"

However, he looked at Alba as he finished speaking and saw the look in her eyes, which prompted him to add:

"You're going to tell me, tell us, that it does, aren't you? You, my dear Alba, can link Eddie's vehicle to being at the manor during your time there – no doubt to the very time your former university tutor fell to his death."

"Yes," said Alba simply.

*

"Four seemingly insignificant details combined in my head that prove – well, prove to me at least – that his vehicle was present at the manor on that critical Friday night."

She paused to take a sip of tea.

Then, once she had placed the cup and saucer back down on the table before her, she continued:

"First, you will recall that when I turned up at 'Kingsbourne Cars and Motorbikes' on Saturday morning to get my brake light fixed, Eddie was washing his car."

"Yes," said Sam, "and you were worried he would soak you with his hose as he turned round."

"Oh, completely but thankfully he didn't. Still, log the fact that he was washing his car. Note also that when Ash turned up a bit later, Ash commented that Eddie was washing his car again. *Again*, Ash said, for he claimed Eddie had only done it the day before – that was the second insignificant detail. Third, was that Eddie himself acknowledged he was washing it again as it was covered in something like sugar, for it was all sticky to the touch; he even accused Ash of foul play."

"Which Ash denied," recalled Matthew. "Insisting he hadn't gone to the shops the night before and bought a bag of sugar and sprinkled it all over Eddie's car."

"Said he went to the cinema," added Sam. "However, he couldn't recall the ending of the film as he fell asleep – well, so he claimed."

"Well, whether he fell asleep or not," considered Andrew, "we can excuse him from playing the same trick on Eddie that May accused Henry of playing on her – if we attribute it to the leaf sap coming from the lime trees. Yet, how does that place him at the manor? That's a very precise location."

"It is," agreed Alba. "However, if you recall that in the village of Kingsbourne, the common limes themselves only grew in a certain location. This is the fourth seemingly insignificant detail. They only grew along the drive to the manor and bordering the parking area to the front of the house itself. Remember a previous owner of the manor had removed all the other limes from the village – mostly through threats and coercion. In his desire to have the approach to his home as a bold horticultural statement, he had orchestrated the removal of all the other lime trees from round about. In the village of Kingsbourne, the only place you could get leaf sap on a vehicle was at the manor itself; not only was the village devoid of a memorial cross, it was also devoid of lime trees growing anywhere apart from in front of Kingsbourne Manor. The car – Eddie's car – just had to be there. Furthermore, if he'd washed it on the Friday and then again on the Saturday morning, it had to be there on the Friday; specifically the Friday night, for he didn't turn up whilst we were playing kubb earlier in the day, nor when Connie and myself were looking for Isabel to return her handbag, nor when we were all, with Connie being the last, heading off for the meal at the 'Earl of Clarendon'. Plus, what compelled him to visit the manor hadn't yet materialised. That sad trigger had still to occur."

"I guess that was someone smuggling out the diamond earring from the manor. My money would be on the maid or Connie–" began Andrew.

"Or Isabel herself," added Sam.

"Oh, yes, the actress playing the victim," said Andrew. "So, maybe Isabel, well, one of them, took the diamond earrings to Ash. He then got greedy for more – perhaps he'd got wind that there were claims other jewels were sloshing around the manor – and went back in his mate's car. Once parked up, he headed for the study, perhaps because the maid or whoever had told him that there was a hidden compartment behind a picture, and was confronted by Dr Sunday as he searched."

He got an agreeing nod from Sam and his summation of events at Kingsbourne Manor were agreed with by Matthew – though Matthew added:

"Yes. I agree, Andrew. However, I am conscious we're working from a lot of circumstantial evidence. The only hard facts, so to speak, were literally washed away by his friend and business partner, when Eddie washed his car on the Saturday morning. It's a shame we don't have any hard facts – that classic set of fingerprints, so to speak. Still, I agree with you all, that Ash, not satisfied with the diamond earrings, went hunting for more. We know he missed the end of the film – meaning he had opportunity – and he, though Eddie too, I seem to recall, had had a few run-ins with the police over the years; suggesting Ash might well have had a few handlers he knew he could pass things on to. So, all in all, then, we're agreed, it was Ash."

Andrew and Sam nodded their agreement. Having got it, Matthew added a further thought:

"Ash then! I thought so. However, I'm conscious I'm a man of the cloth and, to be clear, I wouldn't want it to be anyone. Still, if it were anyone, I was rather hoping it would be one of the family. To my mind at least, they always seemed to be the darker characters in this sad tale, a tale which Alba has been elegantly recounting to us. It's a shame you identified it was Ash, Alba."

"I didn't," she responded.

*

"But he missed the end of the film," said Matthew.

"Because he fell asleep," insisted Alba.

"Really? Alba I'm surprised at your naivety," offered back Matthew.

"He said he fell asleep – surely you've had people fall asleep during one of your sermons, Matthew?"

"Well, yes. Not too many, I might stress in my defence. If you can't preach a good sermon of three points in twenty minutes, twenty two at tops, it probably isn't a good sermon. A waffly introduction doesn't help anyone – set the context, explain who the first hearers of the passage were and then move on to how we should be applying it in our lives. But, yes, I accept, even working to those guidelines, people have been known to nod off and miss the end of one of my talks."

"So, it wasn't Ash for he said he was at the cinema but fell asleep," reiterated Alba.

"Possible–" began Andrew.

"Yes, possible," agreed Alba. "Still, rest assured, I would always wish to corroborate something like that. I haven't, Matthew, rest assured, gone dopey now I'm well past being bean straw and winter forage."

"Sorry," said Sam. "I know it isn't key to the mystery but what do you mean by that saying? It's–"

"Oh, sorry, Sam. Yes, I should have said. It's a line from one of Geoffrey Chaucer's 'Canterbury Tales'. It's a line from 'The Merchant's Tale'; the character is telling his listeners that he seeks a wife who is young – preferably under twenty – and that an older woman, especially one who has reached thirty, is, to him at least, no more than the leftovers from the harvest."

A look of shock on the faces of those around her, prompted Alba to explain:

"Chaucer was writing in a different time – the fourteenth century - and his character, not him *per* se, regarded a woman over thirty as old. In a way, with the harshness of life as it was then, perhaps, thirty was old. So, the teller of 'The Merchant's Tale' described any woman reaching that age of being winter forage and the dried leftovers from the broad bean harvest. I'm two years past being bean straw, I might add."

"Hardly," insisted Andrew. "You are in your prime!"

"Thank you," said Alba in reply. "Still, back to the matter in hand and, to be clear, whether I am young or old, I haven't lost my marbles. So, yes, Matthew, in a tragedy like the one that happened during my time at Kingsbourne, I wouldn't just take someone's word for where they were. I would want proof for what happened. I accept I can't prove where Ash was – I have no eyewitness but I do believe he was at the cinema. However, I can prove who was at the manor that night."

"Everyone was staying at the manor," said Andrew. "Everyone but Ash, who you're now ruling out."

"And Eddie," said Alba sadly.

*

"You know," said Alba quietly, so quietly the others were not sure if she were talking to them or more to herself. "When I identified Vaughan's killer, back here in our village a couple of years ago, not only did I identify the guilty party but, more important than that, well, more important to my mind, was that we established the innocence of someone else. Whereas this time, in one sense, I wish I'd left the shadow of doubt rest over the whole of the Sunday family. To leave them all suspecting one of their own did it. However, what I've achieved – or will achieve when the news breaks – is that it was not one of them, rather it was an outsider. Isabel will be cock-a-hoop that it was the publican's son; that it was Eddie, that tattooed, dirty fingered local, someone she couldn't envisage stepping into a theatre to watch her perform. It saddens me to think that when she hears, she will be, as they all will be, filled with a sense of self-righteousness and arrogance."

"What? They don't currently know you've solved it?" asked Andrew.

"Not yet," confirmed Alba.

"Oh, we'd just assumed you'd gathered them all together in the dining room or out on the lawn," said Sam, "and performed some 'great reveal' and explained what had happened and, critically, who had performed the dastardly deed."

"No," said Alba. "Perhaps I might have, had it been Isabel herself or Henry. Had it been Alice or Johanna, definitely and nothing would have given me more pleasure than had it been Hugh. Had it been Hugh, I would, absolutely, have gathered them all and established his guilt in the matter before their eyes."

"I was rather wishing it was him," said Sam. "He sounded a horrible creep."

"Oh, he was; I mean is," agreed Alba. "And, to be clear, he did assault me in the snooker room. Yes, he was teaching me snooker but he did so in a way that allowed him to assault me."

"It was uncomfortable listening to that part of the story," stated Andrew. "I'm surprised you didn't turn round and—"

"And thump him?"

"Well, er, yes."

"I wanted to but, in that moment, I knew if I had, I would have had to leave the manor and yet Terry and Eleanor wanted – needed – me there. Also, I felt I would defend myself and his future victims better by writing a statement as to what he had just done and getting Eleanor to witness me sign it and date it. To get it documented as contemporaneously as possible was important. Therefore, as soon as I left the billiard room, I went and found Eleanor and got her to witness me write something down and she countersigned it."

"And you've handed it in?" enquired Matthew. "You ought to submit it."

"Yes, don't worry yourself on that front. However, I didn't know anyone in the Wiltshire police force to liaise with but I felt I did want to hand it over to someone I knew or, if not know, at least recognised. It was, is, a rather sensitive matter after all."

"Who then?" asked Andrew.

"Officer Day. You may recall, he was the policeman who stopped me on my journey to Kingsbourne. He'd given me his card, you see. So, I gave him a call and he agreed to meet me on my journey home; we met at Fleet services. I know he's a traffic officer but I felt he was someone I was comfortable handing my statement over to. He explained he would have to pass it to the other Force but he understood the sensitivity of the matter and why I had approached him. He thanked me for taking such a courageous step."

"I wished you'd also walloped Hugh," stated Andrew.

Matthew wanted to add something but felt a discussion on where righteous anger stopped and violence started was for another time.

"So did I. Don't think I didn't or still don't want to but I wanted to protect future victims; whether my statement will or not, who is to say but at least it is on file," said Alba wishing to draw this part of her time at Kingsbourne to a close.

"Annoyingly, Hugh wasn't involved in his brother's death. I still wish it had been him," said Sam.

"It wasn't him but he was the trigger to what happened, so to speak. But for his lewdness I don't think the tragedy would have happened at all," said Alba. "I'll explain."

CHAPTER 24

Alba sheds light on the matter

"Hugh was as unpleasant an individual as I think I have come across. Not wicked, in one sense, but obnoxious, a lech and a danger to us women. Perhaps he had never murdered anyone but the number of lives he must have ruined, the number of us he must have made fearful to venture out from our own front doors and the emotional, psychological scars he must have left on May, his own daughter, and Connie, his niece, must be legion."

Alba paused, closed her eyes for a moment and felt a chill run up and down her spine – even talking about him made her feel violated but she knew, that to explain Dr Sunday's death, she had to start with Hugh.

"Yet, in another sense," continued Alba, "perhaps he did kill his brother. If you imagine the Sunday family as a tower made out of playing cards, Hugh's actions blew through it and the whole thing collapsed. His actions, specifically towards the most vulnerable of those present at the manor, led to the person at the top of the pyramid, his brother John, figuratively falling the furthest; that was truly borne out when John fell to his death. Had Hugh not been present, it would never have happened."

Alba felt his chill once more.

"Other people," continued Alba, "will pay a price for what they did on Friday night – what that price is, is for other people to decide – but Hugh, in a way Hugh seems to be able to do, will slip effortlessly away without anything attaching itself to him. Life is not fair at times, it really isn't."

"When you say other people will pay, Alba, you are referring to–"

"Eddie and Sandy," said Alba unhappily. "Eddie and perhaps Sandy," she corrected herself. "I think Sandy could be left out of things. The only people who so far know what happened at Kingsbourne Manor are myself and the two involved in John's death – Eddie and his girlfriend, Sandy. The sad thing is, they really were just starting out in their relationship. Sandy had been away at university for a year; a year which hadn't worked out for her and financially ruined her. They were just tentatively getting to know one another; just soulmates who seemed to have found each other in a quiet Wiltshire village. They were, I reckon, each other's first real loves."

"But everyone else will surely know by now, as well – you have told everyone else, haven't you?" said Andrew.

"No," stated Alba. "The only people who know – present company excepted – are, as I say, myself and Eddie and Sandy."

"You left the manor before telling anyone else?" asked Sam.

"Yes," acknowledged Alba. Her simple 'yes' conveyed if not defiance then certainly a self-assurance. She then continued. "Thus, when Eddie admits his involvement to the police, which I've told him he must, if he leaves out Sandy's involvement in things – specifically that she was the one who took the earrings and that she lit the candle on the landing to cover his tracks – no one else will ever know she was involved at all."

"Why would he feel able to leave such facts out when confessing to the police, if you know, Alba?" enquired Sam.

"Because I told Eddie it was his decision. I said I would trust his judgment – I said to him 'judgment' but maybe I meant chivalry.

Either way, if he opted to shield her, then when, or if, the police came and spoke with me, I told Eddie I would not mention anything about Sandy's involvement to them. I told Eddie I wouldn't lie but I would simply omit to mention any involvement on Sandy's part. It's tragic enough that Eddie's life is going to be, if not completely ruined, ruined for a number of years. Why bring Sandy into it as well?"

"Because the cold hard facts are that they murdered Dr Sunday and are thieves," suggested Andrew. "Sorry, Alba, don't take that the wrong way. I accept you know them as people and I've never met them but they did some nasty things, didn't they?"

"Nobody murdered John, at least not as I see it but I will explain. Yes, Sandy stole but when I see it within the bigger picture of things that were going on at Kingsbourne, I can understand her actions. As for Eddie, as far as the jewels were concerned, he was actually trying to return them. I'll explain but trust me, Eddie is not a bad person. When he is charged, society will see him as such but he's not, really he's not. He will need people to stand by him, if he's to get through it. Matthew, I will need your pastoral skills to support him, for starters."

"Absolutely," said the Reverend Quinn. "You only need to ask, Alba, you only need to ask. That said, I will attach two conditions."

Alba quizzically looked at Matthew – she did not enquire what they were as she knew he would explain.

"First," said Matthew, "I will ask a friend from my days at theological college to assist us in this matter. Steve, he's a minister in Pewsey, so more local than myself. That local connection will help, I sense. I will, of course, not share anything with him about Sandy until you, I and Eddie are ready to do so; rest assured, Steve will maintain our confidence."

"If you're recommending him, that's fine by me. Makes sense as a plan," said Alba. "And second?"

"Second," added Matthew, "though I accept my points might seem back to front, is that you tell us why Sandy should be left out of this affair and, more generally, that you tell us what exactly happened at Kingsbourne Manor; for starters, where does a candle come into things?"

"Ah, yes, the red candle. It kind of finishes with the candle. That said, it could, alongside Hugh's behaviour, be said that it all began with the candle."

Alba paused and took a deep breath.

*

She then began her monologue as to the events surrounding the death of Dr John Sunday.

"The mystery kind of began from the moment I arrived at Kingsbourne Manor on the Wednesday. Not only was I aware of the presence of the lime trees and instinctively parked my car to avoid the falling leaf sap, but, at the front entrance, I was met by a flustered Sandy as she opened the door to me. Having greeted me, one of the first things she mentioned was that she had been cleaning Dr Sunday's gold candlesticks and what a chore it had been. She said the chore had been made worse by the arrival of John's wider family throughout the day, which had constantly interrupted her. Repeatedly up and down to the front door to welcome them, without so much as a thank you or a smile in return, had dragged out a mundane task. Dragged it out to a point where, when finally opening the door to me, the last to arrive, she said, though as much for herself to hear as for my interest, she had cleaned them all, down to the very last ones on the landing. She had said it out of relief at a task being finished but, crucially, if she'd cleaned them on the Wednesday, any fingerprints on them thereafter meant that the person whose prints they were must have been at the manor sometime after – agree?"

"Yes," confirmed Andrew.

"Good. Now park that fact and let me jump to Friday. We'd just come in from the garden, having played kubb. We were having lemonade in the dining room and Sandy came in to replenish the drinks. I sense, not for the first time, Hugh molested Sandy as she entered – he had that ability to brazenly act in full sight of everyone and somehow get away with it."

Alba grimaced as she recalled the sadness on the maid's face.

"I asked her if she were alright and she said she was; it wasn't for me to force her to formally complain – it must come from her, it wasn't for me to force the matter. Sandy needed to be empowered to protest with her own voice."

Sam gave Alba a nod of agreement and prompted Alba to continue.

"So, we were in the dining room. As Sandy sorted out the drinks – and, I seem to remember, getting myself some more ginger biscuits – she found Isabel's handbag. It had fallen out of sight; I think it had slipped down in Isabel's excitement the day before when she had started to tell me about her upcoming play 'The Wootton Wives'. So, Sandy found it. She had it in her hands at a time in her life when she was under significant financial pressures; a low wage coupled with the fallout from her leaving university, which included still having to pay her accommodation fees."

"Tough," reflected Andrew.

"Yes. All in all, Sandy was under long term financial pressure. Now, that doesn't excuse theft–"

"It is the eighth Commandment, after all," said Matthew.

"Well, yes, I'm just putting her actions in context. So, she was under pressure, and working in a house where she was constantly being sexually harassed. Harassed, to my mind, in the full view of the rest of the family and no one cared, including Isabel. Thus, when Sandy discovered the missing handbag, temptation took hold of her and she put a hand in – perhaps, though here I speculate, the clasp had come undone and she saw a little blush pink suede pouch within the bag. It was a spur of the moment act, not thought through and, having extracted it from the handbag and looked at the contents in her room later, probably couldn't believe what she had taken. Even to the untrained eye, they were obviously worth a small, if not large, fortune. Having taken them, though, what was she to do with them?"

"If, as you say," reflected Sam, "it was a spur of the moment act, she wouldn't have known what to do with them and perhaps regretted taking them quite quickly."

"Yes," agreed Alba. "That's what she said to me when I spoke with her at the end. All she said she could think to do was to take them to Eddie and see what he suggested. Her first opportunity to get to see Eddie was Friday night, shortly before the meal John had organised at the pub for the family. Sandy had no reason to go to the 'Earl of Clarendon'; all the arrangements for the celebratory meal were in place and, even if they weren't, it wouldn't have been for the lowliest maid to sort them out. Nonetheless, she claimed she had wanted to check on things – that was her flustered explanation when I turned up early for the meal and saw her at the pub."

"That was just before you went and sat in the beer garden?" checked Andrew.

"Yes; I'd needed to get away from the manor, myself. Anyway, once there, I saw Eddie come out to continue talking to her but his conversation died when he saw me. He told me later, when I confronted him over everything, that he had come out to give her the earrings back. He said to me that he was going to tell Sandy that they weren't to keep them, that he was not going to reassociate himself with contacts from his past and that Sandy should return the items soonest. He wanted her to place them back in the handbag or, at least, return them to the manor and leave them somewhere for someone else to inadvertently come across them. However, with my arrival, Eddie said he did not want me seeing him hand over a little pink bag so kept them on his person for the time being. He said he planned to return them himself that night – that the shorter the period of time they were missing, the better for the house staff. Eddie added that he knew, from his time working on the garden machinery at the manor, how to get in through the servant's quarters and would place the jewels somewhere near Isabel's bedroom, tucked under a curtain or as if they'd been kicked under a piece of furniture that was against the wall of the long landing."

"But he didn't return them," stated Andrew. "Sorry, Alba, just one of those cold hard facts I need you to help me get past."

"Yes, I know. I found them in the tray of keys at his garage, didn't I, the following morning? He stated it was his intention to return them but things didn't turn out as he planned. He insisted he went to the manor late Friday night to return them but he admitted he also went with a desire to confront Hugh. You see, he had heard repeatedly from his girlfriend what she was experiencing at the manor and then he heard it himself as Hugh was talking about Sandy at the meal he was waitering at."

Alba took a sip of tea.

"Eddie," she continued, "as he started to clean the table, listened to Hugh drawl, fawn and generally be very crude about Sandy. Whether Hugh knew she was dating Eddie or not, I don't know. Hugh probably didn't know but he cared not a jot for who heard his foul lusting after the housemaid. Eddie said it left him, Eddie, fearing for Sandy's safety and it tempted him, given he was now planning on going to the manor in any case, to try and confront Hugh in person but away from his father's public house."

"Given, Alba, you've told us Eddie had a general grudge against the rich family at the manor and that they'd all left without paying for the meal, probably didn't help Eddie's handling of the situation, either," suggested Matthew.

"No, it didn't. A perfect storm was brewing, as you are beginning to understand," suggested Alba.

*

"So, late Friday evening," continued Alba. "Whilst Eleanor and I were still in the pub car park, as we waited to have my puncture repaired, Eddie drove himself to the manor. He parked alongside all the other cars – he said to me that he felt one extra car would be less obvious if it were on the end of a long line of vehicles, rather than if he had parked all by itself somewhere else in the manor grounds."

"And in that decision of his," said Andrew, "by parking under the lime trees in the month of June, he basically told a keen horticulturalist, like yourself Alba, that he had visited the manor since he had washed his car earlier that day."

"Yes," agreed Alba.

"Fascinating," considered Matthew.

"Once parked, he got in through the servants' entrance without Sandy's help – Eddie stressed that point to me. He said, it was not something they had planned between them. He insisted he had not come to harvest more jewels, nor to assault Hugh and definitely not to murder Dr Sunday. He stressed and stressed again, he went on his own volition to the manor to return items he had not himself stolen, to verbally confront Hugh and warn the man off his, Eddie's, sweetheart."

"But it didn't work out like that, did it?" reflected Andrew.

"No," acknowledged Alba. "As he made his way up onto the landing, he saw the door to John's study ajar and the light on. It was quiet and everyone else had retired to bed; he couldn't find Hugh. In the silence and stillness of the moment, Eddie knew he had an opportunity to confront John at least – an opportunity he should never have taken and one he definitely should never have taken with a rashly seized golden candlestick in his hand. Eddie said, in that crazy moment and without any real thought on his part, he grabbed the nearest object to hand as he wanted to threaten Dr Sunday – threaten him over the non-payment of the meal earlier in the evening, threaten him that if he, Hugh's brother, did not control his brother's behaviour towards the female staff in the house, then he, Eddie would and, generally, to tell Dr Sunday what he, the publican's son, really thought of him coming into the village with all his unearned wealth."

Sam, Matthew and Andrew listened in silence as they knew what Alba was about to conclude in her narrative of the tragic events that night.

"It goes without saying, the *conversation*, which Eddie foolishly imagined in his head that they would have, did not go to plan. John was not at his desk, rather he was beyond that discrete little door which opened out onto the lead covered roof. Eddie found him out there – the other being lost in wonder at the night sky above him. John did not appreciate being disturbed nor having Eddie tell him what he, Eddie, thought of him or his brother. The exchange became heated; Eddie insisted he did not hit Dr Sunday with the candlestick but in a tussle they tragically had, Eddie pushed him and John stumbled and somehow, due to the slope of the roof and the gully round the base of the parapet, Dr Sunday fell."

"Ah," voiced Matthew.

"Eddie said he looked over, could hear no groans coming from below and, not knowing what to do, simply went and returned the candlestick to where he had taken it from. With his elbow he turned off the study light and left the room. He said he went and knocked on Sandy's door, unsure what to do. He told her what had happened and, rightly or wrongly – but remember she was panicked herself by now – she told him to leave the way he had come. He said he did but once he got to his car, he sat there for hours, frozen in indecision. He must have still been there when Eleanor and myself finally returned. However, as I parked away from the other cars we didn't notice one extra car on the end of the line."

"Why didn't he just flee the scene as Sandy suggested?" asked Andrew.

"I don't know – I don't think he really knows himself," reflected Alba.

"Maybe," offered Sam, "he felt, if it were an accident, or at least something he hadn't intended, why should he flee; perhaps he wanted to call the emergency services. Equally, the desire to get away must have been so strong. He probably came down on the option of fleeing as Sandy suggested; perhaps he felt he might get away with it, especially as he had had the foresight not to touch the study light switch with his fingers on his way out. Maybe he felt, forensically, he might get away with it. Any prints on the door to the servants' entrance would either get smudged the very next morning or, even if they remained, as Sandy's boyfriend, it would be plausible they might be there."

"But not on the golden candlestick on the table on the landing right near to John's study," said Alba. "He replaced it, not wanting to be found with stolen property and accused of murder out of a robbery gone wrong. Yet, in replacing it, he'd forgotten he'd handled it."

"Which Sandy realised once she had sent Eddie away," suggested Andrew.

"Exactly," agreed Alba. "Equally, she didn't want to be accused of stealing it or hiding it herself. So, what did she do? Well, her first thought was simply to go and clean it once more but then she heard Eleanor and me come in and make our way up the stairs. She couldn't risk being seen by us to be removing it or cleaning it in the small hours of Saturday morning – such bizarre behaviour would naturally stick in our minds. So, with the swiftness of thought – inspired, almost – she lit the candle. She gambled that by the morning the candle would have burnt down and covered the candlestick in the melted wax, perhaps even sealing it to the table itself, and no one would think to check for fingerprints underneath the wax."

Alba paused, looked round the room she was in and then added:

"So, how did I make that connection – that the candlestick, not the paintings, the tapestry nor the talk of missing engagement rings, was critical in unravelling the events at Kingsbourne Manor? Well, consider what a glorious summer day it is once again."

"Yes," said Matthew in reply and on behalf of the others as well.

"Tempted to put the log fire on or light some candles for warmth?" pursued Alba.

"Don't be daft. It's far too warm; it's June after all."

"Oh, definitely – even the nights are warm," added Sam. "Anyone else find it hard to sleep last night?"

"Exactly," stated Alba. "So why on earth, would any of us, at this time of year, go round lighting candles – be it here at the vicarage, in Sam's bedroom or on the long landing at Kingsbourne Manor? The manor had electric lights, for goodness' sake! Things had moved on from the thirteenth century when it was first built – even if it were in Wiltshire! Why would anyone light a candle? There had to be a reason for it to be lit; you don't get your staff to light solitary candles for *atmosphere* around midnight after everyone has retired to bed. There had to be another explanation."

"I never considered that detail," said Matthew. "You mentioned it to us but it didn't tell me anything, so to speak."

"Oh, it added atmosphere, I'll give it that," continued Alba. "As Eleanor and I studied the pictures, especially her favourite one, the woman leaning against the tree, it became more romantic still with the flicker of the candlelight. Yet neither Eleanor nor myself looked at the candle and asked ourselves why it was burning in the first place. Yet, it had been lit by Sandy in a desperate act of shielding her young love; we'd even passed Sandy on the stairs as we went up – she must have literally been holding a burnt match in the palm of her hand as we passed her. Incredible!"

"Indeed," agreed Andrew. "Grandfather would have recruited her in an instance during the war, more so if she were fluent in French or German, for the SOE, the special operations executive. That level of quick thinking and brazen gamesmanship in the face of the 'enemy', if you like, would have caught the eye of grandfather's wartime department. Still, I digress."

"So," continued Alba, "once I'd worked out where I had seen the bag containing the diamond earrings – at the village garage – I knew

Ash or Eddie were involved. Eddie and Sandy were connected and Eddie had grudges against more than one member of the Sunday family; plus, it was Eddie's car covered in sap from the leaves of the lime tree. When I challenged him about it, that was when I saw him with Sandy late on Saturday, they admitted what the significance of the candlestick was all about; I accept I hadn't lifted his actual fingerprints off it but I knew they were there."

"If," pondered Matthew, "Eddie confesses to the police his involvement but doesn't mention grabbing the candlestick as he entered John's study, the police would have no reason to be looking for an accomplice of his, who was helping to cover his tracks after he'd fled the scene. The police wouldn't bother looking for forensic clues on random household items, if Eddie had already admitted his presence. He could shield his girlfriend, couldn't he?"

"Absolutely," agreed Alba. "As I say, I said I wouldn't mention it, either, if the police asked me for a statement. If I'm not the one to alert the police about him, I have no obligation to tell them what I can now 'see'."

"One question, Alba," said Sam.

Alba encouraged Sam to ask away.

"What made you work out where you'd seen the missing diamond earrings? What suddenly made you go, 'oh, hold on, they're in the tray at the garage'? Something must have triggered that connection, surely?"

"Yes," acknowledged Alba. "It was Saturday afternoon; once the emergency services had gone. I'd been for my solitary walk along the drive and had worked out that it was the sticky sap from the trees blighting people's cars. Once back in the manor, I went to check on Eleanor. As I walked the long landing, seeing the tapestry, the fine pictures and the burnt down candle, I sat outside Eleanor's bedroom, on the floor, just puzzling over things. Then I reached down to the tray Eleanor had placed outside her bedroom door – the one Sandy had taken her with some drinks and biscuits on – and helped myself to one of the remaining shortbreads. As I looked down on the tray to select a solitary biscuit amongst the clutter of the other items on the tray – a serviette, a half drunk cup of tea in a china cup on a saucer, a small milk jug, sugar bowl, plate of nibbles, teaspoons and so on, I remembered seeing a different type of tray, equally cluttered, at the village garage and then it came to me – came to me exactly what I'd seen on that tray. I suddenly knew where I'd seen the missing blush pink suede bag. In placing the earrings there, at the garage, that gave reason for why Ash or Eddie had come to the manor."

"Yes," agreed Sam.

"So, Eddie's car had been at the manor the night before, for it had succumbed to the sticky sap – that was why he had been washing it the very day after he had already washed it. There was now a 'motive', one of untold wealth, and then, finally, as I sat on the landing, I looked up, not to Eleanor's favourite painting, but to the burnt down candle beneath it and wondered what the significance of that was."

"Which was when you remembered seeing Sandy on the landing the night before," contributed Andrew.

"Exactly," said Alba. "As I have said, I really didn't want either of them to be involved but I knew I could prove it if I could get back to the garage and have a look myself on that tray. So, I had to orchestrate a reason to go back and get Eddie and Ash out of my way whilst they repaired my car and I sat in reception – so I told them in a grumpy way that I wanted them to sort my car out properly and didn't want to see either of them until they had."

"And you got Henry to loosen the brake light for you, so you could go back to the garage and say 'sorry guys, I'd like you to do it properly this time'."

"Words to that effect," said Alba. "Let's just say Eddie and Ash were puzzled at my reappearance; I ensured they had their tails between their legs as they both went to deal with it and I, in the solitude of the reception-come-shop area of 'Kingsbourne Cars and Motorbikes', successfully located the diamonds."

"Well done, you," said Andrew.

"Once back at the manor, I went and found Sandy. I told her to tell Eddie to come over as I had to speak to both of them. Perhaps Sandy sensed I suspected something but she did as I asked, perhaps solely because I wasn't one of the family. Once Eddie had joined us and we sat in my bedroom, I told them what I knew, what I suspected and presented them with the earrings."

Alba stopped and shook her head slowly.

"Anyone else, I'd have been pleased to unmask, so to speak, but they were the nice people in the tale. I wished, still wish, it was not them. In the past, I've encountered murderers who are dangerously opportunistic. I've met ones who were detailed in their planning but this, well, I'm still not sure this was even murder. Perhaps, in that single moment, he wished him dead as he pushed him but did he really mean to push him over the parapet? Did he really desire his blood? I felt those questions were beyond my remit – Terry had written to me from Tashkent and asked me to look out for Eleanor. I had tried to fulfil that task; I had definitely removed any finger of suspicion ever pointing at her. That might be significant, were John's will to be found and everyone learns he had already amended it to make Eleanor sole beneficiary. To be clear, I don't know whether that is the case or not, still, either way, the finger of suspicion could now never fall on Terry's sister. I had also done what I could do, to protect Eleanor and others from John's brother, Hugh. As for Eddie's culpability? On that point, I could at least mitigate, well, maybe not mitigate, at least leave him in control of how it played out from that point on. Dr Sunday was dead and Eddie, however you packaged it, was involved in that fatal event. I stressed to them that it would ruin both of their lives if they tried to run from the fact; that they would forever live a life of looking over their shoulders. That is no way to live – it surely would eat away at them. Better, as painful as it would be to begin with, to admit involvement and leave it to the police, the Crown Prosecution

Service, ultimately the courts, a jury of his peers, to determine the level of culpability. However–"

Three silent faces waited for Alba to continue.

"I added, if they stayed calm and Eddie kept things simple when he spoke to the police, Sandy could be kept out of it. Were she not mentioned by him, I said, in my opinion at least, that didn't constitute her running away or hiding. Enough truth would come out to keep everyone 'happy'; it would allow the Sunday family – as unpleasant as they all are – to know no one from the family was involved in John's death and it would allow the authorities to conclude matters without troublesome loose ends. Somehow," and with that, Alba looked to Sam, then to Andrew and finally to the Reverend Quinn, "I felt Sandy had suffered enough at Hugh's hands and would *live* whatever punishment Eddie served, with him. Maybe I'm wrong. Maybe it was not for me to act as either arbiter or judge and jury but I just felt she could be spared; that the world wouldn't be a worse place if she were."

"I don't think life is always clear cut – there are often grey areas," said Matthew. "I think, Alba, you were aware that, in this case, there was a difference between pursuing the law and the pursuit of justice. Sometimes the law can be a hard beast. Sometimes what we, what society, are in fact after is not the stern application of the law but rather of seeing justice done. By way of illustration, in *Les Misérables* do you cheer for Javert or Jean Valjean? From a legal point of view, shouldn't a parole breaker be brought to account and yet you read Victor Hugo's novel – which I never have I might add, I've only seen the play – wanting Valjean to escape the law."

"Thank you," said Alba softly. "Thank you. That was how I saw it. So, I told Eddie and Sandy that I would leave it to them as to how much they told the authorities but that I expected them to tell them enough to ensure no finger of suspicion could point at anyone else. I added I would be reporting Hugh for what he had done to me, and Sandy should do likewise but that it was her decision."

"How long have you given them?" asked Matthew. "I don't want to bring my friend Steve in too soon."

"A week from Saturday, which was when I sat the pair of them down in my room at the manor."

"And that was that," said Sam. "Well, apart from–"

"The earrings, yes, I thought you'd be curious what happened to them; no, they are not still in my safe keeping. Once I'd spoken with Eddie and Sandy, I deliberately, blatantly, if you like, went out into the gardens and made a point of sitting out on the garden furniture on the lawn. After a period of time, having made sure one or two of the family had seen me – usefully that included Anthony – I went and returned the pink suede bag, with the earrings, to Isabel. I said I'd found them out on the lawn, under the garden chair she herself had been sitting in on Thursday afternoon, as she had been telling myself and Johanna about her upcoming play."

"Decided you would keep it simple, rather than try to smuggle them back into her handbag or bedroom, yourself?" mused Andrew.

"Exactly. She – as no doubt Andrew was – was thrilled to get them back and she never stopped to wonder quite how they had come to be 'found' out where I claimed to have come across them. She was just so grateful; sad, if you think about it, that some sparkly stones brought her such joy when she should have been mourning her brother. Still, joyful she was – she even said she'd send me four complimentary tickets for 'The Wootton Wives' when the play makes it to Guildford!"

"Four," considered three voices at once.

"Yes, four. I expect the acting will be wooden and her accent, well, I doubt the audience will be able to place it. Furthermore, I fear the run won't even last to the Guildford dates. However, if it does, would anyone like to come and see a Tony Verdie play with me?" asked Alba. "I will have three spare tickets."

Epilogue

A couple of days later, in the shelter of the now perfectly summer-pruned wisteria, Andrew knocked on Alba's front door.

He had meant to be attending a meeting up in Whitehall but he had said he could no longer attend that morning – 'pressing estate matters had arisen', or so he claimed and he had got the thing pushed back to the afternoon. The reality was that, not having seen Alba since their time at the vicarage, he was missing her – he knew she had been up at the Hall, helping to harvest in the kitchen garden and leading a garden tour for the paying visitors, but that did not count for he had not seen her himself. Whatever the government minister wanted his input on could wait at least until the afternoon; matters closer to home seemed more important to him today. So, he had come to surprise Alba and ask her to come up to London with him, to lose herself in a gallery whilst he attended his meeting and then have a meal together – perhaps down the lower end of Regent Steet, maybe one of the places in Waterloo Place, and then just go wandering through St James' together.

He knocked again.

Just as he was about to give up and head up to London by himself, the front door opened. Alba did not speak; she simply smiled, beckoned him in, directed him into the kitchen. She made a 'capital T' sign with her hands but remained in the hall to continue a conversation she was having with someone on the telephone.

Given she had not shut the door to the kitchen, Andrew took that as a sign that, once he had put the kettle on and had emptied out the teapot around Alba's roses, he was 'allowed' to lean against the doorframe to the hall and listen in on the discussion Alba was having.

*

"…yes, Andrew has just turned up, which is a lovely surprise. You remember him, surely?"

"…"

"That's right, he turned up unexpectedly at 'The Jupiter', remember? Just after, well, I hardly need to remind you! We were in the bar enjoying a pot of tea and–"

"…"

"Oh, I agree, the cake we had was scrumptious – Alan's Victoria sponges are delightful, aren't they? Then, if I remember, we had bacon sandwiches to follow."

"…"

"Yes, it was one of those mornings. Anyway, Andrew has just turned up again–"

"…"

"No, he doesn't always do that. Normally, we know when we're seeing one another but today it's a pleasant unexpected surprise. Oh, hold on, Daniel, I had better tell him who I am speaking to; he's looking at me with a puzzled expression on his face and mouthing 'who?' to me. Hold on a mo."

Alba lowered the telephone. She did not bother to cover the mouthpiece for she was happy for the person on the other end to hear what she said:

"It's Daniel Jones. Remember Daniel? He's that private investigator you met down in Cornwall."

"Course I remember Daniel. Good chap; likes his—"

"Food?" joked Alba, with a glint in her eyes and loudly enough to ensure Daniel would hear – whereupon she brought the receiver back up to her mouth and said into it:

"Just teasing, Daniel."

Andrew could not hear Daniel's reply but, given Alba was still smiling, he sensed Daniel was happy with the comment. Still, Andrew felt he, Andrew, should clarify matters:

"His mysteries," stressed Andrew and audibly enough for Daniel to hear down the wire. "He dealt with the Trelyn affair admirably; likes his mysteries, was what I was trying to say."

"I know," agreed Alba. "He was a whizz with regards to Trelyn, wasn't he? That is sort of why I was calling him."

"Well, let me not interrupt further," said Andrew. "I'll go and make the tea now the kettle has boiled."

Andrew returned to the kitchen but he stayed attuned to the conversation Alba and Daniel were having over the telephone.

*

"So," continued Alba, "to summarise. Expect to get a call from an Alice Sunday. She was a sister-in-law of Dr John Sunday."

" … "

"That's right, it was John who fell to his death. Alice – she's the solicitor – will no doubt be giving you a call soon. Well, it will probably be her secretary to begin with but never mind. Alice is looking into John's affairs; not just as a result of his, John's, death but also going back further, into the death of John's uncle Leonard."

" … "

"That's right, Leonard was the successful miner, unlike John's brother Anthony, who's mining business is failing. Leonard left John as his sole heir but the wider family believe Leonard also left John assets – specifically gemstones – unofficially so to speak; jewels that the tax office, Customs and Excise and the southern African nation they were mined from knew nothing about. They were squirrelled away. Small in number but vast in value."

"…"

"So, Alice, as are the rest of the family, is keen to locate them."

"…"

"Yes, Daniel. I do believe, despite John's claims to the contrary, he had stashed away a sizeable fortune from the rest of his family. John had inherited everything anyway but still he enjoyed the deception of keeping the existence of further untold wealth from the others. No doubt Eleanor's engagement ring was made up from some of the stones in question – which was why he did not want her to show it to anyone from his immediate family. To the random person on the street or people Eleanor studied or worked alongside, well, they would neither know nor care where the prized jewels came from. However, John was not willing to take that chance with his siblings and their children – enough of them knew enough about the mining industry to notice if new gems suddenly appeared within the family."

"…"

"Yes, I had described John as the nice one. I suppose he was nice to me and academically he was brilliant. However, I now realise he had his flaws, like the rest of his family did; John's were greed and deception. He must have been thrilled to keep gathering his family around him and not only flaunting his known about wealth but, more so, he must have got a kick from knowing he had other wealth hidden away within the manor that no one else knew about apart from himself."

"…"

"I agree, Daniel, not a nice character trait. Still, as was said to me, they were all cut form the same cloth. Talented they all were – well, I'm not sure about the actress but hopefully we'll decide that for ourselves in Guildford in a few months' time – but flawed with it. Different talents, different flaws but all unpleasant characters at the end of the day."

"…"

"Yes, and this is where you come in. Alice mentioned you over dinner one evening I was there. Said she had heard about you through the Bristol solicitors you work for – Alice had met one of their partners at some do in London and they'd been singing your praises over a case."

"…"

"Yes, Trelyn."

"…"

"Anyway, Alice said she will get your details from that other person and added, not to me but I heard her say it, that she would look to bring you in on this case to seek out these missing jewels at Kingsbourne."

"…"

"No, you're right there. I didn't let on that I knew you. So, I'm phoning you to give you a 'head's up', that's all. Up to you whether you get involved in the case or not but, if you do, and whilst you are entirely free to form your own opinions, be aware Alice is not a nice person. As for her husband, don't let him in the same building as any of your female colleagues – I'm serious, there."

"…"

"Yes, I'll fill you in on why if you do take on the 'Kingsbourne case'."

"…"

"Ideas? Ideas for where he might have stashed the jewels? Daniel, are you losing your touch and need my help?"

"…"

"No, I'm teasing. Of course I'm happy to give you some pointers, given I've stayed at the manor. Plus, you're our good friend, after all."

"…"

"Oh, absolutely. Next time I intend to go to 'The Jupiter' I'll let you know; it would be lovely if you could come down and stay at the same time for a few days. As for the jewels–"

"…"

"Don't be silly – I don't want payment for what I'm about to tell you. We're friends, so stop being daft."

"…"

"Where are they? Well, I don't think he'd be foolish to put them all in one place. There will be other stashes as well but one I'm sure of is in the billiard room."

"…"

"Yes, the billiard room. Look at the cues in the cue rack, they're not all the same length and it's one of the longer ones you want. There is one that doesn't balance in the way the others do – if you lay a certain one across the palm of your hand it doesn't rest as the others do. That one, I believe, has a hollowed-out butt, plugged obviously, but containing jewels of unimaginable wealth. John must have revelled in seeing his brothers play snooker, yet never knowing how close to Leonard's fortune they actually were."

Acknowledgements

Thankful villages – sometimes called Blessed villages – are those villages in England and Wales where all those who went off to serve in the Great War, survived. Around fifty such villages exist. To my knowledge, no such villages have been identified in Scotland or Ireland. 'Doubly Thankful' are those villages where no one was lost during both the Great War and the Second World War; there are around a dozen.

The happiest – maybe *most alive* would be a more fitting description – such village I have so far been fortunate enough to visit is High Toynton, Lincolnshire. It is a doubly thankful village and the congregation of St John the Baptist Church are still at the heart of the community. From my novel, Dr John Sunday would have appreciated the fact that the first mention of a church at High Toynton dates from 1231 when a charter was granted to the Bishop of Carlisle by Henry III.

By contrast, Knowlton, Kent, is the saddest one I have visited. This is because the church has died and the building is now all that remains. Sad because, as my character the Reverend Quinn would say, it is the people who are the church and yet they have gone. They have gone within two, perhaps three, generations of such a momentous cause for thanks. I hope there are people round about who do pause in thankful appreciation that all the sons of Knowlton came back from the Great

War. The Church of St Clement, the building, is maintained by the Churches Conservation Trust; see www.visitchurches.org.uk. The war memorial, known as the 'Memorial to Nobody', is located on the main road which separates Knowlton from Chillenden. It remains a fine tribute to those who went off to war and returned.

Kingsbourne is a fictitious 'doubly thankful' village.

*

Operation Manna saw the RAF, RCAF and RAAF dropping relief supplies to western Holland towards the end of World War II, where 3.5 million people were facing starvation; indeed, tens of thousands had already died. The Operation began on 29th April 1945 and lasted until 8th May. Avro Lancasters and de Havilland Mosquitoes, crewed by men from across the Commonwealth as well as Poles and one Dutchman, flew 3,000 sorties, delivering 7,000 tonnes of food into that part of Holland still under German occupation.

Operation Chowhound, from 1st May until the 7th May 1945, saw 4,000 tonnes of supplies dropped by the United States Army Air Force over the same part of Holland. Operation Faust was the subsequent relief effort by Canadian land forces.

Four (though some accounts state three) allied aircraft were lost during these Operations. The following seems most accurate:

The only loss from the RAF's Bomber Command, was an Avro Lancaster from 576 Squadron (NN806) piloted by P/O Scott. It crashed on take-off but the crew survived.

From the American Eighth Air Force, two collided and one, a Boeing B-17 'Flying Fortress' (48640), piloted by F/L Sceurman, flying from Horham, Suffolk, ditched in the sea following an engine fire; from that plane, only two of the thirteen on board survived.

Operation Manna is touched on in John Nichol and Tony Rennell's book 'Tail-end Charlies: The Last Battles of the Bomber War 1944-45' (2004).

Further accounts can be found on the RAF Museum Hendon's website: www.rafmusuem.org.uk and also the International Bomber Command Centre's website: www.internationalbcc.co.uk.

Operation Chowhound is documented in Stephen Dando-Collins' 2015 book of the same name.

*

For anyone, like Miss Alba White, who has a soft spot for the A303 road, I would recommend Tom Fort's most charming of books 'The A303: Highway to the Sun'. It is published by Simon & Schuster UK Ltd (2012).

*

For those wishing to understand the game of Kubb, the following websites may help: www.ukkubb.org and www.kubb.world.

Specialist toy and sports shops sell the game.

*

'The Wootton Wives', a play about Richard Wootton's two wives meeting in a vision he has towards the end of his life, is something that maybe one day I will write; for now, it is no more than a work of fiction within this work of fiction.

However, the Wootton family were real people. I hope I have not done them or their descendants any disservice by using Richard's life as an inspiration for a fictitious play set within 'Sunday Falling'. I believe the following information is correct about the family:

Richard Rawson Wootton (1867–1946) married, first, Catherine Johnson (1873–1909). They became parents to Frank, Stanley, Stella, Brenda and Richard Johnson 'Young Dick' Wootton. Tragically, Catherine died giving birth to their fifth child, 'Young Dick'.

Richard (senior) originated from Taree in New South Wales, Australia. He was a dairy farmer and a horse trainer. He had success as a trainer in both Australia and South Africa before moving to Epsom, England in 1906. By 1913 he was Champion Trainer.

Frank (1893–1940), as a jockey, won the 1903 Germiston Handicap at Turffontein, South Africa, aged just 9 years and 10 months. In England he went on to become Champion Jockey for four successive years, 1909-1912. During the Great War, he served with the Australian and New Zealand Army Corps in Mesopotamia and was Mentioned in Dispatches. Post-war, Frank became a National Hunt jockey.

Stanley (1895–1986), whilst starting out as a jockey, had greater success as a trainer of horses and jockeys. He also became an accomplished breeder. Like his older brother, his early career was interrupted by the Great War; Lieutenant Stanley Wootton, when serving with 17ᵗʰ Battalion of the Royal Fusiliers, was awarded the Military Cross for rescuing a fellow officer during the Somme campaign, 1916. He was presented with his medal by Queen Alexandra at Buckingham Palace. After transferring to the cavalry, Stanley en route to the Middle East, survived the boat he was on being sunk; many others, as well as several hundred horses, were not so fortunate. In the 1960s, alongside George Wigg, Chairman of the Levy Board, Stanley was instrumental in saving Walton Downs for the nation. Today, at a spot on the Downs where there are fine views across London, a memorial stone to him and Lord George Wigg resides. Stanley is buried in Epsom with his mother, Catherine.

Richard (senior) married, secondly, Frances Young in 1931 and they had three daughters; Jean, Betty and Peggy.

*

Once again, I would like to thank my brother-in-law, Nigel Head, for the original cover design that he created for this book and which forms the basis of the cover design which we now have.

I would like to thank Sybil Coombes for being an excellent teacher of English. Any remaining mistakes within the text are entirely my own.

Thanks, also to Katy Brandham for answering my questions concerning motorcycles. Katy, having ridden her BMW F650GS from the United Kingdom to Japan, knows her bikes. I only wish my limited questions in number and depth had challenged her more.

Finally, I would like to thank the team at Troubador Publishing Ltd. They have guided me through the post-writing stage expertly once again and are a pleasure to work with. Here's to working together again on the fourth book in the Alba White series –

The search for Quicksilver

One Thousand Moons

In between jobs and living alone in a quiet village on the Surrey and Sussex border, thirty-year-old Alba White is drifting through life. At the other end of the village, Hillstone Hall is in a precarious position. Edward Chapman, the 7th Lord Hartfield, is in a financial hole and literally selling the family silver to keep the place afloat.

Then, when during a charity cricket match, one of his own elderly garden volunteers, still mourning the loss of his brother, who flew with the RAF in the war, is murdered, things take a further turn for the worse until an arrest is made. Yet Alba, who found the dying man and whose blood stained her beautiful white dress, is not convinced the police have arrested the right person. Suddenly she has direction but will she discover the truth in time?

Sandcastles by The Jupiter Hotel

Alba White returns.

Holidaying at her favourite Cornish hotel – perched as it is on the cliffs above a remote beautiful, quiet cove – Alba is surprised and embarrassed to bump into an old school friend. Surprised because they have not spoken for years and embarrassed because Alba herself was the cause of their estrangement.

Yet, when the husband of Alba's former friend fails to return to the hotel one evening, Alba senses there might be an opportunity to help and, in so doing, redeem herself.

For whilst a missing husband does not generate much interest from the other hotel residents or even the small tight-knit members of staff who work at 'The Jupiter Hotel', Alba, by contrast, believes something is not right.

A trail of mystery and danger lie ahead but what happens next catches even Alba out.

The trail encompasses a deserted country house, a gifted artist, the hotel's chef who perhaps is wasted at such a small establishment, two young brothers whom Alba takes under her wing and an old map. All of which, somehow, lead Alba to the truth. However, she has to put herself in harm's way to get there.

Or does everything, in the end, come down to the turn of a card?